Teach Me
By
Iris Bolling

SIRI Enterprises
Publishing Division
Richmond, Virginia

This is a work of fiction. Names, characters, places and incidents are either the product of the author's imagination or are used fictitiously, and any resemblance to actual persons, living or dead, business establishments, events, locales is entirely coincidental.

ISBN-13: 978-0-9801066-6-4
ISBN-10: 0-9801066-6-4
Library of Congress Control Number: 9780980106664

Cover design by:
Chanin Richel Creative Design and Judith Wansley

Page design by: Judith Wansley

Books by Iris Bolling

The Heart Series

Once You've Touched The Heart
The Heart of Him
Look Into My Heart
A Heart Divided
A Lost Heart
The Heart

Night of Seduction/Heaven's Gate

www.irisbolling.net
www.sirient.com

Acknowledgements

Thank you my heavenly father for family, friends and supporters.

A special thank you to the sisters of
ARC Book Club Inc. of New York

English
Locksie
Shai
Simone'
SiStar Tea

Thank you for your support and innovative thinking!
May God continue to bless you with books, authors
and an abundance reviews.
You are truly CERTIFIED!

Dedication

Building Relationships Around Books is an on-line book club that has this contagious positive energy that draws me into their world daily. I have met some really wonderful people from this site. Thank you Sharon Blount, Madame Prez as they call her, for sharing your dream with us.

Dear Readers:

Webster dictionary defines a family as: the basic unit of society traditionally consisting of two parents rearing their children. With that in mind, meet Joseph and Sally Lassiter, a couple who took the saying "be fruitful and multiple" seriously. They are the parents of Samuel, Joshua, Ruby, Pearl, Diamond, Matthew, Luke, Opal, Timothy, Jade, Adam and Sapphire.

If you did not notice, all the males are named after men of the bible and will be referred to as The Gents in this series of novels. Why? I'm glad you asked. Well, not only are they your typical Alpha males, with their tall, dark good looks and arrogant ways, they are all true southern gentlemen that wisely open their hearts and welcome love—from the right woman.

Now, the females, well, they are all named after precious gemstones and will be referred to as The Gems in this series. Why? Simple. They are precious gems to their father and brothers. Any man that enters into their lives must treat them as such or deal with the males who all stand over six feet tall. But, putting aside the fear factor, any man that is fortunate enough to have the heart of a Lassiter woman will have in his possession the priceless gift of undying love.

To assist you, my readers from The Heart Series, this story takes place during the time when JD. Harrison was Attorney General. Samuel was working for Brian Thompson and had just won the heart of Cynthia Thornton from a Governor and a Prince, no less. That should give you some idea of the power of a Lassiter man.

The first book in The Gems and Gents Series begins with the middle daughter Diamond, who chose the man she wanted to teach her about love. Unfortunately, Zackary Davenport wants nothing to do with any woman who is after his heart.

Whose willpower will triumph? You'll have to read Teach Me to find out.

Enjoy!
Iris

Prologue

The fire could have destroyed his life. If not the fire, the investigation that commenced afterward certainly would have. Fortunately, for Zackary Davenport, people believed in him enough to invest in his projects to provide affordable quality homes for anyone that desired them. The pending meeting in New York was of the utmost importance for accomplishing the first phase of his goal. However, once he reached Richmond International Airport he found a stumbling block—a small one to his thinking, but a stumbling block all the same. And one he planned to move immediately.

The Department of Motor Vehicles was not as crowded as Zack expected. He smiled thinking, *I should be in and out in no time,* as he took a seat to wait for his number to be called. The receptionist at the information desk had given him an application to complete to renew his expired driver's license. His driver's license had to be renewed to board the plane to New York. *It was a good thing his secretary JoEllen had allowed a few hours between his arrival at JFK and the meeting with his clients,* he thought as he completed the application. He was really pissed when he was not allowed to obtain his boarding pass for the plane. The wonderful feeling he woke up with that morning almost deserted him. But then he took responsibility for the delay. He was the one who allowed his driver's license to expire.

The automated system announced his number. Zack looked up to see his number on the monitor for window three. Checking his watch, he smiled knowing the next flight for New York was in two hours. That was plenty of time for him to renew his license and be back at the airport in no time. In a few minutes he would be on his way.

"Good morning." The clerk said with a smile. "How may I help you?"

"Good morning," Zack replied as he gave his application and license to the clerk. "I need to renew my driver's license."

"I'll be happy to assist you with that." The clerk took a moment to look at the license, then looked back up at Zack. "Mr. Davenport, your driver's license has expired. Do you have proof of legal presence with you?"

A frown creased Zack's face right above his eyes. "No. I don't. I don't think. What is it and why do I need it?"

"The law requires proof of legal presence in order to renew your driver's license. A birth certificate or passport or..."

"Look," Zack interrupted, "I'm not getting a new license. I just need to renew the one I have."

"Yes sir, but you will be receiving a new license."

"I don't want a new license. Just give me this one back with a new date on it," he said pointing to the license the clerk had in her hand, on the verge of losing the little control he promised himself he would keep when he left the airport.

The clerk smiled, "I'm sorry sir, it doesn't work that way."

For some reason the clerk's smile pushed him closer to breaking his promise. "Do you find something funny about this situation, because I don't?" Zack stated.

The clerk didn't frown, but quickly removed the smile. "Not at all sir. I was just smiling."

"I don't need your smiles. I need my license renewed," he replied in a near shout.

"Yes sir," the clerk sobered, "and I will renew your license once you bring in proof of legal presence as required by law." The clerk pulled out a list. "Here is a list of docu..."

"Look," Zack cut the clerk off and looked at her nameplate, "Ms. Shabazz, I have a plane to catch and don't have time for the red tape. I need this renewed and I need it renewed now!" He yelled.

"And we will comply with your request once you present a form of legal presence," the clerk sternly replied. "Would you like for me to review the list with you?"

"No! I don't want to review a damn list! I want my license renewed!" The look the clerk gave him let him know she was not going to budge. "Do you have a supervisor?"

"Several," the clerk curtly replied.

Zack gave the clerk a look that would make most people run for cover. But the clerk stood there after responding to his question. It dawned on him she was not moving. "I want to speak with one of them, now!"

The clerk looked at Zack and smiled as if she knew something he didn't. "Certainly", she said and walked away.

Looking at his watch, Zack shook his head. "This is ridiculous," he said to no one in particular. He did not have the time or patience to deal with DMV. There was an hour and a half before the plane would take off. The financial paperwork in his briefcase needed the clients in New York's signatures. Those signatures would fund his next project for his construction company. There was a small window of opportunity to get it. The clients had a two-hour stopover in New York. If Zack did not get their signatures today, he would have to put off the closing on the property for sixty days until they returned from Paris. That meant his crew would not be available for the next project in the timeframe allocated in the contracts. The new project consisted of approximately fifty homes and a shopping mall. The acquisition would take the already successful construction company firmly into the land development area. The anger he felt earlier at the airport that he promised he would contain, was returning. "If I miss that plane someone is going to..."

"Mr. Davenport?" A voice called out from behind the teller counter before he could complete his thought.

Zack turned and saw the most delicate form of a human being he had ever seen. She was a vision in a red pantsuit that seemed to have been tailored just to fit her body. Her face was oval- shaped with the cutest little nose and smoothest brown skin he had ever seen. If that wasn't enough, there were her lips. Sensuous and suckable were the words that came to his mind.

"Mr. Davenport," the woman extended her hand to him. "My name is Ms. Lassiter. I understand we have a situation."

Zack shook the hand she extended then immediately pulled away. The touch of her hand sent an unwanted desire throughout his body. The shock brought him out of his momentary stupor. He frowned at the woman as if she had caused him bodily harm. "We don't have a situation." He angrily stated, "You do."

She smiled. "I'm sure it's nothing we cannot work out. Tell me what you need Mr. Davenport."

If that question were asked under different circumstances he would have told her that was a loaded question. However, this could be a costly situation and he didn't have time to act on his unexplainable physical reaction to the woman. "Simple. I need my license renewed and Ms. Shabazz is refusing to do that."

"Unfortunately the law will not permit her to renew your license without the proper documents. To renew your license we will need proof of legal presence. There are a number of documents you could provide to accomplish that."

Zack looked at the woman as though she had suddenly grown two heads right in front of him. "Ms. Lassiter you are apparently as inconsiderate as your clerk. I have wasted enough time on this. I am a citizen of the United States. I have been a citizen of the United States all my life and plan to continue for the rest of my life. Now, I don't care what it will take, but you will renew my license within the next thirty minutes or I will have your job." He yelled with an air of authority.

"Mr. Davenport, would you join me in my office?"

"Will you renew my license in there?" His anger peaked as he asked the question.

"Please Mr. Davenport," she slightly tilted her head to the side, "join me in my office." She asked undaunted by his anger, then walked toward the office at the end of the counter.

Zack watched for a moment, realizing that was not a question but a steely spoken demand. He grabbed his application off the counter top and walked in the direction of the office. He was determined to complete what he considered a simple task and be on that plane in, he glanced at his watch, the next hour and fifteen minutes.

The door to the office opened allowing Zack to step inside. "Have a seat Mr. Davenport."

"I don't have time to take a seat Ms. Lassiter. I have a plane to catch. You and your clerk are interfering in my plans. And if I'm not mistaken, I believe you may be stepping on my constitutional rights. Now," he stated as he placed his hands on her desk, bent over and stared directly into the woman's eyes, "are you going to renew my license or will I have to call the Governor's office?"

"Well," the woman exhaled, "you are mistaken. There is nothing in the constitution regarding driver's licenses. I don't believe motor vehicles were around at the time the constitution was framed. And if the Governor's office can provide you with the document you need, then by all means make that call." She sat back in her seat, "I however believe your call would be more beneficial if it was placed to Vital Statistics. They will be in a better position to get the document needed."

If Zack could have snatched the woman up out of her chair he would have, that's how angry he was at this point. Didn't she know the scowl on his face was supposed to make her bend to his will? "You are actually enjoying this aren't you? This menial job is the only place you have to assert your authority. I suppose that gives you some sense of importance," he snarled.

"Mr. Davenport," she sat up and smiled, "let me make a call on your behalf." Zack straightened as she picked up the telephone. She was having a conversation on the telephone as Zack angrily paced the office. Looking at his watch, he saw the window of opportunity slipping away. That was an issue, but now there was a more profound one. The woman sitting on the telephone was raising his curiosity, and a few other things he did not have time to deal with. He needed to get out of this office and away from her as soon as possible.

"Mr. Davenport what time is your flight?" the woman asked.

Zack angrily answered, "Two-forty-five."

"Vital Statistics is about twenty minutes away. My contact could have your birth certificate ready to pick up within that timeframe. In forty-five minutes, you could be on your way to the airport. Would you like for me to have her to prepare the document for you?"

"Where is the office located?" he lashed out.

"Willow Lawn Shopping Center on West Broad Street," she calmly replied.

Zack looked at his watch. He pulled out his cell phone and dialed a number. "Where are you man?"

"Good," he exhaled. "Vital Statistics is across the street, could you run over and speak with a" he looked at Ms. Lassiter for the name.

"Ms. Lassiter," she replied.

"I don't need your name. I need the name of your contact."

"Ruby Lassiter," she smiled.

He looked at her then spoke into the cell phone, "Ruby Lassiter. Bring the document to the DMV on

Laburnum Ave." He listened then replied, "I'll explain when you get here. Hey, hurry up the plane takes off in an hour." He hung up the telephone and looked at Ms. Lassiter. "I take it that was a family member. Does your entire family work as public servants who like to create delays for the poor citizens in the state?"

Ms. Lassiter smiled then stood up. "You are more than welcome to sit here in my office while you wait for your document to arrive. I need to check on my staff."

"I don't need to sit in your office. I will wait outside. The Governor will hear about this incident Ms. Lassiter," he said as he slammed the office door behind him.

Twenty minutes later Zack walked into Ms. Lassiter's office without knocking. He threw the document on her desk just as she was looking up. "May I please have my driver's license now!" he demanded.

Ms. Lassiter stood and smiled, "Yes sir. I will have this processed right away."

"Thank you for your kindness," he snarled.

Ms. Lassiter walked past Zack into the lobby. She handed the document and the application across the counter to Ms. Shabazz and asked her to complete the transaction. She turned to Zack "Once we take your picture and process your transaction you can be on your way. I do apologize for the inconvenience Mr. Davenport."

"Diamond?"

She looked over Zack's shoulder and smiled brightly. Zack looked back; she was looking at his brother.

"Xavier?" she called out, briskly walked over and hugged him. "My goodness you look wonderful. What are you doing here?"

"I think I'm here to save you from my brother," Xavier Davenport smiled back still holding her by the waist.

Zack looked at the two, and for some odd reason was bothered by the intimacy the two were sharing. "I take it you two know each other?" Zack growled as he posed for the camera.

"Yes we went to college together." Xavier beamed as he pointed to Diamond. "She was my savior whenever I got into trouble with classes." He turned back to her, "What are you doing here?" he asked as Zack took his picture.

"I'm the manager here," she smiled proudly.

"That must be interesting," he laughed, "especially dealing with people like Zack. Did he bite your head off?"

"My head and a couple of other places," she whispered with a smile.

"His bark is worse than his bite. Don't worry about it."

Zack, with his renewed license in hand, was hurrying towards the door. "I would worry Ms. Lassiter if I were you. You will be hearing from me again regarding this incident. Let's go X-man," Zack stormed out of the door.

Xavier looked at Diamond, "I'll take care of it." He reached inside his suit jacket. "This is my card. Call me soon. We have a lot to catch up on. Right now I need to get him on that plane."

"Xavier!" Zack yelled back through the door.

"I'll call you," Diamond smiled as Xavier ran out the door. She looked at the card that read, Davenport Industries. *Xavier started the company he wanted,* she thought and smiled as she walked back to her office. *Zackary must be the older brother he always talked about. He never mentioned how handsome his older brother was.* "I don't know how you put up with people like that," LaFonde Shabazz said as Diamond walked behind the counter. "I was ready to give him a piece of my mind."

"I was ready to give him a piece of something else," Deidra, another clerk joked. "That brother was fine."

Diamond gave Deidra a high five, "Hey," they both laughed. "Indeed he was."

"His brother wasn't bad either." Deidra look questioningly at Diamond, "How well do you know him?"

"Very well, but not in the way you are thinking."

"The way he was holding you suggested something else," Deidra smirked.

"No, just a friend." Diamond turned to walk away, "Ladies I do believe we have more customers waiting." Letting each of them know the excitement was over. It was time to get back to work.

Sitting at her desk, Diamond stared at the card. The excitement may have been over in the office, but the build up in the lower part of her body was still kicking strong. She put the card in her purse as she massaged the hand touched by Zackary Davenport, trying to rub away the sensation that lingered. Professionalism dictated that she not react the moment she saw him. But the urge to go to him and ease his fears was overwhelming. Diamond didn't know who or what had hurt the man, but she was certain the scars ran deep. She could see it in his eyes. Then, for the brief moment his eyes held hers, she knew—down in the gut knew, those were the eyes of the man that would teach her how to love. "Mommy said it could happen like this," she whispered. Shaking her head and smiling, the thought she kept at bay as she was dealing with Zackary Davenport burst forward. He was the man she was waiting for. She laughed out loud, "Finally."

$$\mathcal{L}$$

Damn! The article in the newspaper was disappointing. "After months of speculation, Davenport Construction has been cleared of any suspicion in the blaze that destroyed several homes at the Franklin sub-division. Sources close to the investigation stated there was no clear determining factor in the blaze. Therefore, it's been ruled accidental." *How in the hell could that be?* "Sources further state Chief Hasting indicated one of the determining factors to his final decision was the unblemished record of Davenport Construction. There were no code violations or complaints against the company. In its five years of business, this was the first incident on record." Unblemished! They don't know Zackary the way I do. He turned his back on me without any thought to how I would survive. Stop raving like a maniac and think—think! Where did I go wrong? Hmm—maybe I was too clever. Yeah. I should have left something pointing directly to him, indisputable evidence that would lead the authorities directly to his door. What is it going to take to bring him down? Put him exactly in the same position he put me—living in a two bedroom shack roaches wouldn't call home. Just the thought of him living high and mighty sends streaks of rage through my veins. I don't want to be like this, but I need to hold on to the rage, the humiliation he and his father caused. Hell, I can't make his father pay, but I damn sure can disrupt Zackary's life. I need to hold on to the rage to take him down. Unblemished my ass! Wait—that's it. His good reputation needs a mark or two. Yeah, that's it. The fire could be the beginning now that it's on record. Hmm, I'm feeling better already. Let's see, what destructive things can happen in Mr. Perfect's life?

L

Diamond

Chapter 1

One month later

Zack appeared in the office early for the nine o'clock meeting. Normally, he would be on the construction site at seven each morning and not in the exquisitely plush office building that they recently renovated to accommodate the additional staff. It was good to have his baby brother, Xavier, in the business now. While Zack was an excellent builder, Xavier was the one with the business mind. Davenport Construction had grown to the next level and was now Davenport Industries thanks to Xavier.

The construction company was started five years ago by Zack at the age of twenty-six during Xavier's last year of college. Zack worked hard to learn the construction trade when he was forced to leave college to raise Xavier. Their father passed away when Zack was nineteen, leaving a fourteen-year-old brother to care for. Zack worked construction to pay the bills and keep the family home. He made sure Xavier did not want for anything, while he went without just about everything, including women. Yes he had those that would be around whenever he was in need, but he learned early not to depend on any one of them to hang around for any amount of time. His mother left when he was fifteen and his girlfriend left when the dream of the professional football career ended.

None of that mattered now, Zack thought as he took a seat behind the desk in his office. Xavier was on board with short term and long term goals for Davenport Industries and Zack could not be happier. He loved his business, but for the life of him, he could not get used to dealing with his clients. All he wanted was the plans for the homes and his crew. The customer service end of the business anyone could have and Zack could care less about it.

X-man, his nickname for Xavier, had structured the company into two sections. Section one, construction, Zack would handle the building of all projects and the hiring of his crew. Section two, development, X-man would handle the staffing of the business offices, designs, and land acquisition on new projects. It was a perfect setup as far as Zack was concerned. He was especially happy with the idea of not having to talk to clients. X-man had hired an intermediate to handle that. No more deciphering through customers' mind changes. That would now be someone else's headache. There were other aches he would have to deal with, like the fire that nearly destroyed his business. The authorities were still uneasy about the cause of the fire and to be honest so was he.

Zack stood, unbuttoned his suit jacket, put his hands in his pockets and looked out the windows that encased one entire wall of his office in downtown Richmond. He could see the site for the new project in the distance to the north. Looking west across the James River he could see the homes of South Bend Estates, the project his construction company just completed. The very last house of the project was the one that burned to the ground. It was never clear to him how the fire started. The authorities stated the cause was faulty wiring, but he knew the sub-contractor that did the wiring job for him and they were top notch. He also knew faulty wiring was at times used as a catch all when the actual cause cannot be determined. His gut was still telling him there was more to the fire. Once the investigation was closed, Zack and his crew rebuilt the home at his expense and in record time to ensure the developers did not take a loss. His quick action quieted the whispers surrounding his construction company's possible role in the fire. Fortunately, the incident had not stopped the investors from taking a chance with Davenport Industries.

"Hey big bro. It's a big day for the Davenports," Xavier's excitement was clear as he walked into Zack's office. "Here I brought you a black coffee. What's with the intense look?"

Zack turned at the welcomed interruption to see his six-one, slim little brother, with his shoulder length locs secured at his neck, dressed in a tailored suit and Italian loafers. The thought, *when did X-man get so tall and when is he going to cut his hair,* crossed his mind. But he did not voice them, for his brother was right. This was a special day for the Davenport brothers. "Thanks man, I appreciate it," Zack exhaled as he sat back at his desk and took a drink of the coffee. "Nothing to be concerned with," he waved off the feeling. "The crew is itching to get started. This project will keep them working for the next twenty-four months, non-stop. You did good with this one X-man, I'm proud of you."

Xavier looked at his older brother with pride. He always wanted to make sure Zack knew how much he understood the sacrifices made on his behalf. If it took him the rest of his life, he wanted to make sure Zack never regretted the actions he took ten years ago. "Man, it's the least I could do. You put your life on hold to raise me. Now it's my time to give back."

"I don't need back from you. I need you happy with your life and what you want to do with it."

"Zack, this is it," Xavier smiled. "Pulling this project together is something I have dreamed about since I was in college. It's taken me five years to get it started, but the day is here. And I'll tell you, we have a hell of a team. I can't wait for you to meet everyone."

Zack smiled, which in itself, was a rarity, "You did your part by gathering the team. Now it's time for me to do my part."

"Hmm speaking of your part," Xavier spoke cautiously. "Do you think you could possibly be a little pleasant today?"

"I'm always pleasant," Zack snarled.

"Yes, to me you are." X-man quickly stated, then cautiously continued, "However, you are a little rough on women. The board members consist of five people; our attorney and customer relations specialists are females. I'm asking you to put forth an effort to get along with both of them. I have put in a lot of time and resources with headhunters to bring this staff together. I don't want to lose any of them because of your temper."

"I don't have a problem with women!" Zack yelled.

"Of course you do," Mrs. Carson said as she walked into his office and placed his messages in the center of the desk. JoEllen Carson, all five feet three inches of her, was the only woman Zack allowed to say whatever she wanted to him. She had worked for the construction company Zack worked for and decided to come on board as his secretary when he started his own company. JoEllen kept all his paperwork in order and the bills paid on time. If it had not been for her, the business would have folded soon after he started it. Not only did Zack depend on her for his business, but personal ethics as well. She was the mother he never had. "You could simply try lowering your voice. No one is really afraid of you anyway," she said while walking out the office.

Xavier laughed at the bewildered expression on Zack's face. "She's lucky I respect my elders," Zack yelled.

"I'll be in the lobby meeting the new employees and showing them around." Xavier stood. "We will be in the conference room at nine sharp," he stated as he walked towards the door. "And by the way, you look good in a suit, my brother. You should wear them more often."

Zack preferred his jeans and tee shirts any day to the comfortable but confining suits he had to wear for business meetings. Zack stood and posed for his brother. "Take a good look. After this meeting today, it will be a while before you see this again."

Chapter 2

Zack stood in the conference room talking with Jake Turner, the Human Resources Director and Charles Meeks, Director of Finance. He found both to be professional and very astute in their individual fields. His attention was with Charles, who was discussing investments and the merits of diversity in your personal portfolio. Zack wasn't an expert in the field, but had acquired a very nice portfolio for himself over the years. He invested well and those investments had paid off. They were interrupted when Julia English approached them to introduce herself. Zack's first impression of her was how very articulate she was and with that her intelligence became evident. He was impressed X-man was able to bring her onboard. Julia was a very confident sought after Corporate Attorney, who expressed how thrilled she was at the prospect of working with a minority owned business. Her rationale for leaving a very lucrative six-figure income to take a chance on an up and coming company was simple. She wanted to help build something from the ground up. That's the legacy she wanted to leave for her unborn child. That's when she announced she, and her husband of four years, were expecting their first child in six months. The announcement did not necessarily sit well with Zack. In his mind, he questioned X-man's decision on her hiring. However, remembering the request from his little brother, he would hold his tongue and hope the woman could not read what was on his mind. Before he could respond, Reese Kendrick, Zack's best friend from high school, walked over. A pleasantly surprised Zack immediately shook Reese's hand. "Man what are you are doing here?"

The ex-police officer smiled and gave Zack a pat on the back. "I'm your Security Director. X-man asked me to keep it from you. He wanted to surprise you."

"Damn man. It's a good surprise, welcome aboard."

"X-man has come into his own. You did a good job with him Zack."

"Yeah, I'm proud as hell of him and I know Pop would be too."

Zack suddenly felt odd. The bottom half of his body was filling with desire and his body immediately tensed. That bothered him since the only person he was talking to was Reese. He released Reese's hand, took a step back and frowned. Taking a look at the small group around him, he noticed more people were in the conference room, but couldn't account for the reaction his body was having. He raised a questioning eyebrow at Julia. She was very attractive, but not quite his taste in a woman. Besides, she was married and carrying a child. His body wouldn't react to her—would it?

"You okay Zack?" Reese asked puzzled by his friend's reaction. Before Zack could respond, Reese's attention was drawn away. "Whoa. Who in the hell is that with X-man?"

The group turned towards the door. "Oh," Julia exclaimed, "That's the Customer Relations Director. I met her a few days ago and she is awesome."

Zack turned. A look of disbelief appeared on his face, then it changed to something a lot stronger—RAGE! "Awesome or not, I hope like hell he did not hire that woman to work for this company."

Xavier caught Zack's reaction and knew there was going to be a battle. He only hoped Zack would contain himself until...

"Xavier Davenport—my office, now!"

"So much for hope," Xavier chuckled. "As much as I would like to accommodate you big brother, I'm afraid we need to start the meeting."

Zack was half way out the door when X-man finished his statement. He stopped and glared at his little brother and bellowed, "NOW!"

The room fell silent as Xavier held his brother's glare. "Oh—you meant right now?" Xavier asked wittily. Zack stomped off. Xavier turned to the people looking on curiously, shocked at the outburst, and smiled. "This is a family matter." He smoothly stated. "Please forgive us. Take a seat and we will be with you in a moment."

Xavier walked into Zack's office behind JoEllen, as she asked, "What on earth happened? I heard you yelling down here."

"I'm afraid I'm what happened," Diamond Lassiter smiled from the doorway with her hands clasped behind her back. "Hello Mr. Davenport," she said as she took a step inside the office.

Zack's body went into battle stance. He folded his arms across his chest and stood with his feet apart. Anyone with good common sense would have run from the six-two, two hundred and twenty pounds of muscle that was beginning to growl at them. But not Diamond. No, not her, Zack thought as he watched her stroll over with her hands behind her back. She stopped in front of him and had the nerve to smile at him. Didn't she know that it was against the law to have a smile like that? But damn if it wasn't a pretty smile. He shook the thought from his mind. This was war. The woman was after him. He could see it in her eyes.

"What in the hell are you doing here?" He snarled as he looked down at the woman that may be five feet four inches, one hundred ten pounds with every inch of it in the right place and a gleam in her eyes that could save a drowning man, and she had the nerve to have dimples. Dimples—his mind screamed!

Diamond prayed her outer body did not show the turmoil of her inner body. There was something about being in the same room with Zackary Davenport that made her want to kiss all his anger away. She felt it that day in her office and it was even stronger here. Man, he was pissed or scared, Diamond wasn't sure which. But she didn't care. She was put on this earth for this man. "Xavier was so impressed with the way I handled your situation the last time we met that he asked me to join the company. You made such an impression on me that day, I simply couldn't turn away the opportunity to work with you."

What he wouldn't do to kiss that smirk off her face. The thought angered him. He looked over her head at his brother, "Xavier, what in the hell could you have been thinking. First you hire Julia English who is either very much out of shape or is a few months pregnant. Here," he glowered down at Diamond and frowned at the dimples that called out to him, "in Ms. Lassiter you have a woman I consider inconsiderate and incompetent. Have you lost your mind!"

Before Xavier was able to reply, Diamond turned to him, "Did he have a run in with Julia also?"

"No, I did not have a run in with Julia," Zack snapped, "just you!"

Diamond turned back to Zack and smiled, "I guess that makes me special."

JoEllen looked at Xavier and coughed to smother her laugh. She could not believe this young woman who looked to be all of twenty—maybe, was standing there confronting Zack's anger like it was nothing.

Xavier shrugged, "I figure if she could handle him as a customer, she could certainly handle any client we may have," he whispered.

Zack unfolded his arms and clenched his fists at his sides. "The only thing special about you is that you will be the first to tender your resignation. Whatever contract you have with this company will be paid out up front." He pointed to the door, "There's the door. Use it!"

Diamond exhaled. "Mr. Davenport, you seem to be a reasonable man." She paused as she stared at him. "Well, maybe not. But, I haven't done anything in the first ten minutes of employment with your company to warrant a dismissal. Would you at least consider the fact that Xavier has put a lot of time and effort into assembling this team? He wouldn't do anything to jeopardize his dream or your confidence in him. Do you honestly think I would be here if I was not the very best in this field? Is your belief in your little brother that low?"

Zack's stance relaxed a little as his glance shifted to X-man who stood there with a questioning look on his face. Of course he believed in his brother. X-man had his unconditional support. Xavier has worked on this project for five years and he knew there was no way he would hire just anyone unless they were qualified. He never wanted X-man to question the confidence he had in him."Exactly what position is it that you are filling?" Zack asked staring down at Diamond.

He believed her dimples deepened when she smiled up at him. "Customer Relations Director. I believe you and I will be working very closely together."

"Hell no! It's not going to happen. It was because of you that we almost lost the financing for this project." He took a step closer to her and growled. "You are an inconsiderate, control freak, who let a little power go to your head."

"Well, I think," Diamond started then stopped as he stepped even closer.

"What, do you think Ms. Lassiter," he spit out.

The man was standing so close that if she tip-toed up just a little, she could kiss him. But, that would put more fear in his eyes and that was not her intent. So, she had to do something just as outrageous to get him to listen to reason.

Diamond stepped closer to him and sweetly replied, "I think you are a ridiculously handsome man. A woman wouldn't stand a chance against you if you ever smiled." She watched the play of emotions go across his face and was satisfied with knocking him off balance. She took a step back and shook her head, "Nope a woman wouldn't stand a chance." She turned and walked out of the room saying, "I will see you all in the conference room."

Xavier looked at the stunned expression on Zack's face as he watched Diamond walk out. Most men had issues speaking their mind to Zack, much less women, but not Diamond. She was as straight to the point as they come. He was sure she would be able to handle Zack's resentment towards her and do an outstanding job for Davenport Industries. He grinned at Zack, "Hmm, you have any other questions big brother?"

JoEllen looked up at him, "I don't think she is scared of you Zack," she beamed.

Zack stood there shocked at the bluntness of the woman who had shown him her back for the second time since he met her. Just like the first time, her presence stirred desire throughout his body. That was something he did not have the time or patience for. If she was going to work for this company, and it appeared she was, Zack had to make sure he kept his distance from her. The last thing he needed was to know she was attracted to him. Zack looked at JoEllen and Xavier. "You two find something funny?"

"Not funny. But that look on your face is hilarious." Xavier smiled.

Zack frowned and stormed out of the room. "Let's get this damn meeting over with!"

Chapter 3

*W*alking into the conference room at Davenport was equivalent to walking into a boardroom on Wall Street. The carpet was so thick your feet literally sank with each step. Surrounding the twelve-seat conference table were leather ergonomic chairs, drop-down electronic whiteboard and monitor. However, unlike the boardrooms on Wall Street, the ambiance was impressively soothing, not stressful. Everyone was seated when Zack entered the room and took his seat at one end of the table with X- man at the opposite end. Reese, Charles and Julia sat to Zack's left at one side of the table while JoEllen, Jack and Diamond sat on the opposite side of the table. The positions, unfortunately, put Diamond directly in Zack's vision path. That proved to be a problem for Zack. However, it placed Diamond to X-man's right, which helped her immensely, since he was the one leading the meeting.

X-man started the meeting apologizing for the delay, and then proceeded introducing each member of the team. Then he moved on to the introduction of the long awaited presentation. "I would like to officially welcome all of you to Davenport Industries. My brother and I look forward to a rewarding future for you, for the community and of course for us. I would like to share a short story with you. Our father passed away when I was fourteen. Zack had just begun his sophomore year at Virginia Union University and had captured the starting quarterback position. Rather than continuing with his education, Zack opted to leave college to finish the daunting task of raising me. At the age of nineteen, he became the father of a resentful little brother. To this day

I have never heard one complaint from him." He paused, then glanced down the table at Zack. His brother simply held his gaze as the silent thank you was received. Then X-man continued. "To support us he began working in construction. One Saturday he took me to one of his work sites as a punishment for something I had done and made me work. I was not a happy camper. However, I was not foolish enough to buck him. As you can see he is a rather large force." Xavier smiled and looked at Zack. "That day I discovered construction was not just a way to pay the bills for him. Every nail he hammered was done with pride and conviction. He was building someone's home, a place for them to find refuge from the outside world. A place where people can raise a family and create memories. It was then that I decided I wanted to be a part of that and I began drawing designs for houses.

"During college, I met Diamond Lassiter. At first I thought she was there simply for my enjoyment; however, she quickly altered that thought by wounding my young male ego and we became very good friends. We talked a lot, sharing ideas and dreams. One day I felt comfortable enough with her to show her some of my home designs. To my surprise she was very impressed. She told me about her eleven brothers and sisters and how they lived in a five-bedroom house because her parents could not afford a larger home. Then she said the craziest thing." He looked at Diamond. "Wouldn't it be nice to have a community of homes like these that anyone would be able to afford?" He smiled warmly at her then continued. "We began developing a community, with homes, a school, shopping center, banks and a movie theater. It was a rough draft and from time to time over the next four years, I would go to the design and make adjustments. By the end of my last year of college the community had become my dream. As always, I turned to Zack for advice. This time he not only gave me advice, but also assisted with getting the financing needed to help me realize my dream. For a number of years I have been searching for a way to show my appreciation for all he has done for me during my life. I hope this small gesture will give him some idea of my love for him."

X-man pushed a button on the remote that sat at the end of the table, then turned to watch the forty-two inch plasma monitor ease down and stop. At the push of another button an aerial image of land still covered with an abundance of trees appeared. "Our first community will be located on 100 acres of land in eastern Henrico County. It will consist of fifty homes each on an acre lot. In addition to the single dwellings, there will be a community of thirty townhomes, a community center, which will house a daycare and senior care facilities, a shopping center, restaurants and Davenport Towers Condominiums." X-man turned back to the group and smiled. "Ladies and Gentlemen, it is my honor to present to you—Z Estates." X-man took his seat.

The layout of the community with a wrought iron fence with the letter Z circled in the middle appeared on the screen with Diamond leaning against a 1965 cherry red corvette convertible dressed in a matching red dress. The virtual tour began playing. As Diamond welcomed people to the virtual tour, she eased inside the convertible, began driving through the iron archway double gates as they opened. She followed the road to a circular fountain situated in front of the community center, then turned left driving by the townhomes, a shopping mall, a grocery store, a bank, a theater and several small restaurants. On the far end of the complex were home sites that ranged from expansive ranchers to two and three level mansions. At the very back were an elementary school, middle school, a football stadium, baseball diamond and then the high school.

Zack watched the tour and was amazed at the details of Xavier's plans, from the design of the homes, to the landscape, the community center and Condominiums including the inside of the mall. He had seen the individual plans for the different homes and facilities in the community. However, this was the first time he had seen the entire scope of the project, and he loved it the moment it was revealed. His focus remained on the screen.

Once the virtual tour was completed, everyone sat quietly. For a moment, Xavier wondered if he had over reached, were he and Diamond the only ones that believed this community could exist. Diamond looked at Xavier who was looking to Zack for approval. She glanced down the table to Zack. His face was expressionless, but his eyes were not. She could see the pride shining through. She lowered her head and smiled, *Xavier is going to build his dream.*

Zack stood and walked over to his little brother. Xavier stood as well waiting. Zack shook his hand and hugged him. "It's amazing, X-man. I can't tell you how proud of you I am at this moment."

Xavier smiled and hit Zack on the back, "Thank you big brother." The room erupted in applause.

Zack walked back to his seat, "I would change two things", he said as he sat. "The name should be Davenport Estates and the virtual tour should be done by a virtual model."

Xavier looked at Diamond and frowned. He knew she put a lot of work into the presentation. He wanted to make sure she received the deserved recognition. "I think Diamond did a great job in describing the estates."

"Then use her voice, but use a virtual model," Zack replied.

"Are there any other issues?" Diamond asked interrupting the argument that was about to ensue.

Zack shook his head without looking up, "No."

"Then a virtual model it will be," she replied. There was no way she would allow Zackary's displeasure with her to interfere with Xavier's plans.

Xavier looked at her understanding the sacrifice she was making for him. Shaking his head and moving forward he continued with the meeting, but made a note to speak with Zack about his comments. Each member of the team presented his or her initial reports to the group. All were accepted without comment or question, until Diamond gave her report. Her initial report of possible clients for Davenport homes created murmurs around the table.

Charles, the finance director thought the number was a little too ambitious. "I'm not sure the economy will support the push for thirty homes, thirty townhomes and the shopping center in the first year."

"I think with the right PR campaign, it will." Diamond stated, undeterred by the comment. "To date I have received several bids from chain grocery stores for the site, several retail merchants are interested in leasing space and I'm fielding calls from potential home buyers. We may not be able to keep up with the demand for these homes," Diamond enthusiastically declared.

"Whatever demand you bring in, my crew will be more than capable of handling," Zack stated. "Frankly I must agree with Charles. I think your numbers are not realistic. Revise your report to the thirty townhomes, the shopping center and possibly ten home sites."

Xavier looked at Diamond, who nodded her head agreeing to make the adjustments. However, he could tell her enthusiasm was being stomped on.

After Julia gave her report on the legal aspects of the project, Zack smiled and thanked her. Zack advised the team that the ground was broken on the model home and the first set of town homes. "Within a month, the first set of town homes will be ready for dry wall. The model will be completed and ready for decorating for show. Within ninety days, the first home site will be at the same point. In the meantime, Ms. Lassiter, your public relations will have to take place from a trailer. Will that be an issue?"

"Not at all," Diamond replied, refusing to allow his sour mood to spoil the special day.

Xavier smiled and then stood, "I believe we are done. Ladies and gentlemen thank you for your input. The ball is now in your court."

Diamond walked back to her office a little dejected. "Hey girl, hold your head up. Don't let the men on this project determine your worth," Julia said as she walked along. "You know we are working in a man's world here. They will doubt you until you prove yourself. If you think you can truly sell thirty town homes, and thirty home sites, do it. I'm certain Zackary Davenport will not turn the buyers away."

"Thank you for the encouragement Julia," Diamond replied with a faint smile. There was a feisty, kick-ass attitude about Julia that Diamond liked. *That must have been how she survived the male dominated corporate world she came from,* Diamond thought as she walked past LaFonde, whom she brought along as her assistant in a package deal to Davenport Industries. It really was a sucker move on her part, but she wanted someone at the job who knew and liked her.

LaFonde followed her into the office. "How bad was he?"

Since Diamond was to play host to customers, her office was a large open space that incorporated a sitting area of two sofas with a table in the center. A model area that held framed pictures of each of the homes being offered, a table with the actual land layout of lots available and an area with a refreshment stand that included a mini-bar, refrigerator and coffee pot. On the other side of the room was a cherry wood desk sitting in front of a wall of windows, a small conference table with four chairs around it and a cherry secure credenza that held customers financial documents. In front of her desk were two comfortable chairs, one of which LaFonde took up residence in as Diamond sat in the chair behind her desk. "Hell on wheels." Diamond replied as she sat back in the chair and turned towards the window wondering what in the hell had she gotten herself into.

"Are you sure you want to continue with this?" LaFonde huffed. "In case you forgot, the man was not pleasant the first time you met him."

Diamond exhaled and turned back to her desk. "I know. Nevertheless, Xavier has asked me to help him realize this dream and I am committed to doing that. Zackary Davenport is not going to scare me away. Besides, that man needs me in his life." Diamond opened the folder she brought from the meeting.

"But does he want you?" The look Diamond gave her was not pleasant, so she changed directions. "Well, this is the first time he has been in this building since we started. Maybe he won't be here that much."

"He has an office here, but most of his time is spent on site. With all the houses I plan to sell, he will continue to spend most of his time there."

"Once the models are complete, won't you have to spend most of your time on site too?"

Diamond exhaled, "Yes, but hopefully some of his dislike for me will have disappeared by then. In the meantime, we have to redo the report. He feels my estimated sales numbers are too high and wants them adjusted showing more reasonable numbers." She gave the report with notes she'd made to LaFonde. "Also, he wants a virtual model doing the virtual tour, not me. See if you can get the site designer to develop a model and change the voice over too, just to be on the safe side."

"I thought the demo was good. It received positive responses from the test group. Why the changes?"

"Mr. Zackary Davenport liked the virtual tour. He just did not like me on it."

"Does he know how many hours you put into that demo? Does he know how good you are at this? Does he doubt your ability to do this job?"

Diamond knew the answers to all of the questions LaFonde had bombarded her with. However, she did not want to answer any of them. It was hard to admit a man she was personally attracted to, not only did not like her, but had very little respect for her abilities. "He may not know any of those things. It's up to me to prove how good I am. You get started on the web people and I will redo the report and start the media blitz."

LaFonde took the report, "I'll redo the report. You start the media blitz. We need to show this man who he's dealing with. Humph, he don't know who he's messing with," LaFonde continued mumbling under her breath as she walked out of the room.

Diamond couldn't help but smile at her friend who was upset over the insult on her behalf. The smile faded as Diamond stood and looked out of her window with her hands clasped behind her back. She was the over achiever. There was no obstacle she could not overcome. With six brothers and five sisters, she knew how to be patient and wait her turn. That's what she had to do with Zackary Davenport. She had to be patient and wait for him to learn what she already knew. He needed her in his life. "Okay Zackary, I guess it's up to me to teach you how to love." All that anger and mistrust he displayed towards her was his protective mechanism. "I'm about to melt your armor Zackary." With that planted firmly in her mind, Diamond sat down to begin her journey.

Chapter 4

a week later Diamond received an e-mail indicating that the trailer on the site was up. Since the report had been revamped and the presentation with the virtual tour guide was just about complete she decided to ride out to the site to see what was needed to prepare the trailer for clients. The article in the newspaper had sparked more interest than she anticipated and she wanted to make sure everything was ready for customers.

Pulling into the site, Diamond was pleased to see the trailer was placed at the beginning of the worksite. The road was still gravel, which made the area and anything near it dusty, but she could work around that. She approached the trailer, but found the door locked. Looking around she saw another trailer and the frame to the first model home. The project was underway and she couldn't be more excited. It was a nice day so she decided to walk to the model to find a supervisor or someone with the key. As she walked in her heels and skirt suit, she immediately decided a change of clothes would be kept in the trunk of her car until the street was paved in.

Marveling at the construction going on around her, she was not paying a lot of attention to her surroundings. She walked over and asked one man who was in charge of the site. The man pointed to a man with his back to her. Recognition was immediate—it was Zack. He was standing with his legs apart giving directions to one of the workers. Something in his stance reeked of total control and confidence in what he was saying. He was a man's man; nothing but pure masculinity. She sighed and shook her head. It was ridiculous to keep having this type of reaction to this man every time she was around him. For some ungodly reason she could not stop her attraction to Zack Davenport—nor did she want to. She inhaled and walked towards him.

He must have sensed her approaching because he turned around before she could say anything. The frown on his face indicated he was not happy to see her.

"Hello Mr. Davenport," Diamond managed to say before Zack grabbed her by the arms, pulling her forward, crashing into his chest just before a stack of lumber fell from a forklift behind her.

While trying to compose herself, she heard Zack order one of the men to help with the removal of the fallen lumber. He turned to her while she was brushing dirt from her skirt and growled, "Are you that dense? Do you know anything about construction sites?" Before she could answer, she was being dragged by the elbow towards the construction trailer. Once inside Zack continued with the assault. "You can't wear something that distracting on a construction site. Men work here. Don't you know how men on a construction site react to a woman with legs as long as yours? Don't ever come to my site dressed like—like that. In fact don't ever disrupt my site again."

Diamond stared at the man. It wasn't clear to her what she had done to disrupt his site. She looked down at her black silk suit and heels, which was now covered in dust and decided the sight of her legs, must have displeased him. Whatever it was, did not give him enough reason to man handle her the way he did. If one of her six brothers had grabbed her that way she would have kicked his ass. But this was her boss, at least one of them. She was out to prove herself and whatever it took to do that, she would do. So before she said something that he would regret hearing and she would regret saying, Diamond turned and walked out of the trailer without speaking a word. When she reached her car, she looked back and saw Zack and Reese, the security man standing outside the trailer watching her. Diamond wanted to release the tears that were threatening to flow, but she held back. Not sure what hurt the most, the embarrassment in the way he spoke to her or the realization that this man who stirred her so deeply inside really did not like her being around.

She went to the mall, which was located just a few miles from the site, purchased a pair of jeans, a tee shirt and a pair of timberland boots. She changed her clothes and went back to the site. This time she drove directly to the construction trailer and marched inside.

Zack and Reese were standing at the desk reviewing some paperwork when she walked in. "Mr. Davenport, do you happen to have the key to the host trailer?" She asked without expressing the angry emotions that engulfed her. Later she would pat herself on the back for being so professional when all she wanted to do was kick him.

"I have that key Diamond," Reese responded quickly, hoping to prevent another scene between the two.

She stared at Zack. Deep down she wanted to ask him if it was just her or did he hate all women. She decided against that and turned to Reese instead. "I would like to prepare the trailer for clients. May I have a key to see what's needed?"

"Sure," he replied while pulling a ring of keys from his pocket. "I'll walk down with you."

"That won't be necessary Mr. Kendrick, I won't be long," she replied and walked out of the trailer.

Zack stood in battle stance the whole time Diamond was in his presence. When he turned and saw her standing behind him, an immediate surge of desire rode throughout his body. But it wasn't the unexplainable desire that had him frowning. He couldn't explain why but his heart damn near jumped out of his body when he saw the lumber falling towards her. Hell, it was her own damn fault. That skirt she was wearing revealed too much of her perfectly formed legs.

The man driving the forklift couldn't help but be distracted at the sight of her, at least Zack couldn't.

"Did she think changing into those jeans would keep men from reacting to her?" Reese asked looking out the window at the departing woman. When Zack did not reply, Reese turned and noticed the crease in his forehead and his stance. "Are you all right man?"

Zack glared at Reese. "You were looking at her ass weren't you?"

Reese laughed, "You damn right I was. Did you see that? Seeing a woman like that will make you stare."

"You have a wife and two children at home."

"What?" he chuckled, "That's supposed to make me blind or something? Hell, you're the only one walking around trying to act like she doesn't affect you. Don't try to lay your inhibitions on those of us in the male species that happen to like looking at a fine woman like Diamond."

"Your eyes should be for your wife only."

"And they are, but ain't nothing wrong with appreciating a work of art."

"She's just another woman." Zack said as he looked back down at the report on the desk.

Reese stared at him. "You like her don't you?"

Zack's head snapped up, "You want to finish going over this security detail. If not, I have homes to build."

Reese held his friend's stare then sat in the chair in front of the desk. "You know, at some point you are going to have to give some woman a chance. Diamond wouldn't be a bad choice."

Zack sat back in his chair and folded his arms across his chest. "Security Reese—security."

"All right man," Reese pulled one of the reports out and began reviewing his plans for security shifts. Zack listened, but his mind was still on the damn skirt Diamond had on and the feel of her body against his when he grabbed her. The fact that he was still thinking about it pissed him off.

Diamond made a note of things needed to make the trailer presentable. The media blitz had created interest already. Fifteen calls had come through with questions on the proposed community. As a result she wanted the trailer ready for visitors by the weekend. The trailer was a double wide with two rooms. One room would be used as her temporary office and the other to display models and floor plans of the homes being offered and the community layout with home sites marked.

Pulling out her laptop Diamond sent an e-mail to LaFonde giving a list of items to order, before leaving the trailer. It had taken her a moment to settle down to work after her run in with Zack, but now that she looked around, Diamond noticed it was a really nice place. A desk and file cabinet were already in the space to the left and a nice oval shaped table in the room to the right. Actually, there was a partial wall with glass at the top that separated the two rooms. With the right furniture, the space could be staged just right for customers. Once her plans were made, she placed a call to Xavier, to get Mr. Kendrick's cell phone number. There was no way she could take another confrontation with Zack Davenport today. She called and asked Mr. Kendrick to meet her outside the trailer to retrieve the key. He advised her to keep the key and to make a copy. He would keep the copy with him. Grateful for the small reprieve, Diamond left the site and headed straight for her parent's home. Today she needed to feel the love of her family.

Chapter 5

*L*ike most children, whenever Diamond began to doubt herself or her decisions, she went for reinforcement. For her that was the loving arms of her mother. Her decision to pursue Zackary Davenport was weighing heavy on her heart and she needed to talk with someone who knew her well and would advise her if it was a bad choice.

The day she met him at DMV, there was no question in her mind he was the man she was waiting for. Throughout her younger years Diamond never played with love. She knew exactly what she wanted and did not mind waiting for it. She wanted the forever love, like what her parents Joseph and Sally Lassiter had. They were about to celebrate their 35th wedding anniversary. Not a day had passed when Diamond did not see her father caressing her mother or her mother lovingly looking into her father's eyes. She refused to settle for anything less.

Twenty-six year old Diamond was the fifth of twelve children. Her oldest brother Samuel, was an ex-navy-seal who now worked for a security agency, was thirty-four and a newlywed. Joshua, the next in line, was thirty-two and worked for the Central Intelligence Agency. No one but Samuel ever knew where he was, but Joshua had a way of showing up right when you needed him. Ruby, her oldest sister, was thirty, single and worked for Vital Statistics. Her sister and roommate Pearl, was twenty-eight. She currently works for JD Harrison, Attorney General of Virginia. Matthew, twenty-four was a basketball coach for a local college. Luke, twenty-two was just drafted by a professional football team and currently lives in Michigan. Of her eleven brothers and sisters, only five remained at home, well technically only one. The first set of twins, Opal and Timothy, twenty, were away at Hampton University. The second set of twins, Jade and Adam, eighteen, were in their first year at Spelman and Morehouse respectively. Sapphire the baby at sixteen was still in high school.

The family was very close knit and no one wandered too far from home. All major holidays were spent at their parent's home. Each of the older children took on the responsibility for one of their sibling's education, to relieve their parents of the financial burden. For an anniversary present, the children planned to have an addition added to their parent's home. They knew once the children start getting married they would need a bigger house for their grandchildren to visit. It seemed all of the children that were at a marrying age were holding out for the same thing—that special love that their parents shared. They were each other's best friends. There was never a shortage of someone to talk to when life dealt a blow. Today was one of those days.

Diamond walked into the kitchen through the back door, dropped her purse on the counter top and reached for a bowl from the cabinet. Reaching into another cabinet, she pulled out a box of Frosted Flakes and the milk from the refrigerator. She sat at the breakfast bar and filled the bowl to the brim. Forgetting to get the spoon, she got up, retrieved one from the drawer, and sat back down. She exhaled and began to eat.

"Well, hey stranger," her mother beamed as she came into the kitchen from the family room. It was rare to see her children in the middle of the week, but Sally Lassiter was always happy when her grown children ventured home.

Diamond returned the smile then stood and hugged her mother. "Hi Mom." The hug went on a minute longer than just a casual hello and Sally immediately recognized her child was in need of her counsel. This was unusual for this particular child. Diamond was so independent. Whenever she made a decision, she just dealt with the consequences and moved on. Sometimes it seemed Diamond was the forgotten child. Even as a child, Sally rarely had to do anything for her. A quick learner, Diamond always had her chores done and was ready to help with the younger children, while she handled the older ones. It was indeed a rare occasion for Diamond to seek help and Sally could see, her daughter needed to talk.

Sally pulled out of the embrace, sat on the stool next to Diamond, picked up the box of cereal and began eating it dry while Diamond ate out of the bowl. "You've been pulling some long hours at work since you started the new job. How are things going?"

Diamond looked at her mother and exhaled. "I met a man a few months ago." She hunched her shoulders and sighed.

"Sit up straight baby," Sally instructed. "Don't stop there, tell me more."

Diamond sat up, as she was told and continued to eat her cereal as she talked to her mother. Spoon in motion, she continued. "I don't know if there is such a thing, but mom, I felt an immediate attraction to him." She stopped with spoon midair, as if she was deep in thought. "There was something in his eyes that made me smile and feel hurt for him at the same time." She shrugged her shoulder and continued to eat the cereal. "Anyway, I decided to pursue him. Unfortunately, I'm pretty sure he doesn't like me."

Offended for her daughter, Sally huffed, "Why would you say that? You are a beautiful confident young woman. And as Matt would say, you have the body to die for."

Diamond did not acknowledge the compliment as she looked up at her mother, "Those things don't seem to impress Zack." She said while putting a spoonful of cereal in her mouth. "He's been hurt somewhere along the line and he wears it on his sleeve. Besides, he has made it quite clear I am not one of his favorite people. The problem is I can't seem to shake the man. Every time I see him, I want to touch him—feel him—taste him. Hell mom, I dream of being with this man at night. This of course means I'm not sleeping at night. That means I go to work irritable. I don't know what to do. He clearly doesn't want anything to do with me and I can't seem to think about anything but him. Hell, I don't want to stop thinking about him."

"Stop talking with food in your mouth and don't curse in my house." Sally was amazed by the depth of her daughter's feelings for this man. Diamond, her sensible child, who did not play around with men, was lusting after one. "Is he a good man?"

Diamond smiled, "Yes ma'am he is. He's Xavier's brother."

"Zackary Davenport?"

Diamond nodded, "That's him," she sighed, "the one and only man for me. You know, he quit school and raised Xavier when his father passed away. Then about five years ago he started a construction company and now is in partnership with Xavier on the community project. I know people don't see it, but Zack is such a caring man." Warming up to the conversation, she stopped eating and turned to her mother. "Do you know," she swallowed what was in her mouth, "after working all week at his construction site, he helps to build Habitat homes and still finds time to coach the little league football team. And the whole time Xavier was in school he never had to work. Zack would send him money every week." Her eyes grew big and a wonderful smile appeared like a ray of sunshine, "He even has a nickname for Xavier. He calls him X-man. Now is that adorable or what?"

Sally couldn't resist returning the smile. "I remember Zack. He was a friend of Sammy's when they were younger. He is a good man Diamond." Then she reached over and covered her daughter's hand with hers. The serious mother face appeared. "However, from what I hear, he is also a man that has a way with women. He doesn't keep them around very long."

Diamond's smile faded. "I know. I hear the same thing all the time around the office." Diamond shook her head, "I can't shake this man mom. He needs me and I need him. I don't know what to do."

Sally looked at her daughter, "Why this man Diamond?"

Diamond exhaled, "His eyes, Mom. I see myself through his eyes. And I love what I see."

Sally sighed, "I saw myself in your father's eyes too."

"Did you?" Diamond smiled.

"I still do," Sally blushed. Remembering how her parents told her that Joe Lassiter was going to break her heart and to stay away from him, she squeezed Diamond's hand. "If you really want this man, then don't give up on him. You said this has been going on for a month, right?" Diamond nodded. "Well that's not really a lot of time. Give it a little longer. However, don't let anyone make a fool out of you. If after another month or so you begin to feel as if you are in this alone, walk away. He may not be the man for you."

"What man?" Joe Lassiter asked as he entered the kitchen from the front of the house. Diamond smiled as her parents kissed each other. "Well, what do you know; one of my precious gems is home."

"Hey Daddy," Diamond smiled as she hugged her father. At six feet eleven inches, he practically lifted her from the floor to complete the embrace.

"I know sad eyes. What's on your mind?"

"A man," Sally replied.

Joe looked at Sally, surprised by the statement, then back to Diamond. "Not my Diamond. I thought you were going to be daddy's little girl forever."

Diamond smiled at the remembered promise she made when she was six. "I will always be your little girl." She sighed, "I'm a little into this man and don't know how to go about getting him to notice me."

"Oh that's easy." Joe shrugged his shoulder as he reached into the cereal box. "Don't be available." Joe threw the handful of cereal into his mouth. "Knowing you, in some way, you have already made it clear to this person that you are interested in him." Diamond smiled and lowered her head. "Un huh, that's what I thought. Okay, now ease back. Let him come to you baby."

Hmm, that will be the day, Diamond thought as she stood to leave. "I don't see that happening Daddy, but thanks." She placed her bowl in the sink. "I have to go now. You two take care." She kissed both of them on the cheek and left.

"Who has my Diamond tied up in knots?" Joe asked his wife.

"Zackary Davenport."

"Sammy's friend?"

"The one and only as Diamond says."

Joe shook his head. "He's a good man. But, I'm not sure he's ready to settle down. And Diamond is old school. She'll want the house, kids, white picket fence and the dog."

Sally smiled up at her husband. "Therein lies the problem, my handsome husband."

Zack walked into his three bedroom rancher and welcomed the quietness. X-man was still at the office. Man, he was tired. For the last month the same thing had kept him up all night—dreams of Diamond in the red pants suit, or the green dress and tonight he was sure it would be a double feature—black skirt and jeans. It was well after ten when he kicked his shoes off in the mudroom, then walked down the hallway to his office. He grabbed a beer out of the mini refrigerator, dropped the top into the waste basket and slumped down into the overstuffed chair near the wet bar.

Swallowing the cold liquid down eased the tension a little, but nowhere near enough to relax him. Zack placed his head back and closed his eyes. Thoughts of the day filled his mind. The damn woman, in that damn skirt, with those damn long legs, then those damn jeans that fit like a damn glove on her apple bottom behind. Then Reese was looking at her. He wanted to punch his eyes out. The man has been his friend for twenty years and he wanted to deck him. Damn. Damn. Damn. He sat up and finished off the beer, threw the bottle in the trash then walked down the hallway to take another damn cold shower, wondering how in the hell was he going to keep this woman at bay.

L

There's the light in the front bedroom. He must have moved into his father's old room. This is easier than I thought it would be. I could follow him around and he would never know. I wonder how easy it would be to get into the house. I need something of his to leave at the scene. This is a good spot, across the street behind these trees. It's so easy to watch him. I should have done this before. I can't believe he still lives here. Why hasn't he moved into one of those houses he builds for everyone else? For the life of me I don't understand small minded people. If you have the money, live like it. Another light came on in the bathroom, at least that's what it used to be. Tomorrow I'll get a closer look. I wonder if the insurance paid off the house. Hmmm, it might be worth a little something. I'll have to take a trip to city hall and check out the deed. If it is, I want him to lose that too. It sure feels good to have a plan in place that will bring his righteous ass down. I want public humiliation for him. Yes, I want his so called good name dragged through the mud. Let's see how he handles that. The cigarette was thrown to the ground and doused out as the lone figure walked off between the trees smiling.

Chapter 6

The trailer was set and the first round of visitors had arrived. Knowing the next few months would be spent in the trailer, Diamond wrapped up as much as possible in the office. It was the end of March and the weather was unusually warm for the time of year, but she was enjoying it. A week had passed since her last visit to the site. Taking her father's advice, she steered clear of Zackary Davenport whenever possible. If she knew he was going to be in the office, which his secretary JoEllen made sure she did, Diamond would make sure she was out of the office.

On the weekends, the construction crew was usually off, so she set her appointments for the site. She was pleasantly surprised to see the paved driveway when she pulled up early on Saturday morning. Parking her car, the site seemed deserted, which was fine for her. Getting out of the car, she pushed the button to open the trunk and unlocked the trailer door.

Zack watched out of his trailer window as Diamond carried box after box inside. For a moment, it crossed his mind to help her with the boxes. Fear stopped him. The last week was hell on his sleep. Whenever he closed his eyes, some version of Diamond would enter the deep recesses of his mind. It did not matter what he did, she would not leave his thoughts. The thoughts would get him so riled up he had to take cold showers throughout the night to calm himself down. Since she had not visited the site for a few days, the dreams eased up in their intensity.

X-man mentioned that Diamond would be expecting prospective buyers this weekend, so Zack decided to pave the driveway. He knew she would have to dress professionally to receive clients. The timberland boots would not look good with the black pants suit she was wearing today. He could see her smile from his window and that pleased him. He wasn't sure why, but it did.

It was eight in the morning, and he had a lot of paperwork to catch up on so he sat down at his desk and began reviewing plans. Around ten Zack decided to check on the progress of the model home. When he stepped out he noticed there were several vehicles parked at the visitor's trailer. It seemed like a good start for the day. Finding things progressing in the model, he walked the site for a while. From time to time some construction sites had a few unwanted visitors, some homeless, some kids messing around and at times thieves looking to steal supplies. So he made it a habit to check the area, especially once the shell of the homes was constructed. With Diamond on the grounds he wanted to make sure the area was safe. He wasn't sure why, he just did.

After walking the site, he returned to the trailer to review more paperwork. Around five he noticed vehicles were still at the trailer, so he pulled out another set of blueprints and began working on them. He looked out his window around eight and only saw Diamond's car parked. The thought of her being there alone concerned him; it was getting dark. He decided to stay until she left for the day, so he continued to work. A few hours later he looked out the window, the car was still there. Checking his watch he noticed it was after ten. A frown creased his forehead. "She shouldn't be working this late." He grabbed his keys off the desk, locked his trailer, and drove down to the model trailer, then parked next to Diamond's car. He stepped into the trailer and heard the music coming from the office.

Diamond was sitting at the desk diligently working on documents and never heard him enter. The trailer looked very cozy. No wonder people were just hanging around. The place was as nice as his home. To his right were a sofa, two chairs and a table with pastries, cups, napkins and a floral arrangement in the center. The walls were covered with pictures of the homes planned for the site and tasteful art next to them. Curtains were at the two windows of the trailer. Next to the door was a refrigerator and mini-bar. On the left was a glass partition separating the sitting area from the office.

He stood in the doorway and watched as Diamond worked. Observing her without her knowledge gave him the opportunity to really study her features. An oval shaped face with long lashes resting against her dark chocolate skin that appeared to be as smooth as the best quality leather. Her hair framed her face, cascading around her shoulders, with her long legs extended under the desk, crossed at the ankles. It was those legs that kept him up at night. Zack closed his eyes and exhaled. The woman was going to be the death of him. He opened his eyes to her bouncing her head to the music, smooth jazz. How could he hate anyone that loved smooth jazz? Her hands moved gracefully across the paper as she wrote, and he wondered what those hands would feel like on him. Moving his focus back up, he stopped at her lips which were more enticing as she bit the bottom one, concentrating on what she was doing. He was focusing so hard there, he never noticed when she looked up, until her lips formed into a smile. His breath hitched as he looked into her eyes. *What in the hell was it about her?* He thought as they stared at each other.

Zack was content to stand there for a minute, then he stepped further into the trailer. "You're working late tonight."

Diamond was grateful to be in his presence without hearing harsh words from him. "Yeah, I um, have a few contracts to put together for the office on Monday."

She had a wonderful silky voice, like a singer. "You made a few sales today?"

She smiled and nodded. "We sold five town homes today." *He has the manliest stance of any man she had ever met, just like her daddy,* Diamond thought glancing at him from head to toe. The black t-shirt fit snuggly against his chest, with the muscle defined arms extending down to where his hands hung by the thumb from the loop of his jeans. She wondered what it would feel like to have those hands on her. Caressing, kneading her.

"Congratulations," he replied as a slight smile curved his lips. "Are you about to wrap up?"

She looked, jerked her head up. Did he notice she was checking him out? She sure hoped not. Looking around her desk, she replied, "I'll be ready in a few minutes."

"Alright, I'll wait outside for you."

"You don't have to do that, I'll be fine."

"I'm not going to leave you out here this late at night alone." A frown creased his forehead. "I'll wait outside until you are ready to go."

The tone was one that she was sure persuaded most people to see things his way, but unfortunately it did not faze her. She had six brothers and a father that all stood well over six feet. He did not intimidate her. However, sensing the first decent conversation between them about to change, Diamond decided to let it go. The contracts were ready and she was only making notes on those potential customers who had shown interest, but did not commit. That could wait. "I'll leave now. I don't want to hold you up."

After locking everything away and turning off the lights, Diamond locked the door to the trailer and walked over to her car. She looked around the area before getting into her car and thought she saw something move.

Zack, sitting inside his truck, noticed her looking around. He rolled down his window. "Is everything okay?"

Diamond hesitated before she replied. "Is Reese still here?"

"No." He frowned. "Why?"

"I thought I saw something move near the construction trailer."

When in the hell did she start calling him Reese? What happened to Mr. Kendrick? He looked back down towards the trailer, but didn't see anything. "It was probably the wind blowing something up."

She nodded as she began to get into her car, "You're probably right."

"Have you eaten yet?" Zack asked hesitantly. Why in the hell did he do that?

"Not since this morning." Diamond replied as she stood back up in the opened door of her car.

"Do you want to stop to get something before going home?"

Surprised by the invitation, she didn't want to appear too eager. "Is something around here open this time of night?" She asked.

"Follow me. I know a place."

"Okay," she smiled as she got inside her car. "Lord, please hold my tongue while I'm with this man," she prayed silently.

L

I've got to be more careful. I thought she saw me for a moment. Whew! Some dark clothes from now until this job is done. An attempt to open the door to the construction trailer proved fruitless—it was locked. Trying the windows proved to be just as disappointing. But unlike the door, the windows could be broken. Damn, he doesn't lock the windows at his house but the trailer is locked up like Fort Knox. I'll bring more tools tomorrow.

Chapter 7

Zack and Diamond walked into Doc's restaurant, that according to Zack serves the best macaroni and cheese he has ever tasted. Smooth jazz was playing to the almost capacity crowd. A few of the occupants sitting at the bar in the front of the establishment spoke to Zack and shook his hand.

"Two tonight Zack," the waitress asked with a questioning brow raised.

"Yes Barbara," Zack smiled.

Diamond wondered what it would take to get him to smile at her like that. The way she turned and gave Diamond a once over let her know this was someone Zack had been with before. But, she refused to let that bother her. Zack was a grown man with certain needs. Besides, everyone had a past—except her that is.

The waitress led them to a booth in the back of the restaurant. As they sat the waitress asked Zack if he wanted the usual. "No," he replied. "I'll try something a little different tonight. Could you leave the menus and give us a minute?"

"Sure," she replied and walked away.

"What's the usual?" Diamond asked.

Zack picked up the menu, "Nothing you would be interested in."

"And you would know because you know me so well," Diamond smirked as she reviewed the menu. "So, what do you recommend?"

He hesitated for a moment as he stared at her. "Everything," Zack replied with a devilish grin. "I just figured you were one of those women that ate green grass like stuff all the time."

"I take it you are referring to salads. Which are very healthy but some can carry as many calories as some full course meals. However, I tend to enjoy meatier meals. Now, I don't suppose you could be just a little more specific."

Damn she was feisty. "The smothered chops with mashed potatoes and greens, is my favorite. But that's a little much to eat this late at night."

Diamond smiled, "Okay, I'll try it."

Zack frowned at her, "It's a lot of food."

"Good, because I'm starving."

Zack stared at her for a minute. There was no way a woman her size could eat that much food. "When I say it's a lot of food, I mean it's more than enough to satisfy me."

"Okay, and?"

Sitting back, Zack motioned for the waitress to return to the table. He gave her the menus. "Two number threes with ice tea." Zack sat back and exhaled, "So which model did you sell today?"

Diamond began to share the news with Zack. They talked as they ate as if it was the most natural thing in the world to do. It was hard not to see the excitement in her eyes or hear the exhilaration in her voice as she talked about the families that she contracted today. Zack could feel her genuine happiness in assisting people to purchase their new home in her voice. It was difficult not to smile along with her as she talked. After he finished eating, he stretched his long legs out under the table and relaxed. Just the sound of her voice was soothing to him in a way he couldn't explain.

The more she talked, the more he realized not only was she beautiful and intelligent, she was a deeply caring person. Not once did she mention anything about herself or the commission she was to receive. Everything was about the families and their new homes. She may have appeared to be arrogant that first day in his office, but there was nothing self-centered about this woman. For the first time in a long time, he found himself laughing with a woman when she talked about the antics of her brothers and sisters. He could sit there all night listening to her, watching her very kissable lips move. *What? Where did that thought come from?* He shifted his position in the seat and his leg brushed against hers. The sensation was a direct hit in his southern regions. Their eyes connected and he knew she felt it as well. Not liking where his mind was going he sat straight up. "It's late. It's time for you to go."

The simple touch caused ripples in Diamond's stomach and a touch of an ache between her legs. He felt it too, the shock was very evident on his face and the anger was back in his eyes. The same eyes that were warming her soul a few moments ago as he intently listened to her ramble on about her family. The moment he sat up she knew the reprieve was over.

In her mind she thought to tell him she was a grown woman who had a father that did not tell her when it was time to go. Why did he think he could? But before she could, a man called out to him. "Hey Zack, you sitting in on the set?"

"Yeah, King Arthur is in the truck. Let me wrap up here and I'll be with you in a minute." He stood and looked down at her, to let her know he meant what he had said; it was time for her to go.

Diamond stood and reached to pull her wallet from out of her purse. "I have this," he stated as if she had insulted him.

Trying to keep the delicate peace between them she simply smiled and said, "Thank you," then she asked, "What's a set?"

"Not your type of thing."

"There you go again. How would you know what my type of thing is? Today is the first time you have said a civil word to me."

She was right. He had been rough with her. Unfortunately he didn't know why, just that she made him feel strange every time he was within five feet of her. Like now, as she stood staring up at him with those doe like eyes, questioning him.

"A few guys get together on the weekend and play a few sets here. Doc is a friend who owns this place, changed the place into a jazz club when he purchased it. He allows us to play a little for relaxation."

Grateful he shared that small bit of himself with her, she pressed on a little. "What instrument do you play?" she asked recognizing a softness that touched his face.

"Sax."

"I'm not surprised. It's the most intimate instrument there is, in my opinion," she replied looking up at his caramel brown face. A smile replaced the anger that was in his dark brown eyes a few moments ago, but his lips remained in a firm thin line. Even so, they were nice, smooth, and powerful. She could imagine those lips on the mouth of a sax, she sighed inwardly, and on other things.

As if reading her thoughts he spoke close to her ear so no one could hear. "Don't go there baby girl. You have no idea what it would take to satisfy a man like me." He grunted, "Come on, I'll walk you to your car."

She stood there watching him walk away knowing he was right. She didn't know what it would take to satisfy him. But watching him walk away in those jeans made her want to find out. "You named your sax King Arthur?" She asked causing him to stop and turn back to her.

"Yes." He replied, as he wondered why she was not behind him.

"Why? Do you feel like the king of the round table when you play?" She joked.

He looked around and saw a number of the guys setting up the stage area had taken an interest in the conversation they were having. He walked back to where she stood. "I named it after my father. Now let's go."

"Oh, your father's name was Arthur? That is so sweet."

"Aren't you the sweet one, Zack," his friend Lee teased from the stage then looked away when he received a warning look from Zack.

More than a little agitated he stared her down. "There is nothing sweet about it. My father's name was not Arthur. It was King Arthur Davenport. And yes, he was very deserving of that royal title. And no, playing does not make me feel like I'm the king of the round table. It's a release for me."

"What kind of release?" She asked before she could stop herself. Having this little insight into him was so pleasing to her.

"Yeah Zack, what kind of release?" Lee glared at him with laughter in his eyes.

"What the hell is this, twenty questions?" He growled. "I brought you here to get something to eat. You ate, now it's time for you to go."

Not daunted by his words or tone, Diamond looked up at him with pleading eyes. "May I stay to hear you play?"

The request caught him off guard and sent him off balance again, just like the statement she made in his office about him being handsome. "Why?" he asked abruptly.

"I'd like to see how you release yourself," she replied as she placed her blazer across the seat at the table that was close to the stage.

He'd never shared his music with a woman before. It was what he did to release the pain of his mother leaving him and X-man and his father's premature death. That pain he did not share with anyone. Here she was asking to share his pain. He wondered for a moment if she knew what she was asking.

"Let her stay Zack," Lee egged him on. "It would be nice to have a beautiful woman in the audience just for us."

Raising an eyebrow he turned to look at his friend, "Us?"

"Well you. I mean she's your lady."

"She is not my lady."

"She's not?" His friend Doc walked up behind him and hit him on the back. "You could have fooled the hell out of me. I thought for sure she was your lady from the way you been all lovey dovey eyes all night long."

Diamond took a seat and enjoyed the friendly banter going back and forth between the seemingly close friends.

"What kind of eyes Doc?" Lee asked laughing

"Lovey, dovey ones. You know when you don't see anything else going on around you."

You could feel the steam radiating from Zack, which was a telling sign that he was not enjoying the conversation. "I don't have loving eyes for any woman, especially not her," he angrily declared.

That declaration let her know it was time to go. She really did want to hear him play, if for no other reason than to be in his presence a little longer. But it seemed she had worn out her welcome. Diamond stood and weakly smiled, "I better go. Have a good set guys." She walked towards the door.

The three men watched as she walked out. "Well if she ain't your lady, do you mind if I get her number?" A man sitting at another table asked. The look the man received from Zack caused him to throw his hands up in a surrender sign and turn away.

Zack exhaled then stomped out the door behind her. "I'll be back."

Diamond unlocked her car door and was about to get in when Zack called out to her from the door of the restaurant. She put her hand up, "I get it," she said and got into the car.

His long strides had him at the driver side of her car before she could close the door. "Look, I didn't mean to be disrespectful."

Why not, she thought to herself. That's all he had been since the first day they met. Turning the key in the ignition she replied, "Don't worry about it Mr. Davenport. You said several times it was time for me to go. I was the one that forced you to show me. I enjoyed dinner. You have a good evening."

"Hello Zackary."

They both turned to a woman's voice.

Diamond tried to look around Zack to see the woman, it was dark and he blocked her view.

"What in hell are you doing here?"

"I thought it was time for us to talk." The woman replied. "Are you going to introduce me to your friend?

Without turning around Zack growled through clenched teeth. "It's time for you to go Diamond."

The tension generating from Zack's body was so intense Diamond did not consider questioning him. She put the key in the ignition and pulled off.

Zack stood there and watched until her car was out of sight. She never looked back at him, but he knew he had hurt her feelings. He saw the deflation in her spirit just as he saw at the conference room table a month ago. He exhaled, why did he treat her like that? Why did she seem to bring out the worst in him? Turning back to the woman, he knew the answer. He sighed. "Hello mother. How much do you need?"

"Why do you always assume I want money from you?"

"History." He replied as he pulled his wallet out of his back jean pocket.

"I want to see Xavier." She said as she dropped the cigarette to the ground and doused it with her foot.

Zack looked at the woman who still looked to be in her late twenties body wise, but the street life clearly showed on her face. "No."

"He is my child, not yours!"

"Really," Zack angrily took a step towards her. "Where were you when he needed his mother? You were too busy with your life to be bothered with him or me." Zack threw five twenties on the ground. "Go back to your life." He growled then walked away.

"He can make his own decisions you know." She shouted to his back.

Turning around abruptly, he stalked back towards her, seething. "Go anywhere near him and your funding will stop." He stopped directly in front, towering over her. "Do I make myself clear?"

Ann Davenport stared at her son, not backing down. She bent to pick up the bills from the ground and stuffed them inside her bra. "Has your friend seen this side of you? Somebody should warn her about your temper."

"Stay the hell away from her!" He angrily warned with his fist clenched at his side.

Ann wasn't a fool, she took a step back and smirked. "Like that one do you?" She turned to walk away. "You'll push her away with your anger for me just like you do the others." She continued walking with her hands in the pockets of the short jacket she wore over her jeans. "One day that righteous attitude of yours will backfire." She turned back, facing him as she walked backwards. "Like it or not, I will see Xavier."

That's what drugs will do, turn son against mother and mother against son. Zack learned the lesson the hard way. He knew exactly what the problem was. He remembered the caring mother. The one that tucked him into bed at night, taught him to read, kissed his knees when he scraped them. But that mother slowly disappeared before his eyes. He knew what was happening to her before his father did. The memories were ingrained in the forefront of his mind, as deep as the memory of his good mother was buried in the back of his mind. The drugs meant more to her than her own sons. Xavier was only six when she took off for good. But he was eleven the day his father found him on the corner waiting for his mother to come out of the drug dealer's house, paying him for the drugs the only way a woman without money could. That was after the third rehab center had failed. King Arthur took his son's hand and told his wife, not to ever come near his children again. Just like his father, Zack turned his back and walked away from his mother—again.

Chapter 8

*J*t was well after midnight when Diamond entered her apartment. She closed the door quietly, not wanting to wake her sister Pearl, whom she assumed was asleep. Walking into the kitchen she reached into the cabinet and pulled out the box of Frosted Flakes. Not bothering to get the milk, she opened the box and began eating the dry cereal. *How I am going to save him from himself,* she thought. It was so clear to her that that man needs her, but he is too bull headed to see it. Laying her head back she reclined in her favorite chair and began to rock. *Apparently some woman had damaged him so deeply in the past he wasn't willing to give her a chance. In order to face the future, he had to deal with the past. Was the woman that approached him tonight a part of his past?* She continued to weave the situation through her mind. *How do I get him to open up? Well, first I need to know about the past, who the woman was, and what happened. While doing that I have to keep him close. I've already gotten under his skin,* she smiled. *There was no way he could deny his reaction to her, she felt it and knew he did too. If he was honest with himself, he felt it that first day when their hands touched. How do I find out about the woman?* She asked while looking to the ceiling. *I could ask Xavier, but I don't want to put him in an awkward position of discussing his brother's old ladies with his soon to be future wife.* She thought a little more. A knowing smile crept onto her face. She walked back into the kitchen and placed the closed cereal box in the cabinet. Walking into her bedroom, she quickly took her shower and put on a Jordan t-shirt that was about three sizes too big and slid under her covers. She had a plan in mind. This is what she should have done in the first place. Some problems can't be solved alone. Satisfied with her next steps, she closed her eyes and waited for the dream of the man she was going to marry to invade her sleep.

Sundays in the Lassiter house were always the same. Breakfast, church, dinner and whatever game it was for the season. Today, March madness. The top sixteen basketball college teams around the country were competing for the final four elusive top spots. All the Lassiter men, including Joshua, who was usually on a secretive assignment for the government somewhere, were home on this particular weekend and Diamond could not be happier. With everyone home, they could call a council meeting to help solve her dilemma. During a council meeting everyone gets to voice their solution, then the person who calls it selects the top two. The family then votes between the two. If there was a tie, mommy and daddy would deliberate and break the tie.

Sally marched into the family room where her men were seated and announced, "Diamond has called for a council meeting. It is taking place in the dining room now."

"Now?" Matthew yelled.

"Yes now," Sally replied looking at her son as if he had lost his mind.

"Can it wait until after the game?" Luke pleaded.

Joe turned to his wife, "The game will be over in ten minutes. What's happening with Diamond can wait."

All five feet three inches, one hundred and ten pounds of Sally Lassiter stood in front of her husband with hands on hips and stared at him with a raised eyebrow.

Joe, whose attention had gone back to the game, looked up at his wife. Without a word being said he understood her meaning. He picked up the remote and turned off the television. "Boys, you heard your mother."

His six foot eleven frame stood and smiled at his wife, "I don't want you to think you're in control, I run this house."

Sally walked away as Samuel, the oldest, standing at least six five, walked by and hit his father on the back, "Keep thinking that Dad."

"Yeah, it's going to be true one day," Joshua, standing six three, laughed as he walked out the door. "I don't know why you're laughing," he said to Samuel. "Cynthia controls you too." He walked by Samuel and laughed.

Samuel nodded, "I love every minute of it. And one day you will too."

Joshua froze. Samuel and his father laughed at the look on his face.

Once everyone was seated at the table Joe had built to handle his large family, Sally placed the voting box on the table as Ruby gave out the pens and index cards. "The meeting is now called to order. You know the rules, no telephone calls or interruptions until a decision is made." Joe stated. "Diamond you now have the floor."

"Thank you daddy and I'm sorry guys, but this is important." She hesitated then smiled, "I'm interested in a man."

"No!' Joshua shouted, "My vote is no!"

"You haven't heard the problem yet Joshua, you can't vote no," Sapphire the baby girl stated.

"I can and if it involves a man my vote is no," Joshua stated.

"Hear her out Joshua," Samuel quietly ordered.

There were only two men in the world and one woman that would speak to Joshua in that tone and get away without bodily harm-his father, his mother and Samuel, his older brother. Joshua looked at Diamond. This was the sensible sister, who never had issues with men. He wasn't sure he was ready for this conversation. "Sorry Diamond, go ahead."

She exhaled and looked around the table. Ruby's smile encouraged her to continue. "Like I was saying, I'm interested in this man and everything in me screams he is just as attracted to me, but he won't let down his guard. Now, in thinking this through I need to know about his past and what I can do to get him to open up to me."

Joe and Sally looked at each other, they knew who she was referring to and were concerned how the older boys would take the news. "You can't make a man interested in you if he is not," Mathew stated as he sat back in his seat.

"Oh, please, of course you can," Jade smirked. "Any woman can."

"I know that's right," Sapphire agreed with a huff. Everyone at the table turned and stared at her. "So I heard," she quickly added.

"At sixteen that better be all you heard," Joshua scowled.

Diamond smiled at her little sister, trying to smooth over the scowl from Joshua then continued. "The man is interested, he just doesn't know it or want to admit it," she explained.

"How do you know he is interested Diamond?" Samuel asked hoping his question came out more calmly than he felt inside. After all this was one of his little sisters and he was not thrilled at the thought of her being with a man, it didn't matter how old she was.

With a gleam in her eyes, Diamond told her family about the times she had been in Zackary's presence and how he had reacted. After listening, Samuel, Joshua and Luke looked at each other with knowing stares. Matt, Timothy and Adam were lost in the conversation, neither of them had experienced those feelings and did not understand Diamond's dilemma. Ruby, Opal, Jade and Sapphire all smiled the "awe" look at her.

However Pearl had a question. "Why would you want to be with a man that spoke to you publicly in a

disrespectful manner, not once, but twice?" She sat forward
to emphasize her point. "See that's where we go wrong as
women. The man shows you up front that he is
disrespectful, but we think we can step in and change them.
There's no changing him, Diamond, move on."

Most of the occupants rolled their eyes upward.
They had all been privy to Pearl's opinion on men. "That
may have been your experience Pearl. It may not be the
situation for Diamond," Sally surmised.

"Who is he?" Joshua questioned in a harsh tone.

Diamond looked to her father for help. "Joshua,"
Joe cautioned.

"I'm just asking a question, who in the hell is he?"

"Joshua, don't speak that way in this house," Sally
chastised.

"Sorry Mom."

"I have to second Joshua on this." Samuel, who sat at
one end of the table while both his parents were at the other,
spoke calmly. "In order for us to advise you wisely, we need
to know who we are talking about Diamond."

"Will you guys promise not to confront him?"

"No," Joshua replied.

Samuel touched Joshua on the shoulder, "I'm not
going to say we will not speak with him Diamond. You are
our baby sister. It's our responsibility to protect you. But we
won't confront him in a negative way. I take it he is someone
we know."

"You guys do," she pointed to her older brothers
and sisters at the head of the table. Samuel, Joshua, Ruby,
and Pearl sat up.

"Who?" Ruby asked.

"Zackary Lassiter."

"You mean Xavier. He is so fine with his dreads,"
Opal said with a "you go girl" look as her sisters Jade and
Ruby agreed with her.

Diamond inhaled nervously and looked at her mother. Sally smiled and encouraged her on.

"No, not Xavier. I'm talking about his brother Zackary."

"Zack?" Joshua asked, "Huh, you better mean X-man."

"Diamond," Ruby sat up concerned, "Zack is handsome, but honey, he is a full grown man, with manly needs that he satisfies regularly, from what I understand," Ruby explained, hoping her baby sister would not be one of his next conquests.

"He screws them and leaves them, Diamond." Pearl emphasized the words as she spoke. "He is not a forever kind of man. Like I said before, little sis, move on."

"Who is he?" Sapphire, who everyone called Phire and Adam, asked.

"He owns Davenport Industries," said Timothy, the brother in school for business. "He has a success story for the books. He was at Virginia Union on a football scholarship, a shoo in for the NFL when he ups and quit school. He then started working construction, now he owns one of the top construction companies in Virginia. I mean multi-million dollar company."

"Whoa...You go Diamond," Phire laughed.

Samuel looked in Diamond's eyes. He could see she was serious about this man. "Everybody quiet down," Samuel ordered. "Before we start giving Diamond options, you all need to know the entire story on Zack."

The tone in his voice alerted his younger siblings that he was serious. They immediately quieted down, sat up and listened. "Here's what I know. Zack has every reason to be guarded with his feelings." Diamond stood next to her mother and listened intently to Samuel. "When we were in junior high Zack's mother left his father with two young children to raise, for her drug dealer. His father had to take a second job, leaving Zack to care for his little brother. He became X-man's mother and father. After football practice, we came home to a hot meal and a family. Zack went home to cook a meal for him and his little brother. After the games, we got to hang out with the girls, but he had to go home. When Zack got the full ride scholarship, his father refused to allow what he believed to be his responsibility to stop Zack from going to school. That's when his father quit the second job to be with X-man. Things were good for a few years and Zack was tearing up the yards as a receiver. The scouts were at every game, anxiously waiting until they could get their hands on him. Unfortunately, his dream was derailed when his father died from a massive heart attack. I think he was nineteen, maybe twenty, when he had to leave school to take care of X-man. His girlfriend at the time, Celeste Crenshaw, saw the NFL disappear and so did she. Not only did his mother walk out of his life, but so did the woman he loved."

Diamond had tears in her eyes as she listened to her brother. She knew a woman had hurt Zack, but his own mother? "What happened to his mother?," she asked.

"Hmm, that's the interesting part," Joshua chimed in. "His mother is still on drugs. Every now and then when she is in need Zack will give her a few dollars to keep her away from X-man."

"How do you know that?" she asked.

"Every now and then he would ask me to try to locate her, just to make sure she was still alive and okay." Joshua sat up and sighed, "Diamond, Zack is a good brother, and a damn decent man," he looked at his mother. "Sorry Mom. However, he is not going to willingly open up his heart to any woman. He may use your body, but he will not give you his heart."

Knowing his little sister the way he did, Samuel knew her mind was already made up. She was going to have Zackary Davenport's heart, one way or another. That meant he was going to have to see where Zack stood. He exhaled,

"We now know the past, which solves one part of Diamond's dilemma. She knows what she is up against. Now, the question is how does she go about accomplishing her goal unscathed?"

Shaking his head Matthew stated, "You can't get the man if he don't want to be got."

The girls waved their hands at him, "Oh please, yes you can," Jade declared. "There are two ways to a man's heart," Ruby stated, "his stomach...,"

"Or his pants," Phire added.

Again all eyes went to the sixteen year old, "Sapphire, you better watch yourself," her mother warned. The men shook their heads knowing that little sister was going to be a handful.

"All I know is, today's man wants a woman that can work beside him, think with him, satisfy his body, give birth to his children, cook and keep a nice home—all for him." Luke stated firmly emphasizing his statement with a slap on the table.

"You and those Neanderthal teammates of yours in the NFL would think like that. If the woman is going to do all of that, pray tell, why does she need a man?" Opal asked.

"My point exactly," Pearl chimed in.

Jade with her quiet wisdom decided it was time for her to answer. "A woman needs a man to take care of her mental, emotional and sexual needs, first and foremost. In addition to bringing home the bacon, so she can fry it up in a pan."

"Huh, today's woman needs a man that has a job, is not in jail and definitely not on the down low." Again all eyes went to Phire after she made the statement. "I'm just saying," she added.

"A woman needs a man that can find that spot, continuously, that's what a woman needs a man for." Ruby stated as the girls gave her a "hey" and high fives.

Not one to be out done by the girls, Matthew stated, "A man needs a woman that is not afraid or too timid to allow him to explore that spot continuously. And for the record," he turned to his sister, "I don't think Diamond should be pursuing this or any other man. Let him come to you."

"I disagree, if this man is what you want go for it," Phire suggested, "Huh that's what I would do."

"That may be too aggressive," Adam shyly stated. "Some men may be turned off by an overly aggressive woman."

"See you all have to make up your mind," Opal sighed with frustration as she sat up. "Let me make sure I have this straight. You want us timid in the relationship, but aggressive in the bed." She shook her head. "You can't have it both ways."

"Why the hell not?" Joshua laughed. "Women can do all—right? At least that's what all of you keep telling us."

The family laughed along with him. Pearl looked to her mother and father. "What do you guys think? You are about to celebrate thirty-five years of marriage and you still can't keep your hands off each other. What's the right combination?"

"Yeah," Matthew laughed. "If it was physically possible you two would still be spitting out babies."

Joe frowned, "When did we become physically unable to produce children?" The question caused a hush over the room. Sally seconded the question simply by raising her eyebrow at her son.

"I just assumed," Matthew, stammered out.

"Assuming makes an ass out of you and me," Phire informed him. When the room remained quiet, she looked around and shrugged her shoulder, "I'm just saying."

Joe and Sally shook their heads and laughed at their youngest child. "To answer your question Pearl," Sally began, "it takes love, that's it. All those other things you mentioned are secondary. None of it is important or will not do you any good without love." Her children looked at her with knowing eyes. They witnessed the bad and good times of their parents. The one thing that was always constant was the love they had for each other. "The question you need to ask yourself, baby girl is this," Joe stated to Diamond. "Do you want Davenport for forever and days after, or is this just a physical attraction. Your answer to that will determine your next move."

Diamond wondered if her brothers could take her response. Exhaling she replied, "I am deeply attracted to this man physically. But the physical attraction is fueled by what is in my heart. He won't let me get close enough to determine if it is love. If it was only about sex, I would have stripped and placed myself at his feet the first day I met him. This is more than a physical attraction."

Everyone went into deep thought. "I say go for broke," Phire offered. "Put it in his face."

"Sounds like she's done that," Opal said.

"No she hasn't," Phire replied. "She said he would be handsome if he smiled more. They have touched hands and sparks flew. Wow, that's telling him," She added sarcastically.

Samuel chuckled at his baby sister, realizing she was going to be hell on wheels. "She's right," he looked down the table to Diamond. "I say take the direct approach. If he's not interested, he will tell you. However," he held Diamond's eyes sending a direct message, "there will be no stripping at his feet."

"That's right," Joshua joined in the stare.

"I don't know about putting your heart on the table like that. I say take the subtle approach. Spend whatever time you can in his presence. If something is there, it will eventually show itself." Pearl suggested.

After giving them a moment to ensure there were no further suggestions, Sally spoke. "Well, there you have it.

What will it be, the direct approach or the subtle approach? You all realize your sister's heart is at stake. With that in mind, you have your cards, cast your vote."

While she watched others place their vote in the box, Diamond held hers. She knew what steps she wanted to take, but her family was wise and she would follow their decision. Folding her card, she placed it in the box. Sally shook the box up and then began counting the votes. The cards in each pile seemed to mount at the same rate. The decision was not made until the very last vote. "Seven to five for the direct approach," she announced. "Samuel, you and Pearl will act as advisors on this for Diamond."

"Is there anything further, Diamond?," Joe asked. She shook her head no. "Then the meeting is adjourned."

Joshua turned to Samuel, "We are paying him a visit tonight." Samuel nodded his head in agreement.

Jade and Opal turned to Diamond. "You are taking tomorrow off. We are going shopping."

Joe turned to Sally as they walked to the family room. "What are you going to do about your daughter Phire?"

Sally gave her husband an incredulous look. "Why is she my daughter when she acts out, but your daughter when she gets awards?"

L

Zack sat in the office at his home viewing the original tour video for Davenport Estates for at least the hundredth time. He could not understand for the life of him why the woman on the screen fascinated him so. The attractiveness was apparent, but he had been with plenty of attractive women and none of them had held his attention the way this one has.

Of all the scenes in the video, the one where she was getting into the vehicle in the chic red dress that flowed around her hips captivated him. It was her inner spirit that showed predominantly in the scene that had him mesmerized.

He frowned as he realized the treachery that lurked in women did not show, but he knew it existed in her just as it had in his mother, Ann, and his ex-fiancée, Celeste.

Ann's betrayal of his father was not something that entered his mind regularly until lately. Every time he was around Diamond it would appear. If that wasn't enough, the unforgivable acts of Celeste played on his senses as well. He could never forget or forgive her for aborting his child and lying to him in the mix.

The week after his father's funeral he was granted custody of X-man. Celeste told him she would not play stepmother to his brother. She wanted him to turn his back on his own flesh and blood because a few NFL scouts had shown interest in him. When he explained his responsibility was to his brother, she stated his responsibility was to her and their unborn child.

Shock set in at first and then elation. He had lost his father, but God had given him a child. He asked Celeste to marry him and she said yes. Weeks later when she realized his plans had not changed about not returning to school, she had a change of heart. She could not understand why he would settle for a simple life when he could have it all. He simply had to give up the notion of raising his little brother. When he questioned her about the baby, she stated she had lied, there was no baby. She simply said that to get him to see reason. A few months later, he ran into a girlfriend of hers who told him she did have an abortion and was now seeing an ex-teammate of his. When he confronted her, she admitted it was the truth. Anger so intense racked his body. To this day any thoughts of the incident still affected him deeply and any ideas of trusting another woman were lost on him.

He clicked the pause button on his computer with Diamond's smiling face staring back at him. There was nothing insincere about her. Her smile was as genuine as her laughter and caring nature. The other night at the restaurant he had hurt her. It was unfair to take his anger with Ann and Celeste out on her. He owed her a real apology for this behavior.

"Hello Zack," Joshua spoke from the doorway.

Zack looked up, but was not startled by Joshua's sudden soundless appearance. Over the years, Joshua had appeared from time to time with information on his mother. "What has Ann done? It can't be money, I just gave her some the other night. By the way, there is a doorbell on the front and back doors," he smiled.

"Ann was fine the last time I checked in, still doing the street thing when she runs out of money. I'll drop in to check on her before I leave on my next assignment." Joshua took a seat on the arm of the sofa by the window as Zack curiously watched him; he was not a man to visit without reason. "You might want to get that," Joshua motioned towards the door.

"Get what?" Zack asked confused. A second later the chime to the front door bell sounded. He smiled and shook his head, "You never cease to amaze me." Zack said as he hit the button to turn off his computer monitor, and then left the room to answer the door.

Opening the door, Zack was pleasantly surprised to see his high school friend Samuel standing there. Extending his hand and smiling he welcomed him in. "Sammy. It's good to see you. It's been a while man." They gave the traditional male embrace. "I understand congratulations are in order. You married Cynthia Thornton. Who in the hell would have ever thought that would happen?" He laughed.

Pleased with his welcome, Samuel took the extended hand and accepted his invitation to come inside. "It's good to see you, too Zack. And believe me, I was more surprised than anyone when she agreed to have me. She made me a happy man." He exhaled, "I'm not so sure you're going to be too happy once you hear what I've come to say."

Confused at his words, Zack frowned. "Well come on in anyway and thanks for using the door." Now Samuel looked confused. "Come on in", he laughed.

Upon entering the office, Samuel looked at Joshua and just shook his head. "Do you ever follow orders?"

"Only when I agree with them."

Zack retook his seat at his desk and listened to the two brothers talk. They had not changed one bit. Joshua was still trying to outdo his older brother. Zack picked up the glass of Remy Martin he was enjoying before the interruption and said, "Don't mind me, it's just my house." Then he pointed to his glass, "Do either of you want one of these?"

Samuel chuckled, "Zack you are still just as cool as ever."

He saluted them with his glass. "Thanks, now to what do I owe the pleasure?"

"Mind if I take a seat?" Samuel asked.

Nodding he replied, "Not at all and thanks for asking."

Joshua threw up his hands in a questioning gesture. "What, you would have said yes."

Zack and Samuel laughed.

"What can I do for you Sammy?" Zack asked.

"We need to discuss Diamond," Samuel replied with a stern look.

Zack sat back in his chair as he returned Samuel's glare. There was no reason to pretend he had no idea what they were talking about. "What about her?"

"She has it in her mind that you are the man for her," Joshua explained. "The question is what's on your mind?"

Zack held Joshua's stare. "The last time I checked my driver's license I'm pretty sure the date of birth indicated I was a full grown man. What's on my mind is my business."

"That may be, but in this case your business may involve one of our sisters. That in and of itself makes it our business." Joshua explained.

Neither man conceded any ground on the topic. Joshua wanted to know Zack's intentions and Zack was determined to keep his business to himself. Samuel had to be the voice of reason. "Despite how my baby brother is behaving, we are not here to interfere. At least, I'm not." He exhaled. "I agree, both of you are adults and know what you want. If what you want is Diamond, you have my full support. However, if she is not what you want, I'm asking you as a friend to let her down easy. And I have to tell you as her brother, there will be an issue if she is hurt."

Zack turned from Joshua to look at Samuel. "I hear you."

Samuel stood and extended his hand. "I appreciate it Zack."

Zack shook the extended hand. "Not a problem." He looked at Joshua who was still in the chair frowning. "You finished trying to intimidate me?" Zack asked.

"Did it work?" Joshua asked as he stood.

"Yeah, mmm hmmm," Zack replied. All three men broke out in laughter.

Once outside the door, Samuel and Joshua stood on the sidewalk in front of the house. "That man is so gone and he doesn't even realize it," Joshua said with a sigh.

"Why do you say that?" Samuel asked.

"He's sitting in the house drinking Remy watching a video of Diamond on his computer." Joshua shook his head as he walked off. "Damn. Another one bites the dust."

Chapter 9

The clock on her desk indicated it was well after eight in the evening and night had descended upon them. Opening the email reply to her request, Diamond re-read what it said. "I'll be there." Sighing she closed the message and decided to wait in his office. She stopped at LaFonde's desk and checked herself out in the mirror. Her sisters thought the red suit with the skirt that fell right above her knees and the low cut, white draped blouse was tastefully sexy and would catch any man's attention. If the looks she received throughout the day were any indication, they were right. The question in her mind was would it catch Zack's attention.

Satisfied with what her reflection revealed, Diamond exhaled and began the walk towards his office. She requested the meeting in the office because she wanted him to take her seriously. The lateness of the meeting was to ensure the employees were gone and the conversation would not be overheard. The trailer at the site would have been a private location, but that was where they had to work every day. If this went terribly wrong, she did not want to have to spend day after day in the place where she was rejected. Doing it here was best, she thought for the hundredth time. Stop second guessing yourself, this is the right thing to do, the right side of her brain told her. There is nothing wrong with thinking this thing through, after all, this is your life you are about to put on the line.

The wait had put Diamond's nerves on edge, but she had come this far, there was no turning back now. To her way of thinking her plan was a win-win. If he decided not to take her offer, then no loss. If he decided to accept her offer, then regardless of the outcome, she would have won—even if it turned out to be a hollow victory.

The light from the moon was shining through the window behind his desk as she walked into his office, giving the room a serene aura. For a moment she thought to leave it that way, but then decided to turn on the light switch. To her surprise, he sat in his chair staring at her with an unreadable expression. The sensation she had come to accept when he was around flowed through her like hot lava. All she could think of was how devilishly handsome he was. "Hello," she smiled nervously.

"Ms. Lassiter," he replied.

She stepped further into the room. "I didn't know you were here," she smiled.

"You asked me to come." Shaken by the distance in his voice, she hesitated. He propped his elbow on the arm of his chair, rested his head in his hand, then raised his eyebrow as if in anticipation of something. "I'm waiting."

Something about him told her to proceed with caution. "How was your day?"

"How was my day?" He repeated the question sarcastically.

"Yes."

He assessed her from the doorway the moment she stepped in. Even in limited light, her silhouette enticed him. When she turned on the light, it took all the will power he could gather not to get up and strip the red skirt off her body. He prayed his eyes did not betray him to reveal just how well she was wearing that suit. The low cut blouse was daring in a respectful way, the skirt fell just above her knees, but still left some room for the imagination; and those legs. For a moment just the thought of them caused him to close his eyes to gain some control. For his own sanity, he could not let this woman get any further under his skin.

Two nights ago, if she had been anywhere near him he would have strangled her pretty little neck with his bare hands. If it had been any other men in his home with questions about his personal life, he would have beat the hell out of them. But her brothers were two men that he respected and considered friends. Exactly what she had said to them to give them reason to invade his privacy, he did not bother to ask. Yet, the fact that they came let him know two things, one they took their responsibility as her big brothers very seriously and two, he had to keep his distance from her. That was becoming increasingly difficult. He didn't blame her brothers; if he had a sister that looked like her he would have done the exact same thing.

The last time he'd seen her was Saturday night and after three days it angered him to admit he had missed her. When he received her email he thought not to come, but he was scheduled to leave on a flight in the morning and he wanted to hear what she had to say. The brothers' visit asking his intentions towards her had him wondering. Now she stood here looking sexier than sin asking how my day was. "My day was exhausting," he finally replied.

His words were so long in coming she wondered if she should leave. The look on his face was intense and she wasn't sure if she should continue with her plan. "You know," she smiled, "It's late. We can talk another time." She turned to walk out of the door but he called out to her.

"Diamond, we are here. I'd like hear what you have to say."

Although there was an edge to his voice she wondered if he knew how musically he spoke her name. That encouraged her, for only a man with passion for her could make it sound so sensuous. Gathering her will, she turned back. "All right," she began. "I'm attracted to you," she exhaled, "very-very attracted to you. I have been since the first day we met and if you were honest with yourself you would admit that you are attracted to me also." She stepped forward and bit her bottom lip.

He swallowed trying to concentrate on her words and not the signals her body was sending.

"With that in mind, I have a proposition for you."

He sat up straight, "Really."

"Yes, really."

"I'm listening."

She inhaled and pushed forward. "The other night in the restaurant you said something that I did not appreciate at the time, but I now realize is true."

"Which was?"

"You said I would not know how to satisfy a man like you." She paused. "And you are right, I don't know how. So teach me."

"What?" He was sure he did not get her meaning.

"Teach me how to satisfy you."

"Satisfy me how?" The curiosity had his heart racing, echoing in his ears.

"The way a woman would satisfy a man."

"Physically?"

Shifting her footing, she firmly replied, "Yes."

Yes, he had heard her right. He prayed he was the only man she had ever made the ridiculous proposal to. "What makes you think I can teach you?"

Smiling seductively she replied, "You are a very accomplished man Zackary. I believe you can do anything you set your mind to. Even teach an inexperienced woman like me to satisfy an unapproachable man like you."

The temptation to take her up on her offer was strong, but he wouldn't. For his own sanity he couldn't. But he was curious to see how far she would go. Did she have any idea what she was asking for? He tilted his head to the side, "How far would you go to satisfy me Diamond."

"Excuse me?" There was a chill in his voice that made her hesitate.

"You're an intelligent woman, and you heard my question. How far would you go to learn?"

"As far as you are willing to take me."

Damn, that's tempting. But, he had to teach her a lesson. You don't go around giving grown men proposals like that. A different type of man would take advantage of her. "Really? Take off your jacket."

Diamond hesitated, not sure what to do. She wanted this man, but her nerves were shaky. She had never disrobed for a man before. Reaching up she began to remove her jacket.

Zack had no idea what she would do, he hoped she would turn and run out the door. But, she didn't. When she began to remove her jacket he lost his temper and yelled. "Are you in the habit of going around offering your body to men? Is this what you are about?" He slammed his fist on the desk as he shot up from the chair. "Are you so desperate to get a man that you are willing to do anything they ask?"

"No," she replied, shocked by his sudden outburst of questions.

"Standing here with you about to remove your clothes, you want me to believe that answer? You should never be so desperate for a man to be willing to do any and everything he asks just to have him. The answer is no to your proposition and don't ever assume your body is that irresistible."

It took her a minute, but then Diamond realized she had never been so insulted or angry in her life. Here she was offering her heart to this man and he had the audacity to insult her, accuse her of being desperate for a man. Didn't the fool understand she was desperate for him, not just any man—just him. Well she was not going to allow his fears to stop her. She stomped over and leaned across his desk. "You, Mr. Davenport are a one hundred percent, unadulterated ass." She turned and walked towards the door.

"Stop," he commanded without the volume raised. He walked to where she paused in mid motion near the door. Taking a battle stance, he crossed his arms over his chest. "You dare to call me a name after you just stood here and offered me your body. There are names for women like that; stop acting like you are one of them, because you're not. And another thing you just used two phrases that mean the same thing." Her eyebrows as well as her blood pressure elevated. "I would think a woman with the intelligence you claim would have a vocabulary range that would afford her the ability to use words without repeating herself."

Stepping closer to bring herself toe to toe with a man who had grown men shaking in their boots, she looked up, placed her hands on her hips and proceeded to give him a full range of her vocabulary. "You want words, how about pompous, ostentatious, egotistical, arrogant, overbearing, exasperating, aggravating jerk!"

The vicinity of her lips to his was more than he could take. Without a second thought, he seized her arms and captured her lips with his. Anger the likes of which Diamond had never experienced began seeping through her veins. She parted her lips to tell him just that, and his mouth took complete control.

The touch of her lips softened under his relentless assault. His intent was to teach her a lesson for using that mouth against him. Somewhere during the kiss, the initial intent was lost. Once she began to relax her lips, he released his grasp of her arms and moved his hands to her waist. She parted her lips to speak and he plunged in, taking care to explore all the regions within. He pulled her closer as her hands enclosed around his neck, bringing their bodies intimately together. He knew the moment she felt his rising desire, but instead of pulling away she stepped even closer. The softness of her breasts touched his chest. The thin tee shirt offered no defense. The contact caused such a surge through his body he began to grow harder against his zipper.

He ran his hands down the sides of her breasts, then across her nipples and they hardened against his touch. Her uncontainable moaned response ignited a fire in him. He pinned her body between him and the wall and lifted her until the junction between her thighs reached his manhood, which was growing by the minute. He groaned at the touch and she moaned. Holding her in place, he reluctantly released her lips and kissed her neck, moving lower to the crest of her breast until reaching what he sought. Through the silk blouse, he enclosed the tip of her nipple between his lips. Her moan echoed his pleasure of the touch. He moved the lower part of his body more intently against hers as she held his head securely to her. It wasn't enough; he had to touch her just this once. He guided her to the plush carpet and took the assault inside her blouse. Pushing the lace bra aside, he took the hard nipple into his mouth and savored the taste. Both their breaths caught at the gentle tug of his lips, as their desires heightened.

Things were getting out of control, he had to stop. His conscience would not allow him to leave her in this state. He eased her skirt up her legs. Roaming up her thighs he could not ignore the silky feel of her skin. A groan lodged in his throat, but he wasn't surprised to find no stockings and a thong underneath. His hands rested at her center as the heat and moisture penetrated his senses. Perspiration was forming on his forehead as he switched to the nipple on the other breast which he had now taken captive. She raised her body and held his head as if she was afraid he would pull away. That was exactly what he needed to do. But he couldn't—wouldn't leave her like this. He had to give her the release she needed and then he would let her go.

His finger touched the core of her first, then she gasped as his finger entered her. Lord he loved the way she was responding to him. Her body was as uninhibited as her mouth was. It was clear his assault down below in addition to that of her upper body was sending her into overload.

"Zackary," she cried out. He left her breast, kissed the throbbing vein in her neck and whispered in her ear, "ride it out, precious—ride it out." She did. She raised her hips to the motion of his finger and thumb that was fondling her core. The feel of her eagerly rising to him made it difficult to ignore his own need, but he would. This was for her. With his free hand, he held her hands above her head and continued to whisper in her ear. "Let it go, don't be afraid, release for me Diamond. I want to feel you lose control." He kissed her right below her ear and that was all she wrote. She shattered beneath him, like glass from a broken window. He captured her lips and held her while she rode the waves. As her ride eased, he rolled away from fear of his own desire taking over. They both laid still on the carpet in his office until their breathing returned to normal.

Zack was the first to recover. Standing, he held his hand out to her. When he helped her up, she stared at him with a bewildered look. He disregarded it, avoiding her eyes and began to right her clothes. As he smoothed her skirt into place he teased, "Now, I know how to shut you up." He fixed her blouse, then tossed her hair neatly over her shoulders. "Lesson number one, don't ever tease a man." They stared at each other for a long moment. "Go get your things. I'll meet you at the elevator to walk you to your car."

The next morning Zack was on a plane to Los Angeles. He needed to inspect some granite he wanted to use in one of the homes at Davenport Estates. The memory of the night before played through his mind. Never had a woman stirred so much desire in him. The thirty-minute cold shower did not quench the wanting, nor did the dream that followed. Turning the page in the sales catalogue, he was grateful for this trip. The time and distance would cure the longing to touch her again. A smile tugged at his lips. If he were willing to open his heart, she would be his choice. He liked her spunkiness and determination. The most troubling fact was he loved the way she responded to his touch. Her pleasure intensified his. There was no way he could tell her or anyone how the look on her face when she exploded in his hand, touched him. Male pride, the likes of which he had never known, surged through him when she opened her eyes and the look of wonder brightly shined through. Even afterwards when he was adjusting her clothes, the remnants of what she felt rendered her speechless. Now, hours later, the moment was still on his mind. Truth be told, she was right. He had had an immediate attraction to her the first day they met and it had only intensified since then. It would be easy to take what she was offering until he got his fill of her and then let her go. But she was X-Man's friend; Samuel and Joshua's little sister, an employee at his company and worst of all a woman you would love, not leave. That sealed the discussion in his mind.

L

Diamond stood at the window of the model house, looking out the window of the office. It was magnificent. The five bedroom home was a dream house and Zack had built it. One thing was for sure, Zackary did wonderful work with his hands, not only on wood but on her as well. The work he did the night before still had her body soaring just thinking about it. "Diamond," Pearl called out again. She turned to her sister. "You called me over here and now you want to ignore me."

Smiling shamelessly, she apologized. "I'm sorry Pearl. My mind was somewhere else."

"Or on someone else. Tell me what happened."

She hesitated for a moment, not sure if she should tell Pearl all or a clean version. Since high school Pearl has had a hatred for men regardless of how good they were. However, if she wanted to get good advice, she had to tell all.

She was glad Samuel couldn't make the meeting for fear of what his reaction would be.

She relayed to Pearl all that had happened, word for word, action by action, kiss by kiss and waited for her to explode. When her sister stood and joined her at the window, she was surprised at her gentle tone. "Well, that was pretty decent for a man."

Diamond turned to her sister, "I'm not sure what you mean."

"Come sit down. Let's talk on the up and up." As they took a seat at the table in the office Pearl exhaled. "This is not going to be easy so let me get it out and don't ask any questions until I'm done. From what you just told me, Zack put your best interest at the forefront, that indicates to me he cares about you. See, men are dogs. If you put a bone in front of a dog, he is going to snatch it up and gnaw on it until all the flavor is gone and then he will bury it away, out of sight out of mind." Pearl exhaled then covered her sister's hands that were folded in her lap. "Zack didn't do that. He could have taken your offer, enjoyed himself until he was tired, pushed you to the side and moved on. Instead he became angry that you'd lower yourself to do what you did and then he turned you away with some very good advice. Those are the actions of someone who cares. To add to the mix, when your hormones kicked in he still could have taken what you offered this one time, then sent you away. But he didn't. According to you he took control of the situation, let you know he was apparently very attracted to you, and then made sure you were satisfied without satisfying himself. That's the action of an unselfish lover. Any woman would be fortunate to have such a man."

"Even you?"

"Especially me. But men like this don't come around for me." She looked at her baby sister and smiled, "But it seems one has for you. You should do all you can to grab and hold on to him. It's just that the way you are going about it will not work on a man like him. He's going to have to discover his feelings for you. You can't shove it down his throat."

Diamond agreed. "After last night, I know I don't want to play a game with Zack. I want to feel all that he has to give."

"Girl don't be stupid. You have to play the game, just not the one you planned."

Diamond looked sideways at her sister who had a silly grin on her face. "Do you have a game in mind?"

"I'm so glad you asked. It's called the attack of the Lassiter Sisters. You see men tend to want what they can't have."

"Daddy said something similar."

"That's because he's a man and he knows how mom caught him."

Diamond frowned, "I don't know Pearl. Games have a way of backfiring on you. Look what happened last night. If I didn't learn anything else, I know Zack doesn't like games."

"He'll like this one. Because you are going to give him exactly what he wants."

"But he wants space." Diamond said confused.

"And that's what you are going to give him."

Chapter 10

*T*hree weeks had gone by since Zack had entered his office or seen Diamond face to face. The week he spent in LA was torture, for she slipped into his dreams every night. Once he returned things were a little easier, he was busy and she seemed to be keeping her distance. When he stopped by Doc's last Saturday night, Lee and Doc told him Diamond and her sisters had come by a few times. Doc said Diamond apologized for causing a little ruckus the last time she was there. Of course he blamed all of it on him, but Zack didn't mind, he knew his actions had been a little out of line. All the same it was thoughtful of her to apologize for something she could not control.

He only knew one of the sisters, Ruby, and had seen Pearl in the news with J.D. Harrison, the Attorney General of Virginia, but he had never met the other sisters. According to Lee, each one of them was a woman you would turn your head twice to see. And the youngest one, they call Phire; he said she was just that, a ball of fire. Zack laughed at his friend's description of the Lassiter sisters. But today he was only concerned with one.

"Hey big brother, you are looking good in Armani. Must be a special occasion," Xavier said smiling as he took a seat in front of Zack's desk.

"What's up X-Man? I checked out the design for The Tower." He shook his head, "You are a deep brother and I'm not saying that because I love you. It's real." Xavier stared at his brother as if he had grown two heads. Zack looked behind him to see if something was there and then turned back to his brother. "What's wrong?" he asked with a concerned face.

"You just said you love me," Xavier stammered out.

Frowning, Zack waved him off, "You know I love you."

"Damn, you said it again. I mean I know, but you just never said it."

"Well, now I have." Sitting back in his chair, he asked, "When are you going to cut your hair?"

Now, this was the Zack he knew and loved. "My locks—never. You ready for the meeting?"

"Yeah, I'm looking forward to everyone's report." He hesitated, "Is everyone here?"

"Yes Diamond is here and she will give her report." Zack looked up from the papers on his desk and gave his brother a warning stare. "Look, why don't you ease up on her. She is one of the best people I know and she is one of my closest friends. I hate that you two are at odds with each other."

"I'm not at odds with her."

"Well what do you call it? Every time she opens her mouth you jump down her throat. You got her to the point that she's calling in each morning to see if you are in before she decides if she is working in the office or at the site. I asked her to come with me the other night to Doc's to hear you play and she refused because she knows you don't want her around you. She met a major milestone and was going to have her assistant present the information at the board meeting because she did not want to cross you. Let up on the sister Zack. She is damn good and she has made a lot of money for Davenport Industries."

He sat back in his seat, "What money are you referring to?"

"This is all in her report, but in a month's time Diamond has sold thirty home sites and half of the town homes. As of last week there are twenty-two on the waiting list for condos in The Tower. You and Charles made her change the figures in her initial report. What you didn't know was that she had already scaled them down before that meeting." He stood and adjusted his suit blazer. "Give the girl a break Zack."

Listening to his little brother defend his friend, Zack realized that X-man had grown into a formidable man. Maybe he was ready to handle the truth about his mother. But that can wait. At the moment he had to deal with this growing need to see Diamond. He exhaled and ran his hand down his face. "I don't know if I can let up on her."

"Why the hell not?" Xavier glared down at him.

Zack sighed as he sat back in his chair. He stared at his brother for a moment and then stated, "I want her. I want her in the worst way."

Xavier nodded at his brother, "I know. But staying down her throat is not the way to get her."

Zack stood and walked over to the window. "I don't want to get her. I've had my share of heartache. The last thing I need is a woman like Diamond in my life."

"Diamond is exactly what you need in your life. She is not like Celeste. You have to stop holding every woman responsible for what she did to you. Hell, I had a hand in your fate too, but you don't dismiss me."

Realizing he was making statements based on limited information, Zack simply replied, "You had no hand in my decision. You are my blood and nothing or no one will ever come before that."

There was never any question in Xavier's mind about his brother's love for him. "I know that man. I realize your demons are your battle, I have my own. All I'm saying is give the girl a break and she might surprise you."

JoEllen stepped inside the door, "Zack everyone is in the board room."

"Thanks JoEllen, we'll be right there."

"Let's go," Zack said as he picked up his portfolio, "She really sold all the lots that fast?"

"Deposits, signed contracts, approved loans. The girl is making dough."

The meeting took place and Diamond received a standing round of applause at her news. Being the very shy person that she was, she only took five bows and bravos. She announced everything was in place for the ribbon cutting ceremony and the after party at the Community Center a month from Saturday. The list of guests that had sent in RSVPs was quite impressive.

There was one point in the meeting when Xavier thought things were going to flare up between Zack and Diamond, but it was avoided by Diamond giving in. Apparently there was a site that had a hold put on it by Zack and when Diamond asked why, he sternly replied, "Because I said so." Everyone was ready for her to challenge him on it, but she didn't. She simply replied, "All right." After a moment of silent shock from everyone at the table the meeting continued.

Once the meeting was over Diamond left the room. Reese stopped Zack to talk about the security on the lot and to advise him that Fire Chief Richard Hasting would be stopping by the site to see him. It was now May, the weather was breaking and that was usually the time a number of thefts and other incidents would increase on construction sites.

Zack stopped by Diamond's office to congratulate her on her accomplishments, but she had left the building. He knew she was a dedicated worker and would not have gone home early, therefore there was only one other place she would be. It angered him that she was intentionally avoiding him, but he understood why. Her staying away from him was what he wanted; or was it?

"Oh hell!" Zack exclaimed as he pulled up next to the Fire Chief's car. Richard Hasting was a decent man,

Zack knew that. He also knew the man was only doing his job. But when that job questioned his integrity, Zack became defensive. Yes, Davenport Construction had been cleared of any wrong doing in the fire from the last project, but his integrity had been called into question publicly and that was something Zack would not tolerate. To Zack, a man's word was his bond. If people lost faith in a man's word, there wasn't much left.

Zack parked the truck and walked inside the trailer. The sooner he could get this meeting over with the sooner he could find Diamond. Not seeing her had him on edge. He didn't know why, but it did. Zack filled the doorway to find Richard sitting in the chair in front of his desk laughing and Reese at his desk at the other end of the trailer just as jovial. That eased his mind a little, maybe this wasn't a professional visit.

"We all seem to be in a good mood this morning." Zack spoke as he reached out and shook Richard's hand. "Richard."

The Chief stood, shaking Zack's extended hand. "Zack. It's good to see you."

"I would say the same, however, that remains to be seen."

"It's a semi-professional visit." Richard, who stood just an inch below Zack, replied as he released his hand.

Zack turned and walked over to his desk. "In that case, it's semi-good to see you." The two men laughed. "What brings you here?" He asked as he sat behind his desk glancing at messages.

"This is a site visit we will do at different phases of the project to ensure that all fire codes are being met." Richard explained as he took a seat in front of Zack's desk.

Zack looked up, "I don't recall doing this at other sites."

"You're at a different level now Zack. You're a developer, not just the head of a construction crew. There's a whole set of different codes you have to adhere to and issues you have to deal with. Such as the headache of seeing me from time to time."

"That's all there is to it?" Zack raised an eyebrow with the question.

"Not all, but that's the majority of it." Zack didn't respond, he just held Richard's stare and waited. Richard exhaled. "Zack, come on man. You know I have to do these visits. The fire on your last project put a blemish on Davenport Construction. In fact, some believe the insurance money from the incident financed this project."

"You know damn well that's not the fact."

"I know that Zack, but the question is out there. And you and I know if anyone else had been in the chief position, the conclusion of the last investigation could have gone very differently. Let's be honest here, there was something questionable about that fire. As Chief, it is my job to make sure something of that nature doesn't happen again." Zack started to speak, but Richard held up his hand to stop him. "As your friend, I'm taking every precaution to ensure your name and reputation in this business stay intact. If my doing that pisses you off," Richard sat back in the chair, stretched his legs out and smiled, "that's just an extra."

Zack shot a glare over to Reese when he heard him stifle a laugh as a cough. Turning his attention back to Richard, Zack sat back and folded his arms across his chest. "To this day, I wonder about that fire. I know my men, none of them are careless with the equipment. And the fact that it skipped houses is still baffling."

Richard tilted his head, "That's the very reason arson was considered. And the call."

Zack sat forward. "What call?"

"A call came in stating you set the fire for the insurance money."

"You never told me about a call." Zack stated as Reese walked over and stood next to the desk.

"Who did the call come from?" Reese asked.

"It was anonymous," Richard replied to Reese, then turned back to Zack. "You know I couldn't share the facts about the investigation..."

"Was the call from a male or female?" Reese interrupted him.

Both men turned to Reese. "Why?" Zack asked.

"Answer the question," Reese insisted."

"I don't recall," Richard replied as he stared at Reese.

"What's going on Reese?" Zack could see the worried look on Reese's face.

Reese leaned against the file cabinet and folded his arms as he looked at Zack. "While you were in LA, I received a call. The caller was a female. She said you destroyed property to get the insurance money on the last job."

"And you are just telling me this!" Zack yelled.

"It's my job to protect this site. I'm not going to tell you about every little thing that happens. I just handle it. To tell the truth, I didn't think much of it at the time. This is the first I've heard details about the previous fire."

"Did she say anything else?" Richard asked.

Shaking his head Reese replied, "No." He walked purposely over to his desk. "But a few days later it rained. I did walk around the site like I always do." He pulled open his center desk drawer and pulled out a plastic bag with a ring in it. "There were small foot prints around the structure on the lot," he looked at the note written on the bag, "Lot number 102c. The size of the prints made me curious so I followed them. Inside the muddy tracks led to a corner of the house. This was lying on one of the studs. If the men had come in before me and put up the drywall, I would have never seen it." He walked over and showed the bag to Zack. "I thought it might belong to one of the men that were working on the house. But when I questioned them, none of them had ever seen it before."

Zack picked up the bag and couldn't believe what was inside. He sat back confused. "How in the hell did that get inside one of the houses?"

"You recognize the ring?" Richard asked.

Zack looked up at him, then at Reese. "It's my father's mason ring. It was in my house, in the jewelry box in my bedroom."

"You must have dropped it one day while walking through the structure." Reese relaxed.

"It's never been out of my house." Zack flatly stated. "I was going to bury it with my father, but decided it was the one thing of his I wanted to keep to pass on to any children I might have."

"If you didn't bring it, how did it get here?" Richard asked, "and why?"

All three men were silent for a few minutes. Reese took the bag. "I'll get a friend at the station to check it for finger prints." Zack held the bag, reluctant to let it go. "I'll make sure it's returned," Reese added sensing Zack's reluctance.

"You think the foot prints belong to a woman?" Richard asked Reese as Zack watched the bag with concern.

"That was my first impression," Reese replied as he put the bag in his jacket pocket.

"Do you have any women working on the site?"

"Just Diamond Lassiter," Reese replied.

Richard relaxed, "Then the footprints could belong to her."

"No," Reese shook his head. "She wouldn't dare venture down here. Our charming Zack here made sure of that."

Richard looked from the smiling Reese to the frowning Zack. "Lassiter. Is that one of Samuel's sisters?"

"Sure is." Reese sneered. "And Zack here nearly chopped her head off her first day on the site and she hasn't come down here since."

"You're exaggerating." Zack frowned.

"Did you or did you not yell at the woman for looking good?"

"That wasn't the reason and you damn well know it." Zack declared. He turned to Richard to explain, "She was distracting my men from their work. Damn near got herself killed in the process."

Seeing the teasing on Reese's face, Richard followed his lead to get Zack's mind away from the ring. "How was she distracting the men?" he asked grinning.

Zack looked from one man to the other. "Let it go." He stated.

"That good?" Richard said as he stood. "I might have to meet this woman if she is that distracting."

"No you don't. You need to do whatever you came here to do and let me get back to work."

Richard smiled, "I guess that's my cue, I've worn out my welcome."

"Come on man." Reese walked towards the door. "I'll walk the site with you and answer any questions you might have."

"Sounds good." He extended his hand, "Zack, as always it's been interesting."

Zack shook his hand. "Keep me posted on any findings."

"I'll do that." Richard stated as he walked outside with Reese. The men walked a few feet in silence. "What are you thinking Reese?"

"I'm thinking I want whatever information you have on the previous investigation."

"It's closed so it's open to the public." He hesitated. "We've known Zack since high school. I don't remember him having women problems. He was too busy with his little brother. Is there a woman out there that has an issue with Zack?"

Reese shook his head. "Not that I'm aware of. The only woman Zack was seriously involved with was back in college and she left him." He stopped. "I can't imagine a woman stooping to arson."

Richard grunted, "You would be surprised what a woman scorned would do. When I came out it was just to make sure Zack stayed on top of things. Now, I'm documenting as this project progresses to cover his ass."

Every time Zack walked into the model he was amazed at how it was decorated exactly as he'd envisioned while he was building it. He didn't know for sure, but he was guessing Diamond had a hand in the decorating as she had with the trailer. All the items from the trailer were now in the garage area of the model house, which had been converted into an office. She had a way of making things feel like home. Like the apple pie smell that was now permeating the house. *It must be a new type of air freshener or something,* he thought as he walked into the kitchen.

To his surprise, there was a steaming hot apple pie on the counter. He opened the door to the garage, and looked inside. No one was there. He closed the door and walked up the back staircase to the second level of the house - still no sign of Diamond. As he walked up the staircase to the third level, he stopped mid way and knew she was somewhere in the area. The fragrance that'd been enticing him in his dreams was in the air. It'd been weeks and suddenly he was desperate to see her face-to-face, one on one. Checking the game room, she wasn't there. He looked in the theater room, still no sign of her. As he turned to go back down the stairs he stopped and remembered the sitting room on the far end of the theater room. Walking through, her special scent was guiding him to her and just as he turned the corner, there she was. Sitting in the window seat with her shoes off, her legs spread out and crossed at the ankles, with a box of frosted flakes cereal, reading a book. He had never seen anything so serene in his life. Apparently she did not hear him approaching because she was startled when he spoke. "Hello, Diamond."

She looked up suddenly at the sound of his voice. No man on earth had the right to look so damn good in a suit less than an hour ago and even better in a pair of jeans now. Trying to hold down the jitters going off in the pit of her stomach was too much to ask. Diamond had been wondering what his reaction would be the next time he saw her alone. Well the time was here. Now what was it that Pearl told her to do? Oh yeah, be cool. Give him the time he needed to discover his own feelings for her. Swallowing the cereal that was in her mouth, she answered, "Hello, Zackary."

They gazed at each other for a long moment taking in the essence of one another, before either could speak, both reliving the night a few weeks ago. Her mind, unsure and nervous about being in his presence again. His mind wondering why he was losing the battle to keep this woman from getting under his skin. "Why are you sitting up here?" He asked.

She slowly turned back to the window. "I love this view. Since that lot is not going to be sold, this house has a direct view of the river. Once they finish the Canal Walk project, you will be able to see the ships come in and out from here."

She didn't have to turn to know he was closer, she could feel his presence drawing nearer. "When we purchased this land, I chose that site for my home, for the very reasons you just stated. That's why the lot is not for sale."

Taking a breath of astonishment, she nodded slightly. "I can see why." A second passed. "I'm sorry for questioning it. I didn't know."

He breathed in deeply, taking the calming essence of her into his system. "I didn't tell anyone—not even X-Man." He put a hand on the window seal above her head, then pointed out, "If you look down there to the right, but left of Canal Walk, that's where another site is being built."

"What site?"

"Another over priced community, that people like you and me could not afford to live in."

She turned to look at him, but did not expect to be confronted by his massive chest, with his hands braced above her head. Her breath lodged in her throat as she slowly followed his chest up to find him looking down at her. Taking a swallow in an effort to remember what she was going to say, she held his gaze marveling in the wonder of his eyes. She closed her eyes as heat seemed to generate through her body, took a deep breath to shake the spell, then reopened her eyes, looking back out the window. "What are you talking about—you could live anywhere you choose. I, on the other hand, can only dream of living here and definitely not over there."

"You make a six figure income, and stand to get a rather large commission for the homes you have sold. Great job, by the way."

She smiled at the compliment. "Thanks." She nodded, "Yeah you guys pay me well, but I have to pay my sister's tuition and it seems to increase every year."

"Why are you paying your sister's tuition?"

"The older children who have graduated from college pay one of our younger siblings tuition to give our parents a break and kind of say thanks at the same time."

"Really," he said as he took a seat beside her. "That's very thoughtful. Your family has always seemed close."

"Oh we are." She beamed as she moved her feet to make room for him. "A family that prays together stays together—That's what my dad always says."

"Is he a minister?"

"Oh gracious no, the way my daddy puts colorful words out, I don't hardly think so. If the pastor knew some of the words my daddy could say he would lock him in the church basement and fill it with holy water then throw away the key." Zack laughed harder than he had in years. The sound filled her heart with so much joy she continued to talk about her family as he listened. Minutes turned into an hour later before either realized it.

The ringer on Zack's cell phone ended the peaceful interlude the two were having. Standing, he walked to the doorway to take the call. Afterwards, he smiled apologetically at her, "I have to go."

"Okay."

Hesitantly he stood in the doorway. There were things he needed to say to her. "The reason I replaced you with the virtual model had nothing to do with you. It's better to allow people to use their imagination when you are trying to sell something. Let them use the ideal person in their mind to sell the product. While seeing you on that screen pleased me, it may not have the same effect on others." Turning his back to her to continue out he took a step down and stopped. "You don't have to avoid me. I kind of like having you around now." He looked back over his shoulder at her, "We are playing at Doc's on Friday, if you'd like to come by."

Surprised by his invitation, it took her a moment to reply. "I'd like that."

Not realizing he was holding his breath for her reply, he nodded and continued on his way.

Outside the closed door, Zack stood and thought of about the last hour. Seeking out a woman just because he wanted to see her was something he just did not do. He sighed, like it or not Diamond Lassiter was under his skin. Okay, he could accept that because it was something he could no longer control. He was physically attracted to her, which was one thing he could quench. He began to walk away and decided to figure out why just listening to or being near her had such a calming affect on him at a later time.

Diamond walked down to the second floor and watched through the window as he walked towards the construction trailer. The man had the most confident stride she had ever seen. He was such a proud man and it showed in everything he did. The look in his eyes when he delivered her first orgasm came to mind. Yes, she was dazed, but the way he held her gaze as she shattered couldn't be missed. As impossible as it may seem, she had the distinct feeling he was enjoying her pleasure more than she was. A giggle escaped her, "Like that's possible." She continued down to her office, dropped her book on the desk and slumped into her chair, telling herself not to get her hopes up. Yes, he'd opened up a little. But it wasn't nearly enough for what she wanted. She wanted all of him, his hurt, his fears, his joy but most of all she wanted his love. Keeping her exuberance down was going to be hard, Diamond was never one to hide her feelings, but looking at the contracts on her desk, she had plenty to keep her busy and hopefully, Zackary off her mind.

A few days later, while working late at the office, Diamond saw a flash through the window that caught her attention. Standing, she looked out the back window to see a woman outside looking around. The woman was small in stature with short cropped hair, dressed in jeans, a top and a thin jacket. It was the end of April and the weather was nice. But the nights were a little crisp. For a moment, she thought the woman could be a client so she glanced at her watch. It was well after nine, the office stopped showing at seven. Not thinking twice about her actions, Diamond walked into the kitchen, opened the French doors and walked out onto the balcony. "May I help you with something?" she called out.

The woman turned, surprised to see her standing there. "No."

Taken aback by the tone of the woman's response Diamond, raised an eyebrow. "Okay." She looked around then rubbed the chill off her arms. "Would you like to come inside to see the model?"

The woman stood there staring at her as if she was trying to make a decision. "I have tea and an apple cobbler waiting to be enjoyed."

That brought a smile to the woman's face, nothing big, but the ends of her lips did curl. Diamond turned, walking back into the kitchen, leaving the door open. Something about the woman made her think of some of the people her sister Ruby worked with at the shelter. Walking over to the refrigerator, she pulled out the cobbler and sat it on the counter. Opening the drawer, she pulled out a knife and two forks. Taking the tea kettle she filled it with water and placed it on the stove. Just as she suspected, the woman took her time but eventually walked in the door. "I've been trying to stop baking because I end up eating it all by myself." She placed two cups on the breakfast bar. "At home there is no such thing as leftovers," she smiled. "Everything my mother puts on the table disappears within minutes." Noticing the woman's hesitation at the door, Diamond put the cobbler she had dished out into the microwave and pushed the reheat button. "Oh, let me close that door, there's a chill out tonight." As she walked by the woman, she could see the pain in the woman's eyes. But she could see something else, too. The woman's eyes were glassed over, which meant she was high. On what, she wasn't sure, but the woman was feeling no pain. While closing the door, it crossed her mind for a moment that this may not be a good idea. But she shook the thought aside, for whatever reason she wasn't afraid of the woman.

"You shouldn't be here this late by yourself." The woman slurred her words.

Diamond hesitated at the door, "I'm not alone. My boss is in the trailer." She walked over to the stove as the kettle whistle sounded. "Do you take sugar in your tea?" Diamond looked up and the woman was gone. "Well...what the..." she walked over to the door and saw the woman disappear into the woods behind the house. She huffed then turned the lock on the door. "That was weird."

The next day Diamond was standing in Xavier's office telling him about the woman, stalling for time. She really needed to talk to her friend about her attraction to his brother, but she was afraid he may not approve and she did not want to lose his friendship. The time had come for her to tell Xavier. Lord knows she could only take so many dreams of Zack at night—dreams about those tantalizing fingers and his succulent lips.

"Diamond?" Xavier called out to her for the third time, pulling her back to reality. "You realize you stopped talking."

Diamond simply stared at him, weighing the option to talk with him about his brother or not.

Laughing inside, Xavier wondered when she was going to talk with him about Zack. Those two had to be the most hilarious couple he had ever encountered. It was abundantly clear to everyone in the office, except the two of them, that they were hot for each other. However, Diamond, with her inexperience in the art of seduction and Zack with his dismal outlook on women kept the two of them apart. Xavier personally believed they would be perfect for each other. *Poor Diamond,* he thought. She knows it, but is just unlearned in the ways of men. Zack on the other hand is just plain blind. The odds around the office had Zack falling from his temple in about a month. Xavier knew it would take his brother, who had issues with women, a bit longer. In fact, he and JoEllen placed their bets on June, by then Zack would fall. Returning the intense look he was getting from Diamond and trying his best not to laugh, he waited for her to speak.

Placing her hands on her hips, she finally spoke. "Would you have an issue with me dating your brother?"

Xavier sat back in his chair contemplating how he would reply. Tilting his head to the side he held Diamond's intense glare. "Why Zack, Diamond?"   He asked. "All through college there were brothers after brothers trying to get next to you and you didn't give them the time of day. So, why my brother?"

Diamond stood and waved off his question. "Those were boys and I didn't have time to wait for them to learn their left testicle from the right. Nor did I want to play the games women played on campus. They couldn't teach me or give me what I wanted. Zack can. He has so much love inside of him he can't stand it. That's why he lashes out at me."

"He's trying to let the love out?" Xavier asked trying not to laugh at the notion.

"Exactly, and I'm going to help him." She took his hand in hers. "Xavier, I didn't know who Zack was when he came into my office that day. But the moment I stepped out front, I knew he was there for me. His license expiring was God's way of bringing us together. If it hadn't been that it would have been something else. Either way I was meant to be in his life and he in mine." She released his hand and walked over to his window deep in thought. "I'm just having a little difficulty getting him to recognize and accept the fact." She all but stomped her foot.

"A little," Xavier laughed. "I believe you have a monumental problem, however, if anyone can put Zack under a spell it's you. I'm just afraid you may get hurt in the process and I'm more afraid of Zack getting hurt."

Turning swiftly to face him, she frowned, "I wouldn't hurt Zackary, Xavier. I just want to love him and teach him to love me."

Chapter 11

The band completed the first set and was taking a break. Every time the door opened to Doc's, Zack's eyes would automatically wander in that direction. It was well after ten and there was still no sign of Diamond. He wanted to kick himself for caring, but he had not seen her since their talk at the model house. On Wednesday, he asked X-man about her. He stated she wasn't feeling well and was working from home. Today was Friday and he spent it laying sheet rock in some of the homes to keep his mind from drifting to her. Now he wondered if she would show. "You okay Zack?" Lee asked at the break.

"Yeah, why you ask?"

"You keep watching the door. Are you expecting someone?"

The door opened again. Xavier and a young woman who resembled Diamond walked through. His heart leaped, but when no one walked behind them, it shrunk. "Hey Zack," Xavier smiled. "I hope you guys aren't shutting down for the night."

"No, just a break," Zack replied somewhat disappointed. He followed them to a table not far from the stage that was used whenever band members had guests. "I'll get someone to take your drink orders."

"Thanks. Oh Zack, this is Diamond's sister Jade."

"Where is she?" he asked with aggravation showing on his face.

Raising an eyebrow, "Hello to you too," Jade responded with a teasing smile.

"Sorry," Zack countered. "Hello. Where is Diamond," he asked as he pulled the chair out for her.

"I'm right behind you. Is there something wrong?" Diamond asked.

Zack turned and wondered why he did not sense her presence as he had before. The answer came to him as he turned. The anger and disappointment in not seeing her earlier was clouding his mind. Praying like hell his joy in seeing her was not showing, he replied, "There is, but we will discuss that at a later time."

Seeing the smile in his eyes was more then she could take. Before she could stop herself, she tiptoed up and kissed his cheek. "Thank you for inviting me. I look forward to that conversation."

Xavier held his breath, as did Lee, Reese and Doc, who were all standing near the stage looking on in shock. Showing emotions was not something Zack tolerated with a woman in his presence, so they knew in public was a definite no-no. Diamond and Jade took their seats oblivious to the fact that the room was about to explode. "Have you ordered yet?" Diamond asked looking at Xavier.

Zack still had not moved from the spot where Diamond kissed him. The initial shock of her action passed as he realized he enjoyed the nearness of her. "No, they haven't ordered. What would you like?" He asked trying hard to ignore the looks on X-man, Lee, Reese and Doc's faces.

"Chardonnay."

"Chardonnay it is." He looked at X-man and Jade.

"I'll have the same," Jade smiled appreciatively.

Xavier was still recovering from shock as he responded, "Remy."

Zack walked by Lee and Reese, "Doc would you take care of that for me?"

"Sure Zack," he replied slowly as he watched Zack walk towards the door.

Outside the crowded club, Zack inhaled deeply and then released his breath. Damn, if the woman did not take his breath away in that red dress. The top hugged her in all the right places with the bottom flaring out like the Marilyn dress. But the back was completely bare. As he pulled her chair out for her to sit down, his hand touched the smooth skin and memories of the night in his office returned in vivid living color. The urge to have her increased tenfold.

He knew all the reasons why he shouldn't want to touch her, one being his slow tortured death at the hands of her brother Joshua, but he had to have her—taste her again, just once or he would surely lose his mind. With that decision the turmoil inside began to settle and he knew what he had to do—teach her just as she'd requested.

The band was on stage when Zack returned. They played a few upbeat tunes and then the spotlight dimmed to focus on Zack. He stood, whispered something to Lee then sat back on his stool. After giving instructions to the other members of the band, Lee stepped back leaving Zack with King Arthur as the lone figure on the stage.

Closing his eyes, Zack brought the sax to his lips and began to play. The smooth sensuous sound filtered through the place like a warm summer breeze. Each note was clear and precise as the tune became easily recognized as "Teach Me Tonight" by Dinah Washington.

Diamond watched as the man and his sax spoke to her. Soothing emotions began to surface as he played. She wanted this man and from the way he was playing, he wanted her too. Tears welled up in her eyes as the lyrics to the song came to mind.

Will it be tonight Zackary, she wondered. *Will you teach me tonight?* The hook of the song lingered on the single note that he held and she felt as if he was expressing what was in his heart just to her. Was it wishful thinking, probably, but Diamond didn't care. She was going to allow herself to have this night. The song ended as the crowd roared to their feet with a standing ovation. The song lasted all of five minutes, but the effect on her heart would last a lifetime. His eyes found hers and she knew the lesson plan had been made. The only thing she wanted at the moment was to feel his hands on her body, anywhere and everywhere.

The band members left the stage as the house music began to play. A focused Zack walked towards the table. A number of people shook his hand and gave him dap as he stormed by, but his eyes were only on her. Xavier leaned over and whispered to Diamond, "I hope you are ready. It looks like big brother is on a mission."

"I've spent a lifetime getting ready for this moment," she replied wistfully as Zack materialized in front of her. "You have some very talented lips, Mr. Davenport."

A quick devious smile appeared on his face. "The better to taste you my dear." Reaching out for her hand, "May I have this dance?"

She placed her hand in his and stood. The heat of his skin swirled through her body and settled right between her legs. Joining the small crowd that gathered on the dance floor, he took her in his arms.

Zack had been waiting for this moment all week. Hell that was a lie. He had been yearning for this since that night in his office. To feel the silkiness of her skin, smell the fragrance of her hair and to taste the sweetness of her lips. Had he craved Celeste this way? Shaking the thought out of his mind, he concentrated on the woman in his arms. He would have to deal with his past at another time, at this moment, he wanted this woman. Pulling her closer, he held her a little tighter. Her head touched his chin and he inhaled her scent. "You smell almost as good as you feel in my arms." She looked up at him with her doe-shaped eyes and he knew that was his undoing. In the middle of Doc's, on the dance floor, with several couples dancing around them, he lowered his lips to hers and slowly tasted what she was offering.

Meanwhile at the table, Jade had a different plan in mind. "Xavier, you know I'm going to have to block the booty call tonight. I mean I like Zack, but I know his reputation with women. I have to make sure my sister is not going to be a one night thing for him—she deserves better."

"No argument from me. But I'm going to warn you, Zack is not going down easy."

"Not a problem." Jade picked up her cell phone. "I have a sure fire backup plan." She stood and rushed out to the floor and pulled them apart just as their lips touched. "Diamond, we have to go. Some boy is trying to push up on Phire and she needs a ride home."

Diamond looked at Jade as if she had grown two heads. "Call Joshua."

Jade pulled at her again. "Did you just hear yourself? Joshua?"

A frustrated Diamond sighed. What was she thinking? Joshua would kill the boy and ask questions later. Turning to Zack with apologizing eyes, "I'm sorry, I have to go," she said as Jade pulled her towards the door.

Xavier joined Zack who was standing in the doorway watching the women pull off. "What's the problem?"

"Some boy is pushing up on their little sister Phire."

"Kind of like her big sister," Xavier smirked.

The stony look Zack gave his little brother was only a small replica of the anguish he was feeling inside. "You see some humor in this face?"

"Not a bit—just a little irony."

"Irony?"

"Yeah," he shrugged. "Diamond has been trying to get your attention for months. Now that you are ready, she has another priority." He looked up at the sky, "Let me think. What is the lesson here? I'm glad you asked." Xavier continued as he enjoyed the scowl on his brother's face.

"Don't let the grass grow under your feet big brother. Let the past go and live for today, especially if a good woman is involved."

$\mathcal{L}$

The place seemed deserted. The lone figure dressed totally in black slipped between the houses. I have to make sure the walls are up. Reaching the house in question, the lone figure smiled. Step one complete. Things are progressing nicely. Zackary is not going to know what hit him. Suddenly, a dog barked. Startled, the figure looked around. The dog barked again, this time closer. The figure stepped back into the shadows of the house. That's when the guard with the dog on a chain came into view. Damn. The figure took off running through the woods.

Chapter 12

By six the next morning Zack couldn't take it any longer. Pulling himself out of bed, he scrambled to the bathroom. While taking a shower, that was not diminishing the desire he had for Diamond, he devised a plan to get uninterrupted time with her. Drying off he wondered why Barbara's offer to come home with him last night wasn't enticing. Any other time Barbara would have sufficed, but right now the only woman that could quench his need was Diamond. Of course it was only a physical want—wasn't it? That's right it's only physical, he continued to repeat in his mind over and over. Zack was never one to drop in on someone unannounced. However, this was an unusual circumstance and Diamond would just have to understand.

Diamond lived in an old warehouse that was renovated into apartments on the north side of Richmond. The building was secure and he had to be buzzed in by an occupant. Zack pushed the number for her apartment—no answer. Taking a look at his watch, seven-fifteen, it was a little early in the morning to be visiting, nevertheless he buzzed again. Patience had never been his forté. While waiting he examined the construction of the building, occupational habit.

"Zack?"

At the sound of his name, he turned to see Diamond slowly walking towards the building in biker shorts and a tank top. He might as well have never taken a shower this morning. The sight of her body had caused the simmering flame to erupt within him again.

Her hair was up in a ponytail and the perspiration from her run was glistening on her skin. "Zack, what are you doing here?" She asked, subconsciously pushing her hair in place with the palm of her hand. *Man, the muscles in his thighs look like they are bulging out of those jeans. Be cool, she thought, don't run and jump in his arms like you want to, just be cool.* When he did not reply, she took a step closer, "Zack?"

He never before thought a sweaty woman was sexy, but she certainly changed his opinion on that. It took him a moment to realize she had said something. "Good morning," he replied, hoping she did not see the affect she was having on his body. "You're up early this morning."

"I couldn't sleep," Diamond replied, winded from her run.

"I can empathize with you. I didn't get much sleep last night myself." They stood there staring at each other for an awkward moment. "How is your sister?" he asked trying to make small talk until his body could calm down.

"She's okay—slept in my bed all night."

"All it takes is for me to have a problem to sleep in your bed?" *Where in the hell did that come from,* he thought. Seeing the look on her face he added, "I'm just joking."

"You don't have to have a reason Zack. All you have to do is ask." *Who said that,* she thought, *somebody put those words in my mouth.*

He watched and waited until she was toe to toe with him. "I accept your proposal. Spend the day with me."

"I would love to." She inhaled, not believing she replied so quickly and aloud. Stepping by him, she punched in a code to open the door. "Would you like to come in while I shower and change?"

"Yes. You may need help with that shower," he sensuously replied.

They stepped inside the building and began climbing the steps to the second floor. Walking behind her, he could not miss the firmness of her behind and thighs. "You keep walking like that and the lessons are going to begin in this hallway."

"Do you mean like this?" She added a little motion to her steps.

Swallowing hard, Zack stopped and simply watched her walk. I must be losing my mind, he thought. The movement of her hips increased his already straining arousal. "Yeah, like that."

She stopped at the door to her apartment, looked over her shoulder and slowly smiled. "You are a special man Zackary Davenport or I must be going crazy. I don't usually allow men to see me sweaty with my hair up."

"I'm glad to hear that," he replied before he thought about what he was saying. It shouldn't matter to him if other men saw her early in the morning, but the thought of it did.

She opened the door then stood to the side as he walked in. "Make yourself comfortable. Would you like some coffee or tea?" She asked as she closed the door.

"Isn't there another option to that question?"

Leaning with her back against the door, she smiled and tilted her head to the side, "Or me?"

He stepped up to her, placed his hands against the door enclosing her within, looked down into her smiling eyes, "I'll take," he kissed the left side of her lips, "a little of, " he then kissed the right side of her lips, "you," then he captured her lips totally.

No other portion of their bodies were touching, but Diamond felt his gentle caress throughout her body as he explored all regions of her mouth.

"Hmm Hmm," Phire cleared her throat. "Hmm, Hmm" she cleared her throat again. It was apparent the man, whom she assumed to be Zackary Davenport, nor her sister heard her enter the room. When the tactful way did not work, she resorted to her norm. "You two need a room."

Zack broke the kiss and turned towards her. "Man," was all she could manage to say with her mouth hanging open.

Diamond stepped around Zack. "Zack this is my youngest sister Phire. Phire this is Zackary Davenport."

Standing in her pajamas and a robe, she smiled and extended her hand. "I wondered what all the fuss was about at the family council, now I understand. You are fineeeeee."

Smiling at the compliment, he shook her hand, "You're not bad yourself."

"Have you registered that as a lethal weapon?"

"What's that?"

"Your smile-it's got to be illegal."

Diamond rolled her eyes. "Phire, would you keep Mr. Davenport company while I take a shower?" Diamond laughed at her little sister. "Try not to rape him while I'm gone."

"Take your time. I'm not making any promises about the boning thing."

Diamond smiled at Zack, "You will think my directness is nothing after a few minutes with Phire. I won't be long," she said as she left the room.

"Well, well, well." She circled him. "Mr. Davenport." Phire exclaimed with hands on hips, toes tapping, "You are one hell of a fine man. Let's talk in the kitchen, shall we." She walked by a questioning Zack as he looked down the hallway, wondering how long Diamond would be gone. "Don't be scared, I won't bite you."

He looked at her raising an eyebrow, "You're sure about that?"

She giggled and that relaxed him. Now she sounded just like the teenage girl she was. "Would you like a cup of coffee?"

"Sure," he said taking a seat at the breakfast bar. Watching the younger girl, he could see her giving the little boys in high school a fit. The bubbly personality alone would have drawn him in. Yep, if he were young he would give her a run for her money. "Are you feeling better?"

"Huh? Oh you mean last night? Yeah, that wasn't a good scene." Not one to lie to her elders she did not say anything more. "Diamond is always there when I need her."

"That's what big sisters are there for."

"Yeah, they are better than big brothers, especially mine," she rolled her eyes upward.

Thinking of Samuel and Joshua, Zack nodded, "I can imagine."

Sitting on the opposite side of the bar, Phire placed the hot cup of coffee in front of him with all the condiments. "You know my brothers?"

Zack nodded, as he sipped the coffee. "I went to school with Samuel and Joshua."

"Then you are a mighty bold man to want to take out a Lassiter." She shook her head as she drank her hot chocolate. Then she shrugged. "Samuel likes you. I'm not too sure about Joshua. But don't feel bad. I don't think Joshua likes any man that looks at one of his sisters. That's why when I do decide to have a real boyfriend, he will be the last to know."

Smiling as he sipped his coffee he studied the young girl. He wondered if she realized Joshua would know the minute a boy stepped to her. "Joshua takes his responsibility as an older brother seriously. It's his job to protect you from harm. With the way his sisters look, I empathize with him."

"Yet, you are here for Diamond. I'm sure Joshua has dropped in to have a sit down with you. He doesn't frighten you?"

"No."

"Diamond is cool people you know. She's not judgmental at all, she just listens and tries to give unbiased advice. Not like my sister Pearl. Man, don't ask her advice about men—she will take your head off." She laughed then looked at him. "Everyone's scared you are going to hurt Diamond. But I'm not. I think you like and respect her. That's why you are taking it slow. Keeping things on the down low until you are sure of your own feelings. That's okay, just don't play my sister Mr. Davenport. She deserves better than that."

There was something about this girl Zack liked. She was not one to mince words and she seemed wise for her age. "You are a very perceptive young lady. It's hard to believe you would be out with a young man that would try to take advantage of you."

She looked down the hallway to see if anyone was coming. "I wasn't. That was a pre-planned block put in place by Pearl and Jade. Pearl thought Diamond would have given into you last night and they felt you weren't ready to take her seriously. According to Jade, they were right. Diamond was going home with you last night. I don't know why they have a problem with that. I mean Diamond is not one of those women that goes from man to man. In fact, I think you are the first I have ever heard her talk about. And it's so clear she is in love with you, so why not be with the one you love. To tell you the truth Mr. Davenport, I can see why she wants to be with you."

Zack smiled at the unpretentious young woman, "I'm sure your sisters did not want you to tell me about the plan."

"Oh, they're not worried about you finding out. But they straight up said not to ever tell Diamond because she would really be pissed. I'm sorry, mad."

"I won't tell her."

"I know."

"How do you know?," he asked smiling.

"You're not a talker. In fact, I'm going to share another secret with you."

"What's that?"

"I decided to follow in Diamonds footsteps. I'm saving myself. But don't tell my family. I like to keep them guessing." She giggled at the smile from Zack.

"Good morning Zack," Jade said as she entered the kitchen, "Hey Phire. What are you laughing at?"

Drinking from her cup of hot chocolate, Phire shrugged, "Nothing," and winked at Zack.

Zack laughed. "Good morning, Jade."

"Are you the reason Diamond is in the shower?"

"Yes," he replied without adding anything further.

"Do you two have plans?"

"Yes."

Phire snickered and looked at Zack who was smiling back at her.

"Do you want to share your plans with us?"

"Not really."

Jade looked from Phire to Zack and back again. "You told him, didn't you?"

"You didn't say not to."

Sighing, Jade placed her glass on the counter top. "Go get dressed, I'm taking you home."

"Aw, man. Why I always have to go home."

"Because you talk too much, now go."

Phire rolled her eyes and looked at Zack, "Bye Mr. Davenport."

"Call me Zack, Phire. We'll talk again soon." When she left the room Zack's attention went to Jade. "I'm not going to hurt Diamond."

"Yes you will Zack. You won't mean to, but you will hurt her. You are not where she is. You are still at the physical attraction. Diamond left that area the day she met you. She is in love with you, the man and all the baggage that comes along with you. So while you are getting your physical needs taken care of she will be getting her heart broken."

What was it with these Lassiter women? Even Jade who might be all of twenty was reading him like a book. "What happens between Diamond and me is our concern, not yours or your family's. I understand all of you are close, as I told Samuel and Joshua, but my personal business is just that, my business. Now, if I give you reason to doubt my intentions with your sister, address me at that time. Until then, back off."

Nodding her head, she rinsed the glass and placed it in the dishwasher. "You are right. It's not our business. But let me give you a little bit of information you don't have. Diamond has never been with anyone. Keep that in mind while you are seeking your physical fulfillment."

"It's clear you are concerned about my involvement with your sister and you have reason to be. I would never take advantage of Diamond or any woman for that matter. Nor am I a man that allows others to dictate my actions. Your sister is a very intelligent woman and just like you, she knows how to take care of herself. Trust her decisions. If she decides to be with me physically or emotionally, trust her enough to know her own heart."

"Do you know yours?"

"Hey." Diamond spoke tentatively sensing the tension in the air. "Is everything okay in here?" She looked from Jade to Zack.

Zack looked to Jade, who stared him down. "Yeah, everything is fine." She replied looking from him to Diamond. "What are you two up to today?" She asked smiling at her sister.

Diamond wasn't sure what was said, but she could feel a little tension in the room. "I'm not sure," she replied and looked at Zack.

"I thought we would take a bike ride to the river. See where we go from there."

Jade snapped around and looked at Diamond, "You are going to ride his bike?"

Diamond nervously replied staring directly at Jade as she cleared her throat. "Yes," she exhaled slowly.

Jade knew that Diamond did not like to ride motorcycles because of a fall she had taken when she was sixteen. "Maybe it will be better if you drive."

Zack looked to Diamond. "No, the bike will be fine," Diamond replied and looked at him. "You ready to go?"

"Let's go," he smiled. "Jade," he opened the door, "I'll make sure she gets home unharmed."

"I would appreciate that Zack."

Dressed in a pair of jeans, a cardigan sweater set and boots, Diamond stood at the bike and wondered if she had lost her mind. She still had a scar from the last time she rode with Matthew and fell off when he took a curve too fast.

"What's wrong?" Zack pulled her into his arms as he saw the color drain from her face. She looked up at him hesitantly and the fear was clear in her eyes. For a moment he wondered if she was having second thoughts about spending the day with him. "Diamond?"

Swallowing hard she pulled back from him. "It's nothing." She said shaking her head.

He held her at arm's length. "That's not true. I can see it in your eyes."

If her foot were long enough, she would kick herself. She had been waiting to spend real time with this man and she would be damned if a little thing like her fear of bikes would keep her from him. "I um--had a fall off my brother's bike when I was younger and I haven't been on one since."

Exhaling with a sigh of relief, Zack smiled. "That's all. I thought you had changed your mind about going."

Pulling him closer, she put her arms around his waist. "Zackary Davenport, I have been looking forward to spending my days and nights with you. Nothing, not even my fear of bikes could keep me away from you today."

Wrapping his arms around her waist he kissed her forehead, "I'm glad to hear that. How about we ride the bike back to my house and we'll drive."

"I have a better idea. How about if I use this as an opportunity to get over my fears."

"You sure?"

"Yes."

"Let's ride." He reached for the extra helmet he brought for her, placed it securely on her head and latched it under her chin. He then put his helmet on and straddled the bike. He helped her settle in behind him and wrapped her hands around his waist. "Hold on tight and move with my body. When I lean you lean in the same direction, okay." He felt her arms tighten around him and could not resist the smile that came with the knowledge that she trusted him unconditionally. "I won't hurt you Diamond," he said as he began to pull off.

"I know you won't."

Chapter 13

𝒫ulling slowly into the traffic Zack decided to take the back roads rather than Interstate 95. It was a way to allow Diamond to become comfortable on the bike. The last thing he wanted was to have her nerves on edge. Once he reached the lower end of Hanover County, the traffic on Mechanicsville Turnpike was clear. They followed Highway 360 through King William County until they reached Tappahannock, VA. They stopped to eat at Lowery's Seafood Restaurant where a relaxed Diamond told him about going fishing with her family and how much she enjoyed the water. She had put her trust in him and he wanted to reward her with more than an exhilarating bike ride, he wanted to share a part of him with her. Riding was what he did to relax or clear his mind. So instead of going back to Richmond, he turned down Highway 17 towards Urbana.

They pulled up to the dock by the river with sailboats, big and small yachts docked there. He parked the bike and helped her off. Diamond looked around and inhaled. The smell of the river filled the air around them. "Wow, this is nice. I've never been here. Do you come here often?"

He secured the helmets and took her hand, "Every chance I get. Come here I want to show you something."

The excited look in his eyes touched her heart. This was the first time she had seen him with a boyish grin. He was always so serious and intense whenever she was around. It was really nice to see this side of him. Running down the dock he stopped when he reached what had to be one of the

largest boats she had ever seen. He stepped onto the boat
and held his hands out to her. Placing her hands on his
shoulders, he encircled her waist and lifted her down to the
deck of the boat. "This is beautiful Zack. Who does it
belong to?" she asked looking around the top deck.

"It's mine," he smiled. "Come see the control
room." He grabbed her hands and pulled her forward. The
enclosed area looked like every electronic gadget available to
man was surrounding the steering wheel. There were two
leather seats near the controls.

As they walked through, Zack told her about each
room of the boat. The saloon had white leather, semi-circle
seating with a glass table in the center. On another wall was a
television panel, above a stereo system with surround sound.
The galley had every appliance that a modern day kitchen
would have including a microwave, refrigerator and breakfast
bar. Walking further back, they passed a bedroom with a
small shower, commode and sink; he called it the VIP room
and mentioned that that's where Xavier would sleep when
he visited. Then he showed her the master cabin with a king
size bed, enclosed shower and commode. Windows above
the bed were covered with blinds that opened and closed
automatically by a timer. When they walked back up the
stairs to the top deck, she was in awe. "This is awesome. I
believe this boat is larger than my apartment."

"How would you like to go to D.C. for dinner?" He
asked with a cocky grin.

"Yes," she replied excitedly.

Pleased with her excited response, Zack began
checking equipment and emergency gear to ensure their
safety. They went to the nearby store and secured food for
the short trip. An hour later, he unhooked the line from the
cleats of the boat, then entered the control room and began
pulling out of the dock. She sat beside him and marveled at
the difference in him. This was his joy, being on the water
made him a different man. He talked about his 62' Sea Ray

630 and the trips he had taken as he eased into the Potomac River.

The view going towards D.C. was breathtaking to say the least. You could see Mount Vernon, the home of George Washington, Rosalyn, and the Lincoln Memorial. Listening to him talk and seeing the essence of the man come alive right before her eyes made Diamond fall deeper in love with him. This was the man she knew was inside of him.

As they pulled into the Washington Harbor, he docked the boat. "Where would you like to dine my lady?" he asked with a sexy smile.

"Wherever your heart desires, my Lord," she replied as she took the hand he extended to her.

Pulling her onto the dock, he held her body close to his then gazed into her eyes. He pushed a strand of hair from her face then tucked it behind her ear. "You are a beautiful woman," he said with so much sincerity it brought tears to her eyes.

"And you are a handsome man, but you already know that." She placed her hand through his arm and started walking. "It's a little early for dinner. What do you suppose we do?"

Smiling down at her as they walked he wondered when he became so touchy feely. The show of emotions came easy for her and surprisingly he liked it. "How would you like a short tour of D.C.?"

"I would love it. I've never been here."

He looked at her with questioning eyes. "You live right in Virginia and you have at least two brothers that live up this way and you've never been to the Capitol?"

"No, I've been to Quantico and Fredericksburg, but not D.C."

"Then by all means, allow me the honor." Looking down at her he said, "We better go shopping first."

She stopped and looked at herself. "What's wrong with the way I look? I have on jeans just like you."

"This is true, but to do D.C. right, you have to walk and your feet in those boots, although they look very good on you, will not survive the tour. Taxi," he called out as a vehicle pulled over to the curb. He opened the door, the two got inside. "Georgetown," he directed the driver.

After shopping in Georgetown where they argued over the amount of money he was spending on her, they toured the Capitol, the museums and walked to the White House. They were in a taxi on their way back to the dock when they passed a billboard advertising the Wizards. Diamonds head jerked back, looking out of the window pointing. "Hey, are the Wizards playing tonight?" she asked as excitedly as a child.

Zack looked in the direction she was pointing, "The basketball team?"

"Yes," she grabbed his hand, "Can we go, please."

The woman never ceased to amaze him. He knew she was beautiful, intelligent and very friendly. Everywhere they went she spoke and carried on conversations with complete strangers and to his surprise they reciprocated. Now here she was almost jumping out of her seat to get to a professional basketball game. "Take us to the stadium," he instructed the driver. To his surprise, they spent the rest of the evening watching the game and filling themselves up on hot wings, french-fries and beer. It was well after midnight when they returned to the boat.

They sat out on the bench on the deck of the boat with a bottle of wine, smooth jazz filtering through the sound system and laughter filling the air as they talked about the evening.

"Basketball has always been X-man's thing. But football, I'll take you out on a football field."

"Hold up." Diamond sat her glass down and pointed her finger to emphasize her point. "I don't think so my brother. You are looking at a wide receiver extraordinaire."

Zack sat up and got in her face. "You have lost your mind if you think you can get by me in a game."

She bent closer in. "Not only get by you, but I will mow you down," she said as she kissed him on the cheek.

The innocent touch ignited the sexual chemistry that surrounded them the entire day. They stared at each other for the longest moment without touching or speaking. As if on cue, the smooth voice of Al Jarreau slipped through the speaker. "Dance with me," he said as he took her hand and pulled her to him. She eased her arm around his shoulders as he placed his around her waist, neither breaking eye contact. With her small hand in his, he pulled her closer and rested his chin on her head as they danced quietly to Al singing Teach Me Tonight. The sweet torture of sexual chemistry continued to crack through the air like a bullwhip being handled by an expert.

It was taking every ounce of Zack's will power to keep his desire under control. The conversation with Samuel and Joshua played in his mind. At the time he had no intentions of getting involved with Diamond and he told them that. Then there was the statement Jade made. How could he take her virginity when he knew this would not lead to what she wanted and deserved—commitment, marriage and everlasting love. Knowing all of that, he still wanted her with a passion that was threatening to consume him.

Perfect. That was the only word Diamond could use to describe the man who was holding her so possessively. He'd let his guard down enough to allow her to see the real man and she now knew—she loved all of him. Not just the caring brother to her friend or the man totally committed to his craft, or the very decisive businessman, but the Zackary he tried desperately to hide from her. She wanted all of him, even the one that lashed out at her to keep her at bay.

"Teach me, Zackary. Teach me to satisfy you," she whispered against his throat.

The request began to weaken his already tenuous control. Pulling her closer, he placed her hand on his heart. "As much as I want to, I can't." He could feel the disappointment in her body's reaction to his statement. He held her a little tighter, "I can't give you what you want Diamond, I can't love you back."

She kissed his throat and tucked her head there, "I know and I accept that. I'm not asking for anything more than you making love to me tonight. I'd rather you teach me the right way than someone else fumbling through." She kissed his throat, "Please teach me, Zackary. Teach me tonight."

Groaning at the touch of her lips to his already hot skin, he greedily took her lips hostage and began a full assault of its inner regions. All thoughts of his mother, Celeste, Samuel and Joshua ceased to exist. Only the woman in his arms, who had taken complete control of his senses, was on his mind and taking root in his soul.

His hands roamed down her back to her firm behind, lifting her until he felt her legs enclose around his waist then turned to the steps leading to the lower level of the boat. Stopping in the doorway, he looked into her eyes. "Now is the time for you to tell me to stop." She responded by taking his bottom lip between her teeth and running her tongue over it. "Aw hell," he growled as he carried her down the stairs closing the cabin door behind them.

They fell onto the bed, still entwined. Breaking the kiss for a moment, he pulled her cardigan over her head, removed her black lace bra and placed his face between her breasts and inhaled. "Diamond," he moaned as he turned and took her nipple between his lips, sucking until it hardened to his liking, while caressing the other, liking the way it filled his hand. Her body squirmed beneath him as her breathing increased. He planted a trail of kisses down her stomach until he reached the opening to her jeans. Unfastening them, he slid them and her black lace panties down her legs then dropped them to the floor. He had to stop, just to feast on the sight of her. The word perfection should have a picture of her next to it in the dictionary. She was perfect, lying there with the look of innocence and arousal so deep it caused him to inhale. This was a sight no man had ever seen, and suddenly, he wanted it to stay that way.

Shaking the thought from his mind, he removed his shirt and his jeans soon followed. She never blinked or showed any signs of nervousness while he undressed. Only the look of wanting him was on her face. What he had done in his life to deserve her level of trust he didn't know, but he would certainly do all in his power to reward her for it.

He reached down, pulled her foot to his lips, kissed the arch, then the ankle and dropped to his knees. Beginning behind the knee on her left leg, he kissed her inner thigh until he heard her call his name. Switching to the other, he followed the same path. He reached out and spread his hands across her stomach, encircled her waist and pulled until the very core of her was at his lips. Not bothering with a sip, he took her as if she were his only lifeline, devouring her until her body jerked uncontrollably. Then he joined her on the bed, holding her convulsing body until the remnants of her first lesson began to ease. The fact that his arousal was about to explode did not faze him as much as making sure she was ready to take him inside her.

Reaching for his jeans he pulled a condom from his pocket and prepared himself. Easing between her legs, he positioned himself at the very tip of her entrance, lay on top of her and wrapped her arms around his neck. Her eyes were closed and she bit her bottom lip. He began kissing the very spot she was biting down on. "Look at me Diamond." She opened her eyes. The fear, need, and desire were all present. And there was something else, but he didn't dare explore it any further.

"I want to see your eyes when we unite." Slowly he entered her and could immediately feel the tightness of her surround him. He had to take a moment. He pulled back, then slowly retraced his path, sinking deeper as her body snuggly surrounded him, pulling him further and further until he reached her treasure.

Neither took their eyes from the other as her muscles sweetly surrounded him like a glove. Perspiration formed on his brow, for he was doing all he could to hold back from pushing further; the last thing he wanted to do was hurt her. She must have sensed his hesitation, for she spread her legs wider, wrapped them around him and lifted her body to his. She cried out as he smothered her lips with his lips, doing what he could to ease her through the discomfort. "I'm sorry," he kissed her on her cheek, down her throat, on her eyelids and back to her lips. When her inner muscles began to relax around him, he began a slow, smooth circular pattern of motion. She copied his movements, slowly, at first, then the two began the rhythm as old as time—moving as one.

Their movements increased as did their breathing while he told her just how good she felt to him. Moving his hands down to her waist he held her in place as he began to move in and out, increasing the intensity with each stroke. Suddenly, being inside her was a matter of life or death; he had to plunge deeper and deeper to satisfy her. Every entry was an effort to please her—to fill her. Nothing else mattered, just the thought of giving everything he had just to please her was his goal. Her nails breaking into his skin cautioned him and he slowed, but she was not having it. She tightened her hold on him, raising her body to him at a feverish pace, rising to meet his every thrust, holding on for her life, allowing him to go further and further until she exploded with a scream. Her muscles began powerful contractions around him, pulling everything from him. With one last thrust he pulled back, slammed in and released his heart, his soul, the very essence of him into her as he called out her name.

Nothing or no one could have prepared him for the euphoria he felt being inside her. The gentle kisses against his face, and throat began to calm the storm inside him. Turning, he looked into her lustful eyes. Cradling her face in his hands he kissed her, long, deep and slow. The action was meant to thank her for sharing the very essence of her with him, but it only ignited the fire that had started and he began to grow inside her again. It took a moment but he realized it was her moving beneath him. Breaking the kiss he stared down at her and that's when he saw that determined look. A slow sensuous smile began to form on his lips, "I can see you are going to have an insatiable appetite Ms. Lassister."

Returning the smile she replied, "You could say that, Mr. Davenport. But I prefer to say I'm downright greedy when it comes to you."

Turning, he pulled her on top of him. "Really, how greedy?"

"I don't know," she replied shaking her head, "I'm liking what we've done thus far—24/7 wouldn't upset me in the least." She placed kisses down his chest and sat up.

Holding her hips with her looking down at him, Zack moved her slowly in place. She held his arms for balance then closed her eyes as the slow rhythm began to stir deep inside her again. "Your wish is my command." Zack smiled as he watched the student take center stage.

Chapter 14

The next morning Zack lay awake watching the woman, who fit so snugly in his arms, sleep. The woman had rocked his world. She was beautiful from head to toe and tasted just as sweet, for he had indulged in every inch of her, so he knew. It had been years since he held a woman like this, and that woman had been Celeste. But this felt different in some way; nothing Celeste had done made him feel this complete, this content. That was an unsettling thought for him. This woman could hurt him deeper than Celeste ever had.

He eased out of the bed and went to cover her body with the comforter when he noticed the proof of her innocence. There was a touch of male pride that entered his mind—this woman had given herself to him completely. Feeling the pull to touch her again, he shook his head then covered her body.

While taking a shower he wondered how she felt, was she sore, if she needed anything to ease her discomfort. As he toweled dry there was one thing he knew he had to do. He called Xavier, who picked up on the second ring. "Hey X-man, did I wake you?"

"It's six in the morning Zack, of course you woke me. What's going on?" he asked groggily.

"I need you to pick up my bike from Urbanna and leave my car there."

"Urbanna? Where are you?"

"I'm in D.C."

"You took Arthur out? Why didn't you tell me, I would have joined you."

Looking at Diamond lying asleep, he shook his head. "Not this time little brother."

Hesitating for a moment, Xavier wondered. "You took Diamond out on Arthur?"

"Yes, I did."

"Zack," he hesitated again. "Is she okay?"

"She's still asleep."

"Is Diamond the reason I need to pick up your bike?"

"Yes." There was an uneasy silence between the two brothers. Zack knew how close the two were and was sure X-man knew of her virginal state. "You have my word she is fine. I wouldn't do anything to hurt her."

"I know you won't do anything intentionally. But Zack your baggage with Celeste has a way of bringing out the worst in you. I don't want Diamond to pay for that."

Rubbing the back of his head and exhaling Zack found himself torn. He loved his brother and did not want to do anything to disappoint him, but he could not tell him what he wanted to hear. "I hear you X-man, I don't know where things stand here. This woman is in love with me and I'll be damned if I know why. All I can say is the thought of any other man being near her bothers me. I can't give you or her anything more than that."

"I love you Zack and I know you are going to do the right thing. If you are not going to commit to her don't stand in her way. I'll leave it at that. Your car will be at the dock when you return."

"Thanks man, I'll talk to you soon." He hung up the telephone and turned to find Diamond standing in the doorway with his polo shirt on. Immediately he wondered how much she had heard of the conversation.

"Good morning," she said, "I was just wondering where you kept the towels."

He tried to read her thoughts, but her appearance in his shirt captured his mind. "How are you this morning?" he asked.

She didn't move. "I'm fine, thank you," but she didn't say anything more.

He pulled towels and face cloths from the cabinet above and walked towards her.

The closer he got the more apparent her eyes gave away her disappointment. He sat the towels on the table and pulled her into his arms. "Diamond, talk to me."

She hugged him and said, "It's okay Zackary. You told me before we made love how you felt. I made the decision to be with you and I don't regret one moment of it." She pulled away, picked up the towel and headed back to the master cabin into the shower.

The words she heard did hurt, but she knew this was an uphill battle. The simple truth was she loved him and she was willing to give him the time to realize they belonged together. One thing was for sure, he was gentle and patient as he taught her how to make love to him. His touch was lethal and he literally killed her with his kisses. All night she longed to be near him just as she did now. But she had to hide the hurt, which would be difficult—she believed in being up front. Her family did not conceal their feelings, they were openly loving. A frown appeared as she stepped out and began to dry off. Was she willing to settle for less than a totally committed, loving relationship? As she was growing up the one thing that helped her parents deal with the rough times was the love they shared. If she settled, what would they fall back on to get them through those times? She put the shirt back on and thought, there was no way a man could be that tender, that loving if he did not have some feelings for his partner. Okay, she was not a person to see a glass half empty. In her way of looking at things, she was half way to having Zackary Davenport's love.

While Diamond showered, Zack cooked breakfast. The look in her eyes nagged at him. He didn't like seeing her sad, he didn't like it at all. Although his back was to her, he knew the moment she walked into the room. Turning he saw her standing there again in the clean shirt he left on the bed for her. "You look wonderful. How are you, for real?"

Shifting from one foot to the other she smiled. "I'm a little sore and nervous."

"The soreness I understand. What are you nervous about?" He pulled out a seat and pointed for her to take it.

"I'm not sure how to be around you now. You know how I feel about you and I know how you feel about me. You did what I asked and taught me how to satisfy you." She hesitated then asked, "Did I satisfy you?"

He placed the rest of the food on the table and took a seat. Explaining to her how deeply she satisfied him would give her false hope and he did not want to do that. Nor did he want to discourage her. "Totally." He placed a napkin in his lap. "Does that mean the lessons are over?"

"You're the teacher, you tell me."

The sadness seemed to have disappeared. He was certain she was masking it and doing a good job of it. Since he was the one that put that look in her eyes, it was his responsibility to make it disappear. He watched as she spread the cream cheese over the bagel then bit into it.

"Mmm," she closed her eyes and moaned as she savored the taste, "this is good."

She was the most sensuous sight he had ever seen. In that moment, all he desired was to be a part of her enjoyment. "Come to me Diamond." His voice was musical. She opened her eyes and saw desire revealed within his. It wasn't intentional, she was sure of that, but it was there, the moisture that began at her core told her so. Pleased with the thought she slowly rose from her seat, walked around the table and stood before him. Not a sound could be heard, just the waves of the water gently lapping against the side of the boat. He remained seated as his hands circled her waist, placing her body between him and the table. His hands slowly roamed over the cotton t-shirt outlining the silhouette of her body.

The strength in his hands was apparent, but there was also gentleness in his caress as his fingers touched her breast. The attempt not to respond, but to concentrate and learn was futile as Diamond inhaled.

As if reading her mind, "Don't suppress what you are feeling, flow with it," he instructed. Like the good student she was, she complied, closing her eyes she felt his hands roam down the side of her breasts, "thirty-four" he continued down to her waist "twenty-four," then down to her hips where his hands roamed over her behind and held it, "thirty-six."

She opened her eyes and stared down at him. "Is that the winning hand?" The smile was unguarded and genuine, it touched her heart so deeply she shivered.

The feel of her, or was it the smell of her, he wasn't sure, but something took over his senses and filled him with a desire so strong he couldn't resist. His hands moved down to her thighs, that were just as silky as he remembered from last night, and pushed the shirt above her navel. As the very essence of her was revealed to him she shivered. "Your body is beautiful, never be ashamed of it." Pulling her forward, he kissed her navel as he pushed the paper products aside and placed her on the table. She laid there willingly exposed to him. For her to be here this way indicated that she trusted him, completely. The thought pleased him and he in turn wanted to please her. Dipping his fingers into the strawberry flavored cream cheese that remained on the table, he spread it down the inside of her thighs. Pulling his chair closer to the table, he licked his lips then began slowly tasting the spread he had created. His tongue delighted in the taste as much as his lips enjoyed the feel of her. When he was done with the first thigh, he placed it over his shoulder and inhaled the scent of her body temperature rising. Enjoying her response to him, he began skillfully removing the cream from her second thigh up to her core. His lips lingered there, savoring every taste of her like a man having his last meal. The rising of her hips to meet the thrust of his tongue pushed him to go as deep as humanly possible within her. As her body began to flow, he drained all her sweetness and savored the combination of her unique flavor and that of the cream. Her release only intensified his desire. He stood and removed his pants then pulled her limp body down to straddle him. He placed her arms around his neck and with the taste of her still on his lips he kissed her. Instead of her pulling away as he thought she would, she welcomed his mouth with a hunger he did not expect. Her response pushed his desire deeper. Now he was a man starving, he had not had his fill. Moving his hands back to her waist, he lifted her until the tip of his desire was at the opening of her heavenly gate. He slowly pulled his lips from hers, "Open your eyes Diamond." When she did as he asked, he almost wished she hadn't. The completeness of her satisfaction showed through her eyes and captured him so completely, he lost his concentration. But his body knew what to do. Slowly he eased her down until he began to fill her. As her inner core surrounded him with her juices still present inside, he closed his eyes to the intense pleasure. "Open your eyes Zackary," he heard her whisper. He did and looked into hers. He wondered, at that moment, who was teaching who. She pushed her body down onto him and time stopped. The size of his desire was more than she expected and he knew she needed to adjust. He held her there, staring deeply into her eyes until he saw the desire return. He raised her slowly, and then lowered her back down, again and again and again, never breaking eye contact with her. Soon the two were moving together as one, slowly to a feverish point. She arched her back as her nails dug into his back, bringing the center of both of them closer, allowing him to thrust deeper into her until they both exploded. Throwing his head back against the chair, he growled out her name, "Diamond!" She slumped against his shoulder as he held her tightly. He wanted to remain lost in the center of her forever; the thought shook him to his soul. She eased the grip she had on his shoulder and gently caressed the area she had bruised. "I'm sorry," she whispered, "I will never hurt you again."

The innocent words played in his mind as they simultaneously touched his heart. The mind versus the heart, he knew one had to take dominance or he would not survive. Still lodged deep within her his desire had not diminished, but he knew he had to pull away or his mind would lose the battle.

Diamond could feel the turmoil in his body the moment the words were uttered. He lifted her from him, and then smoothed the shirt back over her. Standing he pulled his pants up and as he pulled the drawstring he said, "Don't make promises you can't keep."

With those words she knew the lessons were over; she could only hope that he learned a lesson as well. She turned and walked over to the mess that had fallen from the table. "I'll clean this up."

"No," he said a little harsher than he intended. "I'll take care of this. You go clean up."

She looked at him and sadly smiled. "All right," then walked away.

Thankful she had not pushed the issue he exhaled and looked out over the river. He would never be on this boat again and not remember what happened between them. Clearing his mind of the thought, he began picking up the items from the deck. When he picked up the container of the strawberry flavored cream cheese he held it and laughed. "Kraft never tasted so good." It may be just a physical thing, but it was definitely one he would not mind experiencing time and time again.

They easily settled into a getting to know you session on the way home without realizing it. Diamond listened as he talked about the things he and Samuel used to do to Joshua when they were in high school together. She didn't know it, but the three of them had remained friends all these years. She could not contain her laughter when he talked about Xavier and his antics when he was a teenager. She laughed at the way Zack described the way he attempted to discipline the rebellious boy and how he would have a good laugh in his room remembering that he had tried most of the same antics on their dad. "I bet you would make a good father."

The simple statement was meant as a compliment, but as soon as the words were out she saw the same change of emotions on his face as earlier on the breakfast table. Wanting to take some of the hurt away, she stood behind him at the wheel, wrapped her arms around his waist and laid her head on his back. They stood that way for a long while, neither speaking. After a while he reached around, pulled her beside him and began talking about the business.

Relief like she had never known filled her when she saw his black navigator parked where the motorcycle was previously parked. Seeing her reaction, he smiled. She would have never said anything about being sore, but he knew she had to be after the lessons he put her through. On the way home, as they traveled closer to her apartment, it dawned on him; he wasn't ready to leave her presence. Looking at the clock, it was around dinnertime. "Would you like to stop somewhere for dinner before you go home?"

She turned in the seat towards him, "Funny you should ask that. My mom is cooking lasagna today; with apples topped with a little cinnamon, tossed salad and homemade bread. Would you like to have dinner with us? "She asked a little excited at the thought.

He looked at her and knew his response was going to take that ray of hope from her eyes, but it had to be said. "I don't think that would be a good idea. It may give them the wrong impression." Lowering her eyelashes and turning did not keep him from seeing the disappointment. He reached over and captured her hand, "Diamond I don't want you to have any misconceptions about what happened between us." He had just reached the Mechanicsville area and pulled into the parking lot of the high school. Turning off the engine, he turned to her still holding her hand, "To say I enjoyed being with you would be an understatement. You are an amazing woman in and out of bed. Any man would be fortunate to have you. I'm honored you chose me to teach you how to make love. But that's all it was, a lesson." The interior of the car was silent. "Diamond."

Nodding her head she replied, "I know. You were clear your purpose was to satisfy a physical need. I understand."

"Are you sure?"

She touched his hand and looked over at him, "Of course I am. We agreed to the terms before we took the steps. Now would you mind getting me home before Matt and Luke eat all the lasagna," she gave him a reassuring smile.

Starting the engine, he looked behind him to make sure the way was clear and then he pulled back on to the road thinking he almost believed her. There was no further conversation, just the radio playing in the background. When they reached her apartment, he got out to get her bags to carry inside. She stopped him, "I'll take those. Thank you for a very special lesson. I will never forget it." They stared at each other for a moment. "I'll see you at work tomorrow," Diamond turned and walked through the secured doors. Once inside her apartment she closed the door behind her, slid down it, dropping everything on the floor and cried.

Chapter 15

*M*onday morning was a brighter day for Diamond, if it wasn't she was determined to make it so. Memories of the way Zack taught his lessons replaced the tears and hurt of the night before. Zack was gentle with his caresses, tantalizing with his tongue and more than amply endowed. Not that she had anything to compare him to. The closest she had come was heavy kissing with one or two guys while in college. Now, she knew for sure the boys from those days were just that—boys. If she had to describe Zack at this moment, she would say he was a convincingly skillful lover. There wasn't a moment when they were together that she did not feel loved and cherished.

Those are the memories she took to the office with her today. All her efforts were going towards clearing all thoughts of Zackary and the weekend out of her mind. Closing the loan package she was working on, she walked to the closet that had all the samples for the houses and pulled out the carpet remnants. Placing them on the table in the office of the model home, she began writing suggestions for her client. As she flipped through them, one of the samples reminded her of strawberry cream cheese. A smile crept onto her face from blushing as the memory of how Zack had used the cream cheese clouded her mind.

Standing at the entrance to the office, Zack watched as Diamond moved about. Stopping by the model home today was nothing out of the ordinary. It was just one co-worker saying good morning to the other. It wasn't like he just had to see her. No—it was just that he wanted to make sure she was okay today—that's all. He continued to tell himself that as he walked through the front door of the model home. Besides, he wanted to make sure they were straight on the events of the weekend. He taught her a lesson and that was that. "Damn." She was showing her shapely legs today in a form-fitting sleeveless dress with a v-neck. Only she could wear a dress like that tastefully. The memory of being between those smooth thighs assailed his mind with a vengeance. Closing his eyes he could feel her on his cheeks, smell her scent and could still taste her on his lips. His tongue unconsciously glided slowly across his lips. His eyes sprung open. *What in the hell was wrong with him?* First last night she kept creeping into his dreams. Now here in full daylight he was still dreaming about her. More importantly why was he standing there watching her? It was then that her head came up and a blush colored her face. Exhaling with a smile, he knew she was reliving the same images he was.

"Good morning," he said as he walked through the door. "You're in early."

She was startled by his sudden appearance. Straightening from her position of bending over the table, she turned to walk back to her desk. The sight of him in his tight fitting jeans reminded her of his powerful thighs. "Good morning," she replied as soon as she was protected behind the desk.

The air was crackling with tension. Both simply wanted to touch the other, but neither moved. Suddenly remembering the coffee cups in his hand Zack raised one. "French Vanilla cappuccino," and handed her the cup.

"You remembered," she said smiling at his thoughtfulness.

"Yeah." He turned to leave but stopped with his hand on the doorknob. Looking over his shoulder, with concern showing on his face he asked, "Are you okay? I would hate to think I hurt you in any way."

This was why she loved him. Under that rough exterior was a sensitive caring man. She sat back and sipped her cappuccino. "Your lessons were thorough, in-depth and quite satisfying." She lowered her lashes and slowly raised them again. "Will there be more or has the course ended?" She held his stare as she took another sip from her cup.

"You keep looking at me like that and you'll get another lesson here and now."

His reply shocked, frightened and caressed her simultaneously. Smiling, she sat forward and crossed her legs to keep them from going to him. "You don't have to worry about me Zackary, I'm fine."

"That Ms. Lassiter is an understatement."

"What's an understatement?" Richard asked as he walked by taking the coffee from Zack. "Thanks man," he said to his shocked friend as he took a sip of the coffee. "Ahh, it's nice and hot too. Just what I need this morning." Completely ignoring the look on Zack's face, Richard continued. "I saw your truck parked out front. I hope you have a few minutes this morning."

The perplexed look on Zack's face was clear. "What in the hell are you doing here at seven in the morning?"

Richard shrugged his shoulder, then took another sip of the coffee, "I just told you. I'm here to see you and Reese, if he's here."

A frown appeared as he watched a grin appear on Richard's face as he swallowed the coffee. "There are several fast food places that carry coffee. You could have stopped at any one of them."

Richard nodded in agreement, "I thought about that, but I saw you there and I knew you would pick up a cup for me."

Diamond watched as the two men that were similar in height and build greeted each other. It was clear they were friends, for she knew of no one that would boldly take anything away from Zack. Wisely, she remained silent until the last statement was made and she had no choice but to laugh. The frowning Zack turned to her with a raised eyebrow. She cleared her throat, then took a sip of her cappuccino. "He's right," she said after swallowing, "it is nice and hot."

The man returned her smile, walked over, then extended his hand. "Well good morning beautiful. Richard Hasting. Has anyone ever told you those things are illegal?"

Diamond smiled as she shook the man's hand. "What things are you referring to?"

"Deep, dark, delicious dimples." He held her hand just marveling at her.

"I can't say that they have, Mr. Hasting."

"Well, they are." He tilted his head, "And who may I ask are you, but more importantly where have you been all my life."

Diamond laughed at the very charming man. "Diamond Lassiter."

"All right that's enough. Stop ogling the woman," Zack demanded as he pulled Richard's arm away from Diamond. "And let her hand go." Richard hesitated. "Richard!" Zack growled. "Let's go."

Richard looked over his shoulder as Zack walked towards the door then turned back to Diamond. "He doesn't seem to be in too good of a mood this morning."

"He was fine a few moments ago."

"Then it must be me. I tend to have that effect on some people."

"Richard!"

Richard sighed, "I'm afraid I must go. I sincerely hope we cross paths again soon."

"Have a great day Mr. Hasting."

Zack rolled his eyes skyward as Richard walked by. Looking back, Diamond was smiling at Richard; and for some reason, he didn't like it. He didn't like it one damn bit.

As the two men entered the construction trailer Reese and several of the crew were leaving. "Morning Chief," Reese nodded his head then turned to Zack. "One of the men found some items in one of the homes. Looks like we may have a squatter."

"Let's take a look." Zack walked into the trailer, grabbed his construction hat and one for Richard then rejoined the men.

As the men walked to the lot in question, Richard asked Zack, "So what's the story on Ms. Lassiter?"

Reese smiled, "You met Diamond?"

Richard turned to him, talking over Zack who was walking in between them. "Man. Did I." He shook his head. "I could wake up to that face every morning. Did you see those dimples? Seeing a woman like her let's you know there is a God upstairs."

"Yeah, she is a looker." Reese nodded, "Of course, she has nothing on my wife, but if I was a free man, I'd be on that like white on rice."

"Don't you two have something else to talk about like who in the hell's been squatting in the house?" Zack growled and walked off towards the lot.

Reese and Richard just stared at each other. "Is he always in a bad mood?" Richard asked.

"Only when Diamond's around."

"Oh" Richard smirked, "It's like that?"

"Not yet. But believe me, I wish like hell he'd stop fighting the inevitable." Reese said, "It would sure make life a little easier on the rest of us." The men laughed then followed Zack in the shell of a house.

After collecting the items from the site, Zack, Reese and Richard sat in the trailer discussing their next move. "I'll have these items checked for prints and see if we can identify who may be trespassing on the site." Reese stated as he placed the items in plastic bags.

Richard, who sat in the seat in front of Zack's desk, leaned forward. "I may have something for you on that." He reached into his pocket and pulled out Zack's father's ring. He placed it on the desk. "We didn't get any prints from the ring. But we did DNA testing on the cigarette butts Reese sent over and we did find a match."

Zack sat up as he took the ring and put it in his top drawer. "Who is it?"

Reese walked over to the file cabinet next to the desk and waited with Zack for the reply.

"Zack, I want you to listen to all the facts before you jump to any conclusions."

Sitting up, Zack glared at Richard. "You have gotten on my last nerves this morning. Don't push your luck."

"Me? How am I getting on your nerves?"

"First you take my damn coffee. Then you're hitting on my—my—on Diamond, then you won't stop talking about her. Now who in the hell does the DNA belong to?"

"She's your Diamond?" Both Reese and Richard asked together.

"No she is not....." he had to calm himself down, for he was pissed. But he just didn't know why. He sighed and lowered his voice. "Whose DNA did you find?"

Richard sat back in his chair and sighed. "Ann Davenport."

Chapter 16

The week that followed was one of excitement for Davenport Industries. Headquarters was abuzz and after the board meeting everyone descended to the office to pitch in with preparations. The grand opening celebration was scheduled for Saturday and the guest list was growing with VIP attendees. In addition, Zackary was named as one of the finalists to receive the award as Metropolitan Business Man of the Year. There was a wonderful article in the paper detailing how he became involved in the construction business and the sacrifices he'd made to raise his younger brother. As Diamond read the article, she was very pleased to see the reporter was able to capture the true spirit of the man. She was surprised to read about the arson allegations and even more surprised to see that the man in the picture with the reporter was none other than Richard Hasting, the Fire Chief. "Well, I'll be," she had just said when she heard the bellow she thought only took place when she was in his presence.

"What in the hell happened?" The anger was clear in his voice.

"You're yelling," JoEllen calmly said. "Now, calm down and listen. The arrangement was for her to live there until the house was complete."

"Your damn right I'm yelling. I now have to complete a house in five days." With everything else that was going on, he did not have time to deal with stupidity. After finding out his mother was apparently sleeping in one of his houses, he contacted Joshua to find her. So far, there had been not a word. To top that off he asked X-man about his father's ring, and as he expected he had not seen the ring since the funeral. So, how did the ring get from his house to the site? That question was still plaguing him. To make matters worse, he couldn't get Diamond off his mind. He tried keeping his distance from her, that hadn't worked. He tried working from sun up to sun down, but he still found himself stopping by the model home just to see that she was there. Now this.

"It's not your responsibility Zack. You did your part by finding a place for Barbara and her son. You helped with the Habitat for Humanity housing application and process. Since then you have been there every free moment you had helping build her home. I believe you have put in more of the needed hours than she has."

"Hi, I heard the bellow, is everything alright?" Diamond stood in the doorway. "The last time I heard you yell like that it was about me. So I thought I'd save you time and come to you."

Damn if she didn't look good standing there in a simple black skirt and white blouse with those damn legs showing. He sighed, "It's not you." He threw the note on the desk.

"Okay, what's the problem? Is there something I could do to help?"

Yes, he thought, *stop showing your legs,* but did not voice the thought. "Barbara, the waitress at Doc's is being evicted. Apparently her son was fighting and the subsidized housing they live in saw it as another violation and gave her notice."

"Zack was helping her get a house through Habitat," JoEllen explained.

"But the house isn't finished," Zack exclaimed, "and I'm not sure we can finish it by Monday. Damn!"

"Anything I can do to help?" Diamond asked.

Smiling at her offer Zack walked over and squeezed her hand. "No, thanks for the offer—I'll figure something out." He said and then walked out the door very angry.

JoEllen raised an eyebrow and looked at Diamond, "Did I miss something?"

Diamond sighed, "I don't think so. Are you sure there is nothing I can do to help?"

"Unless you have a small army that could help finish the house over the weekend, I don't think so." JoEllen stared at Diamond, "You and Zack seem to be getting along better."

Without responding Diamond smiled then returned to her office. She stopped at LaFonde's desk, sat on the edge and sighed.

"What did you do this time, kiss his feet?" Diamond turned to her with a raised eyebrow. "Anytime you do anything for him, good or bad he yells at you. I heard the bellow just like you did. So what did you do?"

She had not shared what transpired between her and Zack with anyone, not even her sisters. So she knew LaFonde had no way of knowing things were a little different between her and Zack now. "No, he needs help with a friend and I'm not sure if I should intercede."

"What's the situation?"

"A friend of his is being evicted next week and the Habitat house they are building for her is not ready. I know if I call my family together they could have it done by the weekend. I'm just not sure how he would take my interfering."

"Let me get this straight—you want to help him help another woman."

Standing, Diamond sighed, "It's not like that. This is someone with a son that is being put into the streets. If the house isn't finished and inspected by Monday they won't have anywhere to sleep."

"Diamond, Zackary Davenport is a very resourceful man. I'm sure he can get the men from the site to help out if need be. It's not like he has open arms for you. Let it ride."

She stood and walked towards her office, "Maybe you're right."

Sitting at her desk the thought of Zack working on the house alone bothered her. If the truth were revealed, he did open his arms to her, contrary to what LaFonde said. Those arms were gentle, warm and powerful. The least she could do was offer to help with the painting or something. Truth be told, it would give her a reason to spend time with him. She stopped the thought, now that is selfish. The woman needs a place to live and she was thinking of a way to benefit from it. That was wrong, and she kicked herself for thinking it.

After leaving the office Diamond stopped by her parents home and spoke with her father about the situation. He advised her to leave it alone, if Zack wanted her around he would let her know. She went home changed her clothes and went running to burn off the frustration of wanting to be with him.

That evening, Zack and Xavier were placing sheet rock in the master bedroom of the three bedroom house being built on the east end of town for Barbara and her son, when they heard someone enter the house. "I'll check it out," Zack said as he walked out of the room. Walking down the hallway, he stopped dead in his tracks when he saw the six-eleven, Joe Lassiter standing in the front doorway.

"Hello Zackary. I understand you could use some volunteers to help with the house. I figure I have about two hours to spare—I thought I could give you a hand."

Shocked, Zack extended his hand, "I appreciate that Mr. Lassiter. The more hands the merrier," Zack smiled.

"I'm glad to hear you say that." He stepped back out the door and yelled, "We could use a few more hands in here."

To Zack's surprise, in walked Samuel, Matt and Luke Lassiter. After everyone spoke, they laid out a plan for completing what the six of them could by night fall. By night fall the kitchen, living room and bedrooms walls were up. The men made plans to meet the next three nights to get the house completed by Saturday morning at which time the women would join them to help paint and decorate. Between working on the Estate site by day and Barbara's house in the evening, Zack didn't have time be concerned with Diamond interfering. To be honest he was grateful for the help. There was no way he could ask the men from the crew to help out after working all day at the site. So having the Lassiter men there to help out was a godsend.

Saturday morning at precisely seven a.m. Diamond pulled up in front of the three bedroom ranch and parked behind Zack's truck. She knew he would be there as she climbed the steps on the front porch. Knocking on the door, she called out, "Zack."

He walked into the living room and saw her standing in the doorway. She was dressed in a simple pair of jeans, a tee shirt and sneakers—nothing special. He was sure if there were a picture to show sexy work clothes, she would be the centerfold. He smiled. "If I wasn't so tired I would be tempted to take you where you stand."

She blushed. "I don't think splinters in my backside would be a good look. Besides we have a number of people about to pull up and I don't think my dad would appreciate the scene."

This was the first time he had seen her in a few days and it occurred to him that he had missed her. A frown formed on his face, he didn't like the thought.

For a moment Diamond thought she saw warmth in his eyes as he stared at her, but just as suddenly it disappeared and a frown took its place. "I'll get the others," she said as she turned quickly away. She thought for a moment to tell him she did not ask her family to help, but from the look of things she was glad they did; other than painting and the flooring, the house was just about ready to move in. While she was certain he was appreciative for the help, the fact remained he may feel she should not have interfered.

Throughout the day there were moments when Zack was distracted by the sight of Diamond in those jeans. Every time she walked by or he saw her from a distance all he could think about was holding what was being concealed by those jeans in his hand. The softness of her bare skin in his hand caused him to stumble a time or two. At one point she had gotten a splinter in her finger. Without thinking he took her finger into his mouth and pulled it out with his teeth. He then put a bandage on it and stormed off. Touching her sent shock waves throughout his body, settling where his jeans seemed to suddenly become tight. Then he did something that he had not done since he was on his first construction site. He hit his finger with the hammer. The curse that escaped caught everyone's attention. He walked over to his truck and pulled out an icepack.

"Got to be more careful," Diamond said jokingly as she walked over and took his hand to look at the injury.

The smile and her touch was more than he could take or wanted, regardless of how consoling her voice was or the gentle touch of her hand. He snatched it away and stared at her as if she had burned him. "I don't want this Diamond. I don't know what you told your family to get them to come out here. I appreciate the help but I don't want this whole family scene—the caring woman. I made it clear to you that this is not me. I don't need or want a woman in my life. Don't try to get close to me, you won't like the outcome." He threw the ice pack into the cooler and stormed off. His attraction to her was growing and it seemed to be going beyond his control.

By noon the painting was complete, the food prepared by Barbara and the staff from Doc's was being enjoyed by the women on the front porch and the men who sat out back in the yard. They had taken Barbara's son, Jay to task on the gang members he had been hanging with. The men decided his punishment for all the trouble he had caused was spending his summer working at the construction site. Jay wasn't thrilled, but the size of the men surrounding him quickly convinced him it was in his best interest to cooperate.

Zack walked out front to gather the boxes of hard wood flooring to put down. As he looked around he noticed Diamond was not there. All her sisters, her sister-in-law, Cynthia, and her mother were still on the porch, but she was nowhere to be found and her car was gone.

Watching Zack look around Sally smiled, then said to Cynthia, "I wonder if he knows who he is searching for?"

Cynthia looked up to watch Zack, "I doubt it." She laughed. "Shall I school him or do you want to handle it?"

She took the sandwich and chips from Cynthia's hand. "I'll take this one," Sally said as she stepped down off the porch and walked to the back of the truck. "Take a load off for a moment Zackary and have some lunch." The look he gave her clearly indicated that was the last thing he wanted to do, but he took the sandwich she offered anyway. "You have worked non-stop for days and seriously cut into my cuddle time with my husband. Surely you can give me five minutes."

Looking down at the very petite woman it was evident where Diamond's looks came from. She had her father's eyes, but everything from the high cheekbones to the kissable dimples came from her mother. He sat on the back of the truck and smirked, "We have a little ways to go but I can take five."

"This is a wonderful thing you are doing Zackary. How did you get involved with Habitat?"

Biting into his sandwich, he smiled. "It's my way of giving back. Construction kept me off the street and provides me with a way to make a living. The least I can do is use that skill to help others do the same."

"It takes a very caring man to do something like this for a friend."

"It wouldn't be this far along if it hadn't been for your family. I owe you all a lot for this."

She waved off the statement. "You don't owe us anything. We were more than happy to help." She waited a moment and then began talking. "Family is something you don't get to choose—just like love. You can run from it, ignore it or fight it—but if it's real, it won't go anywhere, it will be right there and smack you on your butt when you least expect it. And there isn't a thing you can do about. Just like we don't get to choose family, we don't get to choose who we fall in love with. It's as natural as breathing and in the end you learn, just like air, you can't live without it." She stood to walk away but stopped and looked at him. She could see why her daughter had fallen head over heels in love with this man; he was a mesmerizing specimen. "She did not ask her father to come here, you know. She told him what you were doing and he liked it. He spoke to the others and they came to help on their own. The last thing she wanted to do was upset you, so she left. I wonder what it means when someone puts your feelings before their own. Hmm," she shook her head and walked away.

Sitting on the back of the truck Zack watched the little woman walk away, not sure what to make of the conversation. Neither love nor family had a place in his life-- that reality he had accepted years ago. The only person he needed in his life was X-man. As long as his little brother was happy nothing else was important.

"Zack," Joe called out. When Zack looked up, he tossed him a cold beer. "I thought you could use one of these." He took the seat Sally vacated. "Damn," was all he said. "Every time I look at my wife that one word just sums it up."

"I know the feeling," Zack replied before he thought about it. Joe's laugh was a low rumble that seemed to make the ground shake. He was a big man. But over the last few days, Zack found the man to be easy to talk to and they had had a few serious and not so serious conversations about just about everything. He liked the man. "What?" Zack asked curiously.

"Man, it's a good thing you had the regular hammer and not the nail gun in your hand when Diamond walked by in those jeans."

For a moment Zack didn't respond. Then he thought about it. "Hell, it's no telling what I would have nailed to the wall." They laughed uncontrollably for a minute before either of them sobered.

"Women will do it to you." Joe shook his head, looking towards the house and all the activity going on. "When my daughter told me she was in love with you, I cautioned her." He nodded. "I told her you were a good man, and I believe you are. But I also knew some of what you've been through and I understand the turmoil you are dealing with inside. Been there with that little woman up there." He pointed to his wife. "There are times I wish I hadn't doubted myself, wasting time thinking I couldn't give her all she deserved. It took me damn near losing her before I realized I had no life without her." Just then Matt threw Jay a baseball, which he missed and it went through the kitchen window of the house. A collected group of moans was heard around the yard. Joe never skipped a beat, he just shook his head. "Then there are times," he sighed, "I'm glad I waited, for right about now I would have twenty-four children instead of twelve."

Zack laughed so hard, he choked on his beer. Joe hit him on the back. "Let's go fix the damn window," he said as he walked away.

"I'll be with you in a minute," Zack replied still laughing. He sighed and took in the sights around him. X-man and Samuel were giving Matt a hard time about the window, while Luke and Jay began clearing away the glass. The Lassiters had made this a labor of love. All of this they did for a person they didn't even know before today. No, that's not true, he thought as he watched them. They did this to help him. His attack on Diamond was unfair, he rationalized. It was not her fault that he could not control his attraction to her. It wasn't her problem that every time he saw her he wanted to strip her naked and teach her all there was about pleasuring a man like him—more precisely him. He exhaled, like it or not he owed her an apology.

It was very clear something had to change. Diamond drifted aimlessly around the canal walk that ran along the James River not far from the Davenport Estates. She enjoyed the solitude and welcomed the time to think. Zackary had given her the best moment of her life. He was a generous considerate lover and she could not imagine any other man teaching her how to make love. Shaking her head, what made her think she was so special that the moment they made love he would realize she was the woman for him? "Huh," she smirked out loud, "what made you think?" She walked under the highway overpass towards Toad's Place, a popular venue in the area called Shockoe bottom in downtown Richmond. Apparently something was happening there since people were on the patio area with drinks and they were laughing. It was a beautiful day and everyone should be carefree and loving life. How she wished her mind were at the moment. Walking closer to the edge so as not to disturb anyone's fun, she continued forward, thinking. It seemed sometimes Zackary was fine with her being around, and then other times it seemed he hated to see her. All of this was just so new to her and she had no idea how to handle his mood changes. Maybe it would be best for her to do exactly what he said and give up trying to be a part of his life. But where could she meet another man like Zackary Davenport? She was sure there was only one on this earth. Hell, maybe she should move to Mars. No, that wouldn't work, hell she was from Venus. Hearing a sound, she looked up just as a young man on a bike came barreling through the crowd, right at her. To keep from getting hit by the rider, she leaned backwards, losing her balance. It was a foregone conclusion in her mind she was going to end up in the river. Just as the scream escaped from her throat a pair of hands caught her from behind and engulfed her. Shocked and a little frightened, she grabbed onto very hard arms and exhaled into a massive chest.

Holding on, she heard the voice whisper, "I got you— you're okay." His hold tightened around her waist and he held her head against his chest. She was still shaking, as the holder rubbed her back to ease her fears. "It's all right, just breathe."

The crowd on the patio did not seem to notice anything was amiss as she slowly opened her eyes and began to gather her composure. Never really looking up Diamond stepped away from the man and exhaled, "I'm sorry, I wasn't paying attention." She finally looked up at the man smiling down at her. "Thank you," she sheepishly smiled.

"Not a problem," the man replied.

She nodded and turned to walk off, "I'm sorry," she said looking back at the man. For a second she thought he looked familiar, but did not know from where. She ran up the steps and headed back to her car with her mind made up. As of that moment, she was working Zackary out of her system.

Chapter 17

*M*onday morning ushered in a new set of problems for Zackary. The sound of the rain hitting the roof awakened him from the vision of Diamond on the deck of his boat. The dream was so vivid he could literally taste her on his lips. Rolling onto his back, he threw his arm across his eyes, still not ready to make an effort to actually get out of the bed. Another sleepless night thinking of Diamond left him drained. A few weeks had passed since he touched her, but his body remembered how it felt to be inside her and it was reeling from withdrawal. Before, it was the dreams of what she might feel like haunting him, now it was the reality of her touch that was driving him crazy. Tossing the top sheet aside, Zack sat up on the side of the bed. It was five thirty in the morning. The sun hadn't made an appearance and it didn't seem it was going to, at least not today. Stalking over to the bathroom with only his briefs on, Zack didn't bother to turn on the light. He stood at the commode and was about to relieve himself when he looked out of the window and was startled. It was still dark out, but he could make out a figure standing at a tree across the street smoking a cigarette. He started to look away, but noticed the person appeared to be checking out the house, or was it the neighbor's house. Stepping back from the window so he wouldn't be seen, he peeked around the curtain that hung at the small window to see if he could determine which house the person was staring at. He watched the figure take a few puffs from the cigarette while looking up at the house. Hearing a sound upstairs Zack looked up towards the ceiling. "X-man must be up." He then looked back to see the figure throw the cigarette to the ground and stare intently at the upper part of the house where X-man's bedroom suite was located. "What the....." Zackary ducked low so the person wouldn't see him, then walked quickly into his bedroom, pulled on a tee-shirt and a pair of sweats out of the dresser drawer then put on his slippers. He turned off the alarm system at the backdoor of the house then walked out. "Damn," he swore. He forgot it was raining, as he followed the walkway from the back of the house to the front. Standing under the carport between his truck and X-man's SUV he studied the figure. Though it was dark and the figure was dressed in dark clothes, something in the way the figure stood was familiar. One thing was for sure, it was a woman. The woman tensed and looked down to the lower level of the house. Zack turned as he heard the click of the door behind him. He turned back as X-man walked up quietly behind him.

"Who is it?"

"I don't know," Zack replied absently shaking his head.

"I've seen her out there before. But I never paid much attention to her." X-man stated in a matter of fact tone.

Zack turned to him, "When?"

Shrugging his shoulder, "The first time was when you were in California." He shook his head, "Then again a few weeks ago."

"And you didn't say anything?" Zack questioned.

"I didn't think anything of it." X-man replied defensively, "Besides, my days of telling my big brother when I see the boogie man are gone."

Zack frowned at him, then smirked, as he turned back around. "Point taken." He looked back across the street. The woman was gone. "Where did she go?" he asked taking a step out, looking up and down the street.

X-man joined him. "I don't know." He said following his brother's actions.

"Damn." Zack cursed as he walked back into the house. He walked into his office to get his cell phone. While dialing a number, he turned to X-man who had taken a seat in front of his desk and asked, "Why in the hell would someone be watching this house? And how long has this been going on?" He stopped then spoke into the phone. "I need you to appear soon," was all he said as he hung up the phone then slumped into his chair bewildered.

"I can't answer either of those questions. But I can tell you this, whoever it is –is a chain smoker."

Zack stared numbly at X-man for a minute. He tilted his head to the side, "A few strange things have been happening at the site."

"And you haven't said anything?" X-man laughed. "Is that why you started putting the alarm on when we leave out of the house?"

"I got your point and yes." Zack smiled back.

"So what's been happening on the site?"

"Little things, like dad's ring showing up in one of the houses. Then there were some items found in another lot. But when you mentioned the cigarettes it made me wonder if the ones that were found at the site are the same as the ones we might find across the street."

"Are we going to play CSI and collect the cigarette butts as evidence?"

"No—we're not." Zack grinned, "We'll let the crime scene investigator do it."

"You called Diamond's brother?"

"He's the best at whatever he does."

"Exactly what does he do?" X-man inquired.

Zack snickered, "I have no idea. We work by a code, I don't ask and he don't tell."

X-man laughed, than sobered. Watching his brother closely, he spoke. "I um....ran into Diamond yesterday with a friend of yours."

Zack frowned, "A friend of mine—who?"

X-man cleared his throat. "Richard Hasting." If it had been anyone else, they would have missed the tick in Zack's jaw. But X-man knew his every move. "It surprised me, because I didn't know they were acquainted."

Zack just nodded. "They met at the site."

"Really?" X-man questioned. "Why was Richard at the site?"

"Making sure what happened at the last site doesn't happen at Davenport Estates."

X-man nodded, "So, what was he doing with Diamond?"

"How in the hell am I supposed to know," Zack replied exasperated.

X-man stood and tried to stifle his laugh. At least he knew Zack did not like the thought of Diamond with another man. He walked towards the door, "I'm not one to get into your business, but..."

"You're going to anyway."

"Damn right. Only because I love you like a brother."

"I am your brother."

"I don't know about that, man. My brother wouldn't let another man walk around town with his woman." He turned to walk out and said over his shoulder. "Don't be a fool and let him take what's yours. I have to get to work. See you later."

Zack cursed the minute he thought X-man was out of hearing range. What in the hell was Diamond doing with Richard. He stormed out of the office into his room and was in the shower before he stopped to think. Why in the hell was he mad? He wanted her to move on---didn't he?

L

Diamond arrived at the site a little after six in the morning. The thought was to get in, gather the paper work she needed for the day then go into the office to work. All of her appointments for the day were scheduled for that evening after six. She could arrive a half-hour before the time to work with the customers. However, that did mean she would not be there if a customer came by during the day. But that was the sacrifice she would have to make for her own sanity. There was no way she could do what had to be done if Zack was in her sights all day.

Walking into the kitchen of the model home, the first thing she did was check the microwave. Since the first night of the mysterious visitor, Diamond would leave the French door unlocked and food in the microwave. At first she simply left chips and a drink on the deck right outside the French door. When she came in the next day, the snack was gone. The next night she left a drink outside the cracked door and a sandwich wrapped on the counter. On the third night, she left the French door unlocked and a plate of food on top of the microwave. Since then she would leave something for the woman to eat each night in the microwave. When she came in the next morning, just like this morning, she would take the plate and put it in the dishwasher.

Diamond knew one day she would come and the food would still be there, which as her sister Ruby told her would eventually happen. It simply meant they have moved on. But for now, it felt good to help the woman. This morning when Diamond opened the microwave, there was a small glass jar with a sky blue marble inside. Opening the jar with a huge smile on her face, Diamond removed the marble and marveled at its simplistic beauty. A giggle escaped her throat. Her brothers would kill for such a rare find. Anyone watching the expression on Diamond's face would have thought she was given a rare gem. But it was just a marble and one that Diamond would cherish. The simple gift of gratitude brightened her otherwise stormy day.

Looking out the door at the rain, Diamond wondered if the woman was in a dry place. Shaking off the worry, she took a seat at her desk and began gathering the paper work she would need for the day.

With every intention of seeing Diamond, if for no other reason than to apologize for his behavior on Saturday, Zack was driving toward the site when his cell phone rang. "Davenport," he answered.

"Zack, its Richard. Do you have a minute to stop by my office before going to the site?"

Before he replied, he knew this was not a good idea. But he had no reason to deny the request—not really. Zack glanced at the clock on the dashboard of his truck. "I can be there in ten minutes."

"I'll see you then," Richard said then hung up the phone.

Zack exhaled as he made a u-turn in the middle of the street. If Richard even mentioned Diamond's name, he was going to knock the hell out of him. It didn't matter that he had no right to be pissed about Diamond being with Richard or any man. She wasn't his woman, as X-man had put it. She was just someone he had had sex with and that was that. But Richard was a friend and he should have known not to step in Diamond's direction. Hell, why would he know that. Zack tried to reason with himself. No one but X-man knew about the weekend he spent with Diamond. Richard would have no way of knowing Diamond was supposed to be his woman. Damn, now X-man had him saying that.

Pulling into the fire station that housed the office Richard worked out of, Zack was still battling with himself on the Diamond issue. The frown on his face must have been quite intense, since everyone seemed to step out of his way as he approached the red brick building and walked inside.

Richard looked up to see Zack storming towards him through the glass that surrounded his office. It took everything in him not to laugh at his friend. Taking a sip of his coffee, that was still nice and hot, Richard sat back in his seat and waited for Zack to walk through the door.

"Decided not to use an umbrella this morning Zack?," Richard asked, almost laughing. His friend was drenched from head to toe.

Zack raised a brow. "You called." He stated in a tone that would have let anyone know he wasn't in the mood to play games.

Richard could care less about Zack's mood. He was going to help his friend whether he wanted the help or not. "I need you to listen to something." Richard hit a button on his computer and a voice began talking.

It took a few moments for Zack to register that he was supposed to be listening to whatever the recorded voice was saying. "You called me in here to listen to some woman on the phone?"

Richard pushed a button to stop the recording. "Do you recognize her?"

"Recognize who?"

"The woman on the recording Zack. Where is your mind this morning?" Zack rubbed a hand down his face, wiping away the wetness from the rain. What in the hell was wrong with him? "The voice on this recording matches the voice from the tip we received before. Do you recognize the voice?"

Zack took a deep breath as he sat in the chair in front of the desk. "Play it again," he calmly requested.

Richard played the recording again. The woman was ranting about letting Zack Davenport off the hook with the fire. The woman also accused the chief of covering for Zack.

While listening to the recording, the only thing Zack could conclude was that the woman must be crazy. Most of what was being said was incoherent because the woman was so upset. However, with all that was being said the threat at the end was very clear. *"I will bring him down, one way or another."*

Zack looked at Richard perplexed. "Her voice sounds muffled, but I have no idea who that could be."

"We think she is trying to disguise her voice." Richard became very serious and sat forward. "But one thing is clear. The woman on the other end of that call is out to get you. And you have no idea who it may be? Could she be a jealous lover or ex-girlfriend?"

"No," Zack replied as he began to understand the seriousness of the situation. He exhaled. "You think it's the same person from the Franklin fire?"

"I do," Richard replied. "This indicates to me that this is personal Zack. What woman have you pissed off so bad that she would want to see you professionally destroyed?"

Perplexed, Zack just shook his head, "I have no idea."

Richard knew he had to tread lightly here, but Zack was his friend. "In your past there is a person that believes they were wronged by you in some way. How that individual deals with the hurt, real or imagined, is the unknown factor that could interrupt your life. I know you don't want to think this way, but someone is out to get you. I need you to think, Zack. Who could that person be?" He hesitated, "What about Diamond?"

Zack tensed, "What about her?" he asked pensively.

"Look, I don't know her well, but there is apparently something between you two. Is it to a point where she would try to destroy you?"

"No! Hell no. I didn't meet Diamond until after the Franklin project." He stood, "And if you know anything at all about Diamond you wouldn't even consider her as a suspect in this. That just goes to show you don't know a damn thing about her." He stormed out slamming the door behind him.

Richard sat back in his chair and snickered. "I know you're in love with the woman." Shaking his head, Richard went back to the report on his desk. He would deal with Zack and his love life later. Right now he had to figure out who was out to destroy Zackary Davenport.

L

Zack drove to Davenport Estates thinking who in the hell would want to bring him down? Who was the woman watching his house and how in the hell was he going to get Diamond off his mind? Stopping in front of the model home he jumped out of the truck and stormed inside heading straight to the office only to find it empty. Bending over the desk, trying to determine where Diamond may be, Zack looked at the calendar. No one was scheduled for a showing until later. He stood up, but his hand hit the top of a jar tipping it over. Marbles in the jar fell to the floor. "Oh hell!" Bending down quickly to stop them from rolling away, he began to gather them. As he picked them up one caught his eye. "Well I'll be damned." He smiled as he looked at the marbles. "It looks just like my marbles." His smile spread as he picked up another, and then another. He stood there with a hand filled with marbles that looked just like the ones he'd had as a child. Hell, he knew the manufacturers made thousands of the damn things, but these looked just like his. After a moment, he let the marbles roll slowly from his large hands back into the jar, and then replaced the top. The marbles and the momentary trip back to his childhood relieved some of the tension he was experiencing from the morning's events. Taking a deep breath, a single thought came to mind. There had only been two women in his life that had ever caused him harm. He was going to determine which one was out to get him now. But one thing was certain, it was not Diamond.

Chapter 18

The week went by without any more sightings of the woman outside his home or any phone calls from Richard. That was a relief, but he still could not get a location on Celeste or his mother. Joshua hadn't returned his calls. That usually meant he was out of the country. However, he knew Joshua would show up soon. Until then, he would just sit tight. As much as the no sightings relieved him, no signs of Diamond frustrated him more. Other than sold signs popping up on multiple lots of land, there was no sign of Diamond. Zack knew she was deliberately waiting until he was gone to post the signs. It didn't matter, because tonight she had to see him. The estate gala was tonight and that was her baby. There was no way she would be able to avoid him tonight. At some point, he was going to apologize to her for his behavior and find a way to at least co-exist with her at the office. The truth was he missed her not being around and if he didn't see her, touch her or kiss her soon he was going to lose his mind. Zack looked at himself in the mirror. He hated tuxedos as much as he did suits, but he had to admit he looked damn good. The eyes reflecting back at him were admitting something more. "You are a fool Zackary Davenport if you go another night without making Diamond Lassiter your woman." Zack looked away and shook his head. When he looked back the eyes said the same thing just in one word—fool.

L

The ballroom located on the first floor of the Davenport Towers was decorated in simple elegant black and white. The table linens were white, with mini black house replica weights holding down black and white balloons that reached the ceiling. The chairs were covered in white linen with black bows. Some tables had beautiful calla lilies with black bows tied around them in a crystal vase. Tables with models of each home offered in Davenport Estates were located around the room, along with five models of condominiums available in Davenport Towers, with furniture and lighting in the center of the room. Diamond took one last look around to ensure everything was in place before allowing the bartender and hostess in to prepare for guests. A celebration was the last thing she felt like, but this was an important night for Davenport Industries and it was her job to ensure this event was the talk of the real estate community in the morning.

She looked out the French doors that led to the courtyard and the homes beyond to ensure the lighting was working just right. At some point tonight, she was scheduled to take potential buyers on a night stroll through the estate. She looked forward to that tour. It was the one thing she knew would take her out of the room and away from Zackary. Some way she would have to make it through the evening without crossing his path. After what happened a week ago at the Habitat house she did not want to give him any reason to lash out at her again. So far she had done a good job of staying out of his sight and it had helped—some. It was just moments like now when he stayed on her mind regardless of what she did. However, tonight she planned to spend most of the evening in the background and give the tour when the celebration was at its peak. That way the multitude of people would keep them separated. But just one more thought of him before she closed Zackary Davenport from her mind. She couldn't help but smile when her mother told her the house was complete and the inspectors would be out early Monday to put their seal on things. If all goes well, Barbara and her son would be able to move in on Tuesday. Until then, Zackary had put them up in a hotel. He was indeed a special man, Diamond thought as she sighed. He just wasn't going to be her special man. That was it, no more thinking of him.

"Well, what do you think?" LaFonde asked as she walked up next to Diamond at the doors.

"I think Xavier and Zackary have created a beautiful place for some very fortunate people to call home," Diamond replied without turning around.

"I agree, but I wasn't talking about that. I was talking about me." LaFonde held her arms out and did a complete turn when Diamond looked her way.

"Wow, who's the lucky man?"

"Girl this is for me. I'm not thinking about any man, especially if he's going to put me in a funk like you."

Diamond frowned at her, "This is my doing. Not Zackary's."

"Why do you always defend that man's actions? He talks to you like dirt and treats you worse."

Diamond sighed. The last thing she wanted to do was allow anyone to have such a bad opinion of Zackary. However, she knew LaFonde very well, the more she defended Zack the deeper her loathing would go. "He really is a nice person LaFonde. But let's not talk about him. Let's talk about you and how beautiful you look tonight."

"I do look good, don't I?" LaFonde rubbed her hand on her locks that were up in a crown.

Smiling Diamond replied, "Girl you look better than good. You look like a breathtaking damsel waiting for the right knight to come along and claim his prize."

With the remote, Diamond turned the lights to the grounds off as they both laughed and walked over to the entrance from the lobby to open the doors.

By nine o'clock the room was packed with people dressed elegantly in their evening attire of gowns and tuxedos. No, this was not an everyday open house, this was an event. Invitations had been sent to a number of dignitaries from the city and other prominent citizens of the metro Richmond area. She was surprised to see the Attorney General of the state, J.D. Harrison and his wife Tracy along with his sister and her husband, James and Ashley Brooks. Her sister Pearl was his Press Secretary and informed Diamond that she had invited them, but she had not expected them to attend. It was an honor to have them present, Diamond thought as she watched the action from the kitchen located off the ballroom.

"Looks like a good turn out."

She turned to see Xavier standing behind her smiling. "Yeah, it looks good," she nodded wondering what he was doing there. "Why aren't you mingling? This is the time for you to be talking about the designs for this building. At some point you know we need to show your condo."

"Whenever you are ready the key is at the desk. Now explain why you are in the kitchen and not out there."

"You know me—I like to make sure everything is flowing right."

"Yeah, I do know you. You're hiding from Zack," he replied folding his arms across his chest.

"You look just like your brother when you stand like that." She smiled. He did not respond he just continued to stare at her as a waitress walked by with a tray of champagne heading towards the ballroom. She brushed an imaginary piece of lint from his well fitting tuxedo. "I don't want to upset Zack tonight. This is a special night for him." The strain of holding back the tears that threatened to come forward showed on her face.

Xavier reached out and pulled her into his arms. "I'm sorry Diamond. I don't know what to tell you when it comes to Zack. He's fighting his feelings for you, but neither of us can beat that realization into him."

She smiled shaking her head, stepping back before the tears spilled, "It's not important." She kissed his cheek. "You are a great friend. Now, go out there and be a good little brother and support him. You know he must be going a little crazy around all these people without you next to him."

"You should be out there too," he sighed.

"Right now would be a good time to do the tour of the grounds, don't you think."

Xavier sighed, "Okay, I'll set it up." Holding her hands, he held her arms out, "You are wearing that dress, Hmm," he shook his head and walked out the door.

Xavier walked out into the crowd with the intention of pulling his brother aside and giving him a piece of his mind about the way he was treating Diamond. Didn't he know that she was the woman who could put a permanent smile in his heart? No, he just had to be so damn stubborn and blind. How could he look at that woman and not see the love she has for him? He never thought he would refer to his brother as a fool, but damn if he wasn't acting like one and he was just at the point where he was going to tell him so when he saw the woman that almost ruined his life walk through the door.

Stunned like a deer in a set of headlights, Xavier did not move for a moment, then he looked in the direction of Zack. He had to get to his brother. Pushing his way through the crowd he walked up next to Zack just as he turned towards the door. "Xavier, I was wondering where you disappeared to. You remember Marian and her sister Adriane."

Blocking Zack's view to the doorway, Xavier smiled and nodded as he grabbed his brother's arm. "Yes, hello ladies. I hope you are enjoying the evening and I hate to do this but I need to speak with Zack for a moment. I promise I'll bring him right back."

"Like hell you will," Zack replied as they walked away. "Where in the hell is Diamond? I've been looking all over for her."

Reese walked over just before Xavier could speak. The look on his face showed he saw the same person Xavier had a few moments ago. "Zack let's take a walk in the courtyard," he said almost as a demand rather than a request.

Folding his arms across his chest Zack asked, "Why would I want to do that?"

"Actually, that's what I was coming to tell you, man." Xavier declared. "Diamond is ready to do the estate tour. We need to meet her by the door to the courtyard."

"It's about time she got here. Well let's go," Zack said as he walked through the crowd. Xavier and Reese shared a concerned look.

"She's been here since four this evening setting up and getting the staff started," Reese felt he had to say as he followed behind Zack. "I don't know what your problem is with her, but the girl has worked her butt off around here. You should be singing her praises instead of pitching a fit every time she is around."

Zack stopped and turned to him, "I don't pitch a fit every time I see her." Reese and Xavier stared at him in stunned disbelief. "Let's just get this over with." Zack turned just as the French doors opened and Diamond walked through.

Diamond stepped inside wearing a shimmering gold gown that hugged every curve of her body. The strings at the top of the gown crisscrossed right above her breasts and fell over her shoulders. She turned to close the doors and he could see the spider like pattern of strings that held the gown together, exposing her bare back down to the area where her behind formed into a perfect apple bottom. Her hair was pinned up with a few strands dangling from the crown of her head. The teardrop diamond earrings fell down stopping right above the shoulders he longed to kiss. The makeup was so light, it didn't appear she had any on, but she did—he could tell from the lipstick she was wearing which was right where his eyes were now drawn. She was exquisite. The mirror was right, he was a damn fool.

This was Diamond's first test now that she'd made up her mind to accept that Zackary really did not want her in his life. But she still had a job to do and she had no intentions of failing at that. Doing all she could to keep her eyes from meeting his, Diamond adjusted the microphone attached to her gown and began to speak to the crowd. "Ladies and Gentlemen, thank you for joining us in what we hope will be a memorable evening for you. If you have never experienced the Garden of Eden, brace yourself. This is going to take your breath away." She hit the remote and the lights illuminated the grounds as if it were the middle of the day. "Welcome to Davenport Estates."

Diamond narrated the tour of the grounds creating a frenzy of excitement about the property. The outrageous plan to introduce the Towers as if it were an opening night on Broadway worked. By the end of the evening, there were at least a hundred commitments from potential purchasers for the condominiums. That was more than she had anticipated. For the next hour after the tour, Diamond and LaFonde were busy setting up appointments for the following week. The interest in the property pleased her for two reasons. First, the homes in the Towers would be fifty percent sold before the building was completed and second, working occupied her completely and she did not have a moment to think about Zackary.

"I'll take that," LaFonde offered as she stood, referring to the appointment book they had used for the evening. "You have not mingled at all tonight. Get a drink, take a load off and enjoy the evening you have made memorable for others."

Diamond took the book from the woman she considered a friend, "You worked just as hard as I did putting this together. I'll handle the book. You go dance or something. Enjoy yourself and show off your new look, that's an order."

"Yes ma'am," LaFonde saluted as she walked away.

As she cleared the table, a few people spoke and said what a wonderful time they'd had at the grand opening. Some even said they had never experienced a grand opening like this one and they looked forward to visiting the estates again. Pleased with the comments, Diamond smiled and continued cleaning up the area. Her back was turned and she didn't see him approach but she knew Zackary was standing nearby, she could feel his presence.

"Is it your plan to avoid me for the rest of the night?"

Without turning, she shook her head, "No, I've been busy tonight."

"So I've noticed." Zack put his hands in his pockets and continued. "I had my doubts about this plan of yours but you pulled it off. You did a great job."

She smiled at the compliment, "It was different. People tend to like different."

"Different, like you."

Turning to him, she blushed and a frown immediately covered his face. Why does he do that she wondered. One minute he is sweet, warm, open and then the next he is shutting her out. Wanting to ease his tension, she spoke up. "You know it's okay. I understand and accept what you said about us. I want us to remain friends. So, thank you for the lessons and I promise you I will get past this obsession for you."

He feigned shock as he put his hands to his chest, "You are obsessed with me?"

Rolling her eyes upward, "Well, maybe a little," she returned the smile.

The two held each other's eyes for a moment, until she looked away. "I remind you of something unpleasant in your life. And since I only want to see happiness on that handsome face of yours, I've decided to keep my distance." She picked up the last of the documents from the table and balanced the paperwork in her arms. "I'll see you on Monday," she smiled and literally ran into the ballroom.

Zack watched as she walked away. He had been waiting all night to talk to her and in a flash she was gone. Not sure if it was his conscience kicking in or his libido responding to the sight of her behind in that dress, but something was urging him to go after her. He took a step towards the door but stopped when he heard a voice he never thought he would hear again. "Hello Zackary."

Chapter 19

*W*ith her nerves playing havoc and her heart breaking Diamond's insides were telling her to get to a place where she could breakdown without causing much embarrassment to herself or Davenport Industries. With her head down, she swiftly walked by the few guests that remained in the ballroom. Just as she began to feel freedom she collided with a brick wall, at least that's what it felt like. Papers went everywhere. When she saw her gold sandals that her feet were still in, in the air, she braced herself for the impact of her behind hitting the floor. With her eyes closed a scream escaped her throat, just as a strong arm circled her waist. She grabbed the arm and held on to the hard body for dear life.

"Diamond," Xavier yelled, "Are you all right?"

Realization hit her that she was no longer plummeting to the floor. She slowly opened one eye and looked into the face of—who was he? Oh yeah, he was the same man that caught her before.

Seeing the look of recognition on her face, Grant Hutchison smiled down at the woman with the dimples. "Is this a habit with you?" he asked with an amusement-laced voice.

There was clearly a smile in the statement as she opened the other eye and found herself lodged against his body. She eased down until her feet touched the floor. Adjusting her dress she turned to the concerned faces of people still in the room, "I'm fine everyone. Please continue with your evening." Sure her face was flushed with embarrassment, she bent down to pick up the papers that had fallen. "I'm so sorry. I wasn't looking where I was walking. Please forgive me."

Pearl rushed over, "You okay?" she touched her sister's shoulder. The one thing big sisters could always do was see through the phony smiles. Diamond's eyes told her that all was not well.

"Other than being a public nuisance, I'm fine," Diamond replied without looking up.

Grant also began to assist with gathering the papers she had dropped. "I wouldn't say you were a public nuisance, just my personal damsel in distress."

"You two know each other?" Xavier asked.

"We bumped into each other before. " Grant explained as he held out his hand to help Diamond to her feet.

Pearl and Xavier stood just as Reese called out. "Xavier we have a situation."

"Go on Xavier, I'll get this." Diamond stated too embarrassed to want anyone around.

"Are you sure?"

"Yeah, I have it covered," she replied.

Pearl looked at her sister and frowned as Xavier walked off. "What did he do this time?"

Looking for a reason to not answer her sister she turned to the man who had saved her from injury twice. "I am so sorry this happened again. Please, I promise not to walk in public ever again."

That brought the nicest smile to his face. "I think it would be a crime to withhold such a beautiful face from public viewing. How about I promise to be around to catch you every time you fall?"

Pearl turned on the man with hands on hips and a scowl on her face, "She has six brothers and a father that's taller than you to handle that."

"Really," Grant replied without taking his eyes from Diamond. "Well, just in case you may need me again, my name is Grant Hutchison. Here's my card." He handed the card to Diamond. "I'm very interested in The Tower Condominiums. Please give me a call at your earliest convenience." He turned to walk away but stopped. "My personal cell number is on the back if you need to be rescued before then." He smiled and walked out of the door.

Pearl watched her sister tuck the card away without a second thought. "Do you know who that is?"

Diamond looked at the card, "Yes, Grant Hutchison."

"No, not just Grant Hutchison, he is the Grant Hutchison of Hutchison Plantations. Do you realize that man just came on to you? And what is he talking about—if you need to be rescued again?"

Diamond waved off the question. "It was nothing. I'm going to drop these papers off in The Tower office then begin to close things down. Are you about to leave?"

"Yeah."

"Okay then. I'll see you at home." Diamond walked off.

Pearl watched her little sister and was concerned with the sadness she saw in her eyes. This was the no-drama-always-upbeat sister—the one that helped everyone else through their problems. Now she was dealing with rejection from a man she believes she is in love with and Pearl didn't know how to help her. She went through something similar when she was younger and the only thing that pulled her through was family. Diamond wasn't the kind to respond to sympathy but she always responded to being needed. It was time for the family meeting. They had to do something to make this hurt go down a little easier for Diamond.

Shaking her head Pearl walked out of the door of the ballroom and into the middle of a scene with Zackary, Xavier and a beautiful woman she did not know. As she listened it became apparent that Diamond's unknown nemesis was in the building.

Celeste Blanchard. Zackary stared at the woman he craved with a vengeance during college. There was no denying, she was still a beautiful woman. A little fuller at the top, but that only added to her allure. But he knew what lay beneath, a cold heartless woman that only cared about the status in life a man could give her. Of all the people he expected to see, she was the last on the list. "I can't imagine why you would want to make your presence here known to me." He turned to walk away.

"Do you seriously think I would give you an opportunity to humiliate me if it wasn't important?"

Zack turned back to her anxiety-filled voice. He knew the voice, remembered hearing it when her mother was diagnosed with cancer, when her grades almost got her kicked out of college and the night he told her he was leaving school. He frowned at the feeling he always got to make things better for her. "Whatever your problem is I'm not the man to solve it."

"On the contrary Zack, you may be the only man I know that can."

"This isn't the place for you Celeste," Xavier stated then turned to Reese. "Would you escort Ms. Blanchard from the building?"

"Well Xavier, you've grown up." Celeste sneered as she yanked her arm away from Reese. "Congratulations on your success. It' good to know Zack's sacrifice paid off."

"I was hoping to spare Zack the unpleasantness of seeing you Celeste, but I see your determination prevailed."

"The unpleasantness caused by you ruining his life." She snapped back.

"Enough!" Zack bellowed as he took a step towards her. "Unlike you X-man is wanted and needed here. You are not."

"I have a little girl Zack." She desperately cried out as Reese approached her. "I'm here because she needs your help, not me."

"What could your child have to do with me?"

"She may be yours."

Zack stood shell shocked.

"What kind of game are you playing now Celeste?" Xavier angrily asked.

Ignoring Xavier, Celeste continued to hold Zack's gaze. "She's twelve years old Zack, you do the math."

Anger was the least of the emotions racing through his body. How dare she come here claiming to have his child! Quietly, doing all he could to hold his temper, he replied, "We'll play this round Celeste."

"Zack, she was in an accident and was in need of a transfusion. My husband was not a match." Seeing she had captured his attention, she stepped forward. "I need to know if you are my daughter's father. I'm not here to cause any problems, I just need to know."

Looking at her distressed expression Zackary could not turn his back on her, as much as he wanted to. He looked at Xavier and Reese, "Give us a minute." Out of the corner of his eye he saw Pearl standing in the doorway. Diamond crossed his mind. "Let's take this to a private area." He walked Celeste over to the bank of elevators that led up to the penthouse. Pearl turned and left the building, leaving Reese and Xavier staring angrily at the woman that was about to turn Zack's life upside down, again.

Diamond stepped out of the office just as the elevator arrived. Her heart stopped when she looked up and saw Zackary with what had to be one of the most beautiful women she had ever seen step on to the elevator. Her breath caught at the sound of the elevator doors closing. It seemed she stood there watching the doors, why, she didn't know. Maybe they will open back up and the woman or Zack would come out. The longer she stood there the more she realized that was not going to happen. Looking up she saw Xavier walking towards her with a concerned look in his eyes. She put her hand up, shook her head to stop him. Nine times out of ten he was going to try to explain what she just saw and that was the last thing she needed to hear.

After checking to make sure the room was clear from the events of the night, Diamond returned to the office and retrieved her purse. She looked over at the elevator doors and wondered if they were still upstairs. The sight of Zack with another woman should not affect her so. She had made a decision to get over him. Somebody should tell her heart not to hurt so much. As she walked to her car, the tears rolled and no matter how much she willed them to stop, they just kept coming.

Chapter 20

The sun rose to find Zack, still dressed from the night before, sitting at the desk in his home office. Life had taken a drastic change for him and for the first time in years he wished for his father's wisdom and guidance. Doubt and uncertainty consumed him. Were all women deceitful and vindictive? What he thought was a monogamous relationship had now been revealed to be anything but. God has a way of saving you from yourself without you even being aware. His plans while in college were simple: have his football career, marry Celeste and have children. He took a drink of cognac from the glass he was holding. When his father died, he cursed God for taking his father and his dreams from him. Now, he could only close his eyes and say thank you to his savior for saving him from a life of lies and deceit.

Now Celeste is claiming to never having had the abortion, but because she was sleeping with him and another player, she thought the child was her husband's, Theodore "Teddy" Blanchard. He picked up the glass to take another drink but it was empty. He checked the bottle, but it was empty too. He slumped back in the chair and placed the empty bottle on the desk. Did he really finish off a five-hundred dollar bottle of Remy? Hell, Celeste wasn't worth it.

Xavier walked into the office with the morning paper in his hand. "You've been sitting there all night?"

"You're just coming in?" Zack questioned without answering.

Xavier smiled, "I was giving a private tour of The Towers."

With a raised eyebrow Zack looked at the silly grin on his little brother's face. "Be careful, those private tours can turn into a public nightmare."

"Hmm." Xavier put the paper on the desk and sat in the chair in front of his brother. "So—she's claiming her daughter is now your child?"

"She's saying she is not sure."

"Convenient, wouldn't you say.   Before your financial status improved, the child was always Teddy's. Now that you are a successful business man and Teddy lost his contract with the NFL you may be the father."

Zack heard the caution in Xavier's voice and was hurt he felt uncertain. "Regardless of what she said or how this turns out, none of this was your fault. You are my brother and I would walk through hell or high water for you. I did what I wanted to do when I left school and Celeste. Don't take the weight of any of this on your shoulders. My decision, my burden, you got that?"

Certain things in life will never change and his brother Zack was at the top of that list. Here he sat dealing with his demons from the past, but still concerned about his feelings. "I hear you. But know we go through this together— none of that big brother protecting little X-man from the realities of life."

"Here, here," Zack replied as he held the empty glass up.

Xavier looked at the empty bottle on the desk, "Is that my Remy you have finished off?"

Zack looked at the bottle, then back up at his brother, "Yeah, you got another one?"

Chuckling and slouching with his head back in the chair, "No." He rubbed his sleep deprived eyes and looked at his brother. "So what does she want you to do?"

"She wants me to meet Chanté."

"She's the daughter?"

Zack nodded, "Yep."

"Why meet the daughter and establish a relationship before finding out if she is yours?"

"Because that's how Celeste operates. She knows how I am about children. Once I'm attached there is nothing I wouldn't do for them."

"Ahh, she's after money?"

"That's my take on the situation." He sat up and folded his arms on the desk, "But what if she is my child?"

Xavier saw the uncertainty in his brother's eyes. "You know how I am. I deal with facts. Is it a possibility? According to you it was rumored that she was pregnant but had an abortion. What if she didn't? That makes this a real situation. Just don't allow her to use this child against you. Take the test, but use your doctor, not hers."

Zack looked at Xavier a little suspicious, "It sounds like you have been through this a time or two. Is there something you are not telling me?"

"Nope," he stood. "I've seen friends get caught up caring for a child for a year or two only to find out by accident the child was not theirs. I don't want that to happen to you." He walked over to the desk and pointed to a small article on the front page of the newspaper. "You should read that. You should also know Diamond saw you get on that elevator with Celeste." Xavier walked towards the door leading out of the room. "I don't like seeing my friend hurt Zack. For all she has done for us, she deserves better than being compared to Celeste." He walked out of the room.

Zack flipped the paper over and in a small column of features articles for the community section was a picture of The Towers. Apparently a reporter covered the opening. He pulled out the section and there on the front page was a beautiful color picture of The Tower. With all the drama, it was nice to see his work being recognized. The article discussed the beauty of the small community and the elegance in which it was presented. Diamond came to his mind. She had such a huge part in making the project a reality. He exhaled; he had to begin the journey to close that chapter in his life. It seemed Celeste's lies were catching up with her, but a child's life was in the balance. Even when it was determined that he is not the father, he would do all he could to help the little girl. The statement Xavier made about him comparing Diamond to Celeste kept nagging him. There was no comparing the two as far as he was concerned. The way Celeste held her head was nowhere near as adoring as Diamond. Her voice didn't soothe him like Diamond's. When she was talking about her daughter and smiled, it didn't make his heart jump for joy like Diamond's smile did. There was nothing about Celeste that reminded him of Diamond because they were nothing alike.

Zack turned on his computer and stared at the picture of Diamond smiling in the original video presentation she'd made and it felt like a sledge hammer had just hit him in the gut. From the moment she entered his life, Diamond had done nothing but give him what he needed whether he wanted it or not. She took the steps to make sure he got the paperwork needed to get his driver's license straight. It was Diamond that designed the marketing concept that brought in investors for Davenport Estates. It was her sweat that sold those sites to produce the income to build The Towers. It was her concept that brought in the buzz surrounding the project. It was Diamond that gave him the most precious gift a woman could give a man, her innocence. She trusted him to teach her how to make love.

Needing some air, he stood and stepped out on the back porch of his home. All along the way it was Diamond that was teaching him—she was teaching him how to love. "Damn." He shook his head, "I begged Celeste to stay and pushed Diamond away. How did I miss that daddy?" Nodding his head as he continued to think out loud, "That's alright it's simple," he said not caring that no one was around listening, "I messed up, but I will fix it." First and foremost he had to resolve this dilemma with Celeste, and then he would work on establishing a real relationship with Diamond. But life had a way of not always being so simple.

Chapter 21

*M*onday morning Diamond arrived at the model home with a new determination. Life was supposed to be lived and not squandered away and that was what she was going to do. Zack did exactly what she asked him to do and now she had to be woman enough to accept that was all he was capable of giving her. After picking up the papers from the office, she settled down in the model home office and began setting up appointments for viewings of the condominiums in the Tower and the last available home sites in Davenport Estates.

Around nine o'clock she heard the front door to the house open and looked up. The first appointment for the day wasn't until ten. "Hello," she called out as she stood to walk into the foyer of the home. She froze when she reached the opening to find the woman who was with Zack on the elevator standing in the living room. The woman was impeccably dressed in white slacks, a white shell with a thick red belt and red sandals looking as if she just stepped out of a fashion magazine. Not even one strand of her neatly short hairdo out of place.

"Hello," the woman said with a smile, "I'm looking for Zack."

Diamond was so stunned to find the woman standing in front of her that she hesitated to speak. "I'm sorry, what did you say?"

"I'm looking for Zack. The man you saw me with last night, your boss, I believe."

"Yes," Diamond was able to stumble out. "There are actually two."

"There is only one Zackary Davenport. Believe me— I know," came the reply implying an intimacy.

Not liking the way the conversation was going Diamond looked out of the window towards the trailer the crew worked from. "I don't see his truck, but Mr. Davenport usually works from the trailer. You should be able to find him there."

The woman turned and looked out the window. "Honey, do you see what I'm wearing. I'm not walking over there. Would you be a dear and call him to meet me here?"

There weren't many people in the world that Diamond took an immediate dislike to, but this woman was the first on her list. "Sure," she said then turned back and walked towards her office. After picking up the telephone and dialing the number, Diamond looked up to see the woman walking into her office. Trying hard not to stare at the woman again, Diamond began concentrating on the papers on top of her desk. "Good morning Reese," happy someone finally answered, "Would you tell," she hesitated then looked up at the woman, "Would you tell Mr. Davenport he has a visitor at the model home."

"Zack's not here Diamond. He had a meeting at headquarters this morning."

"Oh," she replied. "I'll let his visitor know."

"Who is it?" Reese asked.

"Hold on." Diamond looked at the woman, "Who may I tell him is visiting?"

The woman laughed sheepishly, "Zack can be such a jokester. He was the one that made the plans for us to meet this morning."

Diamond raised an eyebrow. Zack was a lot of things—a jokester was not one. "Maybe you have your location mixed up."

"He's not here?" the woman huffed with hands on hips and all.

Diamond almost frowned at the dramatics. The woman reminded her of her little sister Phire. No, that was an insult to Phire. "No. According to our security director he has a meeting at our headquarters building this morning. Is it possible that's where you should be?"

Still holding the telephone, Diamond heard Reese speaking. She put the telephone back to her ear. "I'm sorry Reese what did you say?"

"Is the woman there Celeste Blanchard?"

"I don't know. Are you Celeste Blanchard?" she asked the woman.

"I am." The woman replied smiling with a look as if she had scored points.

And she had. Diamond recognized the name from Samuel's story about Zack and his situation surrounding him leaving school. "Yes it is," Diamond said into the telephone but never took her eyes off the woman.

"I'll call Zack," Reese said as he hung up the telephone.

Diamond hung up the telephone. "Our security Director will contact him. In the meantime you are welcome to have a cup of coffee and wait in the kitchen for a return call."

"I think I'll stay here and keep you company while we wait."

Not wanting to be in the woman's presence for long Diamond smiled and replied. "I'm afraid I have quite a bit of work to do before my next appointment and will not make for good company."

"That isn't very hospitable. You're the spokesperson that represents Davenport Estates, I would think you should know how to treat guests. I'll speak with Zack about that when we talk."

No she didn't just threaten her job. "Well, you can speak to whomever you like, but do it from another room. I'm working in this one."

Celeste gave the most devious smile. "I noticed the shocked look in your eyes last night when you saw Zack and me get onto the elevator. Were you involved with Zack before?"

The word before lingered long enough for Diamond to get the impression that something was happening between Celeste and Zack now. "I'm going to get a cup of coffee. Would you like any?" Diamond asked not willing to acknowledge the dig.

"No thank you. But I would like an answer to my question."

Before Diamond could reply Reese walked through the door. "Ms. Blanchard, Mr. Davenport is on the line." Reese gave the cell phone to Celeste who walked into the other room to talk. Reese turned to Diamond, "Are you okay?"

"Of course I'm fine." She replied and sat back down at her desk and began reading, rather just looking, at papers on her desk.

Reese looked at the woman in the living room and then back at Diamond and whispered, "What in the hell are you doing Zack?"

"Here's your cell phone. Thank you both for your kindness. Ms.—I'm sorry I didn't get your name."

The phony air was sickening. But Diamond knew how to play the game, "Diamond Lassiter." She replied.

"What a beautiful name. I bet you are a Diamond in the rough. Well, thank both of you for your help. As it turns out Ms. Lassiter you were correct. Our meeting was scheduled for his headquarters office. But just like always Zack forgave me and is waiting for me there. I have to go. Have a wonderful day." And with that she walked out of the door. Satisfied she had put some doubt in the woman's head regarding Zack, Celeste smiled as she got into her car.

$\mathcal{L}$

Certain the delay had been orchestrated by Celeste, Zack rescheduled the testing with his doctor for that afternoon. Sitting with his back to his desk looking out the window, he wondered what Diamond was doing at that moment. It seemed since he decided to allow her into his life she had played prominently in his mind. He wished he had handled things on Saturday differently. The way things were left was a little too final. That was what he thought he wanted at the time, but now things were a little different.

JoEllen walked through the door and noticed Zack's suit jacket was thrown across the chair near the door. She picked it up and hung it on the rack. "Since when do you throw expensive clothes around? And why am I making an appointment with your doctor? Are you okay?"

Without turning around Zack replied, "Sorry about the jacket. The doctor's appointment is for a DNA test and yes I'm okay."

JoEllen walked around the desk to stand next to him as he continued to look out the window. "DNA test for whom?" She looked at him with a surprised, motherly scolding stare. "I know you well enough to know you are not having unprotected sex. Are you? You know better than that. Hell I taught you better. Life is too crazy out there to be doing something so stupid. How could you?"

He exhaled and looked at her wondering when she would give him a moment to respond to any of the allegations she was throwing out. When she finally finished with her hands on her hips and approaching him as if he was a child she was about to chastise, he replied, "Celeste."

"Who in the hell is Celeste?" she all but yelled.

"I'm Celeste," the voice came from the doorway.

Both turned towards the door with frowns. "My question remains the same. Who in the hell are you and why would Zack need a DNA test done?" JoEllen looked from the woman in the doorway to Zack waiting for an answer.

Celeste stood watching the woman, who she knew was not Zack's mother, but seemed to have the wrath of God waiting to strike if the wrong thing was said. She then looked to Zack. This was his responsibility to explain, but since it didn't appear he was going to take the initiative, she would. Stepping forward and extending her hand, "Hello, I'm Celeste Blanchard. Zackary and I were involved during college and I have a daughter. We are taking steps to determine if Zack may be her father."

"You were sleeping around with more than one man without protection?" JoEllen walked towards the woman but did not extend her hand. "I would think your mother would have taught you better."

"Are you going to jump in here?" Celeste looked over at Zack who had not moved from his desk.

"I didn't plan to."

It took her a moment to take in his response. This was a different Zack, it was not going to be easy to manipulate him. But she had to give it her best shot, her livelihood depended on it. "I'm not here to cause anyone any problems." She displayed the most sincere face of a caring mother. "But I have to do this for my daughter. During my college days, I was a young, silly, materialistic girl that only cared about what could be done for me. Now I'm a mother and my number one priority is my daughter." She then turned to face Zack. "I'm sorry about the mix up this morning. Any place and time you say, I'll have Chanté ready. Once we get the results I'll be out of your life. I don't personally want anything from you. Only what my child needs."

JoEllen stared at the woman now. She hated deceitful women and this one looked and smelled the part. "Zack, I'm glad to see your taste in women has improved."

She looked from Zack back to the woman known as Celeste. "I need a little fresh air. I have a feeling you are going to be knee deep in some bull." It appeared to JoEllen that Celeste was about to say something. "You have something you want to say to me?" she raised an eyebrow to Celeste.

If it weren't for the bigger picture, Celeste would have taken the old broad on. But Zack was the target here, the old bat could wait. "I understand your need to protect Zack. In fact, I'm glad to know someone is looking out for him."

"Un huh," JoEllen replied. She looked back at Zack, "I'll see if I can find a bucket and a shovel—you are going to need it," then walked out of the room.

The scene was so funny Zack could not resist and smothered a chuckle. JoEllen was worse than a protective mother hen. She was armed and ready to pluck out Celeste's eyes at the first wrong move.

"Well, I guess I deserved that." She then looked at Zack. "And I did mean what I said to your—protector. I'm glad you have her." She then flashed that million dollar smile at Zack.

For a moment—only a moment he could almost forget who he was dealing with. "Fortunately, I'm immune to you and your ways Celeste. I've scheduled the DNA test for this afternoon at two o'clock. If you miss that appointment, there will be no other. We will meet here."

Looking at her watch, "You know that gives us a few hours. It would be a great opportunity for you to meet Chanté. She is so adorable Zack. From the moment she took her first breath she stole my heart."

"Since I wasn't given the opportunity to be there during her birth, I can wait. You may wait outside my office until time for the appointment." He gave her a look letting her know she had been dismissed.

Not wanting to waste an opportunity, she simply smiled, "All right Zack, I understand." She reached into her purse and placed a picture of Chanté on his desk. "This is the child that may be your daughter. I thought you might like to have that." Zack did not look up or acknowledge the picture on the desk. Celeste walked over to the door, "I'll meet you back here at two."

"We will meet in the lobby at the front door. There is no reason for you to invade my space here."

Celeste walked out of the office. *You may be immune to me, but let's see if you can resist Chanté.* The thought had just processed in her mind when JoEllen appeared in front of her.

"I don't know what you are after. But if you bring a moment of sadness into that man's life, I will make you my special project from here until eternity." JoEllen walked behind her desk and took a seat.

Celeste had been dismissed yet again. Not one to take being ignored she stepped over to JoEllen's desk and said, "Start looking for another job, you old bat. When I finish with Zack, you won't be needed." She smirked and walked away.

L

Still frustrated by the visitor this morning, Diamond was doing all she could to mask the woman's affect, but she wasn't succeeding. Walking out to her car, she pulled the files collected on Saturday night from the front seat. Reading over the files, she wasn't looking where she was walking and tripped over the cement walkway. The heel of her shoe broke, her ankle twisted and the files went flying into the air. Just when she expected her behind to hit the ground, an arm grabbed her around the waist. Once she realized she did not hit the ground, she looked up into the smiling eyes of Grant Hutchison.

"You know, there really is a better way to get me to hold you close."

Once her heart stopped racing from the near fall, she closed her eyes and exhaled. "You can put me down now Mr. Hutchison. I promise not to fall all over your feet again."

He looked down at her and grinned, "Are sure you can manage without me holding you?"

She couldn't help but laugh, "I'm pretty sure."

He slowly sat her back on her feet. She reached down to pick up the files. "I seem to lose my balance when I'm around you."

Bending, he helped her to gather the files. "I'm not sure if that's a good thing or a bad thing." He put the files in her arms. "But it does tell me I have an effect on you. And that can't be all bad."

Diamond glared at him for a second then frowned. "Are you flirting with me Mr. Hutchison?"

"Apparently not very well."

Diamond smiled, "Why don't you come inside? The very least I could do for you after you've saved my life yet again is offer you some refreshments," she asked as she turned to walk into the house. "What are you doing here?"

"You mean besides failing miserably at charming you?"

"Yes, other than that."

"I want to talk to you about a project," he said as he held the door open for her.

Diamond placed the files on the desk, then turned to Grant. "May I offer you a drink or some blackberry cobbler?"

"I was wondering if that was an air freshener or real."

"It's homemade real." She smiled as she walked over to the kitchen, "Would you like some?"

He followed her into the kitchen and took a seat at the breakfast bar. "Some of the cobbler?"

She looked over her shoulder at him, "Yes, the cobbler."

"If that's all you are offering, I'll take some cobbler."

"I'm charmed Mr. Hutchison but I'm not interested at the moment. Why don't you tell me about your project," she stated as she prepared the cobbler.

"I can't be that bad. Is it possible it's not my game just the wrong woman."

Placing the cobbler with vanilla bean ice cream on top Diamond laughed, "You are charming, but,"

"Your mind is on Davenport. The question is, which one?"

She grabbed a spoon and began eating her cobbler. "Tell me about your project."

"Well since you asked," he smiled. "I'm in the midst of a project on the north side of the city. We've taken several rundown buildings and renovated them into affordable apartments and condominiums. We are in the second phase of the project and I think you could be quite helpful to us."

Diamond sat back in the seat and crossed her legs. "Me? How could I help you?"

"I was very impressed with the way you presented Davenport Estates and I'm hoping you could do the same for Regenerations."

"Um, Mr. Hutchison, I have a job."

"I'm not offering you a job. This is a non-profit organization that helps people with credit or income challenges to obtain affordable housing in a clean, safe environment. What I'm asking you to do is possibly volunteer your skills to assist us in obtaining residents." He sat forward, "You see, the area was once infested with gangs, drug dealers and prostitutes. The kind of residents we want may not find the area attractive. However, with the changes we have planned I'm certain the area is going to be considered prime family living within a year or two. It's imperative to the project that the correct tenants are selected to help the area reach its full potential."

The more he talked the more recognizable he became. Grant Hutchison was the grandson of the patriarch Richard Hutchison of Hutchison Plantations. Deemed to be some of the most beautiful landscape that ran a good length of the James River, Hutchison Plantations continued to be family owned. Twice a year the family allowed the riverboat to dock and curiosity seekers to tour the estates that once housed a number of the slaves sold in the Virginia area. The exclusive family opened the doors to others during the Fourth of July cookout and fireworks, then again with dinner and dancing during the Christmas holidays. After that the doors to the estate close down and the family is rarely seen. Grant was one of four grandchildren; two lived on the West coast while he and his younger brother lived on the compound. It had been rumored that Grant was thinking of running for a local political office. If the news coverage was any indication of his intentions, then the rumors were probably true.

Diamond sat up, "Would you be so kind as to clarify your stand on characteristics of the 'correct' tenants." She was tired of seeing politicians come out to supposedly benefit the under privileged only to have those that are not in need take over the community to make it an acceptable place to live. She sat back and watched it happen to the East end of the city.

"That's just it Diamond, I don't know and I'm not going to try to pretend that I do. I've had a privileged life. To this day, I've never wanted for anything I can't have. I would not be the best person to recognize those in need. From what I've been told and what I've witnessed for myself, I believe you can identify and help those in need. If they see me involved in the selection process, most of those that truly need would not step forward, assuming they would be turned away. With you making those decisions, maybe, just maybe we can do something for those families that really need our help."

Okay, he was thoughtful, kind and generous. She sighed, "I'm not sure how I can help."

"Are you busy this evening?"

Thinking about going home and crying her eyes out again tonight over Zackary was not appealing at all. "No."

"Good," he smiled. "Meet me at this address so I can show you what we are offering and for your trouble I'll take you to dinner."

"You don't have to do that. I'll meet with you and take a look at your complex. Maybe I could suggest a promo to get you started or something."

He stood and extended his hand, "I look forward to seeing you. Let's say around six."

Shaking his hand she replied, "Six will be fine. I'll see you then."

As Grant walked out the door, Diamond watched his six-two frame get into his car and thought, he really wasn't a bad looking brother.

Chapter 22

*a*s Zack assumed, Celeste pulled out the big guns. Standing in the lobby at the receptionist desk was a miniature vision of Celeste by the name of Chanté. Try as he might, he could not contain the smile that was emerging. The pre-teen was beautiful, with her reddish brown hair hanging across her shoulders as she stood with her arms curved in front of her like she was holding an invisible beach ball, then she gracefully spread her arms out wide to the side.

"It's called first position, then she moved into second position." Zack looked over to see LaFonde manning the front desk. "She wants to be a ballerina and from the looks of it she may succeed. Do you know her?"

"No, but I'm sure her mother is about to change that." Just then the child laughed out as she took a leap across the lobby and the people standing around clapped. She gave a curtsy any mother would be proud of. "She's an attention hound just like her mother."

LaFonde frowned, "Do you ever have anything positive to say."

Zack glared at her. "I did once, when I told Diamond you could stay. Look how that turned out." He walked towards Celeste and her daughter. The girl turned just as he reached them.

"Hello," her smile beamed up at him. "You must be Mr. Davenport." She extended her hand to him. "Wow, I can see why my Dad doesn't want you around my Mom. You are fire, whew!"

"Chanté," Celeste warned. "Zackary, this is my daughter Chanté."

Zackary took her hand, "It's nice to meet you Chanté."

"It is a pleasure to meet you Mr. Davenport. I've read a lot of wonderful things about your work with Habitat for Humanity. I think it's commendable of you to share your talents with the less fortunate. I hope to be able to do the same one day."

It was difficult not to take an instant liking to the child who appeared to be much wiser than her age would allow. "Thank you. But I would think you would have better things to do with your time than to read about me."

"I read about everyone Mr. Davenport. I think next to dancing, reading is my most favorite thing in the world." She did a twirl as she spoke then giggled. The sound was joyous and was a reminder of her age. But that was the only give away. She was a beautiful young girl who looked as if she should be on someone's stage.

Zackary had to smile for he was captivated by the child. "How long have you been dancing?"

"All my life, it seems like," she replied with a shrug of her shoulders. "I'll be performing in New York next month and if that goes well I may get a lead in the production when it goes to Europe. Wouldn't that be wonderful mother?"

"Yes, it would. But I don't want you to get your hopes up."

"I know," the light in the child's eyes dimmed a bit. But in a millisecond it returned. "But I believe we can do it and that's the first step to success. Isn't that right Mr. Davenport?"

"That's exactly right," Zack tapped her on the tip of her nose. "And don't you ever give up on your dream."

She smiled brightly, "I won't."

"Would you mind if I spoke to your mother privately for a moment?"

"Not at all. I'll wait outside for you. In fact, I'll be happy to go back to the studio if you two need some time to talk."

"No, that's not necessary. This will only take a moment." Zack replied as he took Celeste by the elbow and took a few steps away from the child. "I have no idea what game you are playing, but to ensure we are all heading down the right track, let's clear the fog. We are here to test your daughter, whom I do not believe for one moment is mine. Once the DNA proves that, you and your daughter will be on your way back to Teddy. Do I make myself clear?"

"Crystal," Celeste testily stated then walked purposely over to Chanté. "We're leaving Chanté"

Chanté looked from Celeste to Zack then back to her mother. As if she knew not to question, she sadly smiled at Zackary. "I'm sorry if I offended you in any way. My father tells me I talk too much and I really do try to control it." She shrugged her shoulders, "But I like talking to people. Please don't be upset with my mother because of my actions."

The way the child spoke bothered Zack. He reached out and took her hand as she walked away to follow her mother out the door. "Chanté," he bent down to the child. "You did not do anything to offend me. In fact I rather enjoyed listening to you. So don't ever stop talking to people." He stood as he asked, "Does your father take things out on your mother?"

Celeste walked back through the door, "Come along Chanté!"

"All the time," Chanté replied as she followed her mother out the door.

For a moment Zack was so tempted to turn and go back upstairs and allow the two to leave. But he knew this situation would remain an issue until he had proof that

Chanté was not his child. Although, after meeting her, he almost wished she was. Then he looked up at her mother and murmured, "Almost." He stormed out of the door, took both Celeste and Chanté by the elbow. "This way ladies," he said as he led them to his car.

L

Joshua received the message from Zack that he needed to locate his mother. Unfortunately, he had been out of the country when the message arrived. As soon as he returned, he checked on the last location for Ann and was surprised at what he found as he began to shadow her. He wasn't alone.

L

I don't know who this woman is that stays on Zack's property, but I can't allow her to interfere with my plans. Zack thinks he's the man with everybody talking about the open house at Davenport Estates and the damn Businessman of the Year nominations. Hmm, that would be a good time to bring him down. The media will definitely be covering the event and I'm sure his good friend the Fire Chief Hasting will be there. Ha-Ha-Ha, wouldn't that be interesting to have Zackary up one day – as the man and disgraced the next as the greedy son-of-a-bitch he is. Yeah, now what's the best way to ensure he is the target of the investigation?

Chapter 23

*D*iamond walked into the foyer of Marco's restaurant, which was owned by Pearl's friends Marco and Roz Marable. Because of their international cuisine, the restaurant had the reputation of catering to an upscale clientele such as CEO's, entertainers and politicians that have a taste for something different. In fact, the last time she was at the establishment was with Pearl and their movie star brother-in-law, Blake Thornton. It definitely wasn't a place Diamond frequented regularly. Therefore, it surprised her when one of the owners, Rosaline Marable walked into the plush foyer and greeted her by name.

"Diamond," Roz extended her hand. "Welcome to Marco's."

"Hello Roz," Diamond replied as she shook the woman's hand. "Thank you. I'm supposed to be meeting someone."

"Yes, Grant Hutchison. He's been seated and is waiting for you." She turned to the hostess at the front desk. "I'll seat Ms. Lassiter." Then turned back to her, "Follow me." She opened the double doors, and the island oasis interior captured you the moment you stepped inside. If you wanted an island escape during the mid-day or anytime, this was the place to come. "Your sister-in-law is in my kitchen bugging Marco to try every dish that is ordered." Roz mentioned as she escorted Diamond to the table.

"You can always send her to the table to get her out of your kitchen."

Laughing, Roz stopped as they reached Grant. "I may take you up on that," she stated as she pointed to the seat. "I'll give you two a moment to look at the menu, while I get Cynthia out of my kitchen."

"Thank you," Diamond replied as Roz walked away. Grant had stood and was assisting with her chair. She thanked him then took her seat.

"Thank you for coming," he replied as he retook his seat. "I took the liberty of ordering an appetizer and drink for you. I hope that's acceptable."

Diamond watched as his smile radiated around the room. "Mr. Hutchison you can put the megawatt weapon of yours away. I have six brothers and I know all their stunts." She grinned. "So what drink did you order?"

"I'll put away my weapon if you put those legs under cover. What I would give to measure them from thigh to toe." She sat back and crossed her legs. "I have to say my imagination has been running rampant with the things I could do with them." He held his hand up before she could reply. "However, as much as I would love to tease you a little longer, that's not the reason, we are here—tonight."

His emphasis on the word "tonight" caused Diamond to pause for a second. "Let's be very clear, Mr. Hutchison, this is a business dinner. If this is some kind of come on, you've got the wrong girl and the wrong game.

"Well, Ms. Lassiter, this meeting really is about business, however, I wouldn't be a man if I didn't notice a good pair of legs and a pretty smile. And make no mistake, I'm all man. Okay?" Diamond smiled.

Diamond held his eyes for a moment and sighed. "Okay, so tell me about Regenerations and how I can help."

He sat forward, "Well I think the marketing strategy you used for Davenport Estates would work wonders for Regenerations. It was high tech. The target market was clear and the outreach was sensational. We need that to get Regenerations off the ground. There are a number of investors and the construction company is literally donating their time. We are not anticipating making a dime off of this project. Our payment will be people living in affordable, safe homes. Not to mention limiting the number of vacant buildings along that stretch of Clay Street."

"Have you spoken with developers? You have to remember, it's not just about a few buildings. It's about the creation of a new community, with convenient shopping, day care, recreation for children or teens. That's what makes Davenport Estates unique. It's a total package."

Nodding his head, Grant replied, "We have spoken with a number of developers about designs, however, none that are willing to donate the time and skills to the project."

"Have you spoken with Xavier? He has tons of ideas about community development."

Grant sat back with a confused look, but did not speak his mind. His first priority tonight was to get Diamond onboard the project, then he would deal with the Davenport brothers. "No, I did not get an opportunity to speak with him or his brother Saturday night. I hope to have an opportunity to speak with them at the Business Man of the Year dinner."

Diamond pulled out her cell. "Let's set up a meeting for you to talk with Xavier. He loves projects like this. I'm sure he would be more than willing to help out if he can."

Grant looked up as Diamond sent her message, to see Zackary Davenport, with a woman and a little girl enter the restaurant. He must have had the signals mixed up. The night of the open house he would have sworn it was Zackary that Diamond was involved with. However, she had not mentioned his name not once this evening. It was the youngest brother she was praising.

L

After leaving the doctor's office where the DNA test was taken, Chanté asked about the Center for the Arts. After taking her for a tour of the facilities, she noticed the restaurant across the street and indicated she was hungry. The look on Celeste's face was telling. Something wasn't right. What, he did not want to know, but the least he could do was feed them both. Fortunately, the place did not have a line outside the door. But it was a week night, so he thought they may be able to get a table. They were lucky, a table was available. Maybe he would be able to get to the bottom of why Celeste was there. He knew as well as she that Chanté was not his daughter, but she was up to something and he had to get to the bottom of it before he could open up to Diamond.

"Well ladies, what will it be?" Zack asked as he took his seat.

"What's good?" Chanté beamed as a waitress approached the table.

"Why everything child," the woman smiled brightly as she spoke in a heavy Jamaican accent. "My son is a culinary genius. He can make hot dogs taste like a porter house steak."

Chanté smiled at the woman. "You have a really nice accent. Where are you from?"

"Why Jamaica, of course child. The most beautiful island, with oceans so clear you can see the bottom. Now what would you like to fill that tummy of yours?"

Chanté stole a look at her mother before she replied.

Zack caught the exchange. "Do you like steak?" he asked Chanté "Or are you one of those girls that has to watch her figure?" he teased.

"Heck no, Mr. Davenport." She waved him off. "I can eat a horse right about now."

"Chanté" Celeste chastised her daughter.

"Well now, I don't think we have any horse meat in the house," the waitress laughed.

"Why don't you bring us three of those porter house steaks you mentioned with some sweet potatoes fries and a salad." Zack took the menus and handed them back to the waitress.

"Will do. And what would you like to drink?"

"A big pitcher of sweet tea." Chanté replied grinning.

"Sweet tea it shall be." The waitress walked away from the table.

Zack saw a flash of something in Celeste's eyes he had never seen before and as quick as it appeared it disappeared--shame. But what did she have to be ashamed of? "So, Chanté tell me about your last dance recital."

"Ah man, it was awesome. I am very proud to say that it was my performance that earned me the audition in New York. I just have to get there." She solemnly replied, then quickly perked back up. "But I know if I make it to New York, I'll get the role and then I'll make enough money for Mommy and I to go to Europe."

The waitress placed the pitcher of tea on the table. "One pitcher of sweet tea. I'll check on your steaks." Then she walked away.

"If I had a young daughter as pretty as you, I'm not sure I would let her go to New York or Europe. How does your father feel about that?"

"What's important is Chanté's talent," Celeste interrupted. "I have no idea where she gets it from. You know I have two left feet Zack." She laughed.

"I know no such thing." He gave Celeste a warning glare.

She clearly ignored it, "You should come to see Chanté perform next week at The School of Performing Arts. She has the lead in the production."

"Oh yes, you should come Mr. Davenport. Then you can see for yourself just how talented I am."

"And modest," Zack smiled. He couldn't help it, the child's enthusiasm was contagious.

"I have to believe in myself Mr. Davenport. If I don't, who will?"

"Your parents."

"Yes, you're right. My mom will always believe in me. Right mom?" she shrugged against her mom's shoulder.

"Always." She smiled at her daughter.

"Ooh the food is here." Chanté clapped. "It smells soooo good," she beamed as the plate was set in front of her.

"Dig in," Zack's command did not take long to be obeyed, Chanté had begun eating before the two words were out of his mouth.

"Chanté did you forget your manners. Say grace."

"Oh, I'm sorry Mommy." She bowed her head and quickly said her grace then continued with the meal.

Zack watched as Celeste ate slowly, but clearly wanted to go full force the way Chanté was doing. It wasn't hard for him to come to the conclusion that they had not had a good meal in a minute. "Eat your food Celeste and when you are done, we're going to talk."

Celeste looked up into knowing eyes. It didn't matter. She was going through with her plan. Sensing Zack was about to ask about her husband again she quickly changed the subject. "Zack I'm surprised some lucky woman hasn't snatched you up yet. Why aren't you married with a house filled with children? I know how much you love them."

"The woman I planned to have that house full of children with decided to marry someone else with more money."

Celeste closed her eyes against the words that were clearly meant to hurt, but now was not the time for emotions. She had a goal and she was not leaving until she got what she needed from Zack. "Well, she was a fool and I'm sure she is not afraid to admit that."

"It's no longer important, I've moved on."

She nodded, "I thought I knew with whom, but I see she is having dinner with a very handsome man across the room." Zack turned and was stunned to see Diamond.

"That has all the markings of a romantic date. The wine, the easy banter and the smooth smiles." She shrugged her shoulders. "I guess I was wrong about you and her."

L

The meal was delicious, the wine was divine and the company was wonderful. This was exactly what Diamond needed after the weekend she had experienced. "You have to tell me where the wine is from, it was magnificent."

Grant smiled, "Magnificent. I'll let my brother know. He has a winery outside of Hanover. This is his latest vintage. It is a Marco exclusive."

"You mean you can't get it anywhere else?"

"No. He made this for a woman he fell madly in love with. When things did not work out he stopped making it and sealed the recipe away. He then sold the entire collection to Marco. Very few people know about it and those that do, pay a hefty sum to have a bottle."

"Really?" She gave him a suspicious look. "Are you pulling my leg?"

He shook his head, "Not at all. Scout's honor."

"What happened to the woman?" she asked curiously.

"She left the country. It was too difficult for her to choose between Raphael and her family."

Diamond sat forward, "What about your brother?"

"Hmm, do you believe in the theory that there is only one true love in everyone's life?"

Diamond sighed, "Yes, I do."

"Well, I think Shadi was Raphael's one true love. I don't think he will ever get over her. He still longs for her to this day."

Diamond's mind was now wondering. She believed with every fiber in her body that Zackary was her one true love. Was she condemned to a life of longing like Grant's brother? "How long has it been?"

"About ten years now." Grant noticed as soon as the light conversation mood changed. He also noticed the moment Zackary Davenport turned and recognized Diamond sitting at the table with him. A sudden chill ran down his back as Davenport stared almost in disbelief. The woman sitting at the table with Davenport seemed to take a little joy in pointing out Diamond to Zackary. The action made him immediately dislike the woman. He could not stand catty women. However, he had to push that to the back of his mind as Zackary Davenport made his way over to their table.

"I believe you are about to have a visitor." Grant whispered.

Diamond saw his lips move, but her mind was still on Zackary and Raphael and she did not hear what he said.

"Good evening," Zackary greeted them in a foreboding tone. "Ms. Lassiter may I have a moment?"

Diamond looked up to see Grant standing and for a minute wondered why until she heard Zack's voice. The first look was one of surprise. Was her imagination that strong to conjure him up? But the look on his face was rather intimidating if not hostile. Then he had the nerve to just walk away. What is his problem? She wondered.

"I believe you have been summoned." Grant smirked.

The look of irritation formed quickly. How dare he command her to do anything after the tears she shed over the weekend because of him? She chose to keep her seat. "He'll realize I'm not behind him at some point." She picked up her glass.

Grant saw the moment Zack turned to realize Diamond, whom he expected to be following him was not there. Now, if Grant were an insecure man, he would take this moment to get the hell out of dodge, but he chose to stay to see who would emerge from this battle alive. So he remained standing.

The look on Zack's face was monstrous when he reached the table. "Apparently I did not make myself clear. I want a moment of your time—now!"

Diamond sat there staring up at him wondering if she should just get up or give him a piece of her mind. Who does he think he is talking to like he was somebody's boss. Oh wait, he is her boss. Damn. Well maybe it was time for her to do something about that, too. "Mr. Davenport, have you met Grant Hutchison?"

If looks could kill, Grant would have been massacred where he stood. "Not officially," Grant extended his hand.

Public arena, Zack said to himself. Otherwise he would have knocked that smug look off of Hutchison's face. He reluctantly took the man's hand. "Hutchison."

"It's a pleasure." Grant said knowing he was just pissing Zack off more.

Trying not to be rude, Zack nodded, then turned to Diamond and raised an eyebrow.

The nerve of him, acting like a Neanderthal. The atmosphere around the table snapped with tension.

Zack bent down to the table and whispered, "Don't test me."

Diamond exhaled and stood. "Grant, would you excuse me for a moment. While I'm gone would you order another bottle of that wine." She smiled then deliberately walked around Zack.

Zack took a moment to control his emotions as he watched her hips sway seductively as she walked away. He turned to find Grant watching as well. "You don't ogle another man's property."

"Property? Hmm, I was watching a woman." Grant said as he retook his seat. He grinned at Zack. "You better catch her before she gets away."

Diamond stomped back to the table. "Are you coming?" Diamond gritted through her teeth, then walked off again.

Grant wanted to laugh, but instead he shook his head. "Damn, I like sassy women."

Zack didn't know which way to turn. He wanted to knock the hell out of Hutchison, but he also wanted to know why in the hell was Diamond there with him in the first place. "Do you value your life?" He walked off following Diamond.

"This is going to be interesting," Grant grinned.

Walking to the back of the restaurant, Diamond saw Roz. "Roz, excuse me. Do you have a private room I could use for less than five minutes?"

It was clear to Roz that Diamond was a little heated. Looking over her shoulder, she saw Zackary Davenport strutting toward them fuming. "Yes, of course." She pointed to a door near the restrooms. "You are welcome to use my office." Zack had just reached them. "Hello Mr. Davenport."

"Hello," he growled.

With a roll of her eyes, Diamond opened the door and stormed in. As soon as the door closed Roz heard the raised voices. She turned towards the kitchen and called, "Cynthia."

Diamond turned angrily on Zack. "I can't believe you would behave like that in public. What is wrong with you?"

"What in the hell are you doing here with him?"

"What did it look like? We were talking and having dinner. Like normal people do. Not that it's any of your business."

"Like hell it's not my business! Anything and everything you do is my business!"

"What?" A confused Diamond exclaimed as he towered furiously over her. She told him before, neither his size nor his anger fazed her; she yelled back just as furiously. "How in the hell is what I do any of your business? You made it very clear that you did not want me as a part of your life. Fine! Your wish is granted. You have no rights in my life."

"Like hell. The moment you propositioned me gave me all the rights I need. And you damn well better understand that." His nostrils flared as he stared down at her. How could she be here with another man? He just decided to allow her into his life. How dare she? "And here's something else you better know." He snarled. "I don't share."

"Oh, that's rich. Like you haven't made that abundantly clear over the last week. You don't share your life! You don't share your love! And you damn sure don't share your heart! As a matter of fact, YOU, Zackary Davenport are a selfish, cantankerous, belligerent, ass!"

"Don't tempt me Diamond Renee Lassiter. You know I don't back down when pushed into a corner." He stepped closer pinning her in the corner. "Or do you need a reminder of what happened the last time you tempted me?"

Diamond's mouth gaped open. "You wouldn't dare. We are in a public place." She hesitated for a millisecond then took a step bringing them only a breath away. "You know, if I didn't know better, you are behaving like you're jealous or something."

"You are damn right I'm jealous. You belong to me, Damnit!" He grabbed her by the shoulders then crushed his lips to hers greedily taking the sweetness of her mouth and drinking as if it was the last thing he would ever taste.

Stunned, then captured in his madness, Diamond had no choice but to surrender to his demanding kiss. The fact that they were in a public place escaped her mind. The only thing functioning was her tongue with his, her arms as they slid around his neck, her legs, spreading as the moisture from her inner body saturated her panties. Her brain didn't kick in until the realization that her body was being lifted against the wall, but even that deserted her when she felt his hardness between her legs. Lord help her she wanted him then and there.

Zack had no idea what in the hell was happening to him and he didn't give a damn. The only thing that mattered was touching her. At that moment his very life depended on it. If he didn't get inside of her his body was going to explode. He unzipped his pants, moved her panties aside and plunged deep inside of her. Lord she was so wet. She was so hot. She was so his. The realization struck him to the core. The past was done, this woman whose inner core surrounded him so sweetly was his future.

Their breathing stopped! The air around them crackled. Neither moved, as he held her against the wall. Her legs wrapped tightly around his waist, her arms clinging around his neck. He broke the kiss, willing himself not to move within her. "Diamond," he murmured against her cheek, "We have to stop."

"No," she almost cried out as she tightened her legs around him and squeezed her inner muscles.

He groaned. It felt like heaven. She kissed his throat and suckled there furiously. With his hands cupped around her waist, he lifted her slightly and eased her body down around him. They both groaned at the feel of her velvety inner core and his smooth as steel life line tenderly merging. She cupped the back of his head, holding his forehead to hers. "Do it again," she breathlessly whispered.

He could feel himself growing inside of her at the request. "Diamond," he moaned.

"Diamond," someone called from the hallway. "Are you okay in there?"

Neither of them heard as the door cracked opened.

"Oh." Cynthia looked on. "Wave your hand if you are where you want to be."

Embarrassed at being caught with her legs wrapped around a man, but unable to care at the moment, Diamond slightly flipped her hand. "All righty then. Carry on." Cynthia replied and closed the door.

Zack knew he had to get them under control. He slowly withdrew from her with a moan. He pulled her legs from around his waist and sat her feet on the floor. After smoothing her dress down, he then pushed himself back into his pants. It wasn't until he attempted to zip them did he feel where the zipper had nicked him. He placed his forehead against hers. "I swear I don't know what you do to me," he shook his head back and forth. "But I'm tired of fighting."

"You're driving me crazy Zack. One minute you're making love to me and the next you're angry with me. What do you want from me Zack?" She pulled her arms away from his neck and walked around him.

"Come home with me." She turned to him.

"Is that what this is about--me being here with Grant?"

"No Diamond, it's about you being with any man."

Exasperated, she just shook her head, "You don't want me, but you don't want anyone else to have me either. I have to freshen up and get back to Grant."

Zack glared at her as if she had lost her mind. "You are not leaving here with him."

She wasn't sure if she was angry at him or angrier with herself for wanting to finish what they started. But one thing was certain; she wasn't playing games with him any longer. "What do you want Zack?"

The look of determination in his eyes caused her heart to race more as he approached her. Standing over her, he looked into those deep brown eyes and said what she had been longing to hear. "I want you Diamond." He stroked her cheek with his hand. "I want you."

She closed her eyes and exhaled, "I'm not leaving with Grant because I didn't come with him. This was a business meeting. Not a date."

It took all the control he had not to laugh at that ridiculous statement. Of course it was a date. He saw the way Hutchison was looking at her. "Come home with me."

Stepping away, she shook her head, "I have to finish this meeting." She walked towards the door. "Pearl's out of town. You can come by later." Still not liking the idea of her being with Hutchison, he frowned. She almost laughed at his expression. Then a thought occurred to her. "What are you doing here?"

"It's a long story," he sighed. But then he remembered he was there with Celeste. Damn, the last thing he needed was for Diamond to see that. "How long are you going to be?"

"It's only going to take me a few minutes to wash up."

"Not that. How long are you going to be here with him?"

Zackary Davenport was pouting. She smiled as she wondered if he even knew why he was so angry. But she knew. "Oh, I don't know. We have another bottle of wine to finish." She opened the door and walked out. Let him ponder on that for a while.

Zackary waited a few minutes to allow himself time to literally go down. When he walked out of the office Cynthia Lassiter was waiting in the hallway for him.

"Zackary," she coolly spoke.

"Cynthia." He testily replied.

"It's not my business..."

"No, it's not." He turned to walk away.

"It is Samuel's business." She walked towards him. "So I hope for your sake this is something more than a quickie."

He turned back to her and smirked, "I don't do quickies," then walked off.

By the time he returned to the table, Celeste and Chanté had finished eating and were laughing. "We need to leave." He said, praying he didn't sound anxious.

"Is something wrong?" Celeste mockingly asked.

"Life is wonderful," he sarcastically replied as he looked over his shoulder. As his luck would have it, Diamond had just returned back to the table and was staring right at him. He could see the look of hurt as their eyes held. He wanted to go to her and explain about Celeste, but Chanté called him.

"Did I say something to upset you, Mr. Davenport?"

He turned to the child who had a serious look of concern on her face. "No," he replied. "I just need to get back to the office. What hotel are you staying at?" he looked at Celeste.

Her hesitation irritated him. He was in a rush to get to Diamond before she thought any worse of him. At dinner with one woman and in an office making love to another, hell he would be pissed. "Celeste, what hotel?"

"We can walk from here."

"Was everything all right with your meal?" Cynthia asked as she walked over to the table. The look she gave Zack was evil.

"Dinner was fine," he replied.

Cynthia extended her hand to Celeste, "I'm Cynthia Lassiter and you are?"

Celeste hesitated as she looked from Cynthia to Zack. "Celeste Blanchard."

Cynthia smiled, then turned to the child. "And who are you?"

Chanté curtsied, "Chanté LaSha Blanchard."

"Such poise and grace. You must be a dancer."

"I'm a ballerina." Chanté smiled brightly.

"We were just leaving." Zackary said attempting to get Cynthia on her way.

She ignored him. "You know, my brother was younger than you when he embraced his talents. I certainly hope you are doing the same."

"Is he a dancer too?"

"No, he's an actor."

"Really. I may get to act some when I reach New York."

"Well, you let me know when you do. I'll be sure to tell him to be on the lookout for a beautiful ballerina."

"What's your brother's name? Is he someone I would know? Like has he been in movies and everything?"

Cynthia acted as if she had to think hard about it. "I think he's been in one or two small movies. His name is Blake, Blake Thornton."

"Blake Thornton, the movie star, Blake Thornton?" Celeste questioned.

"Yes," Cynthia replied not feeling the woman at all. She turned back to the child. "Well, Ms. Chanté LaSha Blanchard, I'll be sure and tell him about you."

"Is he here?"

"No, he is actually in New York making a movie right now."

Zack watched as Diamond and Grant were walking out of the restaurant. Grant looked at him and he could feel the man shaking his head at him. He could almost read his mind as Grant opened the door and hesitated before he stepped out. The gesture wasn't lost on Zack. He had left the door open for Hutchison to step in on Diamond.

"We need to leave--now," Zack said to Cynthia.

"You're leaving before dessert?"

He wanted to kill her where she stood. She was deliberately delaying them. "Yes," he snapped.

Chapter 24

$\mathcal{J}$t was after four in the morning by the time Zackary arrived home. He was tired and furious. After leaving the restaurant, he found out Celeste and Chanté were staying at a rundown motel in the wrong part of town. Without asking any questions, he picked up their bags and registered them in a suite at the Marriott located on West Broad Street. He had a few questions for Celeste, but she was secondary. Only one person consumed his mind at the time—Diamond.

She never came home. He sat outside her place for hours waiting for her and she never showed. Hell, he even rang the bell at her neighbor's apartment until they opened the door. He told them he was concerned something may have happened to her. It wasn't a total lie, he was concerned Hutchison may be with her. The thought of going to Hutchison's place crossed his mind, but she might appear while he was gone and he did not want to take that chance. So he sat there in his truck waiting for her to come home—for hours.

Frustrated with himself for letting things go this far, he parked in the driveway and let himself in the back door of the house. Turning off the alarm, he threw his keys on the kitchen counter and walked down the hallway to his office. Not bothering to turn on the lights, he slumped heavily into his chair behind his desk. Laying his head back he closed his eyes. He checked everywhere he could think of for her and couldn't find Diamond anywhere. "Where is she?"

"If the she you are speaking of is Diamond, she's gone."

Zack sat up to the sound of his brother's voice. He reached over and turned on the lamp sitting on his desk. X-man was sitting on the sofa near the fireplace. A weary Zack sighed. "What are you doing here X-man?"

"Waiting for you."

The coolness to his voice was not missed, but whatever had X-man pissed would have to wait. "We can talk in the morning when my mind is clearer." Then it dawned on him what X-man said. He looked up. "Did you say Diamond was gone?"

Xavier glared at him. "That's exactly what I said Zack," he replied in a cool controlled voice.

Panic struck him. "What do you mean she's gone?"

"Gone Zack," some of the control lost as he spoke. "As in Mommy's gone, Daddy's gone—GONE!"

The anger was evident, although to him, X-man still appeared to be his calm reserved brother. "Gone where?"

"She wouldn't say." He replied.

"What the hell do you mean she wouldn't say X-man?" he exploded as he stood up behind his desk. "I've been looking for her for hours. Did you talk to her? What did she say?"

Xavier could see the concern in his brother's eyes. But at the moment he was so pissed at Zack he just didn't give a damn about his concerns. "What happened tonight?"

Frustrated, Zack yelled, "It's not your business. Now where in the hell is she?"

"You see Zack that's where you are wrong." Xavier stood and stormed over to his brother's desk. "This is my business on so many levels. Whatever happened between you and Diamond tonight is going to affect our bottom line at the company."

"I don't give a damn about the company right now. I need to know, where Diamond is."

"Really, well I don't know where she is, but I do know where she will not be tomorrow. She won't be at the office because as of eleven-forty-five last night she turned in her resignation." He threw the paper on the desk in front of Zack.

Zack picked up the paper and read the one line. "She quit."

"That's right Zack, she did. So do you want to explain to me why Davenport Industries has lost an employee that has brought in over 10 million dollars in sales in six months and I've lost a friend?"

Zack just stared at the signature on the paper. Then he looked up at Xavier. "This doesn't say where she is."

For the first time in his life Xavier heard fear in his brother's voice. It cooled his temper a little. "What happened, Zack?"

Zack sat back in the chair still holding the paper. "I hurt her." He replied as he looked back at the paper in his hand.

"You've been doing that for the last few months. What happened last night to cause her to quit?"

Zack closed his eyes as he remembered the look on Diamond's face when she saw him with Celeste. "Celeste."

"Celeste!" Xavier wanted to explode. "Don't tell me you let that woman back into your life." He turned away from his brother, ready to hit something then turned back. "What, is her stuff lined in gold or something? Because it can't possibly be her sterling manipulative personality that has you acting like an ass!"

Zack ran his hand down his face. "It wasn't..." he began then stopped. How in the hell could he explain this. Sitting back he just started at the beginning of the day.

After hearing the events of the evening Xavier was certain they would not get Diamond back. The one thing he knew about his friend was that she was a proud woman who did not allow any man to make a fool out of her. And from what Zack just described to him, he was sure that was what Diamond was thinking. Zack had just played her. He blew out a long sigh as he stared at his brother. "I'm sure you did not set out to seduce Diamond in the office then return to another woman in the restaurant simply because she was there with another man. But in Diamond's eyes that's what she saw." He shook his head, "I have no idea how or if you can fix this. But from where I stand you have two options. You can let Grant have a chance at making her happy or you can find her and crawl on your hands and knees begging for her forgiveness. However, I think right now, finding Diamond should be the least of your concerns."

"Nothing is more important than finding Diamond right now."

"I beg to differ," Joshua stated from the entrance into the office.

Xavier looked from Joshua to Zack. "Normally I would have your back, but on this, I would probably help him kick your ass." He walked towards Joshua as he spoke. "Don't kill him. He's the only family I have."

Joshua continued to stare at Zack, who had not moved from his seat. "You may want to answer the door."

The doorbell sounded, as Xavier just shook his head. "You have some weird friends Zack." He opened the door to allow Samuel inside. "Only one of you can knock him out, not both." Xavier followed Samuel to the office. As much as he would like to, he couldn't leave his brother without some type of back up.

Zack may not have paid Joshua any attention, but when Samuel walked into the room he stood. "I can explain."

"Really! You can explain why I was called by my mother to restrain my father from coming over here to kick your ass. You can explain why my wife has been bitching at me all night about the way you treated my sister. You can explain why I just spent hours consoling my Diamond because of your actions with Celeste! You can explain all of this!" Samuel yelled as his right fist connected with Zackary's jaw.

Joshua and Xavier took a step back from the office and closed the double doors, for they both knew what was coming. They had witnessed it so many times before. "Whose turn is it to win?" Joshua asked Xavier.

"I believe its Zack's turn." He shook his head, "But I don't think he has the strength to even fight Samuel back." He walked towards the kitchen. "You want some coffee?"

They heard the first crash as both of them looked back at the door. "Black," Joshua replied as he pushed Xavier forward. "You don't want any part of that."

About thirty minutes later, the destructive sounds that were coming from the office died down. "Shall we," Joshua said as he rinsed his coffee cup.

"So what happened to Redbone?" Xavier asked about the woman from the story Joshua was telling him.

"I had to dispense some of my magic," Joshua replied as he opened the doors to the office. Sitting on the floor in front of the fireplace in the disheveled room, Zack and Samuel were sharing a bottle of Tequila. Both were bloody all over, but neither seemed seriously hurt.

"I could have killed you." Samuel passed the bottle "I kill people for a living."

"I know you do." Zack took a drink and sighed. "You know I'm in love with her."

"Hell, I know and she loves you. That's the only reason I didn't kill you." Samuel said as he took the bottle from Zack. "So how in the hell are you going to fix this?"

"I need to talk to her to fix it." Zack explained as he touched the bruise around his eye.

Samuel shook his head. "It's not going to happen no time soon."

"You're not going to tell me where she is?"

"Nope."

Zack punched Samuel in the jaw with his left fist.

Samuel didn't flinch. He took a drink then sat the bottle on the floor. "You're not tired yet?"

"Nope," Zachary replied.

Samuel exhaled. "Close the door Joshua. I'm going to whip your ass again just for keeping me away from my wife and the ass kicking I'm going to get when my father finds out I didn't kill you." He stood and grabbed Zack from the floor just as Xavier and Joshua reclosed the door.

"So, I was telling you about Redbone, but did I tell you about her mother," Joshua said as the two walked back towards the kitchen.

L

Ann sat at the breakfast bar waiting for Diamond to appear. She thought it was time to tell her about the person she's been watching on the property. The last thing she wanted was for anything to happen to her friend. It wasn't clear what the person was up to, but someone sneaking around at night like that was definitely up to no good. Her number one priority was to make sure Diamond was aware of the person so she could tell Zack or Reese to add a little more protection on the site.

She liked Diamond. Any person that would feed and leave a door open for a stranger had a good heart. Looking out the kitchen she saw the sun rising and knew it was getting late. Diamond was normally there before seven, but the sun was up and she still wasn't there. A smile graced her face as the thought that Diamond could be with Zackary crossed her mind. Wouldn't that be something? She had been watching those two and could feel the attraction between them. Yep, that Diamond would be a good woman for Zack. That was important to her. She may not have been the best mother, back in the day, but that didn't mean she loved her children any less then the next mother. She just had issues.

But just like any other mother she wanted to see her children happy. And she was certain Diamond could make Zachary very happy. Now the only thing she wanted was to see her youngest son. When she left home, Xavier had been no more than three. He wouldn't even recognize her, but she would know him anywhere. He was the spitting image of his father, bowlegs and all. She smiled. Her husband was a good, hardworking man. He just picked the wrong woman. She had problems long before they married. King didn't care, he loved her anyway and for a while that was enough. But then the children came and she was just overwhelmed. It was too much with King working two jobs, leaving her home with the boys alone. It was just too much. But that's neither here nor there, it's the past, there wasn't anything she could do about it now. With Diamond in Zack's life, now her only wish was to be able to spend time talking to Xavier.

Both of her sons were handsome, successful men. King did a good job with them and Zack, she had to give him credit, did a good job with Xavier. But, she just wanted a chance to talk with him to see what kind of man he was inside. Seeing him out and about was one thing, but you never really get to know a person until you could sit down and have a conversation to see what's on their mind. That's what she longed to do with Xavier, just talk with him.

Hearing the chime on the front door, Ann walked over to the counter, and began to pour a cup of coffee for her friend. "You're late missy. Now, that's not like you. So have a seat and tell me all about it." She froze when she turned to see Xavier walking into the kitchen.

"I'm pretty sure I'm not the person you were expecting." He said as he stood on the other side of the room looking at her. The woman looked as if she was going to faint. He quickly walked over and took the cup of coffee out of her hand and took a sip. "Hmm, you have no idea how much I needed a good cup of coffee this morning." He looked over the rim of the cup as he took another sip and the woman still looked like she had seen a ghost. She looked familiar, but working on no sleep, he wasn't sure if he knew her or not.

Ann could not believe he was standing there. Her baby boy was standing there talking to her. As she continued to stare into his eyes, she saw a bit of sadness there. Was he okay? Did someone hurt him? What was he sad about? Could she help him in any way? Was he in love and some girl broke his heart? There were so many questions she wanted to ask him, but nothing came out. Zack would have a fit if he knew she was there with Xavier. But she understood his need to protect his little brother from her. He had been doing it all his life. Then something dawned on her. "Where is Diamond?" He turned his back, but not before she saw the sadness intensify.

"She is no longer with us." He walked over to the office that was adjacent to the kitchen, then sat the coffee cup on the desk.

Ann frowned, "What do you mean; she's no longer with us? Did something happen to her?"

"Did you have an appointment with her this morning?" He asked, not wanting to share personal information about Diamond with a stranger.

Ann laughed. "Do I look like I can afford one of these houses?"

Xavier looked her over, "Of course you do," he shrugged his shoulder. "We make them affordable."

She smiled at her son, it was clear he did not have a pretentious bone in his body. Then a thought occurred to her. "Did Zackary hurt her again?"

Surprised by the question, he asked. "I'm sorry I didn't get your name."

"I didn't give it." Ann replied.

Xavier almost laughed at the sassy woman, standing there all of 5'5", maybe 110 lbs staring him down. "Well, who are you?" he asked as he tried to open the file cabinet and found it locked.

"A friend," she replied as she walked over to the file cabinet, reached behind it and pulled the key from the hook.

"Thank you," he said as she gave him the key.

"Diamond is not the type to just up and quit. She's too dedicated for that. So either you fired her, which I doubt or Zackary hurt her real bad. Now, if I was a gambling woman, which I'm not, I would put my money on that stubborn Zack."

Xavier was half listening to the woman while he searched for the password to the computer. Ann picked up the jar of marbles then handed him the slip of paper underneath. "Thank you," he said wondering who the woman was. "Do you know the password?"

Ann reached over him, keyed in the user name and password then looked at him. "Where is she? What did he do? Did he do something with the snotty-toddy that was here the other day?"

"Who are you?" Xavier just stared at the woman.

"I told you, I'm a friend of Diamond's. Now, if you tell me what you are looking for I could probably tell you what you need to know."

"I need to know if she had any appointments today and if so with whom."

"No, because she sold all the lots last week, with the exception of the one Zack said he wanted for himself. I actually thought the fool was planning on building a home for him and Diamond, but I guess I was wrong."

"I don't know." Xavier ran his hand down his face. "I hope he can straighten things out with her. But for now, I have to pull double duty."

"Oh, I can look out for the place for you." She pulled a folder from the middle desk drawer causing Xavier to move back. "This is the folder that contains the potential buyers for the Towers. She normally makes calls in the mornings, then reviews financial reports in the afternoon. On Wednesdays she meets with or touches base with the media to make sure Davenport Estates stays in the forefront of their minds. What else do you want to know?"

Xavier was stunned how much this woman knew about the business. "Do you want a job?"

"Son, I haven't worked in twenty years. And ain't starting now. But if you need me to look after the place, I will until you sell it. But I want something in return."

"Name it," Xavier quickly stated.

"It ain't that simple."

"Try me."

"Stay and talk with me for an hour. Tell me about your life and how you're doing."

"Me? You want to know about me."

"Yeah."

Identical eyes held each other's stare. "I'll do it on one condition. Tell me your name."

"Okay, Friend."

Xavier looked at her, and then burst out laughing. It was clear she was not going to tell him her name. "Okay— Friend, I'll hang out with you for a while. To be honest I can use a good laugh or two right about now."

L

Now that the plans were clearly defined, it was easy to rest. Watching Davenport with that woman and child stripped the last bit of remorse that may have slipped in. Hell, he even moved them into a five star hotel. That was the last straw. There was now nothing left. No reason not to carry out the plan. Just remembering all the times in the past, Zackary Davenport was on top, stirred the longing to see him fall from grace. Once this was done it would be easy to return to my normal life knowing it was me that brought him to his knees. With eyes closed and smile in place, sleep came easy.

Chapter 25

*J*oshua's home was always an oasis in Diamond's opinion. The single level, four bedroom, three bath home, was nestled away on four acres of land in Fredericksburg, Virginia. Only forty-five minutes from Richmond or Washington, DC. Views of the river could be seen from many of the rooms in the home. There was always a calming effect whenever the family visited. She thought this was exactly what Joshua needed in a home. A place like this could very well offset his high-strung nature.

Unfortunately, the calming water views, the twenty-seat state of the art theater room, the indoor heated pool, not even the one-hundred and twenty pound Chow Rottweiler mix, lovable pooch Commando could ease the hurt she was experiencing. Nothing she did would clear her mind of Zackary. It was now Wednesday and she was just tired of crying. At this point it seemed she was just pathetic with the tears. Poor Ms. Lucy, Joshua's housekeeper was beside herself with worry. Even Commando had learned to read the signs of tears about to break through. He would move from his place of lying with his head in her lap, to the table to pick up the tissues, then trotted back over to the window seat where she sat with her books.

"You need to stop reading those sappy love stories." Ms. Lucy huffed as she brought in another cup of tea for Diamond. It was nothing for her to be awakened at all hours of the night with the hours Joshua kept. But on this night it wasn't Joshua, but Samuel and Diamond coming through the door. Normally, it would be a joy to see Joshua's family, but in this instance it was torture. "If you don't eat something today, I'm calling your mother. And I mean it." She turned her petite five-three, maybe one hundred ten pounds wet body, and yelled as she walked away. "You turned my man-eater into a sappy hound! I'm bringing food back and you are going to eat!"

Commando looked up at her with angry eyes, as if he knew what Ms. Lucy had just called him. "She didn't mean it. She knows you're not sappy." Diamond rubbed under his chin. Commando in turn, licked her cheek. A tear dropped on his nose and he audibly sighed and placed his head back in her lap. "I have to get out of this house." She stood as she wiped yet another tear away. "Let's go for a run boy." Commando jumped right up, ready. "I'll go change my clothes."

Fifteen minutes later, Diamond and Commando were running along the riverbank. They began with a slow jog, then increased to a brisk run. It appeared to Diamond that Commando was used to the exercise and apparently the trail. About twenty minutes into the run, Diamond decided to cut through the woods to return back to the house. As she ran between trees, Commando would bump against her also causing her to lose her footing. "Hey, you want to share this trail buddy," she joked with the dog. He looked up at her and barked as he blocked her yet again. "What is wrong with you Commando, move over." The dog barked again as she ran by him. Commando ran in front of her again, but this time she jumped over him. The moment her foot touched the ground, Commando jumped on top of her covering her entire body. He placed his big paws over her face and tucked his head on top of hers. "What the hell....." before she could get the words out of her mouth, an explosion rocketed through the air. She could hear something wiz over her head for several minutes after the explosion. Commando's weight did not allow her any movement. Once things died down Commando shifted his weight off of her and sat on his hind legs waiting for her to move. Diamond slowly sat up, shaken at what had happened. Commando had an expression of irritation on his face, but then a second later he leaned over and licked her arm, then her face. He walked around as if he were surveying the area then sat back down with one paw on her leg as if to hold her in place. Diamond looked around to see a gaping hole where trees were a moment ago. Funny but there was no smoke or fire. She looked at Commando, "Are you okay boy?" She rubbed his head and over his body. She could have sworn she saw him roll his eyes and heard him groan. A few minutes later an SUV pulled up and Ms. Lucy stepped out. She had a handheld device with her. "Stay still until I get to you." She pushed a button and the wooded area seemed to light up. She pushed another button and the lights went out. With hands on hips, Ms. Lucy just stared at her sitting on the ground. "So now you're trying to kill yourself." She shook her head. "I don't know this Zackary character, but he can't be worth all of that. You can get up now." Commando moved his paws and waited for Diamond to stand. As she did she wiped the dirt from the jogging pants and looked at Ms. Lucy. "What in the hell happened?"

"You ran into a mine field. Didn't Commando try to stop you?"

She looked at Commando, who was now walking towards Ms. Lucy as he looked back over his shoulder at her. "I thought he was just clumsy when he kept running into me." She swore, Commando snapped his head back at her and barked. For a moment, she wondered if she offended him. "Why does Joshua have a mine field around his house? Isn't that something they do in enemy territory?"

Ms. Lucy turned and walked back to the SUV. "Nothing for you to worry your little head about. Come on. I'll give you a ride back to the house before you blow yourself up and me along with you." Once they were inside the SUV, Ms. Lucy pushed another button. The woods lit up again, and then seconds later the lights dimmed. She turned to look at Commando, who was lying on the back seat. Diamond knew not to ignore his actions again.

"It's good to be in your company when you're not full of tears. Glad something brought you back to life."

Diamond dropped her head, then turned back to the view of the water and sighed. "Love hurts. It's not supposed to be that way."

"Well now, that depends on the stage of love you are in."

Diamond turned to Ms. Lucy. "There are no stages of love. You either love someone or you don't. In my case, I love him, he don't."

"How do you know he don't?" Diamond began to reply, but Ms. Lucy waved her off. "Don't answer that, just listen. You are young. This is probably the first time you've ever been in love. Now, it could be that this Zack person isn't the one you are supposed to love all your life. He may just be the one to teach you about love. Or he very well could be the one. Only time will tell. Either way, this thing that's going on with you and him will only make you stronger. If it's him you supposed to be with, this will help the two of you to appreciate what you have and not take it for granted. If he ain't the one, then this will teach you what not to do or look for in the one that's waiting for you." She pulled up into the six car garage. "Now listen to me. You take whatever time you need to moan through what you think you have lost. Then you get yourself together, get back on the horse and find the man you are supposed to be with. If it's him, God will make a way for you to be together. You do believe in God don't you?"

"Of course."

"Then stop wasting life worried over something you can't do anything about. Live and let God." She said as she got out of the vehicle. "You either accept what he told you happened or let him go."

"He didn't tell me what happened."

Ms. Lucy stopped and looked at her before entering the house. "Well why the hell not?"

"I was so hurt; I just left and came here." Diamond said as she walked right into Ms. Lucy. She stepped back and saw the incredulous look on Ms. Lucy's face.

"You mean to tell me you haven't given the boy an opportunity to explain whatever happened?"

Diamond frowned, "No."

"You been here crying for two days and you don't even know what you are crying for?" Lucy turned to walk into the house. "Now girl, that's just dumb. I never took you for a dumb one. Thought you had better stock than that." She fussed as she pulled the covering off of homemade vegetable soup she had made. "Nope, never took you for a quitter either." She said as she pulled the bread from the oven. "Sit down and eat." She demanded as she continued to scold Diamond. "I know your mother did not teach you to run from your troubles. I know the kind of men she raised and I can't believe her daughters weren't taught to fight for what they wanted instead of tucking your tail and running away."

Diamond looked at Commando who lay down in the corner of the kitchen and placed both paws over his ears. She almost burst out laughing as a chuckle escaped. Lucy looked over at Commando, then at Diamond. "He thinks he is a comedian." She smiled at Diamond as she placed a bowl of soup and hot biscuits in front of her. "Tell me about this Zackary and I'll tell you if he is worth all these tears you've shed for the last two days."

L

The guilt riding him was more than he could take. Wednesday morning, Zack decided it was time for him to face the music so to speak. Without knowing where

Diamond was he couldn't apologize to her for what she thought happened, but he could certainly alleviate the guilt. Getting out of his truck a strange feeling came over him, the same one he'd had when he got in at the house. It was as if something was missing, or out of place. He just chalked it up to the thought of losing Diamond. It was just strange to have the feeling occur again, he thought as he knocked on the front door of the Lassiter's home. There was no answer. He looked at his watch. It was a little after nine, so he knocked again.

"Good morning Zackary," Sally said from the side yard of the house. She stood there with plants in her hand, in a pair of cutoff jeans and a t-shirt. She could have been easily mistaken for one of her daughters. "You must have a death wish." She shook her head. "I wouldn't knock on that door again if I were you."

"Good morning Mrs. Lassiter," Zack stepped down from the front porch and walked around the house to where she stood. "I was looking for your husband."

Sally laughed, "No you're not Zackary. Joe is the last person you want to see." She tilted her head to the side, "But I see the boys have already paid you a visit."

Zack touched his eye that Samuel had blackened. "Yes ma'am they did."

"You look about as sad as Diamond." She turned toward the back yard. "Come on back. I'll fix you a cup of coffee, while you cry your heart out to me."

He followed her through the side gate into the back yard. There was a flower garden on the left side of the yard, in the middle was a brick walk way leading to a huge gazebo in the back end of the yard. To the right was a large vegetable garden, with tomatoes ripe on the vine. Near the back of the house was a screened in porch with wicker furniture spread from one end to the next in various positions. He pointed to the gazebo as they entered the screened in porch. "I don't remember that being there."

"You haven't been here since you were in high school. Sammy had that built a few years back." She sat the plant in her hand on the table, and removed her gardening gloves. "Have a seat; I'll get us some coffee."

Zack enjoyed the tranquility of the yard. It was the first time in days he felt as if he could breathe. The last three days he felt lost, trapped, unable to think clearly. Here, he didn't feel like hitting anything, or lashing out, he felt content.

Sally walked back out to the porch with a tray containing a pitcher of coffee and two cups with a variety of Danish tarts. Zack stood and took the tray from her. "Thank you Zack."

He sat the tray on the table as she took a seat. Sitting back down he said, "I can't believe how relaxed I feel here."

She smiled, "Well, enjoy the feeling. As soon as Joe wakes up that contentment will disappear, I promise you."

"He's that upset with me?"

"On yeah," she replied as she poured him a cup of coffee. "It's difficult not to be upset with the man that caused his daughter to crawl up in his lap the way she hasn't done in years and cry her heart out." She passed him a saucer with an apple, cherry and pineapple danish on it. "For that daughter to be Diamond," she tilted her head, "that just made it harder."

Zack picked up the coffee and sipped. "It was not intentional, nor was it what Diamond thinks she saw."

"She didn't see you at the restaurant with another woman, after you were about to make love to her in Roz's office?"

"Yes and no." He replied, he sat the cup down. Shaking his head, "I've been wasting time. For months I've been running away from Diamond and just when I realize I love her, she's now running away from me."

"If you love her, why were you out with another woman?"

"The woman was my ex-fiancé. She was here with her daughter claiming the child might be mine. I know she's not, but I had a DNA test done to make that a legal confirmation, not an assumption. We stopped at the restaurant to have dinner afterwards, and Diamond was there with another man." He shook his head, "I was blinded with the thought of her being with someone else. As with any time Diamond and I are in the same room, emotions exploded. One thing led to another and within seconds thoughts of Celeste and Chanté just slipped my mind. Diamond consumed my every thought."

"That's when Cynthia interrupted you?"

"Yes. I won't lie to you Mrs. Lassiter, if Cynthia had not walked into that office I would have made love to your daughter right then and there. It didn't matter where we were."

"So," she sat back in her chair. "How are you going to fix this?"

"First, I'm going to apologize to you and Mr. Lassiter for causing this type of distress on your family. Then I'm going to wait until Diamond comes home. I'm going to explain to her what happened and then I'm going to beg her forgiveness for being so stupid all these months."

"What if she doesn't come home?"

"She'll come home," he replied as he picked up an apple danish.

"How do you know?"

"Because she loves me, and I believe deep down she knows I love her too." He looked at Sally, "Why aren't you mad at me like your husband?"

Sally shrugged her shoulder as she picked up her cup. "Because I know you love her and she loves you. That by itself is enough to get you through this little misunderstanding."

Joe walked out onto the porch. Zack immediately stood. "Sit down Zack, I'm too tired to kill you today." He kissed his wife, then pulled out a chair. He was only into two hours of sleep, from working the midnight shift at the post office when his wife woke him up to tell him Zack was downstairs. His legs were so long, they touched Zack's who was sitting at the far end of the table. "Any man that has sex in public with my daughters' damn well better be ready to marry them. You ready to marry Diamond?"

Zack wasn't a man to be easily intimidated. Neither Joe's size nor his many sons were going to force him to do something he didn't want to do. "Yes sir, I am." He pulled out a blue velvet box and placed it on the table. "As soon as you accept my apology and give me your permission to marry her."

L

The visit with Joe and Sally went better than he expected. Zack was sure Joe was going to injure him for hurting his daughter, but he didn't. They took a walk and talked about Diamond and their future, but neither of them revealed where she was. "You just have to wait until she is ready to come back to you Zack" Joe said. "Once she comes back, she'll be back for good."

There was no choice but to trust that they knew what they were talking about. Pulling into the garage at the building, the eerie feeling consumed him again. Getting out, he looked around the truck, but nothing seemed to be out of place. Locking the truck, he strolled inside to the lobby. There he saw LaFonde manning the receptionist desk. "Everything good here?" he asked her.

"No, things are a little out of order. But it gets that way when two principle parties are missing from the boardroom. Diamond is MIA, nowhere to be found, Xavier is trying to cover things, Julia is out on maternity leave, and you...well I don't know what's going on with you. That leaves Charles in charge and you know how anal he can be."

"Why are you at the receptionist desk?"

"With Diamond gone, Charles doesn't feel that I have anything to do. So he released the temp we had working the front desk and placed me here."

"Xavier let him?" he asked, confused with the turn of events.

"Xavier hasn't been here. He's been handling Diamond's appointments at the Tower."

"Who's at the model home?"

"I have no idea."

"Call Terry from the mail room to handle the front desk, then meet me in my office." He walked towards the elevator.

"Have you talked to her?" LaFonde asked with a raised eyebrow.

"No." he said as he boarded the elevator.

"Well why the hell not?" he heard her yell.

JoEllen met him as she stepped off the elevator. "It doesn't look so bad," she said as she looked at his eye. "I would have done worse."

"Thanks for the warm welcome JoEllen. What in the hell is going on around here?"

"You tell me," JoEllen replied as she followed him into his office. "For some reason with you and Xavier gone, Charles believes he is in charge. He's even threatened to withhold paychecks if people did not comply with his wishes."

"Get him on the phone." He said as he sat behind his desk. "Before you go, has Doctor Rhymes called?"

"No," she replied from the doorway.

"Get him on the phone first, then call Charles."

"Celeste Blanchard has called several times. Would you like for me to return her call also?"

"Not until after I speak with Rhymes." He pulled his cell phone out as she walked out of the office. "X-man, where are you?"

The voice on the phone sounded like his brother had returned back to his senses. "At the tower. Diamond had back to back showings scheduled this week."

"Who's handling the model?"

"A friend," Xavier replied smiling.

"Did you give Charles authority to move resources and or personnel?"

"Of course not. Charles can be a bit anal at times."

"So I've been told. Do we need to send LaFonde to the model until Diamond returns?"

"Did you talk to Diamond?," the anxiousness was clear in his voice.

"No."

The enthusiasm dropped. "Zack you have to get her back. These people are asking for her. Three of them said they will return to sign contracts as soon as Diamond returns. This is clearly not my area of expertise. I design things, I don't sell them. We need her back!"

"No more than I do," Zack replied. "I'm working on it X-man, I'm working on it. What about LaFonde?" he asked as he motioned her into his office.

"Yes, we can reassign her, for now. But we need Diamond."

"I hear you." He disconnected the call. "LaFonde, you will be taking over the model until Diamond returns. Then you will resume your normal duties. There will be a bonus in your paycheck for the reassignment."

"Did you clear that with Charles?"

"I don't have to clear anything with Charles."

"I beg to differ, Zackary," Charles stated as he walked into the office. "With Xavier temporarily out of the office, as Chief Financial Officer, that leaves me to make decisions around here."

Zack raised an eyebrow when Charles took a seat without being asked. "That will be all LaFonde." She left without saying another word.

JoEllen stepped in, "Dr. Rhymes is on line one." She then closed the office door.

He picked up the phone. "Dr. Rhymes are those results in?"

"Yes, you are not the father. Would you like for my office to contact the other party?"

"No. I'll handle that. Would you send that paper work over by secure carrier?"

"Will do."

Zack hung up the telephone, then glared at Charles. "The name of this company is Davenport Industries. The last time I checked your last name wasn't Davenport."

"Now look here Zack. You're line of control ends at the site. Here in the office it's Xavier. I'm next in line."

"Would you like to be next in the unemployment line?"

"I have a contract Zack. You may have been the man in high school, but here in the business world, my word is gold. That's why Xavier hired me."

Zack had to take a minute to compose himself. When did Charles become a cocky son of a bitch? He was sitting in the chair in front of Zack's desk with his legs crossed like he was really in control. Zack stood, walked around to the front of his desk, crossed his arms over his chest and stared down at Charles. "Did I miss something?"

Charles stood, pretended to knock a piece of lint off his lapel. "You haven't yet...but you will soon," he grinned as he walked to the door. "You will soon."

Puzzled by Charles' behavior, Zack pulled out his cell to dial Reese. "You have any idea what's up with Charles?"

"I planned to call you to ask you the same question. He released me from my security duties yesterday. He said it was financially feasible to have security on site now that most of the homes were sold."

"What?" Zack put his hand over the phone. "JoEllen, get Julia on the phone now!"

"What's going on Zack?"

"I have no idea. But I just had the weirdest conversation with Charles."

"Julia on line two, Zack," JoEllen stated as she walked into the office.

"Hold on Reese, I'm putting you on speaker. Julia you there?"

"I'm here and it's already been handled."

"What's been handled?"

"A month or two ago I received a call from one of the trustees at the bank. He suspected some transactions had not been approved by Davenport Board of Directors because they came with only one signature."

"Charles?" Reese inquired.

"Right. I advised him to proceed as if the transactions were processed and to copy me on any additional requests. I called in a friend from Raines Investigations and we've tracked every request. Charles believes he has embezzled a few million from the company and we are on the verge of bankruptcy. He released several employees from the company without cause. I've contacted all of them and asked them to lay low until they hear back from me. They are all still receiving a paycheck from a reserved fund I had established at the bank."

"JoEllen get X-man on the phone. Reese get over here!" Zack demanded. "Julia, why are we just hearing about this?"

"We believe Charles has something else planned. We have a man on him. He's going to show his hand."

"This hand is costing us a few million. I don't need to see another hand!"

"Yes Zack, we do. It ensures a conviction when he is caught red-handed. I was hired to protect this company and I'm pretty damn good. Let me do my job."

"You're on maternity leave! Hell we need you here."

"You're on idiot leave, but that doesn't diminish your ability to do your job!"

JoEllen laughed out loud and Zack couldn't help but chuckle. "Okay you got me on that one. Have you told Xavier anything about this?"

"No details. I did tell him that something was amiss. You know what he said?"

"Handle your business." Zack and JoEllen said at the same time.

"That's right. He didn't question me or insinuate I couldn't do my job because I was on maternity leave."

Zack sighed. "I apologize for the comment. But we're talking millions of dollars Julia."

"This affects our profit share and our retirement fund. I know Zack. I'm handling it."

Reese walked in the door as soon as Zack hung up the telephone with Julia. JoEllen had not been able to reach Xavier. "His phone went to voicemail." She told Zack.

"Is it possible Charles may be connected to the fires? Is he trying to destroy the company and why?" Reese questioned.

"He said something about Zack being the big man in high school. Did you bully him or something?" JoEllen asked.

"No," Zack replied. "I barely knew him in high school."

"He was a bookworm in high school," Reese added. "Never really fitting in anywhere, from what I remember."

"Richard asked me if I had any enemies from the past, but I never thought of Charles as an enemy. Hell I never thought of him at all."

"That's the problem Zackary. You never think of anyone but yourself and Xavier." Celeste said from the doorway. "I've been calling you non-stop for days and you haven't once returned my phone calls."

Zack turned to the door. "Now is not a good time Celeste."

"Is there ever a good time with you Zack? It wasn't a good time back in college when you just left me with no one to turn to and nowhere to go. This time you left me and Chanté with not one word in two days."

"You're under the misconception that I owe you something Celeste. It was you that left me knowing I had responsibilities that I couldn't turn my back on. It was you who decided to sleep around until you got the next NFL contract player. It was you that decided to marry Teddy even though you were pregnant with somebody else's child. So let me stop you before you make a bigger fool out of yourself." He looked at JoEllen and Reese and they both stepped out of the room. "Where is Chanté?"

"Why? Do you care?"

"About Chanté—yes, about you not one damn bit." He sat behind his desk. "Look, it's been a rough few days. I do plan to meet with you. Right now is just not a good time."

"Because of Diamond Lassiter." She sneered bitterly. "You would choose that woman over your daughter?"

Zack sighed. "You and I both know Chanté is not my daughter. I got the results today. But you knew that before you even came here. Why did you come, Celeste? After all these years, why now? What could you possibly gain from all of this?"

"Seeing you suffer for at least a few days like I have suffered for years!" she snapped. "And it's not over Zackary. Not by a long shot. I will see you crawl before this is over with." She turned and walked out of the door.

JoEllen stood in the doorway, "Is Mercury in retrograde or something. All hell seems to be breaking lose around here."

Zack had no idea what JoEllen was referring to about Mercury but he knew that he seemed to be in a backward motion and he was really beginning to feel the effects of these eventful days.

Chapter 26

Celeste was stepping off the elevator when she saw Diamond walk into the ladies room on the lobby level. She appeared to be distracted and a little upset. What a perfect opportunity. She turned and walked into the ladies room.

"Well, good evening Ms. Lassiter. Working late?"

Diamond turned to see the one person she could really do without. After speaking with Lucy, she decided it was time to face life. She never ran away from her problems or put them on anyone else's shoulder. When she had issues she would deal with them and move on or take the issue up with her family. The woman of the last few days was not her. After all, like Lucy said, if she really loved Zackary the way she claimed, she couldn't run away from it. Wherever she was or whoever she was with, the love for Zack would still be there. Looking past her reflection in the mirror as she washed her hands, she replied to Celeste. "Good evening."

Noticing the shadows around Diamond's eyes, Celeste dug in. "You don't appear to be at your best this evening, is something wrong?"

"I really don't have time for conversation Ms. Blanchard. Would you mind moving out of my way?"

Standing in front of the door with her arms across her chest, Celeste smiled. "Were you on your way to see Zackary? I just left him upstairs. We had a ...brief office meeting," she smirked while touching her lips as if she had just had a tasty meal.

"Really, I hope you enjoyed it." She attempted to step around the woman, but Celeste pushed her away.

"I don't think I'm finished talking to you just yet."

"Whoa, losing your cool. What's wrong? Things are not going your way? I would think you would be happy. You accomplished what you came to do, make Zackary's life miserable—again. For whatever reason you could not stand the thought of him being happy."

"Why should I." Celeste snapped. "He ruined my life when he turned his back on the NFL. We could have had it all, but he wanted to play daddy to his little brother. No, I don't want to see him happy. I want him to suffer like he has made me suffer. I loved that man and he turned his back on me."

Unable to take another minute of the woman or the hurt she had caused, Diamond pushed her against the door and got dead in her face. "You loved him. Bull! You loved him so much you aborted his child and lied to him about it. You loved him so much you left him at the very time he needed you the most. You loved him so much you hurt him so deep that he never wanted to love again. It's women like you that make a good man turn bad. If that is what love is about I don't want no parts of it. Now get the hell out of my way."

Celeste was so blinded by anger because Zack had not done what she needed from him, that she missed the warning signs in Diamond's eyes. "Oh please, Zack could never love you over me. Look in the mirror", she pushed Diamond backwards toward the mirror. "You don't have anything on me."

Diamond jumped right back at her. "You are gorgeous, that's real. But baby, beauty is only skin deep, but ugly—now that's to the bone. I'll take my average looks over your ugly ass soul any day."

"The question is, will Zack?"

"Apparently not, but that's okay. I'm tired of crying over him and don't give a damn about you. Have a nice life." Diamond held her head high and attempted to walk around the woman—again, but Celeste blocked her way. She snatched Celeste by the hair with one hand and threw her to the floor. Standing over the woman on the floor she spoke softly. "I'm a damn Lassiter. We don't take prisoners, we kill them." She paused for emphasis. "Don't make me hurt you." She stared at Celeste a moment longer then stormed out of the ladies room.

Now, she was really ready to give Zackary Davenport a piece of her mind! As she reached the elevator someone called her name.

"Diamond, it's about time you came back."

"I'm not back," she stated to Xavier as she stormed towards the elevator.

"Like hell you're not," he exclaimed as he joined her. "All hell is breaking loose around here. Have you spoken to Zack?"

"No."

"Julia?"

"No."

"LaFonde?"

"No."

Puzzled he stared at her, "Then why are you here?"

"To kill your brother!"

"Hell, you may have to get in line for that."

"Why all the questions? What's going on?"

They could hear the bellow when the elevator door opened. "I don't know all the details. But we are both about to find out."

"I can hear not much has changed in the last few days," Diamond said as she walked in the office. "You really ought to think about putting in sound proof walls or something in this office."

"Diamond," the whispered name escaped as Zack's head snapped up. He stood.

"You stay right over there Zackary Davenport. Don't you come near me. And if that woman, ever comes within fifty feet of me I'm going to finish what she started downstairs."

Ignoring her request Zack walked towards her. "Diamond, you can kill her for all I care."

Diamond stood behind Xavier, but moved towards Reese as Zack continued to walk towards her. Normally she would stand her ground with him, but there was something in his eyes that indicated danger. "I will kill her the next time she jumps in my face. What the hell is up with you and her anyway."

"Nothing," Zack spoke softly as he followed her movement around the room. "I know what it looked like, but that's not what it was."

She spoke, but her voice was not as intense as before, "It looked like you were trying to have your cake and eat it too. Do you know how I felt when I saw you with her right after taking me in the office? Do you have any idea how confused I was before that even happened, then to see you leave me and walk into her arms. It was too much."

"I know," he continued to speak softly, "But I never walked into her arms. Your legs are the only thing I want around me."

She stopped behind JoEllen. He wasn't supposed to say that. All eyes, JoEllen, Reese and Xavier traveled between Zack and Diamond.

He stopped in front of JoEllen as he held her eyes. "I know I was supposed to teach you, but as it turned out, you taught me Diamond." His lips curved at the end, but Diamond didn't see it. Her eyes were riveted by what was in his. "I don't know when it happened or how. I just know I don't want to spend another day of my life without you." JoEllen smiled and stepped from between them. Zack took a step forward closing the distance between them. He cupped her face between his hands, "Your smile with those deep dimples breathes life into my veins. For the life of me I don't know why I kept trying to push you away." He gently kissed her lips. "I'm so sorry for all the harsh words and forever making you doubt choosing me. Will you forgive me Diamond? I'm willing to get on my knees and beg if you ask me to."

The room was silent, then suddenly Xavier and Reese spoke at the same time. "Beg."

Then JoEllen nodded her head. "Yep, make him beg."

Diamond's hands covered his as she held his gaze. "Did my daddy beat you up?" She whimpered as she touched his eye.

"No, he didn't."

"Did Joshua?"

"No, Joshua didn't beat me up either."

"Then who did?"

"Samuel," Xavier stated from where he had now taken a seat.

Zack shoulders slumped as he exhaled, "Samuel did not beat me up. We just had an intense conversation."

"Like the one I just had with Celeste? What was she doing here anyway?" Diamond asked as she slightly pulled away from Zack.

He held her close, not letting her out of his grasp. "Declaring her hatred for me." Zack replied.

"As a number of people seem to be doing today," JoEllen added.

Diamond looked around Zack. "What are you talking about?"

"That's what I was trying to tell you about on the elevator. It seems Zack has a few enemies coming from the woodworks."

Diamond looked at Zack. "What are they talking about?"

He took her hand, took his seat behind the desk and sat her in his lap. "We all need to talk about some events that have us a little concerned." Zack first told them all about

Charles and all Julia had shared with him. He then told them about Celeste and the paternity test. Last he told all of them about the fires and what had happened since the last investigation.

"You're forgetting something Zack." Xavier said. "Did you forget about the woman that's been watching the house?"

Zack had not forgotten, for he knew that probably had nothing to do with the other situations. He was sure the woman watching the house was his mother. "No, we'll discuss that later. For now we need to determine what we are going to do about Charles."

"What do you mean what are we going to do. We should fire his ass," Xavier said.

"No." Reese replied. "I think Julia is right. Let Charles play out his hand. When we take him down, let's get him for everything. In fact Xavier, I think you should place a call to him, thanking him for handling things while you've been away. Tell him you will be out a few more days, so you will appreciate it if he continues handling things."

"Why in the hell would I want to do that? He's got to know Zack is ready to kill him after the way he spoke to him today."

"I have to agree with Xavier. He knows Zack will be after him." JoEllen added.

"Well, Zack could always call and apologize for his behavior towards Charles." Diamond offered.

"No, he cannot," Zack replied. "He will know something is up then."

"Why?" Diamond questioned.

"Because I don't apologize to anyone for anything."

"That's not true. You just apologized to me."

"And I don't think I've received my just reward for that." He smiled at her.

"If you come home with me tonight I may be able to remedy that."

"Excuse me," Reese interrupted the two, "focus—here," he motioned to Zack. "We want Charles comfortable enough to continue with his plans. I think an apology from Zack will not get us anywhere. However, If Xavier could convince him not to worry about Zack, he'll feel secure, safe to continue."

The room was quiet as everyone contemplated the idea. "Are we sure Julia has the accounts on lockdown?" Xavier asked.

"I spoke with Nate Raines," Reese stated, "the investigator she is working with. I know him from the precinct. He's good. According to him the accounts are locked down and the bank investigators are watching the case as well."

Xavier pulled out his cell phone. "Charles, I'm glad I caught you." He nodded to the people in the room. "I know this is not fair to you, but I need you to continue to hold things down at the office. I'll have to handle The Towers for a few more days." He listened for a minute. "Don't worry about Zack. He knows construction not business. That's why I need you to handle the office."

Joshua picked up the figure again. After a few days of following the person he knew whatever was happening was connected to the site, not Ann. Evidence showed she was staying at the site. The person following her was just making sure she was not going to interfere in whatever plans they had. Ann was no longer Joshua's concern. He would report back to Zack on Ann's whereabouts once he was able to determine what this mystery person was up to.

L

Not seeing anyone about, the figure slipped into the model home through the patio door that was left unlocked for the woman. Unfamiliar with the layout, the figure was happy the soft recess lights were on throughout the house. Looking around, the figure was trying to determine where to place the case so it would not be detected. Going to the second level of the house, there was a closet right above the staircase. Opening the closet all the electrical and security panels were located inside. Perfect! Damage at that spot would extend from the top floor to the lower level. Once the explosive device was placed inside the panel, a push of a button at the right time would bring the house down and Zackary Davenport along with it.

Chapter 27

*D*iamond walked into her apartment with the overnight bag she had taken to Joshua's on her shoulder. She dropped it to the floor as she turned to the man who had followed her in. He lifted her body from the floor, wrapped her legs around his waist and leaned against the wall next to the door. "I believe this is where we were interrupted a few days ago." Pushing his body to hers, he kissed her with the security of a man that had come home. This was where he was supposed to be. Right here, between her legs, but more importantly, in her heart as much as she was in his. His tongue took a slow sensuous journey, exploring every luscious corner of her mouth. Clearly his intent was to never let her forget who that mouth belonged to. The plan was to do that with every inch of her body.

Pulling the cool white t-shirt from her body, he broke contact with her lips just long enough to pull it over her head. Capturing her lips again, he unsnapped the bra which hid her golden treasures from him. Only then did he leave her wet, kiss swollen lips to capture the brown peak between his teeth, just grazing, slightly licking, one then the other until he settled on his favorite. He stayed on that right breast, because it fit so perfectly in his mouth, sucking until he heard her moan, only then did he switched to the other, increasing her need to have him inside of her. "Zachary," he heard her cry out as she tightened her legs around his swollen arousal securing him intimately with her center.

"Diamond," he whispered before returning to her lips. "Bed?" he questioned between his now frenzied kisses. She pointed and he followed as best he could without breaking their connection. When he reached one bedroom, she spread her hands out stopping their entrance by bracing the side of both doors. "Pearl's room," she shook her head. He turned and she giggled as he nuzzled between her breasts.

Together, they dropped down to the bed. He cupped her face and stared down into her eyes, "Thank you for teaching me how to love. I love you Diamond."

Her heart swelled at the words she'd waited to hear. "Show me Zackary," she whispered. "Show me."

Beginning with her eyes, he kissed each lid, the tip of her nose, each cheek, each breast, the inside of her elbows, every finger and then her navel. Removing her jeans and panties, he kissed each toe, the arches of her feet, her ankles, her knee caps, behind her knees. Then his tongue traveled up the front of one thigh, across her stomach, down the front of the other thigh, until his lips touched her moist inner lips. He gently spread them apart, kissing the center before taking her sensitive nub between his fingers, then sucking as if his life depended on the substance it was releasing. The relentless thrusting of his tongue into her center had her bucking off the bed. His free hand gently held her in place while he continued to feast on her honey drenched wetness. Nothing was sweeter than Diamond— nothing. And he refused to stop until he had the very last drop of her explosion.

Standing, he began to undress as he reveled at the aftermath of her release. Nothing looked as wonderful as the expression of total satisfaction on her face. That's how he wanted to see her every morning and every night. After joining her on the bed, he pulled her into his arms. His release could wait. There was something more important that he needed from her. "Diamond," he whispered, as her body draped his and her head rested on his shoulder. "Will you be my wife, the mother of my children, my partner for life?"

Her fingers that were stroking his nipple stopped. Her breathing ceased. Then slowly her head rose from his shoulder as she looked down at him. "Yes." She replied, then kissed his lips as her body eased over his. The tip of his manhood flicked at her center. She held his eyes as she eased down onto him, taking a little of him in, then raising back up, taking a little more, then up, and a little more as she gradually took him completely inside of her. She sat up with her hands on his chest, allowing him to go deeper. With him secured deeply in her warmth, she slowly began to move as she held his gaze. "I will be your wife, have your children and protect your heart." She closed her eyes, held on to his arm and began slow circular motions with her body. She could feel him throbbing inside of her. His thickness increased with each swerve of her hips. He grew every time she lifted her hips and eased back down. Throwing her head back, his legs braced her back. She arched her lower body forward squeezing all of him with her inner muscles, tighter and tighter until he just couldn't take anymore. He swung her onto her back and pumped furiously into her, until they both reached that pinnacle of release. Love juices flowed down her legs, the scent of their love making permeated the air around them and they both grasped for the other. Neither wanting to break the connection of their love, he rolled her back into their original position and held her until they both drifted off to sleep. An hour or two later, they awakened and replayed their love making again.

The next morning Zack showered and was in the kitchen preparing breakfast, when Diamond emerged. Standing behind the breakfast bar, he smiled as she walked into the living room. "You are stunning in the morning."

She smiled. A shirtless Zack, with jeans hugging his waist and a huge bulge waiting to break free was a sight to behold. "The afterglow of love making." She walked behind the bar and kissed him. "You're making waffles," she lovingly looked up at him. "I love waffles."

"I know," he kissed the tip of her nose. "Strawberries and whipped cream to dress them." He pulled her into his embrace. Her back to his chest, his bulge nestled perfectly against her behind. One hand covered hers around the wooden spoon, while the other eased under the opening at the top of her robe and began playing a symphony with her nipple. "Do you know the secret to good waffles?"

Unable to really speak due to the sensations he was evoking with his hands, she shook her head. "Well, allow me to demonstrate." He began moving his hips with the motion of the spoon. "You begin with slow, sturdy motions, then as the mixture thickens, you begin to move a little harder to create the desired consistency or thickness as some may say." He unzipped his jeans and they fell to the floor. The thin robe was no barrier to the heat his body was generating. But fair was fair. She wanted to generate a little heat herself. Why should he have all the fun? She dropped the spoon into the batter. Diamond dug two fingers into the cool whip, wrapped her hands firmly around his hardness, then fell to her knees, taking him into her mouth before he could protest. She had no idea what she was doing, but she just let instinct take over. It was like sucking on a Bomb Pop, except he was hot, smooth and moaning. Holding onto his thighs she felt when he stepped back, just allowing the tip of him into her mouth. She continued to revel in the feel of him, the taste of him as she sucked and licked until he fell to his knees. He quickly turned her around and entered her from behind. The power of his entrance caused both of them to sigh, then he began moving within her, like a man possessed. If he hadn't been holding on to her waist she would have gone flying across the floor with each thrust. But he held on to her as if his life depended on every stroke and it did for both of them. At one point she realized her knees were no longer on the floor. Only her hands, her legs were wrapped behind his back, but she didn't care the only thing that mattered at the moment were the sensations that were shattering within her body. They fell to the floor just as the front door opened.

A curse filled the air as someone tripped over something. "Damnit Diamond, why would you leave your bag in front of the damn door?" Pearl yelled through the apartment as Phire and Opal followed her in.

It took both of them a moment to respond. Diamond quickly pulled her robe together as Zack reached for his pants. Peeking over the bar, Diamond, brushed her hair out of her face and found her sisters, Pearl, Opal and Phire frowning at her. She smiled, "Hey. You're home."

"Yes, I'm home." Pearl threw her travel bag on the sofa. "Why is your bag in front of the door?"

"I want to know why you are on the floor." Opal asked still frowning at her sister.

"Hey Mr. Zack," Phire smiled. "Why you don't have no clothes on?"

Zack made it to his knees as he attempted to zip his jeans. "Good morning."

Pearl was shocked to see Zack. She looked from one to the other, but before she could say anything Phire spoke what she was thinking. "Aww, ya'll doing the nasty on the floor," she giggled.

"In the kitchen, around the food," Opal exclaimed with a disgusted look on her face.

"Do you have on clothes?"

"Of course," Diamond said as Zack replied, "Some."

Phire took a step towards the kitchen, put Opal pulled her back. "Go to the bedroom Phire," she demanded.

"I don't think so, I want to see this!"

Pearl getting the jest of the situation, crossed her arms across her chest and smirked. "I'm tempted to stand here."

"Okay," Zack replied as he began to stand.

Pearl, Opal and Phire stood, mouths dropped, "Whoa, nice bod Mr. Zack!" Phire nodded appreciatively.

"Damn," Opal smirked, then looked at Diamond. "Well alright Diamond."

Pearl turned her head, looking at her two sisters, "You two out!" she pointed to the bedroom. She then turned to Zack, "I'll get your clothes. Where are they?"

Diamond playfully hit Zack's shoulder. "He has on jeans, Pearl. You're fine."

Pearl slowly turned back around. "Why are you two in the kitchen like this? You do have a bedroom Diamond."

"We got hungry," Diamond shrugged her shoulder.

"We made waffles," Zack replied as he kissed Diamond's cheek. "Want some?"

"The waffles or you?" Opal questioned.

"The waffles you can have. The man is mine," Diamond stood in front of Zack, for none of her sisters had taken a step to move and were still gawking at his chest. Placing her hands on her hips, she frowned, "Stop looking at him like that!"

"If his waffles are as good as he looks, I'll take some of him with whipped cream on top." Phire responded with a smile. All of her sisters turned the glare on her. "What?" she smirked at Opal and Pearl, "I just said what everyone was thinking."

Chapter 28

Chief Hasting closed the door to the file cabinet, then sat back down in his seat. He scanned through the pictures in the file trying to determine if arson was involved or was this just another mishap. The paper on the edge of his desk moved as if a breeze had blown through. Turning behind him, he checked the office window. It was closed. He turned back to the report. A minute or two later, he had the strangest sensation that someone was in the office with him. Without turning back around, he just shook his head. "I will never understand why you don't use the front door."

"I'm incognito."

He looked back over his shoulder and sure enough Joshua was sitting in the chair by the window he'd just checked. As much as all of them hated to admit it, Joshua was good at what he did. "I see you."

"That's because I want you to."

A frown creased his forehead. Usually when Joshua showed up something was going on that would cause issues for whomever he was visiting. Richard put his picture down and turned his attention to Joshua. "What's up?"

"Do you still have the paper file on the Franklin Sub-division investigation?"

"I do."

"I need to take a look at it."

Knowing Joshua had access to any information ever put on a computer, he was sure he could look at the report at any time. "Why didn't you just pull the report?" Richard stood as he pulled the file from the cabinet. "You have access."

"I need you to look at it with me." Joshua joined him at the desk.

It never ceased to amaze Richard how every time Joshua showed up he was impeccably dressed. "How do you do the type of clandestine work you do dressed to the nines all the time?"

Joshua adjusted the lapel to his suit jacket. "Hey, James Bond was always hooked up when he worked. You should expect no less from me."

"James Bond is a fictional character," Richard smirked as he sat back at his desk.

"Not anymore baby, I'm the new James Bond only sexier." Joshua gave him a devilish grin, which exposed those deep dimples that seemed to run in their family.

Richard just shook his head and turned his attention to the file. "What are we looking for clown?"

"I don't understand why no one takes me seriously. But when you want someone found or dead, you always call me."

"Because we know you are crazy enough to do whatever we ask." He shrugged his shoulders. "We all respect your skills. If I was in the field working, I would want you and your brother to have my back."

Joshua became a little emotional, "That sounded like a compliment. I'm touched."

"You are touched. What am I looking at here?" he pointed to the file.

"You, Zack and Sammy were pretty close in high school. All of you hung out with the same people."

"Yes we did," Richard nodded in agreement.

"Then tell me, do you recognize that person?" Joshua pointed to a person standing in the background of pictures from the Franklin investigation.

Richard held the picture up, taking a closer look. Shaking his head, "I don't think so."

"Take a real close look. You, Sammy and Zack know this person."

Richard pulled another photo taken from a different angle. "Hmm, I still don't recognize that person, but I always wondered about this person." He pointed to another figure in the background. "But I could never identify him."

Joshua pulled out a small computer device and scanned the picture. He sent a message, then placed the device back in his suit jacket. "We'll know his history in a minute. His profile fits the person I've been following."

"What person?" Richard asked.

"Zack asked me to find his mother. In the process of finding her, I detected someone following her. You know me, I start following him. He led me to the construction site. I know why Ann is there. She always hangs out wherever Zack is working. What I didn't know was why the person was following her. I think it's connected to Zack in some way."

"Is Zack still a suspect in the Franklin Investigation?"

"He was cleared, but I've caught a lot of heat from the brass because of it. Some feel the evidence was sufficient to move forward with at least an indictment."

"So if something was to happen on this site Zack will be your person of interest?"

"Definitely."

Joshua's computer beeped. He pulled it out and read the message. The look on his face spoke volumes. "I have to go. We need to find Celeste Blanchard, now!"

L

Xavier had just left The Towers to check on the model. He wanted to let his friend know that Diamond would probably be returning soon. There was something about the woman that was familiar, but for the life of him he could not put his finger on what. She wasn't a family friend or anyone he had spent a lot of time around, but some of her actions and the "shit happens" attitude she took on certain things reminded him of someone. He just hadn't made the connection yet. At the sound of his cell phone, he pushed a button on his console. "Speak to me," he answered.

"Xavier, its Julia. I just received a call from the bank. Charles called to set up a wire transfer to an off shore account in the Cayman Islands for Monday."

"Hold on Julia, let me get Zack in on this call."

Xavier dialed Zack's number then pushed the conference button. The telephone rang three times before he picked up. "This better be good X-man."

"I have Julia on the other line. Julia, tell us what's happening."

"As you may or may not know, the Cayman's is a sanctuary for anyone trying to embezzle funds that cannot be recovered. Our laws do not extend to them. If he is able to make that transfer, the company will lose ten point five million dollars. I don't have to tell you that will put every project we have on the plate in jeopardy."

"Have steps been but in place to ensure that does not happen?" Xavier asked as he heard kissing sounds in the background.

"Nate and his team have all the areas covered. A device has been placed in Charles' computer to make it appear the transfer went through. The bank investigators will be knocking on Charles' door the second after the send button is pushed. This will only appear to be happening on his computer. Nothing will be transmitted to the banks there."

"Did you hear that Zack?" There was no reply. "Zack?"

"Yes. Look X-man, I trust Julia implicitly. If she tells me this situation is under control, then I'm not concerned. Is it under control Julia?"

"Yes it is."

"That's all I need to know. Is there anything else?"

"No," Julia replied. "Hello Diamond."

"Hi Julia," she laughed. "Hey Xavier."

"You two need to get a room," Xavier smiled.

"We're in a room." Zack replied, "Yours." He laughed then disconnected the call.

"How did you know Diamond was there with him?" Xavier asked.

"The edge to his voice is gone. Only a woman can do that to a man."

"You women sure do give yourself a lot of credit."

"It's a proven fact Xavier. You'll find out one day."

"Julia, are we about to lose millions?"

"No, I won't allow that to happen. The president of the bank knows I have subpoenas in place the moment something goes wrong. If anyone loses millions, it certainly will not be Davenport Industries. However, Nate did come up with a very interesting photo of Charles with someone you may know."

"Who?" Xavier asked.

"Celeste Blanchard."

L

Pulling into the parking space at the model home, Xavier's mind was still reeling from the bombshell Julia had just dropped. What in the hell was Charles doing in a picture with Celeste. He didn't even think they knew each other. Shrugging it off, he entered the house and walked straight back into the kitchen. His friend was sitting at the breakfast bar witting for him with a hot cup of coffee. "How's it going little man?" she asked while handing him the coffee.

He hesitated for a moment, shook off whatever hit him wrong, then took the cup. "Good news. Diamond's back." he smiled.

"Hot damn, Zack came to his senses," she smiled brightly.

"Seems like it," Xavier sipped his coffee. "Unfortunately, that means she will probably be returning here. I'm sure it will not be for a few more days. She and Zack are making up for lost time."

She waved him off, "This wasn't a permanent gig anyway. I'm just happy Zack got his girl. So they got the makeup sex thing going on, huh?"

"I'll say," Xavier laughed. "So what are you going to do?"

"Me, same thing I've always done, land on my feet. Don't worry about me son, I'll be just fine."

He flinched again at the term son. But he shrugged it off. "Hey I noticed the front porch light is blinking. You may want to get that checked."

"I'll get right on it. Have you had breakfast?"

"Not yet. I'll grab something on my way to the office."

"Now, I ain't never been a good cook, but I can microwave along with the best. Diamond keeps a few things here. How about a bacon, egg, and cheese biscuit?"

Xavier smiled, "I can go for that." He looked at his watch. "I could do a few things on the computer from here."

"You go on over there and start working. I'll bring this to you."

Taking his coffee with him, he sat it on the table then reached for the password to the computer. In the process he knocked over the jar of marbles. "Oh hell," he said, then proceeded to pick them up. They were rolling everywhere.

As he picked them up he began to laugh. When he was a little boy, Zack would get so mad at him for touching his marbles. A memory hit him so strong his laugh froze.

"Now, little man you know Zackary is going to be upset when he gets home. You know how he is about his marbles. Let's hurry up and get them back in the jar."

"Let's get these back in the jar," Ann was saying as Xavier mouthed the last words with her.

He looked over to where she was bending down to collect the marbles that were rolling away. The silhouette of the woman watching the house from across the street came to mind. Standing, he looked at the marbles in his hand. Closing his hand around them, he looked at the woman walking towards him and he was three years old all over again. "Drop them in," she said.

Xavier did, but held one back. "My brother had marbles just like these when I was little."

Ann picked up on the change in his tone as soon as he spoke. She didn't bother to look at him, for she knew something had changed. "Did he?" she placed the jar on the desk, then turned to walk away.

Xavier stopped her by grabbing her arm. "What's your name?"

Turning back to him, she looked him straight in the eyes and replied, "Friend."

Not ready to deal with what he was thinking, he dropped the marble in the jar and placed the top back on it. The microwave beeped. "I think I'll have that breakfast to go."

Her time with him was up. She knew it couldn't last forever. That was her doing, not his or Zack's. But she was given a few days to see what type of man he was inside and liked what she had a glimpse of. "You know, in life you do reap what you sow." she said as she walked over to the microwave and pulled out the breakfast sandwich. "You're a good man Xavier Prince Davenport. Find yourself a good woman and plant some seeds. You and Zack come from good stock." She gave the wrapped sandwich to him. "You should both be fruitful and multiply. Just make sure it's with the right woman."

Xavier took the sandwich from the woman. What he was thinking was not something he wanted to deal with at this time. Not sure what to say, he held her gaze for a moment then said "Thank you." He turned, and walked out of the door.

L

Joshua placed the case he retrieved from the closet of the second floor of the model home on the bed in his room. While at the model house, he also removed the explosive device. He immediately had his tech friend identify the maker. With an explosive device involved, whatever is going on had become a federal case, giving him carte blanche on whatever he had to do. Not many men had a license to kill, Joshua did. Opening the case he took the instrument from inside. Examining the sax, he found **KAD** engraved on the base of the instrument. Joshua pulled his handheld computer from his inside pocket and scanned the device. Once he was finished he pushed the send button.

Samuel walked into the room Joshua occupied in his house whenever he was in town. Seeing the instrument and the case, he frowned. "What are you doing with King Arthur?"

Joshua looked at the engraving, then at Samuel. "Who in the hell is King Arthur?"

Samuel laughed, "Zack's saxophone. Its name is King Arthur." He walked further into the room. "What are you doing with it?"

"Close the door," Joshua instructed. Samuel complied then sat in the chair next to the bed. "What's up?"

Joshua placed the instrument back in the case, closed it then pushed it under the bed. "I don't know. And you

know how that irritates me." He shook his head, still trying
to piece things together. "I think someone is trying to frame
Zack. On what I'm not sure, but I think Celeste Blanchard is
involved. I just don't know how."

"She's in Richmond," Samuel told Joshua. "That's
the woman that set everything off with Zack and Diamond."

"Interesting, and she just happened to show up now.
Zack hasn't been involved seriously with a woman since her
and she shows up the moment Diamond tells us she's
interested in Zack. I've heard about women's intuition when
it comes to men, but I don't believe it's that strong and I
damn sure don't believe in coincidences."

"You think she is working with someone?"

"I do. The question is who and why?"

"With Celeste the why is easy. Money. Your guess is
as good as mine on the who."

Joshua pulled out his computer. "Do you recognize
this person or this person?" he pointed to the people
standing in the background of the picture from the
investigation.

"I know both of them and so does Zack. But I don't
believe they know each other."

"I think we better find out. I don't want to deal with a
heartbroken Diamond and neither does Lucy."

Samuel smiled. "Lucy told me about Diamond
damn near blowing herself and Commando up."

"We can't have that, I love that dog."

"You love your sister too. Tell me everything you
have."

Chapter 29

Saturday was a whirlwind of activity. The Business Man of the Year Dinner was scheduled at six. Zack and Diamond hadn't come up for air in days, but that was about to end. Xavier was sitting on the patio with the French doors from the kitchen open. The morning was quiet and normally it would be the perfect time for him to work on designs. There were tons of community projects on his mind that he needed to get down on paper, but this morning the friend from the model unit was on his mind. There were unanswered questions swirling around in his mind.

"Well good morning,"

Xavier turned to see a glowing Diamond in the doorway. "Good morning to you," he replied with a wide grin. "You look happy."

Diamond walked out and took a seat on the lounge chair next to him. "I am," she nodded and smiled.

"So is Zack, from what I can see. You're good for him."

She brushed against his shoulder, "Thanks." She watched his gaze go back to the yard. "What's wrong?"

Xavier turned to her. There was no need trying to avoid the question from her. She always had an uncanny ability to read his moods. He sat the cup he was drinking from on the table in front of them then turned to her. "I met your friend from the model home."

"She's something, isn't she?" Diamond grinned.

"That she is. What do you know about her?"

"Not much," Diamond shook her head. "She doesn't talk much about herself."

"Yet you gave her unlimited access to the house, the files, the computer?"

"I didn't give her access to any of those things Xavier." She shrugged.

"She had it. In fact she showed me where everything connected to the model was, even down to how you handled clients. I was curious as to why you would give a stranger that much access to confidential information."

"I just told you I didn't give her access. I have no idea how she knows those things unless she's been watching me when I didn't know it."

"Where do you keep the password to your computer?"

"Under a jar of marbles on my desk."

"Where did the marbles come from?"

"She gave them to me. When she first started coming by I would feed her something and she would leave me a marble or two for payment, I guess."

"Has Zack ever seen those marbles?"

She shrugged "I don't think so, why?"

Xavier sat back in his chair, "I think your friend at the model home is my mother."

A stunned Diamond sat up, "Your mother. Why do you think that?"

"The marbles in the jar look just like the ones from Zack's collection. In fact, I'm sure the shooter is."

"How do you know?"

"There's a nick on Zach's shooter from where I dropped it on the front porch. He kicked my behind for days because of it. I would never forget that shooter."

"Have you talked to Zack about it?"

Xavier shook his head, "Noooo."

"Why not?"

"You don't understand the effect my mother's leaving had on Zack." He chuckled, "For months, everytime my dad mentioned my mother, Zack went into a rage. After a while, my dad stopped mentioning her."

"You didn't know your mother?"

"Not really. I never had any memories of her until yesterday."

"What happened yesterday?"

"I knocked over the jar of marbles on your desk. While I was picking them up, I remembered my mother saying Zack was going to be upset. Let's get them back inside the jar. Your friend was helping me pick them up and said the exact same thing. It was like we went back in time to the moment when I had dropped Zack's marbles."

"Did you ask her who she was?"

Nodding, "Several times, but she never told me her name."

"Her name is Ann," Zack said from the doorway. "I saw the marbles too. I thought they looked familiar, but at the time I didn't pay much attention to them." He leaned against the doorjamb. "How long has she been there?" He looked at Diamond.

Diamond stood and kissed him gently on his lips, "Good morning. She's been around since the model first opened. I had no idea who she was." She exhaled. "Now, would you like some breakfast."

Zack smiled down at her, "Good morning gorgeous. Yes, I'm starving."

She turned back to Xavier, "How about you?"

It was good to see the rough edges around Zack soften at Diamond's touch. "You know I'd like some homemade waffles."

Zack and Diamond looked at each other. "You spoke to Opal yesterday, didn't you?" Diamond smirked.

"Phire, actually. Of course she gave me the run down on you two and the waffles."

"Of course she did," Diamond shook her head and walked into the kitchen.

Zack stepped out onto the patio and sat in front of his brother. This was a conversation he should have had with his brother years ago. "She's been asking to see you."

Xavier nodded, "But you wouldn't allow it."

"No," Zack replied. "I did not want to take a chance on her coming into your life and then running off again."

"I'm a grown man Zack. That was not a decision for you to make."

Zack nodded, "I agree. It should have been your decision. At the time I was doing the best I could to protect you. The thing is, I never understood why Ann would ask permission. I never banned her from the office or the house. She began cleaning up when you returned from college. She was free to approach you at any time." Diamond stepped out and placed a cup of coffee in front of Zack. "Thank you," he said and smiled as he watched her walk away, then turned back to Xavier. "I don't think she wanted to take a chance on upsetting me."

Xavier looked out over the yard and exhaled. "I don't remember anything about her."

"There's a box upstairs in the attic that has "King" written on it. I could never bring myself to get rid of it."

"What's in it?"

"Things that he held dear to his heart. When you are ready, I think you should take a look inside."

Xavier nodded, acknowledging the statement. He looked into the kitchen then turned back to Zack. "I'll be moving into my condo over the weekend."

"X-man, don't let this come between us."

Xavier put his hand up. "I'm not moving because of Ann or my mother or whoever she is. It's time. You have a new life ahead of you and frankly, living here with you is cramping my style." He smirked. "A brother needs a little privacy and so do you. You two are kind of freaky."

Diamond popped him upside the head with the potholder as she walked out with a tray of bacon, eggs and toast. "I heard that."

"I heard you too." Xavier smirked as he reached for a plate. "Oh Zackary," he mimicked her voice.

"You did not," she blushed.

Zack pulled her into his lap. "Pay him no mind babe, he's just jealous."

She kissed his neck. "My sisters and I are going shopping today. I have to find a dress for tonight. Are we still meeting at the dinner?"

"Definitely," he kissed her. "I'll see you tonight." He watched her as she walked from the room.

"Man you are so gone." Xavier laughed.

L

"You told me this was going to be simple. Zack was going to write a check to ensure Chanté and I would be financially set. That hasn't happened and from the looks of things, it's not going to happen. So you have a choice, pay me or I will tell Zackary everything you've been up to!" Celeste paced the floor of the hotel room with her back to the door.

"Look, I told you Zack would fall for your daughter and he did. He immediately moved you from the motel to the hotel, because he's such the caring gentlemen." Charles sarcastically added. "You're the one that lost your cool when you pushed his buttons on the Diamond issue."

Past the point of listening to any reasoning, Celeste insisted. "Cash today or I spill my guts."

The only part of his plans she knew about was her role. She knew nothing about the other player in the game. But if she got to Zack, it could cause a ruffle or two before the last nail in Zack's coffin was in place. "Look, Celeste, you have as much to lose as I do if this doesn't go according to plan. Come Monday, you will have the money you need to get your daughter into that dancing program and more."

"I want out. Now!" Celeste insisted. "This is not going right and I will not allow another man to destroy my dreams for Chanté. Zack turned his back on me, then Teddy and I'll be damned if I'll allow you to do the same. You pay me today or I will tell Zack how you came to me about this plan to bring him down."

"What are you going to tell him? That your husband left you, or the fact that you were about to be evicted from your home? I'm sure Zack is going to be sympathetic towards you. After all you broke his heart, not once, but twice."

"You may be right, but one thing I do know about Zackary Davenport. If I go to him and tell him my situation and why I agreed to this scheme of yours, he will not only forgive me, but he will give me the financial support I need for Chanté. As you said Charles, that's the kind of caring gentleman he is. Either you pay me or Zack will. I don't particularly care which."

"All right!" Charles exclaimed. "Show up at the dinner and you'll get your money."

"Play me and Zack will know the entire story before midnight." She disconnected the call and turned to find Chanté standing in the doorway.

"This trip had nothing to do with me and dancing. This was all about you getting money from Mr. Davenport?" Chanté asked as she stared curiously at her mother.

"Chanté," Celeste took a step towards her. "Darling no, this has everything to do with you."

"Mom, Mr. Davenport is a really nice man. I don't know what happened with you and him back whenever, but no one deserves to be used for money. Didn't you learn anything from Daddy leaving?"

The question stung coming from her daughter. "Yes Chanté I did. I learned that you can't depend on men for anything. That's what I learned from your father leaving."

"Know what I've learned?" Chanté said as she placed the bag of food on the table, "I learned that trying to use people is wrong and it doesn't feel good. That's why Daddy left." She turned and walked out of the door.

Celeste ran to the door and pulled it open, "Chanté you come back here right now."

Chanté turned to look at her mom. She loved her and understood she was only doing what she could to take care of them. But her dad told her, if her mom had just been honest with him, he would have never left. Her dad knew she wasn't his daughter long before he left the family. When they talked, he said he did not know for sure, but he believed Zackary Davenport was her father. She always wondered if she would ever get to meet him. So when her mother said they were going to Richmond to meet with him, she was ecstatic. Chanté liked him immediately and prayed that he was indeed her biological father. But when they did not hear from him after the tests were done, she knew he wasn't her father. Daddy was wrong and only her mother knew the answer to the question that was foremost in her mind. Yes, she loved her mother, but there were times, like now that she just didn't like her very much. "I just need to take a walk Mom."

"Don't be gone long."

Stepping onto the elevator, Chanté replied. "I won't." She saw the relieved look on her mother's face as the elevator doors closed. Pulling out her cell phone Chanté searched the database for the number she had recently stored. "Hi, it's me. Can we talk?"

L

Zack had just walked out of the door when Samuel and Joshua pulled up. "You have a minute?"

Zack looked at his watch. "I'm supposed to be meeting someone, but I can spare a minute." Joshua pulled the case from the car. Zack frowned. "What are you doing with King Arthur?" Zack took the case from him, placed it on the hood of the car and opened it. His shoulders relaxed as he examined the sax. "What are you doing with this?"

"I took it from a closet on the second floor of your model home."

"What?" Zack looked as if Joshua had lost his mind as he placed the sax back inside its velvet case." How in the hell did it get there?"

"I believe Teddy Blanchard put it there." Joshua replied.

"Teddy Blanchard? Celeste's husband?"

"Why?"

"That's something we will have to ask him when we find him." Samuel stated. "Where is Celeste staying?"

"The Marriott on Broad." Joshua took off once he had the location. "What's going on?" Zack asked Samuel.

"I think you are going to be a little late for your meeting," he said as he and Zack walked back into the house.

L

Theodore Blanchard spent his life playing football. He may not be physically able to play any longer, but he still had a lot to contribute to the game. While standing on the sideline of a local high school team camp, he was recognized by some of the players. The gesture made him feel worthy. When the coach asked him to add a few pointers, he was more than happy to pitch in. Just as the practice session wrapped up, his cell phone rang. It was his baby girl Chanté.

She needed to talk. He told her the day he left home, if she ever needed him all she had to do was call. From that day on whenever she called, he made time for her. He knew that he was not her biological father, but he loved her nonetheless. He was the first person to hold her when she was born, the first to see her cut her first tooth, the first to see her take her first steps. Yes, Chanté was as much a part of him as his legs, arms or heart. It was for that reason that he could not stay and allow her mother to make him seem like less of a man in his daughter's eyes.

At first it was the snide way she would belittle his position with the team. Zack would have been a starter; he wouldn't be coming off of the bench when no one else was available. Or Zack wouldn't be wondering if they were going to renew his contract. They would be begging him to stay. Then it got worse, Zack's construction company made Black Enterprise's top ten companies to watch. Then it was Zack isn't even in the NFL and he is still outshining you. The final straw came when they were at a dance competition and Chanté won first place. In front of his child, the child he raised from birth, his loving wife said, Chanté has that same talent, determination and drive that Zack has. The statement cut him so deep, for the first time in twelve years, he said something back. "Zack wasn't the one that married you. I was." The next day, when he was driving Chanté to her dance lessons, she asked him, "Daddy, who is Zack that Mom talks about all the time?" He didn't bother to lie, he told her the truth. That night he packed his bags and left. Why did he put up with it for so long? Simple, he loved Celeste before Zack came along, and he loved her when Zack walked away.

"Hey baby girl," Teddy smiled as Chanté got into the car.

"Hey Daddy," she reached over and kissed him on the cheek. "I'm so happy you're here. Can we just go somewhere and talk?"

"Of course. Would that talk go down better with ice cream and donuts?"

"It sure would." Chanté smiled. As they drove her mind went back to the conversation she overheard. "Daddy, I think Mom is trying to blackmail Mr. Davenport or doing something to get money from him." She shook her head. "I don't understand how Mom can say how much she loved him, but want to hurt him at the same time. It's not right, what she's doing. It's just not right."

"It may not be what you think. Tell me what you heard."

"She was talking to someone named Charles who promised to give her money if she did something to Mr. Davenport."

"Charles?" Teddy inquired.

"Yeah, I don't know who he is, but she threatened to tell Mr. Davenport everything if this Charles guy didn't give her some money."

"Did you see this Charles guy?"

"No they were on the telephone."

"Daddy, I met Mr. Davenport and he really is a nice guy. He's very handsome and funny. I don't know why Mommy wants to hurt him." Chanté did see the vein in her father's neck throbbing, as she continued to talk. "I wish it had turned out that he was my father, but he's not. So now what Daddy? How do I find out who my real father is?"

It took every ounce of will power Teddy had not to explode. Zack had taken his girlfriend, his wife and now his little girl was wishing Zack was her father. How much humiliation can one man take from another? "Daddy? Daddy, did you hear me?"

"Yes, baby girl, I heard you. Loud and clear, you wish Zackary Davenport was your real father."

In all the years, all the verbal attacks her mother made against her dad, she had never seen him break down. Whatever she said made him snap. She had said something to make her daddy mad. Thinking back, she was talking so much she had no idea what had made his face go white with anger. "Davenport wasn't the one that took care of you, taught you right from wrong, took you to your dance lessons, wiped your tears when you were hurt, answered your calls everytime you needed or wanted something. That was me, dammit, not Zackary Davenport!"

"I know Daddy," a stunned and frightened Chanté cried out.

"It was bad enough that your mother always wanted Davenport, now you too. Enough is enough! And I've had my fill of being a shadow of Zackary Davenport!"

"Daddy I'm sorry. I didn't mean to upset you. Please slow the car down!"

"I'm not going to hurt you baby girl, but I am going to take the all mighty Davenport down, once and for all."

The car sped forward and Chanté wondered who was the craziest, her mother or her father. "Daddy no one could ever replace you. But you said I need to know who my real father was." She touched his arm. "You will always be my daddy. Please Daddy, slow the car down," she cried.

Teddy did not slow the car down until they were turning into Davenport Estates. The grounds were beautiful. Circling the turn-a-bout at the beginning of the grounds, the road passed several buildings in different stages of construction, what looked like an apartment building that was named The Towers, then on past what appeared to be a park. Then they drove through another gate that led to really nice single dwelling homes. It looked similar to the area where Chanté and her family lived. "What are you doing here Daddy?" Chanté asked.

"I'm bringing Davenport to his knees." He stopped the vehicle in front of the model home. He looked around as if to see if anyone was there. He then reached into the glove compartment and pulled out something that looked like a small transmitter. He let out a chilling chuckle, then pressed the button. Nothing happened. "What the?" he looked down at the device in his hand, turning it over, then back again. He shook the device and a green light appeared. Smiling he nodded his head and pushed the button again. Still, nothing happened. He looked at the device and yelled, while he slammed it against the steering wheel.

"What is it Daddy? What's wrong?"

"Stay here!" he said. "Don't you move out of this car!" He glared at her and she didn't recognize him.

Chanté watched as he walked around to the back of the house. She pulled out her cell phone and called her mother.

"Mommy, something's wrong with Daddy."

"I can't talk right now Chanté. I'll call you back in a minute."

"But Mommy..." The call was disconnected.

Chanté looked around. No one was in sight. She watched through the window of the house as her father walked up the stairs and disappeared. She had no idea where she was or what was wrong with her dad, but she was too afraid to leave. Then she saw her dad running from the house. "Daddy please tell me what's wrong?"

L

"You think that Teddy Blanchard was involved in the Franklin fire?" Zack asked shaking his head. "I don't believe that. Teddy was cool people, laidback, quiet. We never had any issues."

"Did you know that Teddy and Celeste were involved before you came into the picture?" Samuel asked. "He could be holding a grudge against you for that. My question is how does Charles play into all of this?"

Zack stood and paced the floor in his kitchen. "What in the hell is happening here? Is this about money?"

"I think it's about a lot more." Samuel stated, "The only reason I can see he would take items from your home and place them inside the burning houses is to frame you for the act. That would certainly ruin your business and possibly your reputation. I'll be honest Zack, I don't understand minds like these. If I have an issue with a man, I take it to him. I don't play these games."

"Same here," Zack nodded, "but for the life of me I have no idea what I have ever done to Charles or Teddy. Celeste, I can almost understand. But that's still a stretch for me. She left me, I didn't leave her."

"In a way you did Zack. You chose your brother over her."

"That wasn't a choice Sammy that was life. X-man is my brother, my blood, he needed me and I was not going to turn my back on him."

"I understand that, but Celeste didn't."

"So what do we do now?"

"Joshua is on Celeste. Reese is following Charles. We haven't located Teddy yet, but we will. Joshua believes whatever is planned will take place at the dinner tonight."

"Why?"

"It's the perfect place to embarrass you, especially if you are the winner. We are going to continue to follow the players and cover the event. Until they show their hand, that's about all we can do."

Xavier walked into the room, "Julia is on the line. Charles has requested fifty thousand dollars from the bank manager. Should she authorize the release?"

Zack shook his head and looked at Samuel. "Did he indicate what the funds were for?"

Xavier relayed the question to Julia, then turned back to him. "No, but anything over fifty thousand has to be signed off on by you or I and Charles knows that."

"It could be the break we were waiting for." Samuel stated, "Tell her to release the funds. I'll check with Reese to make sure he stays close to Charles."

Xavier relayed the message then hung up the phone. "Julia indicated Nate Raines requested the bank to record the serial numbers on the bills as a precautionary measure." He shook his head too, "This is just unbelievable. I can't believe people are this vindictive."

"A woman scorned has no boundaries," Samuel stated.

"That explains Celeste. What's Charles' excuse?" Zack asked.

Samuel and Xavier both stared at Zack in disbelief. "You don't know?" Xavier asked almost in a chuckle.

"No, what?" Zack asked.

Samuel just laughed. "I don't have the heart to tell him."

Chapter 30

*Y*ou are rocking that gown and I love those shoes," Phire exclaimed as she watched her sister dress for dinner. "I'm going to have a man like Mr. Zack one day."

Diamond smiled at her little sister through the mirror. "It didn't come easy, but it has definitely been worth the wait."

"You mean you never did the nasty before Mr. Zack?" Phire asked.

"No, I've never come across a man worthy until Zack."

"Girl, you're a good one," Opal stated, "I had my first taste in high school. Wasn't worth it, but I've had fun since."

"What about you Jade?" Phire asked.

"I'm saving myself until that man comes along that is worth giving my gold to."

"Ruby?" Phire asked. All eyes turned to their oldest sister.

"I'm taking the fifth." She smiled. "The ultimate decision is each of yours to make. Opal and Pearl are very strong women and will put a man in his place with one look. Diamond and Jade are more sensitive and follow what their heart tells them. I don't know where you fall in Phire. You pretend to have this hard shell, but you are the most sensitive of all us girls. You can't follow what any of us did unless it's right for you."

Diamond smiled at her sister who always dispensed wisdom, "I always wanted what Mom and Dad have. That love that lasts a lifetime. I never wanted to go back and forth."

"That back and forth gives a lot to work with when you find that man." Pearl added.

"Hey," Opal gave her a high five. "I enjoy my sexual freedom. If men can test the cow before buying the milk, I want to test the bull before buying the meat."

Pearl laughed. "It's not for everyone Phire. You have to know who and what you are getting involved with before your share your goodies. Once you give them cookies away it's no taking it back."

"Yeah and make sure he knows what he is doing." Ruby added her wisdom. "The wrong experience can ruin you for life. So before you decide to share, you talk to someone."

"Anyone of us or Cynthia." Opal advised. "Talk to someone that cares about you, before making that decision."

"And whoever he may be, if he is not willing to wait, then he is not the man for you." Pearl added, "He's a little boy just wanting to get your cookies wet and not worthy."

Diamond stood, "Okay, what do you think?"

All of her sisters took in the total package of Diamond Renee Lassiter and smiled. "Zackary Davenport is going to eat you up." Ruby smiled.

"He already did," Phire said.

The sisters looked at each other and fell out laughing.

L

Zack, Xavier, and Samuel stood at the entrance of the Marriott ballroom where the Businessman of the Year dinner was being held. Heads turned as admiring females walked through the lobby, some on the arms of men, and some entering the ballroom alone. None of them noticed for their eyes were on Charles as he entered the lobby. Not one of them missed the silver briefcase in his hand. They watched as he crossed the lobby and walked around the corner to the bank of elevators. A moment later, Reese walked into the lobby. Looking around, he headed towards the ballroom. "Gentlemen," he spoke then looked at Samuel. "Is Joshua upstairs?"

"Yes." Samuel replied. "We should hear from him in a moment, if we are right." Samuel paused as he listened to his earpiece. "The Attorney General is en route. I'm on the job tonight. Joshua is capable of handling whatever those two are up to quietly. Zack," he warned, "Keep your cool. We'll get to the bottom of this."

Reese looked around. "Where's Diamond?"

"She's on her way." Zack replied.

"X-man, he's yours until I return or Diamond gets here. If Charles comes back down, don't approach him. Let it play out." He looked at Zack. "I'm going to change, I'll meet you guys in the ballroom."

L

The patio door was unlocked. A lone figure entered the doors to the model home, walked over to the kitchen, searched under the cabinet, pulled out a can of oven cleaner, opened the oven door, placed the can inside, closed the oven door and walked right back out the patio door.

L

Diamond was on her way to the dinner when her cell chimed. It was the security company indicating an alarm had sounded at the model home. Thinking it was probably Ann, she instructed them it was probably one of the employees and she would go by to check on things. The agent indicated an officer would meet her there.

Diamond hung up and called Zack. "Hi," she blushed. Just the sound of his voice did wicked things to her. "The alarm at the model went off. I think it's probably Ann. I'm right at the exit, so I'm going to stop by to check on things then I'll be on my way."

"All right, but hurry up. Some issues have come up and I want you here with me."

"And I want to be there. See you in a few."

L

Ann wasn't sure what, but the moment she walked through the patio door of the model home, something didn't feel right. No, that was it. Something didn't smell right. Looking towards the kitchen, she knew she didn't leave the oven on, hell she didn't cook. Walking over to the stove she noticed the oven light was on. "What the he....." she opened the oven door and whatever was inside exploded, knocking her across the breakfast bar, unconscious.

Diamond pulled up in front of the house and could see Ann walking towards the kitchen. "Just what I thought," she turned off the ignition and walked towards the house. Just before she reached the front door, something in the house exploded knocking her to the ground and showering her with glass from the front window. Pain radiated through the arm she'd used to shield her face from the glass. Stunned and shaken, she laid there on the ground just staring at the flames now raging inside the house. "Ann," she remembered. Ann was walking into the kitchen. "Ann!" she yelled as she jumped up and ran to the front door. It was locked. "Ann!" she called out again. Not waiting for a reply she ran to the garage doors. It was locked, and she did not have time to look around for the keys that had fallen when she was knocked to the ground. She ran around the house to the patio door, pushed it open and there was a whoosh sound to the fire. It was so eerie. It sounded as if the fire was telling her to get out. But she couldn't. Ann was in there. Her brother's voice came to her, duck, drop and roll - duck drop and roll. She followed exactly what the voice in her head instructed. "Go low Diamond," she heard Sammy say, "go low and stretch". That's how you reach the goal line. Diamond dropped to her knees, eyes wide, straining to find Ann. The smoke was intense and stung her eyes. She crawled further in calling out. "Ann." The smoke was now thick in her mouth and she felt herself dropping from her knees onto her stomach. Crawling now on her stomach, she stretched and reached, praying as she did. Closing, then opening her eyes again, she thought she saw a shoe. She crawled deeper into the burning house until she touched the shoe. "Please be a foot in there," she thought as she grabbed the shoe that contained a foot. Diamond wanted to cry out, but she couldn't. If she did, it very well may be the last breath she would ever take. And Lord, that could not happen—not now. She couldn't leave Zack. She pulled that foot with both hands, crawling backwards as fast as she could. Unfortunately, she had lost track of where she was. The smoke was thick, the fire was raging and now she was pulling an additional hundred pounds of dead weight. Moving back, and back and back, finally her foot hit the patio opening. She could hear sirens in the background. She prayed they were coming here. She crawled out onto the patio, then pulled Ann with all her might propelling both of them to the ground. Ann's heavy weight falling on top of her took the last ounce of air from her lungs. The night went black.

$\mathcal{L}$

Neither of the occupants of the room knew that the conversation they were having was being videotaped until the damaging information had been gathered. That was exactly the way Joshua wanted it. In his career he dealt with foreign agents with more intelligence in their pinky finger than these two had. Both of them were amateurs trying to play in the big boy's game and neither had the talent to pull it off. He activated his earpiece as he coolly walked from his concealed location. The occupants of the room were shocked when they heard him approach. "All right you can come get these two assholes. I can't take another moment of this travesty against the criminal element of the world."

"Who in the hell are you?" Charles boasted.

Joshua gave him an incredulous look. "Be for real. Look at me. Do you really think you can take me?"

Charles growled at Celeste, "Bitch did you set me up?"

Celeste looked from Charles to the man standing in her room. "No. Who are you and where in the hell did you come from?"

"The who, I'm the last man you're going say was in your bedroom. He doesn't count." Looking Celeste up and down, Joshua smiled. "It's a shame we did not have the opportunity to see just how much fun it would have been."

Charles made a dash for the door. Joshua exhaled as if irritated by the action. Charles had just made it to the door when he felt the collar of his tuxedo jerked around his throat and then found himself flying backwards. Joshua put his foot on Charles' chest and applied pressure. "Don't irritate me again—understand." A knock sounded at the door. He looked at Celeste. "Would you mind getting that? It's for you."

She could not believe how fast the man caught Charles and jerked him back. She was still staring in disbelief when he spoke to her. "What?"

"The door is for you."

Celeste took a wide path around the stranger. When she opened the door, the police and another man in a tuxedo were there.

"Nate," Joshua smiled as he walked over to the man in the doorway allowing Charles to breathe again. "Man long time no see." He extended his hand. "How the hell are you?"

Nate Raines remembered the cocky Joshua from a number of assignments they had worked on. He was arrogant as all get out, but knew how to get the job done and could definitely hold his liquor. "Joshua, what in the hell are you doing here?" he smiled.

"Catching dumb criminals—man I mean dumb."

"I don't know man, this was a fifty million dollar embezzlement scheme you just broke. If it hadn't been for a very smart employee of Davenport, they would have gotten away with it."

"Get the hell out of here," Joshua looked over his shoulder at Charles and Celeste who were now in handcuffs. "I underestimated your dumb ass," he said to Charles. Joshua touched his earpiece. "The AG is about to speak, I have to go. We have to catch up Raines." He pulled a device from his jacket pocket. "I believe everything you need is there. You'll make sure they make it to headquarters. I can't wait to hear this story."

L

Joshua walked in the ballroom just as Attorney General Harrison took the stage. Joshua made his way to the table and noticed seats were empty. He unbuttoned the single button on his tux jacket and whispered, "The wolves have been caged."

"The money?" Julia asked.

"Recovered." Joshua smiled. "Where's Diamond?" he asked.

Zack looked back at the entrance as he had several times and there were no signs of her. "I have no idea. I spoke with her a few moments ago and she said she was on her way."

"She'll be here Zack," JoEllen said patting his hand. "Don't worry."

But Zack was worried. Nothing would have kept Diamond from being there with him. However, that had to take a back seat, for the Attorney General had just called his name as the Businessman of the Year. The applause drowned out the thumping of his heart that told him something was wrong. Something was very wrong. The thought followed him through people extending handshakes and congratulations as he made his way toward the stage.

The honor was a hollow one. A few moments after accepting the award, Reese abruptly stood. He whispered something in Xavier's ear then left the room. Zack thanked the AG for the honor, and then made short work of his speech. "What's going on?" he asked Xavier the moment he reached the table.

"Reese received a call. There's a fire at the site."

Before Xavier could say more, Zack took off. "Zack what's up? Zack?" Xavier chased after him.

"Diamond's there."

All the occupants of the table stood at the announcement. Joshua touched his earpiece. "There's a fire at the site."

"I'll secure the AG and meet you there."

L

The fire was now raging. The left side of the house was destroyed as fire fighters worked desperately to contain the blaze. Chief Hasting was directing his men when one yelled, "We have two bodies back here."

"What?" he yelled. "This is a model home, no one lives here."

"I got two bodies in the back Chief. That's all I can tell you."

Then it dawned on him Ann had been staying on site. But who could the second person be? The Chief took off around the house like a bat out of hell.

They had just reached the entrance of the complex and could see the smoke rising towards the sky, As soon as they turned in, an ambulance raced past Xavier who was driving. Zack looked at Xavier. "Push it dammit X-man!" Xavier stomped on the gas, following the ambulance.

The flames coming from the house caused Zack to shudder. "She's not in there Zack. She's not in there." Xavier exclaimed.

Zack jumped from the car before it stopped. He ran in front of the house and couldn't believe this was happening again. The house he could rebuild, but where was Diamond. "Was anybody in the house?"   He yelled at one of the firemen.

"Two bodies in the back." The fireman said then continued with his duties.

Zack's heart stopped. "Diamond!" he screamed as he ran towards the back of the house. Xavier was right behind him. "Diamond!" He yelled again. By this time Joshua was next to him. He grabbed Zack and followed the Emergency Medical Team towards the back of the house. A group of firemen were looking at something on the ground. "Diamond!" Zack yelled again.

The Chief rose from his kneeling position next to a body. He pushed the EMT tech through the group of men then turned to Zack. "No Zack."

"Get the hell out of my way Richard."

Joshua followed the tech then screamed as he fell to his knees. Zack stopped fighting Richard and stared at Joshua's back. "No." he shook his head. "No," he pulled away from the Chief. Xavier began shaking his head refusing to believe what the scene indicated. Joshua stood, with a body in his arms. "Get a medevac here now!" he yelled into his earpiece. Joshua had Diamond in his arms as he spoke. "We have two injured. One with smoke inhalation the other with second and third degree burns. I need a burn unit ready in ten!"

Zack ran over and fell to his knees in front of him. "Diamond," he whispered as he pulled her from Joshua and held her to his chest where his heart was about to explode.

Joshua took the oxygen mask from the tech and placed it over Diamond's face. He then checked to see the cuts on her arms, neck and upper body. "She's still alive Zack and going to stay that way!" he ordered.

Xavier was watching as they worked on Diamond when he heard, the other Tech say. "She's crashing." He turned to the other body that was on the ground. Something told him not to look, but he couldn't stop himself. They stopped what they were doing and began trying to revive the other person. Chief Hasting stepped in front of Xavier. "You don't need to see that son."

Xavier looked into Richard's eyes. "Is that my mother?"

Richard lowered his head, "Yes."

Xavier walked to the men working on his mother and looked down at the body. For a moment, only a moment, he held no hope that the woman would survive. But then the longer he stared at her, the more his mind willed her to survive. "I need you mother. Don't leave me again." Just as the words escaped his lips, the heart rhythm on the portable monitor beeped.

The medevac could be heard overhead. Samuel jumped off as soon as it landed and ran over to Joshua and

Zack. Once he assessed Diamond's injuries, he went to Xavier. He turned to the medical team and yelled. "I need this victim transported immediately." He spoke into his earpiece. "Call Dr. Amber Nicolas at Johns Hopkins. I want her flown in within the hour." He turned to the men that had now secured the body on the gurney. "Let's move her out." He ordered. He then ran back to Joshua. "She ready?"

Joshua looked at Zack. "I'll take her."

"Zack look at me. Zack! We'll take good care of her. X-man needs you. We'll take care of Diamond."

Zack hesitated, then eased his grip on Diamond. Samuel picked his sister up in his arms and his knees almost buckled. The pain cut so deep seeing her like this. He placed her on the gurney as Zack looked on. He then turned to Xavier. "We'll follow in the car."

So many emotions were flowing through Xavier's mind that he did not know which way to turn. Zack walked over to him, wrapped his arms around his brother and held him. "You're going to have a chance to talk to her. I promise." Xavier believed his big brother, because he had never broken his promises. He returned the hug. Zack hit him on the back. "Let's go X-man."

Chapter 31

*I*n interrogation room number one, Samuel was with Celeste as he questioned her about the fire. "Look I told you I don't know anything about a fire. I told you my only interest here was getting the money to support myself and my daughter that was all."

"Tell me again how you got involved with Charles Meeks."

"He sent me an invitation to the open house with his telephone number on it saying there would be compensation for my time." She huffed, "When I called we arranged to meet in Fredericksburg to discuss the details. He told me he wanted to bring Zack to his knees for something that happened back in high school," She waved her hand as if the information wasn't important. "Then he mentioned how different my life would have been if Zack had accepted the NFL contract and I had married him instead of Teddy. He said if I help him distract Zack for a while, he would guarantee enough money for me and my daughter to live comfortably for quite some time."

"So your role was to distract Zack. What was Teddy's role?"

"What? Teddy doesn't know anything about this. Hell, I don't even know where he is and don't care. He lost his ability to take care of us when he injured his knees. Hell it wasn't like he was an NFL staple the way Zack would have been. He had a contract, but it was only for 2.7 million for three years, then a lousy 4.2 the next four years. Once he busted his knee, the league disappeared. We lost the house and everything else we had. My only savior was Chanté's talent. Once we get her on the right stage, she'll be able to take care of us financially. Since Zack was the one that ruined my life in the first place, I see no reason why he shouldn't be the one to fix it. Hell, it's not like he doesn't have the money."

"Why not just ask him to help you and your daughter rather than trying to run a scam on him?" Reese, who stood quietly in the corner asked.

Celeste narrowed her eyes on him, "The last time I asked Zack for anything he said no and chose his brother over me."

"It wasn't a choice!" Reese lost his cool for the first time during this entire situation. "Don't you get it? It was about love for his family—family, Celeste. Right or wrong, good or bad, there is no choice when it comes to family."

"You're right Reese, and I would do anything for my family." She slammed her hands on the table "Anything to help my baby girl live out her dream. I damn sure am not living mine."

Samuel put up his hand to stop Reese from speaking further. "Would it surprise you to know your husband is here in Richmond?"

A look of confusion spread across Celeste's face, she shook her head, "Teddy is not here, he would have no reason to be."

"Then it would surprise you to know Meeks has also been in contact with your husband?"

L

In interrogation room number two, Charles Meeks, wasn't even sweating bullets. It was as if he still had control of things. That concerned Nate Raines, but it did not show on his face.

"Mr. Meeks I have to say I admire your work. It took my team hours to dismantle your plan to embezzle millions from Davenport Industries. What I don't understand is why you wanted to destroy Xavier Davenport. After all, he recruited you into the company. Gave you a more than lucrative contract and yet, you set out almost from the very beginning to destroy him."

Charles crossed his legs and sighed as if he was bored. "You all still don't get it. This had nothing at all to do with Xavier. He's a decent boy, his only fault is he worships the ground his brother walks on."

Nate frowned as if he was confused, "So this wasn't about bringing Xavier down? It was his project, his baby so to say. If it wasn't about Xavier, who was the target?"

"Don't you know anything? It was Xavier's project, but it was Zack's money. Money that I helped him acquire over the years. That's right, me. The nerd that couldn't even sit at the lunch table with him and his boys." He nodded his head realizing he was now a little heated. He settled back down, then looked at Nate. "My target is Zack, not Xavier. " He held Nate's glare. "You were one of those kids in high school too weren't you?"

Nate was a top notch investigator who knew how to read what people said. It wasn't lost on him that Charles used the word is and not was. "What kids?" Nate sat back and asked.

"You know," Charles turned to face him. "The popular boys. The ones all the girls followed behind. I bet you were a three letter athlete too, weren't you. You look like you could have been one of them."

Nate shook his head. "No, I'm afraid not. I was heavy into math during high school." Nate laughed. "I couldn't dribble a ball for a million bucks back then. Now, give me a calculator, and a Wall Street Journal and I could make you a million."

"So you were like me," Charles gave him a good look up and down then smiled. "They didn't make nerds like you when I was in high school."

"I don't know about all of that. I didn't know you back then, hell I don't know you now. But if you were ignored, or had people walk by you in the hall like you were just a part of the lockers or something, then yes, that was me."

"So you understand how they use you to make them millions then toss you aside, like you never even matter in their life."

"Did Zack do that to you?" Nate shook his head. "At some point enough is enough."

"You're right. And I had enough of Zack's superior attitude. All I ever wanted was to help him, be around him. But he never had time for me. Oh he was nice enough, but he just never made time for me. So when the opportunity arose I took it. I knew Xavier was looking for a Finance Officer and I made sure my resume was in his top ten. When I interviewed with him, I mentioned my relationship with his brother. That surprised him. But I knew I was in then."

"Did Zack begin to appreciate your help once you started working for him?"

"Hell no. He was paying too much attention to Diamond Lassiter and not enough attention to the construction business."

"They had an office affair going on?" Nate acted appalled.

"Well," Charles looked around to make sure no one was in the room. "It wasn't known for a while. But I knew. I saw them."

"You saw them in the office?" Nate sat forward and asked.

"On his office floor," Charles frowned. "How tacky is that? I couldn't stand to watch them going at it like dogs in heat." The expression on Charles' face changed. "That's when I knew, nothing about Zackary Davenport had changed from high school. He would never know or understand my worth to him. A short skirt and long legs was all he was ever interested in."

Nate prayed his expression of total bafflement did not show on his face as he asked his last question. "This plot to bring Zack," he hesitated, but couldn't think of another way to phrase the question. "To his knees was because he did not appreciate the special friendship you believe the two of you could have had?"

"Exactly."

"So you've been secretly in love with him since high school?"

Charles tilted his head to one side. "Infatuated is more accurate."

Nate sat back in his chair. He wanted to take the pad he was writing on and throw it in the air. "Charles I have to say, I've worked on a lot of strange cases in my day. You, my man have set the bar high for originality." Nate stood to walk out of the room.

"Thank you Nathan." Charles smiled and took in all of the man at the door, "You are much taller than I thought before."

Nathan walked into the room next to the interrogation room. Joshua, Samuel and Reese sat looking at the monitors in both rooms. They all turned and looked up at him. All he could do was shake his head and say, "A woman scorned doesn't have shit on a man scorned."

Joshua stood to leave, but could not resist, "I think he was checking you out Nate." The room was silent for a moment then every one of them broke out into laughter at the expression on Nate's face.

Nate joined in for a moment then said. "Neither of these idiots started that fire."

"No, I'm going to find Teddy Blanchard," Joshua stated.

"Don't kill him," Samuel ordered.

Joshua frowned, "Why do you always have to take the fun out of things?"

L

As it turned out Joshua did not have to go far. When he stepped into the lobby of the station, Theodore Blanchard and his daughter were at the front desk.

"I need to make a statement regarding the fire at Davenport Estates tonight," Teddy said.

The officer nodded, "Come with me."

Teddy turned to his daughter, hugged and kissed her. "I want you to sit over there and don't worry. I'll take care of everything."

Sitting in the waiting room of the police station Chanté thought about her parents. Both of them were really nice people, if you took the time to get to know them. She wondered if either of them knew the type of stress their issues had caused her. There had been times when she didn't know who was the parent and who was the child, when it came to her mother. And as for her daddy, well, he lost his mind when he lost his contract. He knew the moment he lost the contract, he lost mommy. Didn't he know if that was the case, he never had her in the first place? But this latest move had her stunned. Her daddy was being a father. What happened was wrong and had caused someone to be physically injured. He always prided himself on teaching her right from wrong and that there are consequences to all actions. With all that he had done, it was his responsibility to keep her from making bad decisions. So now they sat in the police station where her dad had taken them the moment the medevac took off and he realized someone was hurt. He told her he had to do what was right.

Joshua watched the emotions going across the child's face as her father was taken to the back. If anyone had paid attention they would know that the answers to their questions lie with her. He walked over, leaned against the wall next to the bench she was sitting on. "A penny for your thoughts."

She looked up at him with eyes much wiser than her age. Her hair pulled back into a ponytail, diamond stud earrings in her ears, a very conservative shell top for a teenager and a smile so knowing, he really didn't need to hear what she had to say. "My thoughts are worth about a million dollars right now."

"Okay," he pushed away from the wall and sat next to her. He took her small hand into his and gently squeezed. "I'm listening."

She smiled at him then looked straight ahead as she began talking. "Adults make things so complicated." She shook her head. "I don't think we realize how decisions we make when we are young impact not only our lives but others as well. I think if my mother had thought about others when she made the decision to abort Mr. Davenport's child, we would probably not be here today. If my father hadn't made the decision to marry my mom even though he knew she never loved him, just to say he had something that once belonged to Mr. Davenport, we probably would not be here today. Any one of those decisions could have altered what happened here tonight. Tonight when I called my dad, I didn't know he was in Richmond. When he picked me up, I told him about my mom's plan to take down Mr. Davenport. I told him how much I liked Mr. Davenport and asked him what I should do. Instead of him helping me, he snapped. I've never seen my daddy that angry. He took me to the new site and we sat in the car. He must have seen the scared look on my face, because that's when he broke. He told me he never wanted his baby girl to see him a broken man. But that's what Zackary Davenport had done to him. Davenport took his starting position on the football team. Davenport took his girl. And now Davenport was trying to take his daughter. If he was ever to look himself in the face again, he had to make Davenport pay for all the damage he had caused him. He had to make Davenport lose everything, make him a broken man. But you know what my dad and my mom never understood?"

"What?" Joshua asked.

"Possessions, money, houses and cars, are not what break a man like Mr. Davenport. He is the type of man that can lose the shirt off his back, work hard and come back with ten more shirts. It's not about material things with him, it's about the things you can't buy but people give willingly, like love and respect."

"I think your father understood that. He was after Zack's reputation. It was your mother that was after his money."

She looked up at him. "You may be right." She sighed. "But you know my father's plan didn't work. We sat there waiting for something to happen. The longer we sat the more irritated he became. Finally he got out of the car and walked around to the back of the house. I watched through the window as he walked up the stairs. A few minutes later he returned to the car and just broke down. I have no idea what went wrong, but he felt Mr. Davenport had beat him again." She sighed, "I think things just went black for me. I was so angry, so very angry that my parents weren't worth a damn. I've tried so hard not to let their insecurities in life affect me. But they did." She shook her head. "Do you know how many everyday household cleaners are highly flammable? Quite a few I'll tell you. The whole time I was walking into that house I kept thinking how freaking hard can it be to set a house on fire. I walked in, looked under the cabinet, pulled out the can of oven cleaner. Placed it in the oven, closed the door, turned the oven on then walked out the same way I walked in. I got back into the car and said, let's go daddy."

Joshua inhaled. This child should not be going down for this. This was an innocent child with a bright future ahead of her. Her only crime was having assholes as parents. "Did you know anyone was in the house?"

She shook her head, "No one was in the house when I was in there."

Joshua pulled the child to him and kissed her on the forehead. "You wanted to be an actress right."

"No, a dancer," she corrected him. "There's a difference."

"Well either way, it's a performance you have to put on and you have to be in the right frame of mind to put on that performance right."

"Yeah," she looked at him sideways.

"Okay, I want you to listen carefully to what I'm about to say. You are going to have to tell them what you told me. But I want you to add a little something. Now, this is going to be between you and me. Understand."

"Okay."

Joshua talked to the child a little longer. Then he had her to retell the story to him with the added script. Once he was satisfied, he took her by the hand and down to the interrogation room with her father.

L

Joe and Sally Lassiter held each other as they waited for word on their fifth child. "Funny, I always imagined us being here like this for Sammy or Joshua, but never Diamond," Sally whispered to her husband.

Joe held her a little tighter, "Sammy is too skilled and Joshua too cocky to be in this position." He felt the smile tug at his wife's lips. That's what he wanted. He wanted to ease her worry. That was his job, to protect his wife and their children. But it seemed he failed on that note. His mind kept wondering why Diamond was there in the first place. She was supposed to be at the dinner with Zack. He stared at the double doors leading to the treatment area of the emergency room. His heart went out to Zack. The woman he loved and his mother were in danger. People didn't realize that more people died from smoke inhalation than burns. He had a daughter in danger, but Zack could lose both. Then he thought about Xavier and shook his head. "Lord I pray that boy is alright."

"Which boy?" Sally asked.

Joe looked down at his wife, "Xavier. Can you imagine, just finding out his mother is alive and right under his nose to possibly losing her all in the same day. That has to be a lot to deal with."

Sally kissed her husband's cheek. "You are standing here worried about Xavier while your own child is fighting for her life."

"Oh Diamond is going to be fine. Zack is too stubborn to let her go."

"Mom," Ruby, the oldest girl, called out.

Sally looked up to see a team of doctors come out. All of the Lassiter children gathered around. Ruby, Pearl, Matthew, Luke, Opal, Timothy, Jade, Adam, and Sapphire circled around the doctors. Sally reached over and pulled Xavier in with the family.

"Mr. and Mrs. Lassiter?"

"That's us." Joe replied.

The first doctor turned to Mr. Lassiter. "Your daughter is stable. We've done several intervals of chest x-rays to determine if there was any damage to the lungs. So far they have come back clear, however, we have to continue to monitor for delayed lung injury. A pulse oximetry was done to check the amount of oxygen in her blood. The levels were low, but the continued intake of oxygen will raise those levels. If respiratory problems persist, we will perform a Bronchoscopy. All in all, your daughter is stable and should recover from this incident. Dr. Nicolas will brief you on the other victim."

The doctor stepped back and a very young female stepped forward. "Good evening. Which of you are the Davenports?"

Xavier started to step forward when Sally replied. "We all are."

"Okay, Ms. Davenport's situation is quite different. The first thing I'm going to tell you is we are not going to lose her."

A sigh of relief resonated through the group. But then Adam, the shyest member and arguably the most intelligent member of the family, challenged the doctor's words. "How can you be certain of that?"

Dr. Nicolas narrowed her eyes at the man and something in her eyes sparked as she replied. "Because I said so and I'm too stubborn to let her die."

"You may be, but medicine, as I'm sure you know, is an area shrouded in uncertainty. As encouraging as your words are, we need to hear the facts of Ms. Davenport's condition before we are given what could be false hope."

The entire family was staring at Adam as if he were a stranger. He rarely spoke a few words at a time to anyone except his twin Jade and here he was literally challenging the doctor. Jade took a step closer to her brother as a gesture to let everyone know she supported whatever he just said to the doctor.

Dr. Nicolas held Adam's glare for a moment before blinking. "You're right. I apologize." She turned back to Sally. "Ms. Davenport is in grave condition. She sustained second and third degree burns on the left side of her face and torso. Once the burns begin to heal, she will have to endure a series of skin grafts to repair the damage. That's the good news. The smoke inhalation has caused some damage to her lungs. Fortunately, she was not in the fire for a significant amount of time, therefore, the damage wasn't as severe as it could have been." Her eyes shifted to Adam, "If she survives, and I believe she will," she turned back to Sally, "there may be respiratory problems in her future."

"Second and third degree burns are painful. Is the patient sedated and comfortable?" Adam asked.

"Yes, we will keep her sedated while assessing the respiratory damage."

"Once she stabilizes, I take it she will be transferred to the Burn Unit and cared for by the best physician available."

The Lassiters' eyes were riveted on their son. "Yes, once the patient is stabilized she will be moved and I will remain her doctor until she is released."

Adam did not miss the emphasis placed on the word "I" when the doctor spoke. Everyone held their breath waiting for Adam's reply.

"Adam?" Xavier asked before agreeing to the doctors' plans.

Finally pulling his eyes from Dr. Nicolas, Adam nodded. "I'll hang around for a few days to make sure all goes according to the doctor's plan."

Xavier turned back to the doctor. "Do whatever you have to to ensure she is comfortable at all times. Can I sit with her?"

"Not at this moment."

"The patient's mental state is as important as her physical under these circumstances. I think having a loved one nearby would be beneficial to her will to survive. Wouldn't you agree, Doctor Nicolas?"

"I do," Dr. Nicolas cleared her throat, "Once we get her in a sterile environment, we will advise you." She looked around, "Only one visitor at a time. Okay?"

Everyone nodded and replied. "Okay."

The medical team turned to retreat behind the double doors, but Dr. Nicolas paused for a moment to take another look at the man that dared to challenge her. He looked young, but then again she got the same reaction when people discover she is one of the top burn specialists in the country. She wondered if she would ever see him again, then turned and walked back through the doors.

L

It was well after four in the morning when Samuel tapped Zack on his shoulder. Zack was seated in a chair next to Diamond's bed, asleep. She lay there with oxygen tubing in her nose and monitors constantly measuring her breathing. "How is she doing?"

Zack sat up, wiped his hand down his face and nodded. "I think she's good. She's opened her eyes a few times. Your father and mother came in for a while." He chuckled. "Your father called out to her but she didn't blink. Then your mother said, "Diamond Renee Lassister open your eyes this minute", in that tone. I thought Diamond was going to jump out of her skin. The monitor started beeping like crazy. The nurses came running in. Diamond opened her eyes. Your mother smiled, kissed her forehead and told her to rest. Diamond closed her eyes. Your mother turned to me and said, 'She'll be fine, now you get some rest.' I started to protest, and your father gave me one of those, do as she said looks and I just agreed. It's not your father that puts the fear of God in you, it's your mother."

Samuel smiled. "Man I could have told you that years ago."

Zack pointed to a chair for Samuel. He took a seat and the two talked. "Chanté?" Zack asked.

"She's at my house with Joshua. Her father insisted that the child was trying to protect him. He said he set the fire. In a way he did, along with Celeste. That child has been dealing with too much for someone her age. It's a wonder she turned out as balanced as she is."

"She's a special girl. I'll make sure she doesn't want for anything. Ask Cynthia to check into this dance school Chanté talks about. Whatever it takes I want her enrolled as soon as possible. I want her life back to normal."

"I'm not sure that will happen. Celeste is going to be charged with embezzlement. Her father is definitely going to serve some time for arson and that's going to leave her with no parents."

Zack shook his head. "I won't let that happen. If nothing else, Diamond and I will take her. Is there any idea who is her real father?"

Samuel laughed. "You're not going to believe it."

"Try me."

"Teddy is her real father." Samuel smiled at the look on Zack's face.

"After all of this craziness. How did you find out?"

"I didn't, Joshua did. He pulled the lab results from your DNA test, sent them to his tech friend along with a sample from Teddy and within an hour the results were back in. You should have seen the tears from the man when Joshua told him. I'm pretty sure Joshua is going to pull some strings for Teddy so that he and Chanté can eventually be together."

"Hmm, I never thought Joshua had a sweet side to him." Diamond's foot moved and she moaned. Zack jumped up and leaned over her. "Diamond." She blinked, looked at him and smiled. "Hey babe," he rubbed her temple and kissed her cheek. She tried to say something, but nothing came out. Tears formed in her eyes and spilled down her cheek. "Don't try to talk. Here," he poured a little water into a cup. "Sip." She did, but the tears kept flowing. Samuel handed him a pen and pad. He gave it to Diamond.

She wrote: Ann Boom. Tears began pouring as she closed her eyes.

"No babe," Zack kissed her cheek. "You pulled her out. She's here." Diamond opened her eyes and stared at him in wonder. "She's here. X-man is with her. She's safe."

Samuel stood next to the other side of her bed. "Seems like we have another hero in the family."

She reached for the pen and pad and wrote: House.

"We're going to have to rebuild." Zack replied. She frowned. Then wrote: I love you.

Samuel took that as his cue as Zack gathered Diamond in his arms and held her. "Thank you for teaching me how to love."

She wrapped her arms around him and whispered, "You're welcome." Then fell asleep in his arms.

Samuel watched them and smiled thinking, one sister down, five to go.

Epilogue

At first Zack thought the initiation to the family football game was a joke. Today, his body told him it was anything but! Those girls, whom their father, Joe, refers to as his precious gems, should be linebackers on Luke's professional football team. He was sure the men had the game in the bag until Cynthia made the play of the day.

Zack had taken a moment to enjoy a kiss from Diamond when he found himself being dragged away.

Samuel and Joshua grabbed Zack by the arms just as Ruby and Pearl grabbed Diamond and pulled them apart. "There will be no booty bumping tonight!" Phire proclaimed.

Everyone stopped and looked at her. "What? I just said what all of you were thinking."

"You know the rule," Sammy said to Zack, "no contact until tomorrow."

"Don't make me whip you again Sammy." Zack laughed as they huddled for the final play of the game.

The girls gathered around Diamond. "This one is for you." Pearl smiled. "Cynthia, you know what to do."

"We'll handle the other guys," Jade added, "You go get your man."

Diamond smiled as they all clapped signaling they were ready. They lined up with Diamond in the center flanked on the right by Cynthia, Pearl and Jade—on the left with Phire, Opal, and Ruby. Sammy had the ball, Luke was the center with Joshua and Adam on his left, to his right were Timothy, Matt and Zack. Luke snapped the ball and lunged forward to tackle Diamond, but she wasn't there. Instead of pushing forward, she fell back and followed Zack running to the goal line. Pearl and Jade took out Joshua and

Adam. Cynthia jumped over Luke, right in Samuel's face and yelled, "I'm pregnant," just as Samuel released the ball. Phire caught the ball that came up short as Diamond tackled Zack to the ground.

"What?" Samuel stared at Cynthia.

"We're going to have a baby." Everyone went into an uproar, including Joe and Sally who ran off the porch to join the celebration. No one paid any attention to Diamond and Zack as they snuck around the back of the house.

As they rounded the corner of the house they came to a sudden stop. "Going somewhere?" Xavier stood there leaning against the back door of the house.

"X-man," Zack frowned. "You don't see us."

"You expect me to go up against six feet eleven inches of Joe Lassiter. Not to mention, his sons?"

"You damn right I do." Zack replied. He watched as X-man contemplated his next move. "Come on man. Help a brother out."

Xavier looked at Diamond, "Are you sure you want to marry this Davenport?"

Diamond walked over, kissed Xavier on the cheek and smiled. "Yes."

Xavier smiled at his friend then looked at his brother. He still wasn't sure how he felt about Zack keeping his mother away from him, but he loved his brother. That would never be in question. He turned his back, "I see nothing."

Zack patted X-man on the back. "I love you man." He grabbed Diamond's hand and ran towards the back gate.

"Be back in time for dinner, Diamond Renee Lassiter." Sally yelled from the kitchen window.

"And don't come back pregnant," Phire yelled over her mother's shoulder. Sally turned and stared at her daughter. Phire took a step back, "I'm just saying."

The other members of the family, that were now all inside the house laughed, then turned to Ann to tell her the news.

When he finally had Diamond to himself, Zack drove to Davenport Estates and parked by the lot he'd broken ground on to build their home. The temperature was crisp, but bearable. He pulled out two chairs and a table from the back of the truck. He sat one chair facing the river and the other facing the street. He sat a bottle of wine and two glasses on the table. "This is where our bedroom deck will be." He explained as he took her by the hand, sat her in the chair, then wrapped the blanket around her legs. He took the seat facing her with the view of the James River behind her. With Arthur in his hands, he smiled. "This is the view I want to see each morning for the rest of my life."

Diamond poured two glasses of wine. Taking one in her hand, she crossed her jean covered legs, sat back and waited for Zack to serenade her. Zack, licked his lips, placed them on the mouthpiece of King Arthur and began playing his rendition of Teach Me Tonight. With every note, her heart expanded. By the time he hit the last note, her heart exploded with so much love for this man she thought she would die in that spot. Dropping the glass to the ground, she rushed into his arms. King Arthur fell to the ground as Zack wrapped her in his arms and kissed her well into the morning light.

Yes, that was a football game that was well worth the punishment he'd taken from the gems. Now he stood with Xavier at his side and his mother watching on as the wedding procession began.

The bridal party was simple, but nowhere near small. There were six bridesmaids, Cynthia, Ruby, Pearl, Jade, Opal and Phire, six groomsmen, Samuel, Joshua, Luke, Matthew, Timothy and Adam, one dog, Commando as the ring bearer and one very happy little girl, Chanté as the flower girl. It was hard to determine who received the most attention, Commando in his tuxedo carrying the ring pillow in his mouth or Chanté who was breathtaking as she danced down the aisle. The one thing Zack and Diamond had agreed on was that they wanted to keep Chanté as a part of their life in some way. As part of a plea agreement, Celeste signed over custody of Chanté to Teddy's parents. Zack set up a trust fund to ensure the child would be financially able to live her dream. Cynthia kept her promise and connected Chanté with her brother Blake who immediately saw the talent in the child and hooked her up with his agent. Chanté was now an honorary member of the Lassiter family.

    Zack's patience was running thin. There were just too many people in front of Diamond. He wanted, no, needed to see her soon or he was going to start throwing bodies out of the way until he found her. But then, standing in the doorway next to her father, there was Diamond, looking sexier than words could describe. Her dress had a diamond studded, jeweled, halter neckline, The asymmetric body fitting gown, had the sexiest side slit that showed off her beautiful long legs, and a train extending from her knees down. Her shoes were diamond encrusted four-inch sandals that just added more shape to those legs. A simple diamond bracelet and teardrop diamond earrings completed the look. She was the epitome of elegant sophistication. If that wasn't enough, when he stepped forward and placed his hand on her lower back, there was nothing there but skin. Taking a quick peep behind her, he noticed the back of the dress dipped, exposing her bare back. Zack inhaled as he heard Xavier snicker and knew he had read his mind. His first instinct was to take off his jacket and wrap it around her shoulders so no one else could see what was his. But then it dawned on him, she was his. At that moment Diamond smiled up at him and the world was right. Nothing else mattered.

What a day to celebrate. The air was cool and crisp. The sky was sunny without a cloud in sight and another Lassiter had taken the plunge.

After the ceremony, the couple and family took pictures then joined the guests in the reception hall. Joe, Sally and Ann took their seats and watched as their children and their guests partied hard. "Two down and ten to go," Joe smiled down at his wife.

"I like him for Diamond," Sally said.

"Zack's a good man. He loves her and will move heaven and earth to keep what he's found." Joe smiled.

"I think Ruby feels some kind of way about Diamond getting married before her. Now, Pearl couldn't care less. I don't think that child will ever find a man."

"Yes, she will," Joe kissed his wife's forehead. "There is a man that will change her mind about love."

"Is she still sleeping with the Thompson boy?"

"Brian?" Sally shook her head. "I think Sammy put a stop to that."

"Is the boy still alive?"

Sally smiled, "Yes."

"Damn. I think Cynthia has softened him up too much. There was a time when Sammy was harder on his sister's boyfriend's than Joshua."

"That's the one we have to be concerned with," Sally exhaled.

"Joshua is going to be just fine," Joe consoled his wife, not sure if he believed the words himself. "Either way, the family is growing."

Xavier stood at the next table talking to the girls. "I thought the game was touch football. You were hitting like it was the super bowl."

"Oh stop crying like a baby," Opal replied. "You can always take his hits for him."

"Yeah, I'd like to tackle you once or twice." Phire smiled at Xavier. The group stopped and stared at Phire. She shrugged her shoulders, "What?"

Joe laughed. "I love my precious gems. They are just like their mother. Brilliantly beautiful as the stones they were named for and just as rough as an uncut diamond." Sally smiled up at him and kissed his neck. He in turn pulled her petite body into his lap and began to nuzzle her neck.

"Ain't that how you got those twelve that's already here?" Ann said from her seat at the next table.

"Yes it is." Joe replied. "We're going for twelve more."

The room grew quiet as fourteen pairs of eyes turned to them and in unison yelled. "What?" Joe and Sally laughed at the expressions on their children's faces.

The guests were a virtual who's who, including State Attorney General JD Harrison and his wife Tracy, millionaire James Brooks and his wife Ashley, and Senator John Roth and his wife Lena. Even Prince LaVere' from Emure was there to celebrate the marriage of one of the Lassiters. Pearl worked for the Attorney General and James Brooks.

Samuel and Joshua both had worked for Senator Roth and Prince LaVere' at some point in time. Yes, the Lassiter's reach was far and wide and quite powerful, even though they would never use it. Zack really didn't care about any of that. What he wanted to do now, more than anything, was to get Diamond alone and show her just how much love she had in store. However, tradition dictated that they spend a little time at the reception before taking their leave. "It will be time to go soon," Diamond kissed her husband's neck, as they danced. "One more dance, then I need to get you out of that dress." Zack whispered into her ear.

JD, Tracy, James, Ashley, Samuel, Cynthia, Joshua, Prince LaVere' and Pearl were sitting at a table catching up on Brian's condition. As JD's body man, he had recently been shot and was now recuperating. JD turned to Joshua, who had taken the seat next to him and touched him on the shoulder. "Brian sent you a message."

Joshua picked up his drink. "Yeah, what was that?"

"He said you're next."

"Next for what?" Joshua asked just as he put the glass to his lips.

"To get married."

The liquid had just made it to his tongue as he almost choked. JD laughed at the expression on Joshua's face. The table exploded in laughter. "It's not bad Joshua." JD smiled. "I get to wake up every morning to the most exquisite woman in the world." He turned and lightly kissed his wife on the lips.

"I have to disagree Mr. Attorney General," Samuel smiled at his wife, "That honor belongs to me."

James laughed in that rich baritone voice of his, shaking his head, "I'm afraid you both are mistaken." He looked at Ashley. "I'm the fortunate one."

Prince LaVere's cell phone rang. "Saved by the bell!" Joshua exclaimed as he looked disgustedly at the men around the table ogling their wives.

Laughing, Prince LaVere' answered his phone. The laughter faded as he asked a series of questions. Concern was etched on the face of everyone at the table. Joshua and Samuel stood, as LaVere' turned to them. "Zsa Zsa, my little sister has been kidnapped."

The men began moving. James and JD spoke quietly with LaVere, getting details. Samuel went to let his parents know that he and Joshua would be leaving. Joshua placed a call to have a helicopter prepared for a long journey. He walked back over to LaVere'. "Our transportation will be here in five minutes."

LaVere' looked at the men that were all ready and willing to assist his family. "Thank you my friends."

"Let's move," Joshua stated. And just like that, the men were gone.

Pearl looked around the table at the women and shook her head. "Men," she exclaimed. "The more things change, the more they stay the same."

L

Finally, Zack and Diamond took their leave. The honeymoon was to be as unique as the couple. Imagine her surprise when the limo pulled up in the circular driveway of the Hutchison Estate. "Why are we at Grant's house?"

Zack took her hand as he helped her out of the limo. Grant appeared at the entrance. "Congratulations Mr. and Mrs. Davenport. Your chariot awaits." He guided them to the back of the house. To her surprise, Arthur was docked there. The beam in her eyes was all he needed to know he had made the right decision. "We are taking the yacht from Virginia through the Carolinas, docking at different cities in between, until we reach the coastal waters of Florida. Then we are spending the week on a private island where I can make love to you all day and night."

"Look at you, becoming the romantic husband. I like that."

"You're going to like this even more." He threw a hand up and Diamond thought he was waiving bye to Grant, but instead it was a signal. Lights illuminated the area and now she could clearly see the yacht. It was no longer called Arthur. Now in big bold letters and in beautiful script, the name Diamond appeared. Tears filled her eyes.

"Now whenever I want to relax, I'll climb aboard the Diamond."

"Oh, you are definitely getting some tonight and many nights to come."

Hours later, Zack sat on the bed watching as Diamond talked to her family on the phone. At that moment, he could not imagine his life without her. The years of dealing with hurt and betrayal seemed to have vanished as if they had never happened. Love is a powerful emotion, he thought. It can stomp out years of hate and despair in a matter of moments. His life, that was lonely only months ago, was now filled with family, friends and even his mother. Things still felt a little strained with X-man, but he believed that with time his brother would understand his reason for keeping Ann away and that it had been done out of love.

That's the lesson he had learned, love conquers all. Diamond may have been the one to ask him to teach her how to love. But the truth was now staring him in the face.

The look in his eyes is what every woman should see every day of their lives. She could feel the intensity of his look. "A penny for your thoughts," Diamond said as she watched her husband from the vanity in the stateroom of their yacht. His long muscular legs were stretched out, partially covered by the satin sheet from the bed. His arms were braced under his head exposing his chest, which she had the urge to run her tongue across.

His eyes shifted to hers. There she was, his life, his world, his children and his future. "I was thinking you are the most alluring, seductive, luscious tasting woman I have ever known. And I thank God for bringing you into my life."

For a moment Diamond was speechless. She held his gaze as his words settled into her heart. She slowly stood, allowing the white silk robe to drop to the floor. Walking over to the bed, she straddled him, cupped his face between her hands and gently kissed his lips. "You Zackary Davenport are the sexiest, most adoring, magnificently endowed man I know. And I thank God every second of the day for allowing you to teach me how to love."

His eyes darkened as a smirk reached his lips. His hands circled her waist as he effortlessly lifted her onto his engorged shaft. He filled her completely. "It was you who